Very soon, she forg[...] body tingle wheneve[...] he would take her and needing all her pride to refrain from begging him not to wait any longer. She wondered why he waited, hated him for waiting.

He knelt beside her, hands on her shoulders. "Later, Arabella. We shall be devilish hungry later." His hands went from her shoulder to neck, and he kissed her with a great deal more than the careless ardor he had shown before.

Then his hands moved again, to the fastenings of her dress, and even while she drowned in passion she felt a flicker of amusement for his skill: ribbons, sprung metal and fastenings, he never hesitated over their complexity nor did his mouth cease in its quest, rousing each part of her as clothes were loosed.

This he had waited for and intended. He could buy women whenever he desired them, and certainly had done so even while he met her. This must be different, something neither would forget, or it would be wasted.

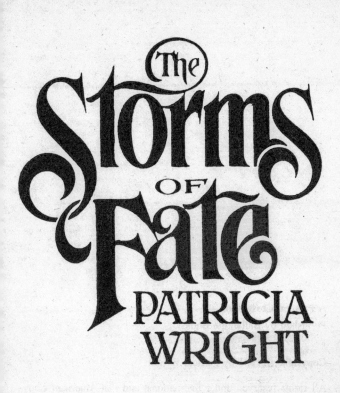

The Storms of Fate

PATRICIA WRIGHT

FAWCETT CREST • NEW YORK

A Fawcett Crest Book
Published by Ballantine Books

Library of Congress Catalog Card Number: 80-1695

ISBN 0-449-20176-7

This edition published by arrangement with Doubleday & Com-pany, Inc.

Manufactured in the United States of America

First Ballantine Books Edition: June 1983

THIS BOOK IS DEDICATED TO
THE BANKERS AND MERCHANTS
OF THE CITY OF LONDON WHO
SINCE 1945 HAVE AGAIN REBUILT
THEIR CITY FROM RUIN AND RESTORED IT
TO COMMERCIAL GREATNESS, DESPITE
THE ODDS SET AGAINST THEIR ENDEAVOUR

A brave man struggling in the storms of fate
and greatly falling with a falling state.

—Alexander Pope

~ I ~

Arabella

1665–1683

Strong be thy wall that about thee stands!
  Wise be the people that within thee dwells.
Fresh is thy River with his lusty strands;
  Blithe be thy churches; well-sounding thy bells.
Rich be thy merchants, in substance that excels,
    Fair be their wives; right lovesome, white and small.
Clear be thy virgins, lusty under kells,
  London, thou art the flower of Cities all.

WILLIAM DUNBAR

Chapter One

Great clouds were rolling over London, and soon it would rain. Then, if the wind continued to rise, chimney pots would roll into the streets with satisfactory crashes, bundles of thatch fly over market stalls and into faces, low-swinging signs force cursing citizens to seek safety in the centre of the street. There green-slimed pools lay trapped by garbage, but at least a cracked head was less likely.

Arabella liked storms. She had climbed up a heap of firewood until she could just see over their courtyard wall into Furnival Alley, which separated her father's Cheapside house from Alderman Cornish's property next door. If she could only climb a little higher and sit on the wall, she would be able to look down the length of the alley and laugh at the slithering haste with which everyone in Cheapside was trying to finish their business before the storm came.

From the top she would also be able to count the number of gables on Alderman Cornish's house, the pairs of carved angels holding up his massive roof timbers, and feel the same warm pleasure she always felt when her counting confirmed that they were fewer than the gables and angels of her own home. Even the gilded corncrake sign over his entry, which announced that John Cornish carried on business as a goldsmith on the premises, was paltry in Arabella's eyes since it was painted on wood, while her father's crossed spurs were crafted in wrought iron. Spurs were more noble too, she decided, though she seldom regretted that her father remained a working goldsmith. Robert Sperling was a common councilman of the City and hoped soon to be chosen alderman like his friend John Cornish, but to his mind there was more pride in being a

3

craftsman of outstanding repute than in lending money to courtiers as other goldsmiths were beginning to do. City and court were closely linked by money, but the two-mile journey between Cheapside and Whitehall Palace was more than an unpleasant expedition, it divided different ways of life. Robert Sperling and his like were happy to have it so, Arabella his daughter decidedly was not.

She watched open-mouthed when noble clients came to call, fingered their silks and ribbons if the chance arose, and hung out of the window to admire their painted coaches and silver-harnessed horses waiting outside. Often, such people lingered an hour or more, examining Robert Sperling's wares and sipping coffee without the least intention of doing more than pass the time agreeably; Arabella's father fumed at the waste of time, she stored their gestures and drawling accents in her memory, to practise later on her brothers and sister. Her elder brother, Rob, simply laughed and cuffed her ear, the little ones had learned to run to their mother with their complaints. Arabella did not cry when she was punished, just felt dreadfully unappreciated in such a place as Cheapside; the sooner she removed to court, the better.

The wind was rising, and Arabella shivered a little in anticipation. Last year a wall of St. Mary-le-Bow Church had blown down, flattening a row of tile-and-timber shops, and she had seen it all. The shops were already rebuilt and crazier than before, thrown together with the cheapest materials, as was so much else in London, and she debated whether to climb down from her woodpile and watch from a front window in the hope of it happening again, but decided against it. Her mother would find some dull task for her to do, and ask why she had not gathered herbs ready for pounding in the stillroom.

A moment later she was glad she had not gone, for the door in the wall opposite opened and Harry Cornish, the alderman's elder son, came out.

He grinned at the eyes and nose notched over brick and kicked enough alley rubbish aside so he could come and stand directly below her. He was tall and already squaring into manhood for all that he was only seventeen; Arabella liked him very much. She liked most males since there were few who did not soften towards her while women treated her with harshness, recognising even in her youth the open promise of lips and graceful body, the challenge of a tough and selfish spirit.

Harry's eyes were not far below hers, despite the woodpile

on which she was standing. "Slipped your leash again, Bella, or has your mother given up beating you for idleness?"

She dimpled prettily. Small and dark, with long curls well suited to the new Restoration styles she aped, it was Arabella Sperling's good fortune that she seemed incapable of an inelegant movement or an unseductive expression. Even when sulking, and she sulked often, her mouth pouted invitingly; when angry her eyes slanted in such a way that Harry Cornish at least sometimes provoked her just to watch them change shape; when she was frightened, she hid it behind tilted chin and defiant expression so anger often was disarmed.

"I've an errand to run for my father," said Harry casually. "It's just to the Royal Exchange, so I expect I'll be back before the storm breaks. If it breaks," he added, glancing at the sky. "It's a strange spring and we've had these alarms before with precious little rain to show for them."

"Do you mean it, Harry? You'll take me with you?" Arabella always recognised an offer however well disguised.

He laughed. "Can you sneak out your pattens? Your mother will never believe you paddled dirt to the ankles in your own back court."

Arabella slid from the wall with a rattle and grabbed a handful of herbs, heedless of whether she pulled plants out by the roots or mixed a dozen different sorts. She wanted an excuse if she was caught and cared not at all that any efforts to make potions from her gatherings would be wasted.

The kitchen and stillroom opened directly into the back court, and close by were the melting shed and workshop, noisy with hammers, where she was likely to encounter her father or Rob. Their home was luxurious by City standards, where even the prosperous lived several to a room, but it was crowded; which made it extremely difficult to do anything forbidden without being seen. For pattens meant the street, and Arabella was not allowed to leave the house without permission and an escort, so she seldom left it at all.

And Harry was going to take her to the Royal Exchange!

Arabella skipped a little in anticipation, then planned rapidly. Pattens hung on pegs between the kitchen and stillroom; Cook and two serving maids were in the kitchen, but not her mother. Arabella wrinkled her nose at the smell coming from the cauldron, but it was only the apprentices' dinner; Mr. Sperling was exceptional in giving his apprentices two good meals a day, even if the unseasoned, musty waft of it made Arabella wish he was less scrupulous.

She waited until the passage was empty, then made a rapid selection from amongst the pattens. These were the platforms which lifted women's unbooted feet clear of filth piled in the street, necessary but distressingly inelegant for a young lady being escorted out by Harry Cornish. She chose a pair tall enough to bring her head to his shoulder but made with metal spikes instead of clumsy wood, then heard footsteps approaching from the melting shed and scuttled into the stillroom as the only escape.

Susannah was there, pounding herbs with the fervent obedience she always affected. It never occurred to Arabella that Susannah might actually like household tasks, only that her zeal was deliberately aimed at making her elder sister's shortcomings more obvious. At nine years old, Susannah was her mother's favourite, a place Arabella considered should be hers by right.

Susannah turned, sweat beaded on her lip. "Have you brought the herbs Mother told you to collect? Wait—there's two I must add to this recipe if you have them." She scrabbled amongst some papers.

"I expect they're here somewhere," said Arabella indifferently, dropping her handful on the bench and holding the pattens out of sight; Susannah would certainly run squealing to her mother if she saw them. Arabella did not mind being beaten when she returned from the Royal Exchange, but her mind already leaped to the thought that Harry might take her again if they were not caught. She eyed her sister with dislike.

Susannah prodded at the clammy bunch of herbs. "I can't even see what you've got here. There is even..." She gave a screech of horror. "You've pulled up the turkey plant by the roots!"

"What if I have? The rest will grow better for the space." Sailors made money out of selling exotic plants which were reputed to cure all manner of ills, and Londoners bought them eagerly since sickness was commonplace in their teeming streets.

"Because it is good for headaches, and I could well do with a decoction from it today," snapped Susannah. "This storm... why doesn't it come? I can scarce see for pain at times."

Arabella seldom ailed and was impatient with those who did, but saw her opportunity in Susannah's complaints. "Pulled out by the roots or not, there's plenty of turkey plant in my gathering. Let me finish pounding while you lie down, and later I will bring some up to you."

"Would you really?" Susannah looked at her uncertainly; helpfulness from Arabella was unusual enough to cause surprise. "I have seldom felt such an ache before, and am mortal chilled besides."

"Well, go and lie down, you goose," said Arabella crossly. "Why wear yourself out pounding herbs which can well wait until the morrow?"

It took several more minutes to persuade Susannah, until Arabella became fearful that Harry would not wait. When she went at last, Arabella shredded a few leaves into the mortar, gave them some perfunctory thumps, before immediately scraping them into a flask to steep in water. No one would be able to say that she had not done what she had offered to do, she thought virtuously.

Then she ran into the back court and scrambled high enough to allow Harry to lift her over the wall. Mr. Sperling kept his side gate locked because of the precious metals in his melting house, and Furnival Alley was a haunt of thieves preying on the rich traffic of Cheapside.

In daylight and escorted by Harry Cornish it was safe enough, and Cheapside one of the few thoroughfares kept regularly scavenged and wide enough for two carts to pass with ease. Arabella enjoyed being with Harry, because he was so sure of himself, and shoved a passage for her through the thickest crowds; the best kind of passage too, close to the walls where she was safe from thrown slops and excited the envy of those escorted by more timid men. Harry yielded respect only to a few rich merchants of his father's acquaintance; he was a Londoner to the core and arrogant as most Londoners were, with the sense of their own power and difference from the rest of the nation.

Unselfconsciously, Arabella slipped her hand under his arm, pleased that her pattens gave her extra height. "Can we go down Bucklersbury? Please, Harry."

He glanced at the eager face by his shoulder. "What potion or physic is it you want this time? A dried toad to draw a fever, or heartsbane and mercury to kindle passion?"

"Oh, I'll never need any of those," said Arabella confidently. "I don't ail and—"

"And you'll discover passion without the need of potions."

"Well, I think so," she replied seriously. "My mother says

I must cultivate humility and a downcast eye before it is too late, or I'll burn in hellfire for bringing men's hearts to lust. But it sounds mortal dull to me."

He gave a shout of laughter, and held her close while battering a way across Cheapside, dodging handcarts and porters trotting head down heedless of anyone in their way, booting a hissing cluster of geese aside and ducking under the slobbering mouths of oxen hauling timber. "A compromise then, fair Bella. No simples for passion, but no downcast eyes, either!"

She glanced at him from under curved lids; she could not be blamed for the warm promise of her look but was very much aware of it. She liked seeing the admiring expression which came to men's faces when they saw her, and especially she liked it in Harry Cornish. Four years' difference in age is a great deal in youth and he had seemed irritatingly proof against her wiles before. "I can promise both easily enough, although not much else. I keep my promises when I make them, so I don't intend to make many." Her eyes went past him and her pace quickened: Bucklersbury was the centre of the apothecaries' trade and lined with shops selling every kind of remedy, quack potions and the dried entrails of beasts; blockaded by old women brewing simples from scummy cauldrons and peddlers hawking such things as pounded dried rats which they swore would cure every ill. "Look, Harry! The latest paints and salves from France! How I've wanted to see the newest mode since the servants tattled of a great load of wickedness come freshly to the stalls."

Harry looked disparagingly at trays of ground pigments. "Leave such things alone, Bella. You'll not take advice, but know your own beauty well enough. Study the next court ladies who come to your father's shop without allowing yourself to become dazzled by gold ribbons and fine velvets. Wait for a lowered mask and see the trenches dug in their flesh by paint, how ugly they look although only a few years older than you. Keep your complexion, my dear, so I may kiss you with the same pleasure at twenty years old as I do at thirteen."

His arm at her waist tightened and he kissed her swiftly while a couple of apprentices jeered from a shop entrance. It was little more than a gesture and in a moment they were walking again, for crowded Bucklersbury was no place for kissing and clods of filth would soon follow jeers, yet even in that instant Arabella yielded to his touch and returned his kiss eagerly. Her body warmed to admiration, although her understanding of desire was limited to the many warnings she had received against feeling it. Now Harry's lips had answered her simplest queries, even while the fleeting touch of him aroused further intriguing speculations. Arabella walked on silently, thinking that as she had suspected, her mother was at fault in presenting fleshly lusts as disagreeable as well as sinful. Harry said nothing either, but kept tight hold on her hand against his arm.

Arabella was never silent long, and forgot everything except her own pleasure once they reached the Royal Exchange, its arcaded walks full of merchants chaffering over bargains while courtiers strolled on the mosaic brick of its courtyard. Lords and their ladies were not ashamed to be seen in this temple of trade, strolling and flirting, buying expensive trifles from shops like burrows dug into 'Change wall, as if traders had started business in the road and chipped their way into masonry as prosperity hurled importunity and traffic at them. The freshest spices could be bought here; silks and drugs unloaded that very morning, ivory from trading posts newly captured from the Dutch in Africa, jet from Scandinavia, jewellery from Aleppo, amber from oceans few could have placed on a chart. The City of London was reaching into new worlds with its gold, and finding the profits very pleasant.

Arabella exclaimed at everything, stared with sudden curiosity at some ladies chatting too eagerly to remember their masks. Harry was right, she decided; she had looked at clothes and jewels before and faces were usually hidden, now she saw wrinkles like scars and skin inflamed by paint which had to be daubed ever thicker to hide the ravages it caused.

"Quite right," said Harry in her ear. "You won't listen to much advice in your life but preserving your beauty is another matter altogether." He watched with amusement as she flushed with fury at having her mind read so easily, and added, "Now I must find Alderman Backwell and despatch my father's trade with him before you are missed."

"I'll be missed, but I don't care. When I'm grown I'll not account to anyone for my doings, even if now I must pay with a beating for what I want."

Harry frowned. "You fool yourself if you think that. A husband is younger and stronger than parents when it comes to a beating. You'll be accountable to someone all your days, Bella, and don't make the mistake of thinking a pout and a kiss from your pretty lips can change it."

9

Arabella scowled and stared hungrily at the shifting throng; if merchants' wives seldom came here, then the women of the court did and not always escorted by their husbands either. Her lips parted and her eyes glowed as she drank in colour and noise and the richness of fine merchandise, longing to look closer at wonders on every side. Unseen hands touched her, one fumbled in her bosom, unidentifiable in the crowd when Harry swung around swearing, poised for a blow.

Arabella laughed from the sheer joy of it. She had felt horribly shabby in her plain-cut gown, and however crude it was, admiration brought back her confidence. "Don't be angry and spoil it all! I've seen the gallants in my father's shop, it's no more than a game to them."

He looked down at her, the swift, expressive yearning of her body still printed on his senses. "A game to them perhaps, but it shouldn't be to you. I'll carry a sword next time I bring you out."

She nodded enthusiastically, she thought it intolerably dull the way merchants seldom wore swords. Harry would look splendid with a chased gold blade at his side, though the red-skirted coat and crisp linen he wore was creditable enough. Older merchants might be content to hide their wealth behind sober colours and old-fashioned dress, but their sons felt no need for reticence: they could buy up most courtiers or ransom the King himself and saw no reason why Whitehall should not have its arrogant nose rubbed in the fact. Sir Thomas Gresham had built the Royal Exchange a hundred years before with the avowed intention of using it to capture trade from the Dutch, and then with typical pride had placed his own bust among those of the Kings of England. Now, City merchants were financing war against the Dutch, English ships foraging far and wide, and the atmosphere crackled with ambition, for this was a war of greed with mastery of trade the prize. A few might shake their heads and talk about common interests and religion with the Dutch, most remembered past losses at the Hollanders' hands and invested in privateers, or borrowed money from goldsmith-bankers like Alderman Cornish to exploit victory when it came.

Arabella stood a little aside while Harry talked to Alderman Backwell, one of the richest men in the City. Harry started by being deferential as befitted a young man, but far from servile. Once, he snapped back some retort, face reddening with anger, then the two argued as equals, raised voices attracting stares and nudges. Harry Cornish had too good an opinion of himself, and of his father's trade, to be capable of deferring long to anyone.

I'll be like that, thought Arabella with satisfaction, as Backwell began to yield; rich and great, let them all come, then we'll see who is accountable to whom.

"You won, didn't you?" she said as they walked home in stifling heat. The storm was passing over after all. "The great Alderman Backwell with the King's treasury at his call, and you won."

"Not precisely won. I made it clear that the house of Cornish does not pay the same interest as he expects from some ignorant country nobleman. He knew anyway, but tried to screw up the rate because that's the way he works, when it should be the other way around."

"The other way around?"

"Backwell demands high interest from his trading clients and accepts lower from the King because he borrows so much. Yet if there is one man in this realm who cannot be trusted, it is the King. At the Sign of the Corncrake we drive a hard bargain with Charles Stuart and his creatures, so they borrow from us only in extremity, but an easier one with those whose livelihood depends on their honesty. And so we prosper."

Arabella thought about it carefully. Harry could be tried for treason for saying such things about the King, lately restored to his realm after civil war, but she was not shocked since both the Sperling and Cornish families had supported Parliament, as had most in the City of London. "So also does Alderman Backwell prosper," she pointed out at last.

Harry gave a gasp of laughter. "Bella, my sweeting, it's fortunate you cannot inherit the house of Sperling and turn its trade towards keeping balances, or we should have to look to our profits. Backwell prospers so long as the King pays his debts."

"I should not want to trade in balances," snapped Arabella. "Fine craft from our furnace is more worthy than scribbling in ledgers."

"Keeping balances and cashes is the way to riches, or to ruin without care; there is also far more to it than scribbling in ledgers. The day our furnace is cold forever will be a sad one for us all, but I suspect it isn't far off; only sentiment makes my father keep the workshop, as well as the need to deal in plate as security. It's hard to give up the pride of seeing the best craft in London set with the Cornish mark, but our profit lies elsewhere now."

"Everyone knows that you find the best at the Sign of the Spurs," retorted Arabella instantly. "The pair of salts Lord Craven bought from us last month made those old-fashioned hacks of Goldsmith's Row green with envy." Her thoughts seldom strayed far from her own concerns, but the splendid wares she had handled since babyhood cast their special spell over her senses.

Irritatingly, Harry refused to argue although this did not mean that he accepted Sperling craft as best. Perhaps he knew he would not easily win an argument with me, Arabella reflected, and after he had helped her over the wall she went by instinct into their melting shed. Her absence for so long would certainly have been noticed, a few more minutes would make no difference to her punishment.

Only a single apprentice was still there, carefully sweeping dirt. When silver was melted it sometimes spat, or lost a trickle in the pouring, so every grain of dust was gathered for reheating; even a few glitters in a pile of dust were worth more than a journeyman's daily wage.

The furnace was hot but dull; tongs, ladles and long-handled puddlers polished and hung back on the wall. Arabella wandered around the scrupulously clean shed, finally stopping by two sheets of silver, the product of a whole day's labour. They had been annealed, beaten and rolled again and again by sweating apprentices, until wafer-thin and ready for crafting. Arabella's father dealt in gold but worked in silver; gold was too soft to take fine detail and those who wanted it paid extra to have items gilded after they were finished.

"What are these sheets due to be crafted into, do you know, Richard?" she asked at last.

The boy propped his broom in a corner and came over. He had a thin, bony face, restless eyes and fair hair which he was growing in imitation of a wig. There had been a fearful fuss a few months before when some chippings of silver were missed and Arabella knew her father believed that Richard Goodenough had taken them. She glanced at the apprentice curiously and wondered whether he knew how closely watched he now was, the fearful penalties which discovery in theft would bring.

He fingered the silver as she was doing, though the feel of it could not equal that of gold. Even blindfolded, Arabella could have distinguished gold from all other metals, and watching the sensuous stroke of Richard's fingers she knew that he could, too. And intended to have riches of his own, one day. Father was right, she thought suddenly; Richard did take the silver and probably the snuffer we missed last year as well.

"It's to be some new style of decoration for my lady of Craven," he said after a pause. "Not a brooch nor yet a buckle but something between the two, all in filigree and twist to loop up her gown and set the court wild with envy. We'll have a dozen orders in a week once a new fashion is set."

"Paid for in security if not in coins, I hope." Arabella copied words she had heard her father speak. This was the rub; a tradesman could not afford to refuse court business, equally he could be ruined by accepting commissions which went unpaid for years.

"The Cravens are sound enough, although I wouldn't say the same for most of 'em," said Richard confidently. "And this sheet is rolled from a pledged salver melted down. Mr. Sperling knows where to trust credit and where to ask security."

His voice was full of admiration. He doesn't realize he is suspect, Arabella thought, surprised. "Perhaps he also knows which apprentice to trust with punching filigree and which to leave sweeping dust."

"What do you mean?"

"Why ask when you must know if you allowed yourself to think? How long since you worked out of the melting shed, Richard Goodenough?" She did not blame him for theft, perhaps admired his courage when she had merely thought him dull before, but could not resist the taunt.

She saw his eyes darken as suspicion leapt from trifles he had discounted before. "It's not true. It's my turn to learn in the melting shed, while Jack and Will are at the bench." She said nothing, only laughed and tapped her foot. Theft from the melting shed was next to impossible, for her father supervised the melt and once the broken pieces were in the pan the metal was molten or else in blocks or sheets. In the workshop it was different, as fragments were punched clear of filigree, edges clipped or trimmed, precious wire twisted into decoration until exact calculation of amounts became impossible. "It's not true," he repeated lamely.

She shrugged. "It isn't me you have to convince, and you haven't even if it was. My father waits for proof, I'd look at you and know. You'd be in Newgate tonight if you worked for me."

"Why would Richard be in Newgate?" enquired her father from the door, how much he had heard they could not tell. "It seems a severe penalty for idling over sweeping the floor, when it was you, my daughter, who led him astray." He glanced at the silver they both were touching and smiled slightly, but his eyes were watchful. Robert Sperling had risen from pewterer's apprentice to pawnbroking goldsmith through his own great skills and some fortunate acquaintance during the civil war, when the aristocracy of England could not melt down plate fast enough to meet the crushing expenses of fighting. Rigidly honest, he was also an awkward man to cross.

"Mistress Arabella was asking me what these sheets were to be worked into." Richard seized the way of escape offered him. "And then we spoke of bad debts and how Newgate did not help a trader who was owed money."

"And my daughter reckoned you amongst the bad debtors?"

"It was a jest, no more." He was as unsettled by Arabella's silence as he would have been by accusation. She's the kind of bitch who would say or do anything for the sheer pleasure of brewing trouble, he thought viciously; then she'd smile like Jezebel or be beaten back to forgiveness and none of it mean anything to her at all.

"It's not a jest I should expect a young man of spirit to accept, or did you wait to ask my permission before you boxed her ears?"

Richard mumbled something and looked away. God, he wished he'd done a deal more than box the jade's ears.

"Answer me, Richard." Robert spoke quite pleasantly, one hand steadying himself against the door. He dragged a foot from a wound taken in battle against the King at Naseby; although he never spoke of it he often suffered pain and measured his steps carefully. Only his lined face and sometimes irritable temper showed the price he paid for Parliament's victory, as his plain clothes proclaimed an old religious loyalty amongst the gaudy fashions of the Restoration.

Richard forced a smile. "As I said, sir, I took it in jest. We spoke of gold and debtors, nothing more, and Mistress Arabella rouses a man to other things than chastisement, as she well knows."

The eyes of father and daughter met and something flashed between them; the stamp of blood clear on totally dissimilar countenances as judicious, principled man and hot-blooded, unscrupulous girl united in contempt for incompetent deceit.

14

After a moment Robert limped over and picked up the silver sheets. "You'd best finish your sweeping then. Arabella, your mother has been searching for you this past hour."

Arabella followed him to the house, slowing her steps to his; her father the only person she loved and whose approval she craved. "Why didn't you call the constable? You know he stole the silver you missed and probably has other scraps hidden away somewhere."

"I haven't caught him with anything," Robert said mildly. "And if I stripped him I wouldn't find anything except the intent in his mind. I was waiting for some slackness to give me an excuse to cancel his indentures without ruining his life by an accusation of theft, but after the warning you've delivered he'll guard himself so carefully that now I'll have him until his apprenticeship ends."

"I wouldn't," said Arabella, scowling. "I'd—"

"Send him to Newgate tonight," he finished for her. "I heard. I shall beat you for the disobedience of going out with Henry Cornish and think little of it, but I am deeply grieved to find that justice and mercy are only words to you."

"How did you know I'd been with Harry?"

She doesn't notice anything but her own concerns, he reflected, I might as well not have spoken. "I didn't believe even you would wander Cheapside alone, so when you were missed I sent to ask Mr. Cornish the whereabouts of his son. If you think to set your heart on Henry, you have misjudged the matter. As the properties adjoin and our affairs are similar, a marriage between you might have pleased both families, but Cornish is not the man to accept a self-willed hoyden for his elder son."

"Oh, I don't want to wed Harry and be shut up with a child a year for the rest of my life; born, wedded and dead all within two patches of Cheapside!" Arabella looked at her father with a mixture of mischief and resolve. "You always said you'd choose for your daughters but not wed them against their will; well, my will would be suited by a more pliant husband than Harry Cornish."

Robert stared at the silver in his hands, not wanting to meet her eyes. He should feel angry, he was angry as she casually weighed principle and found it unnecessary; but above all he felt overwhelming sadness. Arabella was calculating, defiant and selfish; she was also courageous, filled with vitality and never for an instant dull. He wouldn't admit it, but he loved

15

her more than easygoing Rob, submissive Susannah or rowdy Iam. He had lost four children in infancy, and was aware of sin when he thanked God that Arabella never sickened as they did. Even the smallpox which killed little Charity and month-old Joseph had left scarcely a mark on her.

"You will not listen to others, daughter," he said slowly, "so I have never before spoken what has long been in my heart. I hate waste, and wasted words are perhaps the most useless of all. Yet God gives a season for all things and somehow this seems the time, I know not why. I grieve for the sorrows your wilfulness must bring, but when you are overwhelmed by them, remember me. Remember I will pray for you every day of my life, and beyond it, if it be in my power to do so. Remember also that I knew what you were, and would be, and loved you still."

Arabella puzzled over his meaning, frowning. She was glad he was not angered by her escapade with Harry, a little worried by a reaction so different from what she had expected. Then she pushed unpleasant thought aside. What good fortune to find her father in such a mellow mood the very evening she was caught visiting 'Change with Harry. She remembered now that her Uncle Bevil was coming to dinner this evening; if she behaved faultlessly and kept entirely quiet until the morrow, she might not even be beaten.

Chapter Two

*A*rabella *seldom troubled to hide her* feelings and was almost without hypocrisy, yet another way in which she differed from most of those around her in an age when rapid changes of political fortune and religious ascendancy made both necessary arts of life. Only in one matter did she attempt to deceive herself as well as others: she was ashamed of feeling contempt for her mother.

Hopewell Sperling was thirty-eight years old and by the reckoning of the day an ageing woman. She had borne eight children, four of whom had died, yet retained an enviable serenity. She was ceaselessly busy yet never used her cares as an excuse for refusing help, indeed her charity was well known to the Cheapside poor, who blessed or took advantage of her according to their natures.

But she was content with so little, thought Arabella resentfully. She never felt confined if the time between one Sunday and the next went by without occasion for her to leave the house and yard; she never became exasperated by the constant, petty demands on her time when the slightest enterprise could have discovered opportunities for pleasure now that the Restoration brought licence even to the sober City. Hopewell helped polish silver and gold, but never surrendered to the feel of rich metal. She sat up with a sick servant and still emerged from her room faultlessly dressed the following morning; she honoured and obeyed her husband yet never followed him with her eyes or touched him for the simple joy of it. This last annoyed Arabella intensely, for the warmth of her own flesh made her an unerring judge where emotion was concerned, and she was certain that her father would have liked his wife to respond to him with more than dutiful submission. He was devout but enjoyed conversation and laughter; Arabella stamped on the thought that he must often find his wife intensely dull.

As she did.

She wanted to know so much, to ask about the court, about the latest gossip she heard over the kitchen table, to go to market and gatherings which were not religious, see for herself the marvels of a beautiful world. To go out. To go out. If Mistress Sperling had asked her husband for an escort to the Stocks or Leadenhall Market he would have provided one; if she had shown any desire for entertainment he was not narrow-minded over such freedom as was safe and sensible for his womenfolk. But Hopewell was contented by domesticity and did not ask.

Arabella changed her dress and petticoat for dinner with her nose pressed to the window, yearning redoubled by her visit to the Royal Exchange. Carriers, porters, heavy-wheeled carts, coaches, street women, beggar girls, all swirled past endlessly. Other women sauntered and stared, giggled in dark corners and dared the world daily. Court ladies hid behind masks and were guarded by servants but otherwise did as they pleased, drabs and market girls cried their wares openly; only respectability locked its prison tight.

She turned away from the window and slammed across the room, jerking at press doors and spilling clothes on the floor. Susannah was lying on the bed they shared, and consequently Arabella had to dress in the dark. She had not argued when she was refused a candle, fearful that her mother would forbid her to come down for dinner, but she'd look a fearful frump with her hair ill-dressed and her gown wrongly fastened in the gloom.

"Here," she said abruptly. "Lace this, will you, Susie?"

Susannah moaned. "I can't, my head is like an anvil. Wet the cloth again, please, Bella."

"If you'll lace me up, not before."

The mound on the bed stirred and then flopped back. "I can't."

"Of course you can! How do you suppose I'm going to lace my own stomacher tight enough, I'd like to know?" Another moan answered her, so she tried wheedling instead. "Come on, Susie. If you'll do it, I'll fetch some really cold water from the kitchen as well as the philtre you swear does you so much good."

18

Susannah did not reply, but fumbled her laces into annoyingly slack knots. Her breathing sounds really bad, thought Arabella critically, I'm glad I don't get headaches like that.

"Don't forget my water," whispered Susannah as she went out.

"Serve you right if I did," retorted Arabella. "Why should I be running about with pitchers of water when you won't even try to help me?" She ran downstairs, not intending to forget, just keep Susie waiting a few minutes; if she possessed the will of a rabbit she could perfectly well fetch water for herself and feel better for it.

But Uncle Bevil had arrived, there was madeira to be poured, and in the flurry of settling him and his lady by the hearth, Arabella did forget.

Bevil Sperling pinched her cheek when she brought his wine, and looked as if he would like to do more. "You've a fine wench here, Robert, you'd best put her match in my hands, hey? There's plenty of younger sons at court willing to overlook trade breeding for the sake of cash and a pretty face."

"I'll choose for my own when the time comes," replied Robert briefly. The brothers were totally dissimilar, and indeed had different mothers. While Robert was respected for his skill and honesty, Bevil possessed no settled convictions except those related to his own profit, and considered his brother an improvident fool when he joined the Parliamentary army. Bevil also had the good fortune to be a widower when Oliver Cromwell died, so was free to marry into an impeccably Royalist family at a time when this became a sensible precaution for an ambitious man to take. True, he was forced to settle for an impoverished spinster approaching thirty, but he judged that Royalist connections were more important than wealth or looks and his estimate had proved gratifyingly accurate.

Bevil had served an apprenticeship to an attorney and since the Restoration prospered in the legal battles between dispossessed but now triumphant Cavaliers and those who had seized their property during the war years. Corrupt courts and attorneys willing to buy verdicts had become commonplace, so Bevil and his kind flourished, while the jungle growth of vengeance added yet more bitterness to years of national blood feud.

The Restoration of Charles II to his throne had been accepted by all but a handful of his most obdurate enemies; many Englishmen were delighted by the turn of events, some resigned, nearly all cherished the hope of peace at last. Until 1642 England had been a nation where civil war belonged to the past, peace at home the birthright of half a dozen generations. Of course, there were always those who enjoyed fighting, but it was a taste Englishmen indulged on their travels. Then had come the quarrel between King and Parliament, an array of principle on either side which split families, localities and finally the nation.

By the end of the eighteen years of turmoil which followed, the country was united in one feeling only: a deadly loathing of armies. Any armies, all armies. Earlier Kings and Queens had ruled without them in an England men understood before it was lost in a maelstrom of blood and stupidity: pigheaded Scottish, Stuart blood and stupidity, many Englishmen said bitterly. Welsh Tudors, French Plantagenets and Norman conquerors had all learned English habits quickly or slowly according to their natures, only Stuarts seemed incapable of acquiring the touch which made the English compromise work. But in great weariness and believing that only by returning to their heritage could they build afresh, the son of a King beheaded by his people was recalled and crowned, a huge tax raised to pay off the army, and men hoped for better things at last.

But memory was too raw, too many had lost too much for easy healing. Even the King had to pass each day the place his father died. Men called Charles II pliable or easygoing, and said he was interested only in women; he was all those things and far more besides. Like his subjects, he desired peace; like them, he also wanted to win, to be revenged, to profit and enjoy it. He had much in common with Bevil Sperling but needed more patience for success, since his ambitions were higher though equally unscrupulous.

Bevil would never be completely satisfied with success, nevertheless he was well pleased with himself. In the five years since the Restoration he had acquired lodgings off the Strand and cherished hopes of moving to better quarters soon. He dressed like a courtier and hung on the outer fringes of Whitehall snapping up commissions and some of the less reputable government business: litigation was ruinously expensive and swarms of lawyers fattened on its bounty.

Arabella knew nothing of this and would not have cared if she had. Robert did, and only a sense of duty and compassion for Bevil's wife impelled him to entertain his brother at widely spaced intervals. Her ancient family had been ruined by the war and all efforts to regain their property failed: she tried to adapt herself to her unprincipled husband and the vulgar company he kept, but without success. She was a thin, bitter-looking woman who had already miscarried four times in five years of marriage. Bevil did not expect her to live long and only just avoided remarking on the fact too frequently. He was already reviewing his acquaintance in a leisurely way, searching for a profitable replacement.

Since Robert had few illusions about his brother, he went out of his way to be kind to his wife when she came, and this left Arabella to entertain her uncle while her mother was distracted by some crisis in the kitchen.

Bevil regarded his niece with unqualified approval. "I'll say one thing for Robert, he's bred a daughter fit for the court out of ash and Cheapside hammering." He roared with laughter and slapped his thigh at his own wit.

The crude double meaning escaped Arabella but she smiled demurely, mindful of her resolve to be good. "Do you often go to court, sir?"

He looked at her sharply, he made a living out of gratifying desires which were seldom plainly expressed, and read her yearning instantly. "Every day I am not kept from it by affairs. You must beg your father to let you come and stay with me in a year or so and my wife will chaperone you there. A fresh and lovely face always finds a welcome."

"Oh, thank you!" Arabella knew that her father would never grant permission for her to go to Bevil, so kept her eyes downcast to avoid giving the impression of intimate conversation. "I shan't let you forget such an offer, if your lady does not object. If you're of the same mind in a year or two's time..." She risked a swift upward glance through her lashes, excited when she saw his eyes wander instinctively to her bosom, demurely covered though it was.

"I'll be of the same mind," he promised. A wench of beauty backed by Cheapside gold would be a valuable gift to bestow where his interest was served. "I daresay you know better ways of bringing your father to your line of thinking than I do, but if he is overly stubborn, why, we can devise a few tricks between us, eh?" He patted her knee and winked; a clandestine meeting between the chit and a suitable client, then Robert might be glad of any offer to turn the girl off creditably.

Arabella agreed enthusiastically, aware that her father had

not missed Bevil's hand on her knee and glad when the bustle of serving the meal enabled her to leave his side without offence. She looked at her aunt's prematurely aged face and wondered what her uncle could see in such a woman, she wasn't surprised that he only spoke to her in tones of angry impatience.

Robert Sperling still held to the old-fashioned custom of having trestles erected in the parlour for meals, so the whole household ate together. Partly this was because space was lacking, and partly because he considered servants and apprentices as belonging to his family. There were differences but no distinctions between God's children. Bevil was so disgruntled by the idea of being wedged in discomfort on a bench for his repast that he sat without thinking and had to be prodded to his feet again for grace; while they stood with bowed heads, he met Arabella's stare and winked, so even she was slightly shocked.

Robert was not in the habit of praying at such length that good food chilled on the platter, but he was sincere and no fool. He saw his brother's look and Arabella's confusion, and had no difficulty in interpreting both. Brother or no, he never comes to this house again, he thought. May God witness that I will see him dead if he corrupts Arabella. Without warning, his formidable temper unsheathed and he prayed with his eyes open, head tipped back arrogantly, staring straight at Bevil. "O Lord, bless this thy plenty and grant that we never count thy gifts as ours by right. Teach us to recognise evil even at our own board, and punish it; may we always remember that from thy wrath there is no hiding place. Yea, I will punish; yea, I will avenge, saith the Lord, and my anger not be turned aside. I have spoken, so shall I perform. Amen."

Bent heads began to lift long before he had finished, breath held, mouths agape. Never before had they heard a grace like it. For an instant there was the glass stillness of shock, and all the while Robert stood staring at the brother of his half-blood, threat and not prayer unmistakable. Bevil jerked from abstraction with the rest, a superstitious shudder in his guts, followed by fierce rage. They were all laughing at him, the only man of quality in a room full of yokels; blood surged into his face and he opened his mouth to answer threat with threat, then closed it again. Bevil was a winner, not a fighter, and sufficiently shrewd to know that with Robert in this mood he could only lose expensively and unpleasantly. There were other girls less protected than Arabella, even if waste of such beauty made him regretful.

Robert smiled and nodded slightly before pulling out the bench for the ladies. Brother Bevil had understood his meaning well enough. A babble of talk swept over the room as everyone chattered to cover embarrassment, only Bevil's wife still watched her husband, a faint smile on her lips.

She turned to Robert when they were both seated. "You and your brother are very different. I have often remarked it, but never so clearly as tonight."

"There is no doubting our relationship," he replied coolly. "Only the direction of our lives."

"Which now part forever?"

"Perhaps, although I hope you will always feel that a welcome awaits you here."

She inclined her head. "I think it would not be right for me to come where my husband is unwelcome, but I thank you for your kindness. You should beware, though; what Bevil would have done from greed, he might now plot in hatred and revenge. It isn't in his power to forgive such humiliation as he has felt tonight."

"In his power but not in his nature, perhaps," agreed Robert, smiling. "My words were simply a warning, which I trust will keep him from the injury he had in his mind to do." He was not the man to tell a wife that her husband lacked courage to plot revenge if there was the slightest risk the result would prove unprofitable. She knew it anyway and once honour was satisfied by warning him, would consider it shockingly underbred to discuss her husband's failings.

Though meals at the Sign of the Golden Spurs were served on trestles, there was no lack of fine plate to decorate the boards. Light glinted from candelabra and gilt salts, even the apprentices being supplied with forks, a new fashion since the Restoration. Linenfold panelling on the walls shone with the lustre of untold polishings, the floor pleasantly scented by rushes bought that morning in Leadenhall Market. Only, it was stifling hot. The windows could not be opened since they gave straight on the stench of Furnival Alley, while the shop occupied the front of the house and must be kept securely barred.

Hopewell Sperling gave up her attempts to talk to her brother-in-law. She was not sure what Robert had done to annoy him so, but felt too tired for the effort of lifting him out of the sulks. Her back was aching as it had ever since Lucy was born,

23

born and dead in a single day; now she had a dreadful fear she had started another child. Pray God, no, she thought desperately. Robert was a good man and had kept from her more than a full year after she was so ill with Lucy; she wondered whether she was irremediably wicked to wish that he was also a sinful one who would take another woman away from her sight, and leave her to the touch of his hands and lips only, free from the fear of pregnancy. Poor little Lucy. She had looked so pathetic, lying in her arms without even the strength to whimper. Poor Charity and Joseph, dead of the smallpox. Poor baby Diccon, whose face she could scarcely remember, bled to death fifteen years ago by a doctor who said he could save him when the London ague struck. At least Rob and Arabella and little Tam seemed hale enough, although she worried over Susannah. She was so sweet and gentle, looking as if a rough touch would break her bones apart. Hopewell knew the signs, these were the ones whom God took early, as if He could not wait for their company.

"Arabella," she said sharply. "Go upstairs and see how your sister fares. The herbs you prepared this afternoon should be well steeped by now and a draught might ease her." She watched Arabella curtsey with a certain wry amusement although no flicker showed on her face. It was not easy to extricate yourself with grace from a bench on which four others sat, but Arabella managed it, and without saying a word drew all eyes to herself. We'll have scandal on our doorstep with that girl, she thought. Robert does not approve of child marriages, but if John Cornish is willing, the sooner we speak to him for his son, the better. Rob is not the craftsman his father is, and would do best as partner to Henry Cornish in the future, who has thrust and arrogance enough to double his father's gain. Cornish's will need our space to expand, the deal could well be made.

As if in response to her thought there was a heavy knocking on the outer door, and one of the maids scuttled into the room after a shouted enquiry. "'Tis Mr. Henry from next door mindful to see 'ee, sir. I tole 'im there were guests, but he said he would wait an' take no more than a peckin' o' Mr. Sperling's time."

"I'll come," said Robert briefly, and followed the maid through to the shop. Their only outside door was heavily barred at night and he allowed no one else to open it; a guard of apprentices always slept under the counter with staves by their sides, for a goldsmith's premises tempted all manner of thieves.

Talk in the parlour had been limping along anyway, and now died away as everyone listened to catch what had brought young Harry round so late.

"I've come to apologise, sir." His voice carried clearly since it never occurred to him to lower it, or tiptoe around a purpose once his mind was set. "I did not like to think of Arabella punished while I sat at ease, when the fault was mine for asking her."

"Your behaviour is not my concern, while Arabella's is," replied Robert drily. "I accept your apology but it cannot serve as an excuse for her."

"She is young and I suggested the expedition, perhaps she did not realise—"

"My dear Harry, the sooner you understand that Arabella always knows exactly what she is about, the better. Come and drink some wine with us instead of arguing in the dark." He ushered Harry into the room, regretting that he must introduce his disreputable brother but with his mind moving along very similar lines to his wife's. The boy was clearly taken with Arabella and she would not do better; for her own good he might be forced to thrust her into marriage against her will.

Harry wore his own hair, since Alderman Cornish disapproved of vain adornment, otherwise he was as richly dressed as Bevil and in better taste, conversed easily and appeared to feel no embarrassment at breaking in on a private party. There will be some molten metal spilled in that household if they wed, reflected Robert, when both are so self-willed. And was struck by qualms again; at thirteen years old, surely Arabella was too young for choice in such a matter.

Harry was unsurprised to find Arabella absent from the room; he had come because he could not keep his mind from thinking of her beaten bloody and locked in an attic. He could not stop thinking of it now. He made himself ridiculous by coming when he could accomplish no purpose, but had not been able to keep away. Consequently, his astonishment showed when Arabella came into the room, looking even more beautiful than she had in the afternoon and clearly in excellent fettle.

Robert lifted his goblet in ironic toast. "You see that you are not the only one on whom a pretty face has its effect, my boy. Even I sometimes temper retribution with understanding."

Harry laughed. "I'm grateful you've relieved my conscience, sir, and don't suppose I shall be the last fool to make himself absurd for that same face." He returned the toast as if

25

it was a contract they sealed, then dropped his eyes to the silver in his hand and changed the subject. Whatever other kind of fool he might be, Harry Cornish was already skilled in the art of negotiating a bargain. "This is not apprentices' work, sir."

Robert twirled his goblet thoughtfully. He liked the boy and Arabella needed a strong hand: yet, I'll not marry Harry, she had said that afternoon, and meant it. "These are from a set I made before ever I had apprentices or journeymen; I regret sometimes that I no longer have time to grave and scrop as I used, only finish the work of others. Perhaps in my dotage I may return to my pleasure again."

Arabella was aware of Harry the instant she entered the room, knew why he had come and rejoiced in it. But it would do no harm to make him think her indifferent and she had anyway come downstairs with other matters on her mind. It took a great deal to divert her from her own affairs, but she was frightened now. "Mother, I think you should come to Susannah. She says her head is much worse and certainly has a fever." Susannah had looked like a damned spirit under judgment, her face fallen in under the pressure of pain, her coverings soaked from a fever which had risen out of nowhere.

Hopewell shuddered to her daughter's touch, foreboding for Susannah instantly confirmed. Superstition told her it was scarcely worth enduring the routine of nursing and desperate hope, when loss inevitably would follow. "You gave her the decoction?"

Arabella shook her head, tears pricking. Her inadequately pounded herbs stuck in Susannah's throat and made her retch.

Hopewell made her excuses and went upstairs, a signal for uncongenial guests to take their leave; Harry took advantage of the bustle to draw Arabella aside. "Have you ever been to the May Fair?"

Arabella shook her head, dark curls bobbing. "Oh, Harry, are you going to take me?"

"Has no one ever told you what a forward little minx you are? Yes, I'd like to take you if your father will allow it."

"He won't, Harry! Never! I can meet you . . . tell me when and I'll slip out somehow. Say you will, please, Harry!"

"Be quiet, you little shrew. You must know that May Fair Fields are beyond the palace of St. James's, we'd be away most of a day and your father have every right to forbid me his house after the anxiety such a prank would cause. I want him to trust me to take care of you, not think me a rogue."

Her mouth tightened and her foot began to tap on the floor. "Why ask me then, when you know I cannot come? He'll say the May Fair is full of lice-lice-licentiousness and bid me do my stitchery instead."

"So it is," said Harry, grinning. "That's why I know you'll enjoy it, although it isn't a word you should know. I wager you a gilded brooch to a pinch of herbs that Mr. Sperling never used it to you."

Arabella gave a gurgle of laughter. "How wretched of you not just to give me the brooch! Though I daresay I should be ashamed to wear it lest people thought such workmanship came from our bench," she added provocatively. Alderman Cornish might not craft silver any longer, but Harry had served a full apprenticeship and was well capable of making any brooch he gave.

"I'll ask your father in the morning, since this moment isn't opportune, with Mistress Sperling so anxious for Susannah. I hope she is recovered soon, there is a deal of sickness about in the heat." His lips brushed hers, and she felt the touch of his hands on waist and bosom. Then he was gone, calling a cheerful good-night to her father as he went.

Arabella opened her eyes again, she had squeezed them shut while he kissed her, to enjoy the sensation more. She hoped she would be able to go to the May Fair, but wasn't optimistic, since Harry was being stuffy and asking if she might. May Fair Fields were notorious even when cows grazed there during other months of the year, and in fair time it must be much worse; dancing and dog fighting, hogshead rolling and—and fondling under hedges, thought Arabella, drawing generously on her limited imagination of vice. Gallants in velvet coats with bold, seeking eyes, and Harry's lips again.

The slam of her father relocking the door bars roused her and they went together into the parlour, a scene of ordered chaos as trestles were polished and stacked against the wall, and apprentices burnished plate ready for Robert to check back into his chest.

"Go and see if your mother requires help, Arabella," said Robert curtly. "Then come and tell me how Susannah does."

Arabella stuck out her tongue at Richard Goodenough as she passed him on her way upstairs. He had somehow contrived to drink too much although the apprentices were only allowed small beer; he looked half stupefied and Arabella thought gleefully that he would probably puke before his turn came to check in plate. Then there would be a fine-to-do, since her father was already short-tempered from an evening of Uncle Bevil's company.

She pushed open the door to her bedroom reluctantly, she could smell vomit and the sharp stench of sweat, the reek of sweet candles, of syrups and decoctions. She wrinkled her nose distastefully but went over to the bed, driven by curiosity rather than compassion. Although of course she was sorry for Susie.

She stood and looked down at her sister and then, yes, truly she was sorry. She felt uncomfortably guilty too: if only she had pounded the herbs properly, perhaps Susie would have been able to choke down some liquid before it was too late. For her sister was dying.

Her hand lay like curled leather on the coverlet, and she did not hear Arabella's muttered contrition. She ought to hear, thought Arabella resentfully. She was all right this afternoon; if only she would try a little, surely she would live.

Her mother was on her knees by the bed and Arabella shook her in fright, prayer could wait until after Susie was dead. "What can we do? If she could be roused and made to drink or . . . or something, wouldn't it help a little?"

"She can't swallow," said Hopewell dully. "Leave her in peace."

"But—" began Arabella, then abruptly she ran out of the room and clattered down the stairs.

Her father looked up as she half fell down their precipitous steepness. "How is she?"

"She's very ill! She's going to die unless we do something!" She tugged at his arm. "Please come, Mother is praying but I'm sure if I brewed a posset and we made her take it she would be better! She isn't even trying, neither of them are." All the disgust of the tough and healthy for those who surrender without a struggle was in her voice, and Robert felt her tone pull at his own spirit as he followed her upstairs. He did not give up easily himself, either.

Even in the few moments Arabella had been away, the sickroom had changed. Susannah no longer lay as if already dead, but thrashed and moaned; there was fresh vomit on the floor and even Arabella could see there was no hope of forcing anything down her throat.

"Hold her feet, Arabella," said Robert quietly. "We must prevent her from burning up more strength." He grasped Susannah's shoulders and forced them back on the bed, but for all her delicacy he had difficulty in holding her. He ought to send for a doctor but instinct told him it was already too late, and doctors were tormentors who refused to admit ignorance and killed patients with hot coals and emetics long after all hope was gone.

Susannah was talking now, voice rough and angry, not like her gentle self at all. Words were slurred and unrecognisable while all the time she fought against their hands, skin scorching to the touch; how could so great a fever have risen so quickly?

"Go now, Arabella," Robert said softly. "Share a bed with one of the maids tonight." It was not right for her to witness such suffering when she could do no good.

"No," said Arabella, she looked angry rather than upset. "I owe a debt to Susannah. I would pay it by staying while she lives."

He hesitated, and then decided that he had no right to interfere in the first sign of God's grace he had seen in her. "As you wish. Hand me the dipper and I will see whether she can swallow a trifle."

While he held her one-handed, Susannah tore from his grasp, half flinging herself off the bed. Her nightdress tore and he stilled with shock.

Arabella had always admired her father, and felt cheated when he betrayed her into contempt by too obvious dismay at the sight of his daughter's bare bosom under his hands. What does it matter? she thought scornfully.

He recovered himself in an instant, then spilled half the dipper as Susannah thrashed afresh. He looked up, his full weight on her shoulders, face close to hers, his expression set. "Arabella, I want no argument. You must do exactly as I say. Make any excuse you like, the need to brew fresh potions, anything, but take your mother out of here. Shut the door behind you and do not come back. Go straight downstairs and wait in the yard with her until I come."

Arabella had seldom seen him look so, and protests died on her lips; she coaxed her mother to her feet somehow and guided her from the room as if her senses were disordered.

The night air in the yard was infinitely welcome and she breathed deeply. Everyone said air was dangerous to the sick, but if ever she was ill Arabella reckoned that she would prefer to breathe and accept the risk of it. I'll never be sick, she thought in sudden panic. I'll not become a thing of horror in a matter of hours and tamely yield up life to a trifling fever.

29

But it had not been a trifling fever; a quarter of its power would have sufficed to kill Susie. Arabella sat on the melting-shed step and tried to think about Harry and the Royal Exchange, but somehow she could not manage it. Her mother sat by her side with her head on her knees and did not move at all, while London sounds drifted over the wall: even in darkness there was a shuffle of feet on cobbles, loud voices, the call of the watch, an occasional cart bringing country wares for to-morrow's markets. The bells of St. Mary's struck the hour and one by one the scores of City churches took up the sound. Arabella shivered; it was like a toll for the dead.

At last she heard her father's step and stood stiffly. "She's dead?"

He nodded. "God rest her soul." He stooped and kissed his wife gently but she did not stir.

He looked at Arabella measuringly, wondering what to tell her. Only thirteen years old and flowering with life, now she must face death and the long strain of waiting for it to come. But there was no way to hide the truth, and he had always judged her as very strong. "I'm going to strip and wash," he said abruptly. "Then I will bring fresh clothes and you must both do the same. I have brought down Susannah's bedding and we'll burn everything here, at once. I know I can rely on your help, as I have already tonight. As I shall in the days ahead."

Arabella felt her lips frame words which would not come, the chill as her blood stilled with shock. She had lived in London all her life and knew what such desperate measures meant.

The plague. Susannah had died of plague.

Chapter Three

O*f course there had been rumours of* plague for weeks. There always were in London. A year seldom went by without a couple of hundred or so dying of it in the slums of St. Giles or Wapping, nor twenty years without a major epidemic. The hot spring alone was enough to make rumour multiply and decide the fainthearted to retreat to the country unless there was a break in the drought, but most shrugged and expected rain soon; it had after all been dry since the previous autumn. Anyway plague nearly always stayed in the slums and the poor could not afford the luxury of abandoning work to tramp the country for a season.

There had not been a case of plague in the rich ward of Cheap for five years. Susannah had scarcely ventured farther than church or meeting house in months; this was what made the disease so horrifying, the way it remained confined for years, then struck without warning, cure or pattern.

That and the agonising death it brought.

From the moment he saw plague tokens on Susannah's breast, Robert Sperling knew that most, perhaps all, of his household were dead. Their doors and windows would be boarded up for forty days and guarded by armed men to keep them in; if another of the family sickened, then time would be measured afresh. Until they all died, or the survivors went insane from the horror of it all. They could expect no help except a drunken crone sent by the parish, more to report cases than give assistance, a repulsive and obligatory presence as if the disease had taken human form. A masked doctor might call, but those who were honest admitted ignorance of any cure.

These were the regulations, enforced with the harshness of

fear. Plague deaths were often concealed, or households fled before they could be incarcerated when to admit the disease carried such fearsome penalties. So contagion spread, by touch certainly, but how else no one knew. As punishment for sin, some said, yet the good died as easily as the wicked; by self-indulgence, others maintained, though the strong were stricken as swiftly as the weak; by exhalations of air, by fear itself, by the devil's curse as he strode on his way. Only one thing was certain: once in a household, spread of the disease was almost inevitable, so their doors would be daubed with the red cross of contagion and the prayer few expected to be answered: "Lord, have mercy on us."

Certainly, no one else would.

For the first time since he returned from the war, Robert Sperling did not unlock the bars on his door as Bow Bells struck seven in the morning. Instead, he called everyone living in the house to the parlour, from Betsy the simpleton scullion to Hopewell his wife, who suffered herself to be led and dressed but had not spoken since she left Susannah's room.

Robert was uncertain whether she understood the cause of her daughter's death and surrendered to despair because she had not seen one child die, but all of them; or whether quite simply she no longer cared. He had to care; he was master of a household facing a supreme ordeal and must somehow turn his back on the dead to sustain the living. And, unless some miracle occurred, do it again and again as they watched each other die.

Not one of them grasped all of his meaning when he told them how Susannah died, though everyone except baby Tam had seen barred doors and daubed cross before. He spoke quietly and clearly, yet still they did not understand until thunderous blows began to echo through the house, faces peering through distorting glass as piece by piece light vanished as boards were nailed over doors and windows. A murmur went round the room then, feet shuffled and one of the maids began to sob. A single candle was lit, flame blurring before Arabella's eyes as she wept too, she who always scorned to weep.

"Some wine, I think, Betsy," said Robert, watching faces suddenly aged by fear. "Then we must reckon our supplies and decide how best to conserve them. Arabella, you could do that."

Arabella wiped her nose on her sleeve. "Can't—can't some-one go to market in the night? Or someone for us, perhaps?"

"Certainly we will not be allowed out, others may put goods for us to draw up to a window. But we must be prepared for people fearing to touch basket or rope or coins from this house." Except those so depraved they bargained for an extortionate fee and then were never seen again, he thought but did not say. "We have preserves and wine, and took a recent delivery of flour, with care we should do well enough."

"How did the parish know so quickly?" demanded Rob. "Who scuttled off to tell them before we had time to prepare ourselves?"

"I told them," said Robert quietly. "And followed Susannah to her grave in the dawn with the white staff of infection in my hand and a bellman walking before as a warning. No other house in the inner wards is infected, so this we owe our neighbours and our city: to keep ourselves apart and die if need be to save them."

"I haven't seen Susannah in two days and was out all yesterday, surely—"

"No, Rob. All of us together or it is wasted." He stared at them over the light of the candle, shadows all around. They would soon lack candles, too. "Face it now, all of you. Face it and put it behind you. We stay together until forty days have gone by since the last infection, and if I should die then I pledge those who are left to keep faith in this, or await eternal judgment. It is possible to escape from this house, given time and skill. A slum dweller can be boarded in like a rat in a trap, we have yards and back walls which cannot be guarded all the time. Yet if one of you takes his life and goes, he takes murder on his soul. So long as I live, I will stop you and will not be asleep; if I am dead then I will reach out from the grave to curse you, and the Lord will not have mercy on your soul."

Arabella felt her breath stop, and sensed it stop also in every throat in the room as they stared at her father's face, gold and black in the light of a single flame. Then he relaxed and laughed, pouring wine. "A toast to you all! May the Sign of the Golden Spurs turn out the finest craft Cheapside has ever seen while we are working through our time, for be sure I'll not allow you time to brood."

They sniggered uneasily, minds bound to the treadmill of panic. Even as they drank, they studied each other with unnatural earnestness, looking for plague signs as they would not cease to look every hour of the days ahead.

"I still think it is unjust for me to be here," muttered Rob

33

to Arabella. "If I had gone at once I could not have carried infection. Now—"

"Now you can hardly help but rub shoulders with the next victim the moment before he falls," Arabella finished for him, gulping her wine thirstily. She wanted another gobletful immediately, and then another if only her father would move away from the flagon. She was the most likely to be infected, sharing a room with Susie the evening before she died, the feel of stinking bedclothes and scaled skin still on her hands.

Richard Goodenough was standing immediately behind them and agreed wholeheartedly with Rob. He knew he could not yet carry the plague. I'll get out, he thought. Whatever old Sperling says, he has to sleep sometimes and then just watch me go. He looked at Rob speculatively; if he was left as watchman then they might connive something together.

Robert drove them about their business until any spare moment was spent in sleep instead of morbid fears, and at the same time demanded a completely new approach to excellence in their craft. He set them to attempt techniques and designs he had wondered about before but not dared try, since new methods were often unsuccessful and led to wasteful remelting and reworking while customers went elsewhere. Now, waste did not matter. No one would buy from the House of the Spurs for months and his purpose was to deny his household an instant's leisure, so the best use for such silver as he had in stock was to craft it again and again in ever more innovative ways, to disrupt routine instead of enforcing the usual disciplines of production.

So he made everyone take their turn at each process, a heresy on the goldsmith's craft which would have earned him expulsion from his guild if it had become known. And unexpectedly, they were caught by the sheer novelty and originality of Robert's ordering of their lives; no one knew what task they would be given next, what tried habits pitched aside, on which day serving maids would become apprentices or journeymen sweat over cooking pots.

Even baby Tam was given metal to pound into a drunken finger bowl, and after several failures in melting and shaping, Arabella proved herself surprisingly successful in the new technique of carving silver, rather than punching or hammering designs. To her delight, her father refused to allow her to help in the house, so Hopewell was forced to emerge from apathy and exercise authority there, although she performed her tasks as an ox does, blindfold at the grinding wheel.

For the first time in her life Arabella found herself encouraged to perform work she found interesting. Her normal routine of petty chores interspersed by long periods of confined inactivity left her in such a state of frustrated boredom that she was almost unmanageable; now, the satisfaction of seeing her own efforts produce something of worth made this the happiest time of her life—had it not been for terror sunk into bone and sense. Terror which came in great breakers out of the dark and kept her awake even when she was exhausted, and made her fingers fumble just when the utmost precision was needed.

After five days she was allowed to try her skills on a candlestick; Robert fashioned the stem and base, then left her to carve thinly peeled metal into decorative fronds. Vice, punch, hammer, chisel; her hands were toughening and she rejected Richard's help when he offered to hold the pincers while she peeled another leaf. Her head ached from the clang of hammers and when the leaf was edged to her satisfaction she wandered out into the yard to drink from a rain butt.

The water was green and scummy, still it had not rained. Arabella sat in a scrap of shadow and stared dreamily at a butterfly hovering above the herb bed: five days since Susannah died and they were all healthy; no one spoke of it, but with each day hope grew, unacknowledged.

The sun was oppressive, opaque through clouds of dust; heat and glare were everywhere, the physical labour of silversmithing intolerable. Even the sounds of Cheapside dulled in the heat and Rob said plague must be spreading elsewhere now, their incarceration a pointless martyrdom. But when Richard tried to escape one night, he discovered that Robert Sperling rested in the melting shed instead of in his bedroom. He was caught as he climbed the wall and received the worst beating of his life, with the edge of a skimming paddle before them all.

Arabella laid her head against the wall, if only it wasn't so hot. The yard was like a furnace, but she felt disinclined to move. Harry came each day and shouted the latest news across Furnival Alley, threw over little luxuries for her alone; at least they need not fear starvation as Robert had suggested. The Cornishes marketed for them and extended whatever credit they required: she ought to be up and waiting for Harry when he came, he would laugh to find her sleeping like a grandmother.

Someone was speaking her name. She looked up and blinked, how strange her head should feel so heavy and her arms so hot. She was in shadow and gasped with the relief of it, before heat rolled over her again and hands probed her face and body. She cried with pain when she was lifted and opened her eyes to find herself in her father's arms. "I've got it, haven't I?" she said, astonished.

He laid his face to hers and his cheek was wet. "Yes, my sweet, you have. You are strong, though, and will live. Promise?"

Her tongue was like cloth, her throat a furnace. She could not speak, surely she could not speak. "I promise." she said clearly. "Stay with me."

"All the time I'm not beating cowardice out of Richard with a puddler."

She chuckled feebly and snuggled into his arms.

But he would not let her rest, or hide from the waves of sickness. Instead, she must sit when she longed to lie, swallow wine when her throat was so raw she thrashed wildly to escape tipped flasks, suffer change after change of linen as foul-smelling sweat soaked coverings and bed straw.

All the time she was sick. Remorselessly, endlessly sick. Until fire in her throat spread into stomach and chest, until she was scraped of will and strength, until she wanted nothing but an end to it all. Then, from a very great distance she remembered her promise to live and struggled feebly against the dark and back to agony again. She wanted to ask her father to release her from her pledge, knew he was close by and wondered hazily whether he had locked Richard up while he stayed by her side. She could not speak, tongue bleeding as it peeled in thick strips.

She had been burning alive and now was freezing cold. It must be raining at last. Her arms and legs were numb; agony blazing like a torch at thigh and neck. Her eyes bulged and mouth gaped with the pressure of such pain, bones crushed by the power of it; yet at the same time she seemed to be drifting and saw herself lying in a strange circle of death, quite clearly heard her mother say unemotionally: "She cannot last." On her knees, hope given up the moment I sickened, thought Arabella disgustedly.

"She will last as she promised, and do as she said she would," replied Robert, hands on her shoulders.

Arabella wanted to tell him she had heard, and moved slightly. In her mind she took an enormous stride from one place to another, from surcease back to pain, from watching herself die to a measure of sense again. In fact, her lips curved slightly and her eyes opened long enough for her father's face to slide across blurred vision. How stupid to think he would release her from a promise even if she asked, how feeble to want to ask when she despised those who yielded in adversity. Of course she was not ill.

She was, but somehow she lived.

Chapter Four

Two weeks passed before Arabella was well enough to be carried down to the courtyard and sit in such coolness as the evening brought, and even so little effort brought her to the edge of fainting. The air was marvellous, though, and she drew long breaths as if she would never have enough of it.

Her father had ordered that she was to be left quite alone and she was thankful for it, staring at sunset sky, dingy brick and a fleck of green where the single Cheapside tree showed above tumbling roofs, as if her mind would never adjust to a life returned from hell.

She had taken the plague, and lived. Not one in twenty did that, and pride in her achievement stirred. Smallpox and plague both, and just one pit on my chin to show for it, she thought, I'll surely live my threescore years and ten now.

Tam came tiptoeing up, glancing over his shoulder to be sure he wasn't observed. "You should see my bowl now, Arabella. It doesn't wobble at all and has punch decoration round the rim."

She smiled, although normally she found him annoying. "Has it, lovedy? You must show me."

He stared at her. "You look old and faded. No one except Father thought you'd live."

"Well, I did," snapped Arabella, rapidly abandoning charity with all the world. "And you were told to leave me alone."

"Rob's taken it and Betsy's dead," he offered, wiping his fingers thoughtfully on the wall. "I haven't, though."

"Don't say that!" cried Arabella. "Turn round three times

38

and spit! Don't you know better than to tempt the devil with such boasts?"

He twirled obediently and spat expertly between her feet. "Mother says such things are empty super-super-superstitshun."

Arabella thought that the devil needed as much placating as God but refrained from saying so, closing her eyes and refusing to answer until he trailed disconsolately away. Rob. Dear, cheerful Rob terrified and torn apart as she had been. And if less than one in twenty survived the plague then she must have taken all the luck their household could expect.

She had. Rob died during the night when his fever would not gather, and so destroyed him long before its heat was fully stoked. Then one of the maids lasted through three days of agony and was thought to be recovering, but her strength was gone and she slipped out of life while she slept.

Arabella refused to be carried any longer, for she yearned to be well again. Instead she fumbled from step to step clinging to the banister, and consequently was completely spent the whole time she remained in the yard. Although she had survived, her usual buoyancy had not returned and the pit in her thigh where the tumour burst still felt as though a cinder smouldered there. She had thought herself freed from fear, since surely plague could not be contracted twice, yet no one eyed the others more narrowly than she or was thrown into such despair by reports of headaches or an itch. The house stank, too. Lower windows were boarded and the serving maids terrified of touching plague vomit and soiled sheets: the whole of London sweltered in an unprecedented heat, so its customary stench redoubled and there was little relief even in the yard.

Thousands were now dying every week, but at least the inner city remained fairly clear: they need not feel their ordeal was in vain. No other house was reported as infected in the wards of Cheap, Walbrook or Cornhill, and only the odd case had so far appeared in Leadenhall, Gracechurch and Dowgate. Even so, trade was at a standstill, the poor who escaped contagion faced starvation as their masters fled into the country.

Five days after she came downstairs, Arabella opened her eyes from drowsing to find Harry sitting on the wall looking down at her.

"Hullo," he said casually. "I've watched you once or twice, but thought you best left alone."

"Why haven't you quitted London with the rest?" She felt some animosity towards him for being free to leave.

"If your father had compassion enough to imprison his household for the sake of us all, then mine considered that his duty as alderman kept him here where he is needed. He ordered my mother and the children into Essex, but I would not run while he stayed and you were sick. Some things must be left to the hand of God."

"Only some things?" She was tired of God's hand, which seemed to dispense evil easier than good.

"I think so, yes. My decision whether to stay or run, and God's to measure reward or blame afterwards. My father prays that my thinking will not bring me to hellfire."

"Plague fire. Hell would be a pleasant summer outing compared to that."

He laughed. "Poor Arabella. Be comforted that it has left you more beautiful than before. Wan delicacy suits you even better than your usual health."

A sparkle came to her eyes, beyond everything she hated looking ugly. "Really, Harry? You're teasing, you know I look hideous and my skin is like old rags."

He looked at her critically, sensing how much this mattered to her. "Any woman who can make me sit on the top of a wall admiring her from a distance must be out of the common way." He clasped at his heart dramatically and nearly fell. "Ah, Arabella the fair! My bosom throbs with emotion, the pout of your lips brings me to my knees!"

She giggled. "Idiot. It's a long tumble into a plague-stricken yard if you fall on your knees from there."

He flushed. "My duty was to my own house, or I would not have kept away while you were shut up."

"Then you would be a fool! Keep from the plague and be thankful, nothing but bars and a guard would have held me here."

"Are you sure?"

"Of course I'm sure! Are you mad as well?" But as she said it, she knew it wasn't true. She felt no sense of obligation to fellow citizens she had never seen, but would hate to appear contemptible in her father's eyes.

"Good for you, Bella," said Harry seriously; it was infuriating the way he read her thoughts. "We'll go to the May Fair next year, and I will ask your father for permission to wed you as soon as you've stopped being a silly little girl and are willing to accept me."

"I'm not a silly little girl!" she flashed.

"Yes, you are, or you would listen to what I really said, instead of boiling over at the first home truth you hear and pretending deafness to the rest."

She stood up, folding the shawl which had been over her knees with angry precision. "And you are a rude, hateful boy! I'll never wed you, and so I told my father." It was on the tip of her tongue to say she wouldn't go with him to the May Fair either, but she thought better of it. He was tiresome enough to remember and refuse to take her without a grovelling apology. "If you had an ounce of proper feeling you would be talking commonplaces, and doing what you could to divert me instead of being disagreeable."

"I have diverted you," he pointed out, preparing to descend on his side of the wall. "You haven't felt so well since you took the plague, there's nothing like a good quarrel for stripping off the mopes." He disappeared with a slither, leaving her scowling resentfully at where he had been.

Then her expression lightened, and she laughed. She did feel a great deal better, although whether Harry's declaration when she still looked so haggish was at the root of it, or the entertainment of quarrelling, she could not have said.

Cook and the last serving maid died the following morning, and two days later Hopewell fell in the parlour and was raging with fever by the time she was carried upstairs.

As plague tightened its grip on London, the virulence of the disease seemed to increase. Where the fever had taken days, now it killed in hours; where once the purple plague spots had signalled hope that the poison was gathering and the sufferer might survive if he had strength enough, now they became the inevitable prologue to death. If possible, the agony seemed worse, symptoms more varied and baffling than ever.

And of all those who contracted plague, it was generally agreed that pregnant women had least chance of survival, which meant no chance at all. Hopewell Sperling miscarried her child as the convulsions racked her and no one could say whether she died of haemorrhage or fever.

Arabella stood dry-eyed at one side of the bed, her father at the other. She felt utterly exhausted, far too tired for tears or sorrow, only part recovered as she was herself. There had been no one else to tend her mother: the doctor whom she dimly remembered at her own bedside had not been seen in weeks and was presumably dead, the depraved quacks who preyed on stricken households better kept away.

41

Robert stirred at last and slowly began to wrap his wife's body in a quilt. It would be laid by the door and the guard outside told to stop the plague cart on its rounds. "Go to bed, my dear. Wash well, change your clothes and keep away from Tam." He kissed her gently. "God bless you for all you have done tonight."

Arabella nodded, head and neck stiff, groin tender to the touch. God in heaven, she thought in panic, I feel as if I had the fever again myself. She hurried downstairs, desperate to strip and scrub, to be convinced she was not ill again. The plague nurse was snoring by the table, and Arabella kicked her off her stool in a fury.

She collapsed in a heap of rags, then sat up and belched. "What call d'ye have to do that to a poor old woman, hey? What's to do?"

"Get up! Go and help my father with my mother's body, then fetch water and scrub the room. Don't stop until I come and see it done, or I swear I won't allow you a single crust next time we eat."

"Lor' Mam, 'ow were I to know there were owt to do? As for scrubbin' now, precious little water for owt like that, I'm thinking."

Arabella hauled her up and shook her until ragged clothes rattled in their dirt. A moment before she had been exhausted, now rage gave her unnatural strength. "Do as you are told! I know you stole from us to bribe the guard to fetch you liquor, so you just start scrubbing before I beat you as you deserve!"

The old woman went, muttering, and when Arabella trailed wearily upstairs she was slapping water desultorily on the boards. It didn't make much difference. Filth was everywhere, and all through the day eyes had to be averted from the bundle lying by the shop door waiting for its journey to the communal pit. The City churchyards were full; churned and double-dug until the dead were scarcely covered and deeper digging merely turned up bodies from the week before, so the Lord Mayor decreed that the dead were to be taken to huge trenches dug in open ground.

Robert intended to follow his wife's body, however horrific the journey was likely to be, and bribed their guard five shillings to let him pass. Plague was now so prevalent and the streets so deserted that he felt no qualm of conscience, in fact there were long stretches when no guard stood at their door at all. But when the cart came at last he could not go, and had to watch his wife thrown on top of a dozen others, her shroud stripped before prayer dried on his lips.

He could not go because little Tam was ill, and the youngest apprentice too.

They both died before morning.

Arabella slept through the night and knew nothing, since he had given her a posset to make sure she did not hear the plague cart come. She woke with the heat of another day sticking linen to her skin and lay staring at yellow light on the wood of floor and walls, hating it, resolving never to complain of fog or rain again.

Something was wrong. It took a while to identify it as stillness everywhere; stillness in a house where a few weeks before fifteen souls had lived, where a prosperous and noisy trade echoed through every waking hour. Stillness, too, along the length of Cheapside, where usually you had to bawl to make yourself heard. She climbed out of bed straw and went over to the window; it still seemed strange to be sleeping alone but Susannah was already a hazed memory, the maid who had slept in the trundle at their feet a week dead.

Arabella leaned out of the window, uncaring whether anyone saw her in her nightrail. No one would, she reflected grimly, for the street was deserted. No faces peering from diamond-paned windows, no carts, no peddlers or merchants about their business. Only a greenish haze above the cobbles, as if disease grew out of the ground itself.

Arabella stared at it, superstitious fear prickling the back of her neck before she realised what it was; the shock then almost as great as if she had indeed seen plague embodied. Grass was growing between the cobbles of Cheapside, Poultry and Cornhill: the busiest crossroads in the kingdom and no life stirred to keep it from going back to pasture.

She banged the window shut and dressed hastily, surprised by the raw hurt she felt at London's ruin, when she had never consciously thought of this city as hers before.

Downstairs the same uncanny stillness prevailed. The nurse was snoring again but not worth waking; Arabella stoked the fire and went into the yard in search of water, someone should be clattering metal by now. She found Will, the senior apprentice, gloomily filing a minute tendril at an otherwise bare bench: every scrap of silver was locked away at night and work could not start until Robert opened his chest in the morning.

"Where are the others, Will? Hasn't my father come down yet?"

Will went on filing doggedly, refusing to look at her.

Deliberately Arabella tipped some water over his feet. "I asked you a question, Will Leggatt."

He jumped up with a curse, dropping his piece of silver. "Now look what you've made me do!" Muttering, he dropped on his knees and started sifting wet dirt.

"Will!" said Arabella, exasperated. "If it was too small to lock up, it's too small to work on. Where are the others? I must go and wake my father if he's overslept."

"No." He scrambled to his feet. "Leave him be, Mistress Arabella. He's mortal tired and best sleeping if he can. Richard has run and Jack died in the night. Young Tam...he's dead too."

Tam, dead. Thomas Edward Sperling, aged six, dead. He had been completely well last night.

"Mr. Sperling didn't want you waked," said Will awkwardly. "We shrouded 'em and followed 'em to the pits together. There's no guards any more. The plague's everywhere now."

Not much point to guards, thought Arabella dully, since I should be clear and only Will and Father remain from all the rest. And Richard of course, but she was surprised that fear of her father had kept him there so long.

"Tam..." Her voice sounded strange when she spoke at last. "Did he...was it quick?"

"Aye. He knew little and was in a sleep before the end." It wasn't true, and she could tell it wasn't from his tone, but even the illusion that he had not suffered helped.

She sighed and, having sighed, could not stop, found herself weeping instead. She dropped the bucket and ran inside, tears streaming down her face and wanting only to hide herself away. It wasn't difficult, the house enormously large now so few were left to live in it. She sat in the darkened parlour with her head in her hands. This is what sacrifice has brought us, she thought. If Father had chanced very little with the lives of others and sent Tam and Rob away to the country that first night, they probably would have lived. While those he thought to save had died anyway, with plague everywhere now. So much for duty and sacrifice: a bitter wasted gesture thrown in your teeth by God. He won't catch me that way, ever.

The leaning floors and walls of the house were not particularly thick, and after a while Arabella became aware of sound upstairs. At first she thought her father was rising after short rest, but felt too sunk in misery to blow up the kitchen fire. Then, suddenly, she stiffened, transfixed by dread. She shot off the bench and half fell upstairs, threw open her father's door without ceremony and flung back the shutters.

He was lying on his back, still as soon as he saw her, but the bedclothes were in wild disarray, and his face poured sweat.

"Oh, sweet Jesus!" Arabella instantly forgot her defiance of God. "Jesus, have mercy, no!"

His mouth twisted. "Yes, I'm afraid. Send up the nurse."

"As if I'd let that stinking toad touch you! You made me promise . . . you'll promise too, won't you?" She flung herself on her knees beside his bed, felt the scorch of his body before she touched him.

"I'll try." Cracked lips slipped on the words.

He did try; he fought the endless vomiting through a baking day while Arabella and Will trailed up and down stairs with water and fresh linen. He tried to scrape up enough strength to keep darkness at bay while the fever gathered, to endure the unspeakable agony of peeling plague spots on lining of stomach and lungs. Arabella had been young and came fresh to her ordeal, the disease in early summer less malignant than it had since become. Robert was a middle-aged man already in the last stages of emotional and physical exhaustion, who had sustained his household through inhuman strain and been forced to watch them die through his decision, the rightness of which he could not longer judge. However hard he tried, he simply could not last.

As dawn broke, Arabella saw that his eyes were rational again after hours of raving. "Be good," he said, and smiled. "Bless you, Arabella."

"You're better!" she cried joyfully. "Of course I'll be good, I promised God so many things if you lived that I'll have to be as sober as a Presbyterian for months and months!"

His head moved and there was a faint croak, as if he laughed. "Lucky . . . you don't have . . . to keep that resolution. The key . . . the key to the plate chest . . . the slot under the Tudor rose . . . you know. Go to . . . Cornish . . . not—" Not my brother Bevil, he wanted to say, but his throat was so swollen words would not come. He could see Arabella quite clearly, how strange when the rest of the room was lost. Her face was set,

45

almost savage; eyes glittering. Her love had surrounded him as long as he might live, it was lost in fury at the betrayal of his death.

He closed his eyes, he must say something to draw her back from hatred in the years ahead. There was such force in her, which must not be shaped into a weapon of revenge on life. Only he was so dreadfully tired; with all the strength of mind and will he tried to choke out words, and could not.

Only one, and that not what he intended.

Arabella, head in her hands beside him, caught the breath of it.

"Courage . . ."

Chapter Five

Winter was coming at last, and never more passionately desired. First wind and then rain blew through the empty streets of London, when only the week before the Lord Mayor had ordered huge bonfires lit in a vain attempt to stir stagnant, plague-thick air. Unfamiliar sounds of water pouring off the eaves and sluicing over rubbish in the streets brought hope at last to the survivors of the greatest disaster London had known since it was razed by Boudicca and her horde sixteen hundred years before. Yet the disease was so deeply entrenched, London's citizens so demoralised and underfed with most of their employment gone, that thousands continued to die even as infection ebbed. People grabbed at broadsheets giving the week's mortality rate as if at life itself, but although showing improvement after months of terrifying increases, decline remained desperately slow. In November fifteen hundred were still dying every week from plague alone, but as snow fell at Christmas the toll dropped below a hundred at last. Everyone knew that there were, and had been, many plague deaths unreported, but out of the official total of more than a hundred thousand dead, some fifteen thousand had lived in the square mile within the ancient gates, which men called the City.

Arabella found sullen satisfaction in the ruin about her where she had felt personal hurt before. The beggars displaying their sores and besieging any traveller who might have a coin to spare, the great tufts of weeds in formerly prosperous thoroughfares, the rows of empty, looted houses with smashed glass and cascading plaster fitted exactly to her mood. In three

47

short months she had been stripped of everything by malignant fate and only ruin seemed fit framing for the change.

For all its sufferings and the dislocation of trade, the City revived faster than Whitehall, the wealthy network of streets around the Strand, or the slums. The Lord Mayor, who had jurisdiction only within its walls, had stayed and ordered his aldermen and officials to do the same, while court and government had fled, the parishes disintegrated under the impact of disaster. Many merchants too, although they sent their families away, feared for their property too much to go themselves. Some died, the remainder resumed trade as soon as hope released people into the streets again. Rubbish was cleared, pestiferous beggars hounded off main thoroughfares; no one cared where they went so long as it was out of sight. Consequently, the death toll rose again in the outlying districts during January, while in the City the rate was almost back to normal.

A new Lord Mayor was elected in November with a shadow of the usual pomp, but everyone felt it marked a return to known ways. The City voted its thanks to Sir William Lawrence for his courage during his year of office and devoutly hoped that the mayoralty of Sir Thomas Bludworth would see a renewal of God's blessing and a return to prosperity—which in most minds amounted to the same thing.

The week after Christmas, Arabella abruptly snapped out of her gloom.

There were mummers in the street outside, a bear ward leading a mangy bear, and a mountebank who tumbled and shouted on the ice. Snow crisped over roofs and peeled in long slivers off gables, sending paunchy merchants skipping for cover; hot-pie vendors, rabbit skinners and ribbon girls brought familiar cries under her window, the bustle of life irresistible after long apathy.

She hung out of her gable end in the Cornish house, laughing aloud in pleasure, and Harry on his way back from the Exchange felt his heart lighten at the sight. He had accepted her lethargy as natural when she first came to their house and wanted only to comfort her desolation. Yet all his efforts failed to stir her out of glum, resentful courtesy which was so unlike the Arabella he knew that as the weeks went by he began to fear that the plague had left only the shell of her behind.

Arabella jumped as a snowball hit the sill, showering her with crystals, and saw him laughing below. "Hey there, mistress! What shall I ask the mummers to sing for you?"

"Anything!" she called back gaily. "So long as it isn't one of those long-faced Puritan drones!"

He grinned and hoped his father had not heard; Alderman Cornish did not associate religion with good cheer. Arabella leaned still further out while the mummers sang some old round about eating and drinking from the days of Elizabeth, when most men took merriment at Christmas for granted; the fashionable world did now, of course, but few songs from Charles II's court were fit for a woman's ears. The Cornish corncrake sign was just out of Arabella's reach but immediately above Harry's head, for the house leaned sharply over the street, each storey built beyond the one below. If she could just reach a little further... she wriggled perilously, feet off the ground, until she was just able to reach with her fingertips and set it swinging, sending a cascade of snow on Harry below.

He spluttered as it hit him squarely on the neck, then heard peals of laughter from above and the discordant squawk of pipes as the mummers laughed too. He swore and stepped back to shout at Arabella, unused to being the butt of street idlers.

At the sight of her face, anger stilled on his lips. Cold air and wriggling across the windowsill brought a flush to her cheeks, her mouth was curved in laughter where it had been tight so long, her eyes alight with mischief and dark hair sprinkled with snow. He pitied her but had not found her attractive these past weeks, now her beauty struck him to the heart and he stood gaping like a yokel. "Get you inside," he said gruffly, at last. "You'll fall if you lean further."

She wrinkled her nose at him. "You're jealous because I'm a better marksman with snow than you."

"I had chivalry enough not to intend to hit you. I'll know better next time, and all the taunts of Cheapside will not stop me." He began to flick snow from his shoulders; ice water trickled inside his shirt but he did not care at all.

Arabella giggled and began to squirm her way back, already half a dozen boys had gathered, jeering as Londoners easily did at another's discomfiture, and a rich Cornish covered with snow was fair amusement for Cheapside carters and apprentices.

"Mr. Henry, Mr. Henry, Mr. Cornish sends to ask what the disturbance is!"

Harry looked at the meagre little clerk hopping from leg to leg in front of him, and then through thick glasses to his father's disapproving face within. "A chance fall of snow, which gave

49

some pleasure to the vulgar but is naught to worry about." He raised his voice slightly. "You should be careful where you stand, or you may suffer a like accident."

Just above, Arabella had regained the security of feet firmly on the floor. There was not much snow in reach, but she scraped what she could from fretwork and measured her distance carefully. Harry was ushering the little man before him and she dropped her handful precisely on his shabby wig, heard his squawk of dismay as she slammed the window shut. Pity it wasn't Alderman Cornish, she thought, scowling again.

She did not like either the alderman or his wife. They had been kind to take her in when their house was already crowded, as all City houses were crowded when trade and large families were crammed under one roof; but she detested feeling beholden. She had been detached by grief before; as she stood through interminable prayers that evening detachment vanished, and she hated them all. Especially the self-righteous alderman, eyes bloodshot from long squinting over his ledgers, and his bird-like, nervous wife in her dowdy clothes. Hypocritical old fool, droning prayers while good food chilled; no wonder Harry enjoyed eating with us in the old days.

Her gaze swept down the table. It glinted with gold and silver, but that was no novelty to her and roused no interest. Robert Sperling's plate chest had been carried across Furnival Alley into Cornish safekeeping by four hefty men sweating at wooden handles and now formed her dowry. At the far end of the table were the three little Cornishes; Harry was the sole surviving child of an earlier marriage, the rest swept away by the usual London agues and distempers, his mother dead of gilding sickness. Little Sing-to-the-Lord, Hephzibah and Nicodemus were younger than he by more than ten years. What names! Arabella thought. Sing-to-the-Lord had been born while Protector Cromwell was still alive, but that was no excuse when any sensible man must have seen which way the wind would blow. What a mercy that Harry had been born while a King still reigned: his mother at least must have had some particle of sense.

Prayers over at last, they sat down with a clatter. No trestles nor everyone feeding together here. I expect the serving maids and apprentices prefer ease in the kitchen, thought Arabella gloomily. I'm sure I would.

Alderman Cornish did not approve of light conversation while he ate, and usually discoursed on the day's trade or catechised his children on their doings. This was an ordeal which hung over the younger ones all day, like the threat of the devil on Sundays. Arabella had been largely spared so far, but recently sensed a tendency to consider that grief was no longer sufficient excuse for slackness.

They were talking about the Dutch war, she realised, and listened with flickering interest. There had been sea battles without clear victory for either side and trade was languishing in consequence. "Another loan is being raised on 'Change for His Majesty," remarked Harry. "They were full of it there today. I was pressed to set your name to a large subscription, but said you would take up no more than the minimum required of an alderman."

"If there's a shortfall, the mayor will force subscription. I intend to urge a new course in our next council; the City must insist on proper security since there is no end to demands for loans."

"What security can the King give?" asked Harry cynically. "He has no money and his word is worthless, as all those who deal with Stuarts know."

His father's face creased in annoyance. "Keep your opinions to yourself, since they are so ill-judged! The exchequer collects taxes, does it not, and is situated in the Tower within the City's reach? We will insist that if we lend to the King, then tax is appropriated to repay us before a penny is spent elsewhere. Thus will we bring order to the realm's finances, and profit to ourselves."

Harry shrugged, tonight he felt no interest in money. He looked across at Arabella, and she tilted her head under his stare, giving him back look for look. He had thought her eyes completely black before, in candlelight they seemed flecked with gold. He wanted to hold her and discover whether only the candles made them so, he wanted . . . he gulped wine and lost the thread of his father's homily on the security offered by direct appropriation of taxation to the goldsmith-bankers of London.

His abstraction was clear to Alderman Cornish, who was a dislikeable man but not a stupid one. He studied Arabella appraisingly, much as he scrutinised plate brought to him as security. She was adequately though not richly dowered, for he had already valued the contents of Robert Sperling's chest, but above all she inherited the remainder of the long lease Robert had taken on the House of the Spurs when values were

51

low during the war. Unfortunately, the deeds to the property were still in some cache there, whose whereabouts she said she did not know. Alderman Cornish thought her a surly chit and in need of frequent beating, but that was no great matter; now she had recovered he could supply such discipline as was necessary to make her a pliant wife for Henry: the nub of the matter was the expansion of his trade which made extra space necessary.

"Tell me your doings, miss," he said abruptly. "To what good purposes have you given your day?"

Arabella smiled at him sweetly. "Why, none, for look as I would I found nothing but mischief came ready to my hands."

His jaw dropped in sheer astonishment, he had never been so answered in his life. For a moment he wondered whether she was deranged and felt a pang over her property deeds, but her smile soon convinced him otherwise. "I have been too easy with you, and your father as well no doubt. So I give you due warning now and shall not repeat it, that the time of indulgence is over. Apologise for your pertness and go to your room."

Her eyes looked dark as night again. She shrugged and rose. "My apologies then, for speaking the truth. I will endeavour to keep from it in future and so avoid punishment." She stalked out of the room, head high. Stupid old goat, she thought with satisfaction, that'll make his jowls wobble.

She sat on the edge of her bed in moonlight, hugging her knees. Candles had not been set out when she came upstairs and she would get none now, which did not bother her since she had nothing to read; an accomplishment Alderman Cornish considered unnecessary for a woman, who should be able to spell her letters but not exactly read, cast up accounts but not understand money. Since Robert Sperling accepted all God's children as souls, it had never occurred to him that his daughters should not read as fluently as his sons, and Arabella enjoyed reading when nothing more amusing offered, as she had come to enjoy shaping silver.

She did wish, however, that she had had time for more than a few mouthfuls before she left the table, and her stomach growled in tune with her thought. Moonlight moved slowly up the wall while Christmas roisterers shouted outside: one day she would be festive and roistering, not sitting alone in the dark while others enjoyed themselves.

She heard steps in the passage outside, muted voices, creaking of wood. Perhaps when everyone slept she could creep down to the kitchen and find something to eat.

She waited while old timbers snapped into rest around her. She slept in a tiny cubicle under the eaves, the maids in the gable above, the three little ones and their nurse next door, Mr. and Mrs. Cornish and Harry on the floor below: she would have to pass their door to reach the stair leading to the kitchen.

She slipped off her shoes and paused, listening. There was a slither of sound outside. No. Yes. A click from the latch and Harry slipped into her room. "I brought you something to eat."

"You needn't have troubled, I was just going to find what I wanted." She felt deflated, tension ebbing into irritable boredom again.

He glanced at her feet, bare in frosty moonlight, and quickly away again. He did not speak.

Arabella twitched up her dress. "Perhaps you haven't seen below a woman's skirts before. Look your fill and feel paid for your trouble."

She could not see his anger, but sensed it instantly. She had forgotten that, like her father, Harry was unsafe to provoke. He swung her round and held her, hands clamped tight on her shoulders, then deliberately brought his mouth down hard on hers, kissing without mercy, beyond breath and into flame beyond. Then as it lit, his grip changed into tenderness, although she could feel his body trembling through the tumult in her own. "I'm sorry," he said simply. "Not for the kiss, but for taking it like a punishment, of which you have had more than enough this past year."

She refused to meet his eyes, astonished by her own reactions and disappointed by apology. She twisted away from him and sat on the bed again. "Where is the food you brought?"

He hesitated and then sat beside her, pulling a cloth from his pocket. "Don't sulk, Bella. Such airs are wasted on me, since I'll neither beat you nor keep from another kiss when the opportunity offers. You could never convince me you didn't enjoy it."

She chuckled involuntarily. "Oh, Harry! Don't you think this is as good a time as any for finding your opportunity?" She tilted her face and closed her eyes, lips parted and heart beating with excitement.

Nothing happened, and after a moment she stole a look at him. He was grinning at her in the most infuriating way. "You've

53

no idea how ridiculous you look, Bella, waiting with your lips all puckered up like that."

"Oh!" she cried, forgetting the need for caution. "There never was such a rude, ungallant boy as you, Harry Cornish!"

"Hush! For God's sake, you'll wake the household and a pretty pickle we shall be in then." He grasped her hand when she tried to slap his face, and kissed the palm carelessly. "When you are older, I promise you'll not lack my kisses."

"I certainly will, since I don't intend to be kept dangling on your whim for years while Cornish's reckon up my worth in plate."

His lips tightened. "Listen, Bella, for I won't explain again. I respected your father too much to take his daughter like a trollop whatever my wishes—or yours—may be. Marriage is always a question of plate and property, you'd be the first to reckon up your advantage and think me a fool if I didn't do the same. But I trust that if we wed it will be for more than sober reckoning, and I shan't offer for you until I can judge something of what we'll find together. You're a gallant, beautiful, obstinate little vixen; also selfish and uncommonly hot in the blood, a chancy combination, as any horse dealer would admit." He kissed her again, lightly this time, derisively almost. "I'm not to be driven, my dear, any more than you. So I'll wait awhile and be damned to you and your chestful of plate."

He laughed softly at the look on her face, and was gone.

She was very angry with him, but there was no doubt that days sped faster when they were measured by the feel of his eyes on her, the edged jests only they understood. For she was bored; stiflingly, paralysingly bored. The house was full of servants and the tasks she had to do, in her view, either invented or unnecessary. Since John Cornish had turned to keeping running balances for his clients and adventuring credit on their deposits, there was no clangour of hammers or the excitement of a difficult pour, no urgent call to help with bellows or pincers. Arabella looked back on the days of incarceration under the threat of plague almost with longing, and hankered absurdly for skills she had begun to learn as a diversion from fear.

"Will, why does everything seem so dreary?" she exclaimed one day, fingering some silver scrollwork he was repairing. Will Leggatt was the only other survivor from Robert Sperling's household and somehow had escaped plague altogether.

"Depends on the way you look on un, Miss Arabella," he

replied stolidly. "There's a few mercies for me to count, my life first of all." Alderman Cornish had also accepted his indentures though he had no need for the kind of skills Will had acquired. Plenty of men would have turned him away, and so forced him to give up his trade, or perhaps start seven years' apprenticeship again; no matter if the work was only petty repairs, within months he would be his own master and free to hire himself where he would.

Arabella thrust out her lip, glowering. "You're as bad as the rest. At least you have a trade, even if the melting shed here is full of scribbling clerks."

"Aye, I've a trade and my skill in it owed to Mr. Sperling. I won't forget him, you may be sure." He picked up the scroll he was riveting.

Arabella dropped the silver on the bench with a clatter. She was neither resigned nor patient, nor was she able to practise such skills as she possessed. When she asked once for some silver sheet, Alderman Cornish gobbled like water damned behind conduit rubbish, and recommended her to improve her stitchery.

Halfway up the stairs, she paused, looking across Furnival Alley into her own familiar home. She no longer remembered the frustration she had felt there too, and invested her former life with dreamlike happiness. Seized with sudden desire, she went softly downstairs again, across the yard, and slipped the chain on the side door. There was no one in the alley, and after a struggle she climbed the opposite wall where some bricks were loose. The House of the Spurs had been empty only a matter of months and already it was falling down: dark spots like plague on the plaster and a section of tiles had been stripped. Looters had broken in long before anyone was willing to bid for infected furnishings and taken anything which could be moved, ripped panelling and smashed windows. Since then it had been boarded up tighter than during the plague.

Arabella knew that Alderman Cornish was not sorry for its dilapidated state, since he intended to pull it down and rebuild, she supposed into rooms for clerks. At least he had not found the deeds yet, although Arabella knew perfectly well where they were. John Cornish would scrupulously pay her for the improved value of her property, but she had no desire to see it rebuilt and enjoyed watching him search for papers she would refuse to sign even if he found them.

The old Sperling melting shed and workshop had little but

dust left in them, roofs gaping and rubbish blown into corners. As she looked at desolation, a new determination grew in her: why shouldn't it have life again? When Will finished his apprenticeship she could set him up as a master. This place was made for sweat and hammering, for craft handled by men at the stretch of their endeavour, not snotty-nosed clerks scratching percentages. Arabella respected money, it was difficult not to if you were born in Cheapside, but figures on paper meant nothing to her, wealth was something you saw, admired and weighed.

She eased open a couple of boards on the kitchen window, it had not taken looters long to find their way in again. The house reeked of damp, mould flowing down walls and across floors; it smelled also of imperfectly scoured sickness, of squalor left by tramps who slept here sometimes now.

The deeds were under a stone at the edge of the hearth, the space double-lined to withstand even fire if necessary. She knelt and felt carefully for the slot which would give her fingers purchase. The stone lifted easily, everything Robert Sperling made fitted exactly to its purpose, but the space below was empty. She stared at it, then felt around dark edges as if thick parchment could be concealed in a crack of mortar. The deeds of lease were gone.

A board creaked in the passage and she scrambled to her feet, heart pounding, the stone still in her hands. A soft sound she was unable to identify, and another creak; she realised suddenly how foolish she was to be here alone when the house had become a refuge for vagrants. No one would hear her screams above the roar of Cheapside.

"Bella? Are you there?" Harry's voice.

She gasped with relief and then was flooded by the fury which follows fear. "What do you mean by following me! This is my house and not Cornish property yet, so you can just climb back the way you came and leave me alone!"

"You know very well why I followed you, in case exactly what you feared a moment ago happened." He stayed just inside the door.

"How did you know I had come?"

"If you must leave our alley door off its chain and scramble over walls in full daylight, you mustn't be surprised if people discover what you are about."

She dropped the stone with a clatter. "I suppose you followed me once before and stole the deeds when my back was turned. No wonder Cornish's need to expand when they profit by such dealings."

He flushed instantly with anger in the way she was coming to know. He did not enter disputes easily even when his disagreement was obvious, but this came from long training in restraint: he did in fact possess a swift temper and blood as hot as her own.

He crossed the floor in three strides and took her by the shoulders, shaking her so she would have fallen but for his grip. "You believe nothing of the sort, you mischief-making little shrew! It is time someone put a curb on your tongue before we are all at each other's throats." He pushed her against the wall, hand hard on her chest with no lover's touch. "Look at me and say again, if you dare, that you thought I spied on you and then stole what was yours."

She felt dizzy, stays cutting into her ribs, his hand stifling breath. She would rather die than apologise, though, even if shock had spoken the first accusation which came to mind. She shook her head, he could take it as he liked.

His fingers closed on her throat. "Are you too honest or too cowardly to speak it to my face?"

Courage, her father said as he died in the room above her head. "I regret calling you thief when clearly it should be murderer instead."

His hand stayed on her throat but the flush faded from his face, eyes a remote and chilly grey. Then he released her and turned abruptly. "I'll wait for you outside."

She looked around her disbelievingly when he had gone. Well, she thought, I didn't intend to marry him before because I thought how dull it would be, my purpose hasn't changed but perhaps the reason has.

She slotted back stone and joined him in the yard; neither spoke while he helped her over the wall and chained the yard door behind them. She would have left him at once, but he put his hand on her arm. "Bella, I've a devilish temper sometimes, and you a tongue straight from the whetstone. I would never have tightened my hand, although it needed courage to call me murderer with it on your throat. You didn't believe me a thief, but know too well how to cause pain in those who love you. So shall we call it quits?"

She shrugged. "What is it to me whether we do or not?"

"That is what I meant," he said drily, and left her staring. Could he mean he did indeed love her enough to be easily hurt? Damn Harry anyway, she couldn't be bothered with him now.

If he had not taken the deeds, then who had? She did not believe that looters could have discovered so neatly jointed a hiding place, nor would papers interest them if they did. So who? Certainly not Will, who might know the hiding place after six years of living in their household, but his devotion to Robert Sperling's memory was beyond question.

The mystery was solved a week later.

Arabella was summoned to Mr. Cornish's counting room—it was no longer called the shop, although silver and gold wares were on display, the same counter in place. Callers now mostly brought coin and bullion for deposit and took paper credits in exchange: ever since accumulating financial disasters had forced the King to agree to secure his loans against specific sources of taxation, the goldsmith-bankers of the City had felt able to lend more freely and prospered in consequence.

The only real change in the counting room was the high desk on a dais in one corner. Here Mr. Cornish sat with his ledgers and bawled at any clerk who dared let his eyes lift from paper. He glared at Arabella when she arrived, panting with the haste of such an unusual summons. "Come over here, miss."

She went, relishing covert rustlings from clerks as she passed. She was wearing a tight-laced busk over tucked bodice and skirt, all black as became her mourning but so well nipped at waist and bust that the effect was very different from Mrs. Cornish's intention when she drew out the pattern. Arabella loathed sewing but never grudged effort in the cause of her beauty.

Alderman Cornish did not find her attractive; in his mind he labelled her papist, not because he cherished doubts on Robert Sperling's religion but simply as a description of such flaunting immodesty, when her colouring did not conform to his idea of Englishness either.

"See here, miss," he said at last. "I have a letter from your Uncle Bevil, claiming the lease of the Golden Spurs was left to him by special wish of your father. He says he has documents to prove it."

Arabella gasped. Neither she nor Harry had said anything about the missing deeds, and she had begun to think that some tramp must have found and destroyed them, not knowing their

58

value. "That's impossible! Father never liked him, and the deeds were..." She bit her lip as the pitfall gaped before her.

"Yes? Just where were these deeds for which we have been searching and you swore to me were unknown to you?"

"In a safe place by the hearth, but they are gone," said Arabella sulkily. "I looked the other day."

"So when I asked for their whereabouts, you had every reason to believe they were still there?"

"They were there. At least, they were just after Christmas."

He grunted with annoyance. "Why then did you say you knew nothing of them?"

"Because I wanted to keep them myself," she said defiantly. "Of course I knew you wouldn't cheat me over price, but the house is mine to do with as I will. I'm going to see silver hammered there again, not rows of clerks wheezing over figures." She heard quills stop scratching behind her, then hurry faster than before.

"Not now," Cornish pointed out coldly. "Since your uncle claims to have inherited and holds papers to prove it."

"I don't see how he can. Not genuine papers. My father disliked him and would never have left him the property, put his own family in the street. The deeds—"

"Which Bevil now possesses."

"Which he certainly did not possess in my father's lifetime!" she flashed. "I tell you, I saw them just after Christmas."

He rasped a quill across his chin, thinking. This tiresome wench had put all his plans in jeopardy, but there was something very odd here. If Bevil Sperling had forged the will and could be proved to have done so, then he could be sued for possession of the deeds, and there was no doubt that Cornish's had the resources to outlast and outbribe a swindling attorney in the courts. He tossed over the letter to Arabella. "Read it, then. He sends an authenticated copy of the will dated just over a year ago. See whether there is anything which strikes you as strange."

Arabella stumbled through legal phrases, then stopped dead. The witnesses were William Vickery and Richard Goodenough. She choked involuntarily.

"What is it, girl?"

She pointed to the names, finger quivering. "I don't know who Vickery is, but Richard Goodenough was our apprentice who ran off before Father died."

"Taking the deeds with him? No, you saw them at Christmas. He came back then, must have known where they were hidden."

She nodded reluctantly. "He was always skulking around corners and lived five years with us. He stole silver, but my father refused to accuse him on mere suspicion."

"So he either saw Bevil and suggested the scheme, or tried to sell him the deeds for what he could get, knowing they were enemies, and Bevil decided to forge a will to give them value, like the double-crossing lawyer's clerk he is. It's clever, though; if this Goodenough was in your household, he can swear he was called in as witness once when your uncle came to dine, and your father charged him to deliver the deeds when he was dying."

"It isn't true," said Arabella, remembering painfully her father's deathbed.

"What is that to the matter? It would be impossible to disprove."

"Can you fight it?" Harry's voice behind her.

"Difficult, very difficult. I shall have to think about it. As for you, miss—" He turned on Arabella. "You realise you have ruined yourself? If you don't fight, then you forfeit your property; if you do, it is likely to cost you that chestful of plate. The law is a bog where many inheritances have been lost."

Arabella nodded, she knew. "You will be able to lease it from my uncle if he wins, he won't want to live in Cheapside." Her lips felt stiff but she refused to whine.

"And he'll milk me of treble its worth, no doubt. He's sent me this letter because he knows my need of it. That Richard Goodenough is worth a pretty sum to Bevil: I suppose he heard your father and me talking one night." He turned on the clerks abruptly. "Get out, all of you!" They gaped at him, they never left their stools before evening and it was only just turned three. He bellowed at them again, and they made a rush for the door before he remembered to tell them a time to be back. "You get out too," he added brusquely to Harry. "I want a word alone with Arabella, it's her inheritance and none of your affair."

"I think it is," said Harry quietly. "If she doesn't like being sold, then neither do I."

Arabella looked from one to the other. "I'd like him to stay."

Harry's expression relaxed and he took her arm. "Good girl. Sit down, I've an idea that you may need all your wits about you during the next few minutes to decide where your interest lies."

"Well, if you must," said his father grudgingly, leaving Arabella to face a surprising discovery about Harry: he might defer to his father but was far from a mere assistant in the business. "I have a proposition to make to Arabella and as it concerns you too, perhaps you are best here. A business proposition, miss," he added. "Yes or no now, and keep your word on the bargain afterwards."

She folded her hands in her lap and looked at him expectantly. "Of course."

"If I decide to fight this claim on your behalf it will be expensive, and have only an even chance of success whatever the truth of the matter. You have your dowry to risk if you wish, but it may not be enough."

"It won't be," interrupted Harry.

"Hold your tongue! Do you follow me?" Arabella nodded. "So the day I win for you, you wed Harry. If I lose, I dower you with a hundred guineas, take the balance of your plate to recoup some of my loss in fighting on your behalf, and find you a husband to suit your new station. A skilled journeyman hammering silver if you are fortunate."

"No," said Harry lazily. "I'm sorry, Arabella, but that is one bargain I won't be a party to. Keep your dowry, lease the house to us and let us fight for it at our own risk. I told you before, we'll take our own time to discover whether my temper and your tongue bed comfortably together."

For all his calm, he was furiously angry she could tell, but Arabella felt no anger for herself. She possessed a practical mind and the past year had put a harsh edge to an already uncompromising nature; she recognised the risk Alderman Cornish ran of losing his case and then having to pay Bevil an exorbitant rent, after years of litigation. This was trade and no place for sentiment.

On the other hand, she had long ago decided not to marry Harry and nothing since had changed her mind. She did not object to fighting him, every day if necessary, but the whole idea was too tame and constricting. "I have a better suggestion. If you lose, you keep my plate chest and I go to my uncle at no further charge to you. He cannot refuse me, and offered me a home before. If you win, I keep my dower and lease you the House of the Spurs for five years at the cost of a brooch each year, made in our own melting shed, where Will will have licence to work so long as I wish him to do so. After five years, you pay full market rent: I am sure we shall be able to agree a fair figure."

Harry's hand was on her shoulder; his fingers tightened until they dug into flesh. She did not wince but put up her chin and said clearly, "Take it or leave it, now."

Alderman Cornish rubbed his chin thoughtfully. "It's a fair offer." It was more than fair, since it left Henry free to marry elsewhere and recoup their losses. "Very well, I agree."

Harry turned and went out of the room.

Chapter Six

*I must go and see Bevil soon, mused Ar-*abella. She was sitting in the first warmth of summer, sewing on her lap but her mind preoccupied with a pleasing web of plotting. Quite how she could arrange to see Bevil was a different matter. She owed it to Alderman Cornish not to spoil his chances by an inadvertent word or show of anxiety; on the other hand, she had thought for some time that her life would be more amusing under Uncle Bevil's roof. She was annoyed he had cheated her, but not resentful: she too much an adventurer herself not to recognise the same characteristics in another. She was simply determined to outswindle him in her turn.

There was a strange tremble in the air. She stood, tumbling sewing on the ground, aware that the sensation had been there some time without her taking notice. "'Tis thunder, a long way off and naught to worry about yet," said little Hephzibah, continuing to sew. She was a tranquil child, and dull.

Dull. Dull. Dull. Arabella wanted to scream at the ordinariness of women sewing and pounding herbs, of discussing whether fresh-caught eels should be baked or seethed, a busk worn full-laced or only half. How could she live out her years and be satisfied with so little? How work off the bursting vigour she felt within a dozen paces of yard, three flights of stairs and a single walk down Cheapside each week?

At least in two day's time they were all going on the first expedition of pleasure she could remember since a picnic on Islington Heights three years ago. Pray God it didn't rain: she strained her ears, listening. The sound differed from thunder and the sky was brilliantly blue, plague reviving again with heat.

Others had heard, too. Feet were clattering in Furnival Alley, indistinct shouts coming from Cheapside. If only I could see, thought Arabella. "I'm going in," she said abruptly.

"Mamma said we must stay until these cuffs were trimmed," Hephzibah replied placidly.

"Well, say I had a gripe and will soon be back!"

"But you haven't," the child persisted infuriatingly.

"No, I haven't, and you can say that, too," snapped Arabella. "I'm sure I don't care."

The noise was louder in the front of the house, and the shouting, too. Arabella hesitated, not wanting to encounter Mrs. Cornish and hearing voices in the counting room.

". . . the Dutch," Harry was saying. "There's tales of a great loss of ships."

"We'll have them this time, close under our own coast and with the wind onshore." His father sounded as if he was already reckoning the growth of his investment in the rich East India trade, long dominated by the Dutch.

"Perhaps, but ships are hard to replace in a hurry, especially when three years' tax have been anticipated for loan repayment. How much has the Sign of the Corncrake lent His Majesty these past six months?"

"None of your business! You mind your bargains on 'Change and I'll keep our balances safe. I'm not in my dotage yet."

"Of course not, sir. All the same—"

"We've doubled capital in three years, and but for the plague would have done better still, so what complaint have you? If that silly chit had not played jackstraws with Sperling's deeds we'd be building a new counting house this minute."

"If she agreed, and I don't think she would. The house is hers and she fancies keeping it to her father's trade, not ours."

"Faugh! She's a headstrong shrew, but if you were half the man I was at your age you'd have the girl soft enough to sign anything. Her face is not unpleasing and you have her underfoot every day, what more do you want?"

Harry came out unexpectedly, nearly knocking her down in his haste and slamming the door behind him. "Enjoying yourself, Bella?" he enquired sarcastically.

"Yes," she replied coolly. "I need to listen at latches since my affairs are so freely discussed."

"Perhaps, yet those who eavesdrop rarely hear good of themselves."

A glint came to her eyes. "I have your father's word for it

that my face is not unpleasing, and I'll go to others, not you, when I want compliments gracefully turned since you don't know the meaning of the word. But while I live here with my inheritance at your disposal I prefer to know the truth."

He gave a hoot of genuine amusement. "At least you don't confuse compliments with truth, remember that when you seek others to fit your purposes rather than myself."

She smiled, in charity with him for the first time in months. "I will. Is that noise really Dutch guns?"

"At the mouth of the Thames, yes. There's a great fleet battle and the trade of both nations depends on the outcome."

"And Cornish money?"

"All London's money and the nation's lifeblood," he said angrily. "We cannot live without trade, and when there is so much mismanagement everywhere, a damaged ship is a ship out of commission for a twelvemonth. At least Cromwell kept the seas safe and England respected. Charles Stuart tosses his purse at the first pretty face he sees and is too busy cheating his own people to spare thought for seamen a year unpaid and royal dockyards rotted by corruption."

"For God's sake," said Arabella, startled. "Watch your tongue if you are not minded to hang."

"You too, if you are not minded to spend a week locked in your room on bread and water, for blasphemy."

They both laughed, they had not been so easy together since he took her to the Royal Exchange a year before, and they had kissed amongst the apothecaries' stalls of Bucklersbury.

The cannonade continued all day and into the night. Arabella lay awake, listening and praying hard, not for victory but that their river expedition should not be spoiled. She could not visualise a naval battle, or the consequences of defeat, only dread the loss of her only jaunt in years. Next morning she hung out of the window in her nightrail and strained her ears along with most of the inhabitants of London, but the roar of gunfire was stilled. All through the morning rumours swept the City and people stopped in mid-sentence to listen, knowing their livelihood depended on the outcome of the battle. The ravages of plague were bad enough, last year's losses not yet recouped while the disease flickered on through yet another hot, dry summer; the Dutch fleet in the Thames would mean incalculable disaster.

In the middle of the afternoon, the bells began to ring. St.

Mary-le-Bow, St. Sepulchre, St. Lawrence Jewry, All Hallows-the-Great, St. Dionis Backchurch... one by one the scores of City churches joined in the clangour, although the greatest of them all, St. Paul's, was in too ruinous a state for it to be safe to ring the bells. The Dutch were beaten and scampering home as fast as they could tack off a lee shore. The curse of the Stuarts had lifted, it wasn't only Cromwell who won victories after all. Cheers spread through the streets and bonfires were lit, causing some citizens severe annoyance as flames blew under eaves and filled their homes with smoke.

There was a touch of hysteria in the rejoicing, though, which showed how badly frightened Londoners had been, and with the dark more rumours swept through the streets. Bells fell silent as Kentish wherrymen up on the tide told how they had seen the fleet putting in to Chatham, Gravesend and Deptford: battered, leaking, sails shot to pieces, the screams of the wounded clearly heard a mile away.

The Dutch were driven off, but the English had lost too heavily to be reckoned victors.

At least Arabella was able to rejoice wholeheartedly, since their expedition was safe.

Two heavy carriages, looking like leather trunks slung between unsprung wheels, drew up before the Sign of the Corncrake punctually at eleven o'clock; Alderman Cornish and his wife embarked in one with two apprentices as guards, Arabella and the three children in the other with Harry as protection, a drawn sword on his knees. They were going to see the launching of the frigate *London*, built through private subscription by the City merchants, and must travel through the slums before taking a barge at Swan Wharf. No coach was safe in the teeming courts leading to the Thames without at least one armed and active man inside and another by the coachman.

Nicodemus fingered sharp steel admiringly. "How old shall I have to be before I can have a sword?"

"I'll give you one the day you worst me with blunted blades," promised Harry. "I shall grow bloated and have snuff stains down my waistcoat soon, so you should win easily not too many years hence." Since he was tall and moved with easy grace, they all laughed.

"By then Arabella will have a skirtful of children and be chiding them to remember their stitchery, instead of pretending to excuses for herself," chimed in Hephzibah.

"No, I won't," retorted Arabella. "You won't catch me

breeding every year, with nothing more in my mind than the best way to boil beef. Speak for yourself, miss." She hunched a shoulder at them and stared out of a hole in the coach leather, drinking in sounds and sights of the outside world. Several times they passed shuttered houses daubed with red crosses but she refused to look: this was life, the world over the wall she so seldom saw, although she had lived all her days in the busiest street in London.

There were quite a few other things she refused to notice, too. Dingy, tumbledown houses smeared with pitch against the weather and propped up by poles; the filth everywhere, beside which Cheapside looked fresh-scrubbed; green-scummed water standing in stagnant pools, the emaciated children and pus-dripping beggars clamouring for alms whenever the coach stopped, though this was not regarded as one of the poorest slums. Instead she envied how the women walked where they wished and stared bold-eyed at passers-by, how they drank with the men and screamed insults at the coach together as it passed. She saw bright colours instead of dirt and greyness; blue sky, green and silver glint of river, red porters' aprons, yellow milkmaids' smocks. She smelled the sharp salt breeze off the Thames, the acrid brew of beer; heard the smack of hammers on leather and the clank of metal, the yells of draymen and lilting calls of porters touting for trade.

Harry turned his head on dirty squabs and watched her, his face inscrutable. "You would dislike it after a very short while," he said at last.

For a long time she did not answer; when she did he realised she had been weeping. "At least it is life; to hazard something, to win or lose it all."

He was silent, understanding her well enough. He could not imagine his days without the excitement of a profitable bargain, the risk of loss where profit was uncertain. Women were different and content when kept secure, yet Arabella was the most feminine of women and did not value security at all.

The barge Alderman Cornish had hired was chosen for its gilded rails and counter, since this was a day of ceremony when City aldermen measured each other's gilding minutely. Rowed by eight oarsmen, whose oaths fortunately only Harry understood, it tossed alarmingly shooting the rapids under the narrow piers of London Bridge. The bridge itself was crowded with tall houses, here and there a wall tumbling into water, a gap burned at the City end and not yet repaired.

The river was thronged with Londoners come to see their ship launched, and below the bridge rank upon rank of deep-sea ships were tied up waiting to unload. All cargo had to be landed on twenty quays between the Tower and London Bridge so proper tolls could be charged and the congestion was enormous, smuggling brisk and profitable.

Water slapped at planking as their oarsmen drove them forward, the air sparkling after oppressive heat in Cheapside. Arabella stared dreamily across the river, scarcely able to absorb so many impressions when she had lived so long on very few. For a moment rebellion was stilled and she was content with light and air, with ships and salt sea tang, and her own great city polished by the sun and piled on every side. Content, too, with Harry, who stood beside her and did not try to talk, although she felt the closeness of his body when their barge lurched, the wanting touch of his hands when she moved against him. She was briefly happy in the sun and open spaces of the river, yet soon her black mood returned: at the end of the day four walls and a stretch of yard waited for her again.

They saw the *London* launched with all ceremony, pipes shrilling, drums tapping and huzzas rippling over the water as she was levered sideways into the incoming tide. Then the Lord Mayor in scarlet cloth and gold chain led an official procession in his crested barge, the livery companies forming up behind, a splendid sight when each craft had been designed with the intent of outdoing the rest in gold carvings and bright paintwork. This did not make for seaworthiness, though, and they all had to drop downriver and return on the flood, so the merchants of London saw for themselves the torn hulls, stripped canvas and splintered timbers of the anchored fleet. They fell silent as they looked; it would take a year's taxation to pay off and repair these ships, months of work before they were fit for sea again, and everyone knew the scandalous state of the dockyards, the anticipated receipts which sent sailors unpaid into battle.

Arabella felt the gloom around her but cared little for its cause. Ships and trade were not her affair; on the other hand, her own life required a deal of organisation if she was to live it as she wished. She lay sleepless through the night, staring at the ceiling and raging in her heat. I will break out of this cage and soon, she vowed, even if it means letting Bevil sell me to his profit. So long as he sells me to mine as well.

Chapter Seven

Arabella needed to see Bevil, and tried everything without success. Will refused to help her, saying he knew very well that Mr. Robert mistrusted his brother, and no matter how often Arabella stamped her foot or what arguments she tried, nothing would shift him.

Then she made the mistake of asking Harry to take her since she lacked money to hire a coach and, though she would not admit it, courage also to trust herself to an unknown driver all the way to the Strand. He not only refused but watched her closely thereafter, when he had seemed to avoid her since their trip to see the *London* launched. She would have to bide her time until he relaxed his guard, and meanwhile filch such coins as she could from Mrs. Cornish's housekeeping. By October she should have enough and so began to pretend an attachment to the bobble-throated apprentice who kept the day ledger. Soon she would have him so dazzle-eyed he would do anything she asked, and save her the money needed to hire an escort.

She did not sleep well, frustration an ache which seldom left her. It continued fiercely hot, plague trickling nearer every day, and Arabella often sat through the hours of darkness on her windowsill, casement open to air everyone said was so dangerous. No one told her what was happening over her property: Harry angry and scathing if she asked, his father unwilling to waste time explaining legal complications to a feebleminded woman.

There was a fire down by the river. Arabella watched it grow through a whole night with desultory interest: there were often fires in London and provided you were willing to bribe the fire-cart men when they arrived, sooner or later they put it out. Cheapside was deserted, no one else seemed to be feeling concern either. The fire glow did not dim with the dawn, instead palls of smoke driven by rising wind blotted out the sun. Occasionally a dull thud could be heard, and a crackling roar travelled on the wind.

Arabella heard the door slam hours before unlocking time and looked down to see Harry hurrying away; boredom forced her to listen to dronings on loans and balances over meals and she knew that Cornish's lent money against goods as well as coin and plate. Far away as the fire was, they would be concerned in case it threatened warehouses stocked with security for their loans.

As soon as she came downstairs Arabella heard Alderman Cornish complaining about City slackness over controlling fires, while at the same time he tried to convince himself that this one would not cost him money. "They say Mayor Bludworth has been to see it and said an apprentice could piss it out, and he lives in Gracechurch Street close by. All the same, he has not lent balances on oil warehoused at Queenhithe."

Mrs. Cornish clucked vaguely. The Bible used the word "piss" but it still made her feel uncomfortable.

"Has Harry gone to look?" asked Arabella.

He nodded, forgetting to censure interruption. "And to supervise the oil's shifting. He can hire wherries and take it across to Southwark if the danger grows." He went off to his counting room, although not to work, since it was Sunday, leaving everyone else to prepare themselves for meeting house.

Cornish himself was bound by the requirements of the Corporation Act to take communion in the Church of England, a regulation which sought since the King's return to keep Dissenters out of civic office. This he did, although some of his persuasion refused for conscience's sake, but too many of the City's great merchants were Nonconformist by inclination for other laws against Dissenting gatherings to be strictly enforced within its confines. Papists were hated and although the court was full of them, few prospered in the City, where they were regarded as little better than traitors in foreign pay. Even Jews, readmitted to England by Cromwell after centuries of exile, were more easily accepted.

But the Dissenting sects did best of all. They were hardworking, usually honest, and did not dissipate their capital in frivolity. Every Sunday, Alderman Cornish looked complacently around the Wood Street meeting house off Cheapside, and reckoned that his fellow worshippers could command double the wealth of the Anglican congregation gathered a few paces away at St. Lawrence Jewry. It gave him intense satisfaction to make this calculation and helped fix his mind on the minister's exhortation to God's so successful children. Compare Sir William Lawrence with Bludworth, this year's mayor, he thought, and see God's blessing. Lawrence attended Wood Street and did his duty by the City during the plague; Bludworth was a high Anglican and a fool who would run at the first sniff of danger, acclaimed mayor simply because he was next in seniority as alderman. Cornish shifted uneasily and wished Lawrence was still mayor; he would not have left warehouses full of lamp oil, canvas and resin in danger from fire while he went home to bed.

Anxious groups gathered at the corner of Wood Street and Cateaton Street* after the service, Anglican and Nonconformist congregations mingling in their common anxiety. The smoke seemed less, but the wind was still dangerously strong. "Unless every spark is out, the wind will fan it up again," said Alderman Cornish anxiously, when he rejoined the women. Really, he had been unwise to lend so much on a single shipment, yet lending on goods was profitable since few other goldsmith-bankers ventured it. "We'll see what Henry has to say for himself."

But when they returned to Cheapside, Harry had still not come back. They waited for him awhile, smelling the meat burn on the spit, the younger ones running up and down the stairs to report whether the smoke seemed less or not; then Alderman Cornish abruptly cursed Harry for a feckless boy wasting his time gaping at a fire, and declared he would not wait the meal another moment on his son's pleasure.

"Are you going down to the fire later, sir?" asked Arabella when they were eating.

"Me? Certainly not. I've better things to do than look at fires, let me tell you!"

"I'd go, if Harry was my son," observed Arabella in a detached tone. His face mottled alarmingly and everyone else stared at her in fright. Except Harry. She realised suddenly how much she missed him when he was not there, how he was the only one in the household who laughed or knew her mind

*Now Gresham Street.

71

before she spoke. She pushed back her chair. "Someone should go, he may be hurt."

"Don't say so, Arabella dear," begged Mrs. Cornish. Harry was not her son, and she was only tepidly concerned.

"Why not, when it could easily be true? Oil explodes when it catches light." She remembered a lamp which had burst once and nearly burned down the House of the Spurs. She stared at them, hating them all and wanting to go herself.

Harry, my love. No, she did not love Harry, but liked him very much.

The hours dragged by and still he did not come. Alderman Cornish walked to the far end of Walbrook where the slums began, but came back saying the fire was dying down and went to sleep in the parlour as was his habit on a Sunday.

Arabella fidgeted around the house until she saw Will slipping into the kitchen, half drunk since the apprentices spent most of Sunday in the tavern. "Will, I've been waiting hours for you! I want you to come and look for Harry with me."

He blinked. "Look for Mr. Henry? Likely he's in some alehouse and would give few thanks—"

"He isn't! I know he wouldn't stay all this time unless there's some reason for it. He must know how anxious we would feel."

Will looked down the passage at the somnolent scene in the parlour. "Might anxious, ain't they?"

"Mr. Cornish is," said Arabella shrewdly, "but he won't admit it lest it means he's also lost his precious oil. Come on, Will, for pity's sake!"

Will flatly refused. He might be fuddled with ale but knew where his duty to Robert Sperling lay, and with doors and lower shutters barred Arabella needed help if she was to go. Goldsmiths' premises were as difficult to break out of as they were to break into. It seemed as if she had battered at him for hours before he reluctantly agreed to take her to the corner of Cheapside and no further. Smoke was bringing an early dusk, and even apprentices went in groups after dark.

She accepted instantly. Once there, she would argue him onward a step at a time. "How are we to get out?"

He winked. "Apprentices usually have a way." He led her to the Furnival Alley wall and made a stirrup of his hands. "Up as high as you can reach; you'll find handholds and a broken brick for your feet. Wait on top for me."

She scrambled up lithely, heart beating with excitement. When Will joined her, he held her by the wrists and lowered her carefully. "It's a long drop, be careful you don't twist an ankle."

Arabella's bones were crackling and she dropped heavily; she wondered how she would get back but refused to worry about it now.

Cheapside was seething with people, she had never seen it so crowded at night. People were walking up and down, staring at the sky, or gathered in knots, arguing. Everyone agreed the fire was less, but did not believe it sufficiently to go inside. Will stopped where Cheapside conduit sheered off toward Guildhall. "That's far enough."

"Just to the end of Poultry, you promised, Will."

"This end of Poultry, not that."

Arabella coaxed him along Poultry, and then hesitated. The night was alive with hurrying figures, and very dark. Apart from a glow on smoke-thick clouds there was no light at all, and she realised how optimistic she had been. She couldn't see Will's face, let alone Harry if he came past: Cheapside householders placed a lantern outside their doors as a courtesy to passers-by, and in Lombard Street and Cornhill it was the same, elsewhere darkness was complete. No one had troubled them so far, but Will himself would not be safe in the warren of streets which lay between them and the river. Arabella sighed. "I suppose we'll have to go back. How I hate doing nothing when something needs to be done."

"Not afore time. You put a spell on me, Miss Arabella, and no mistake." He took her arm in a grasp like forge pincers, glancing over his shoulder and sidling her from doorway to doorway: thieves were everywhere and shadow impenetrable below gables which almost touched.

Arabella tripped, and only Will's hand kept her from falling. A voice loosed a string of obscenities and a blow missed her by a hairbreadth. Will yelped as some weapon caught him across the shins. "Run!" he gasped. "Watch your feet, don't fall."

It was easy to say, thought Arabella, panting. She couldn't see her feet, and her stays locked out breath. They barged into a merchant staring at the sky and he immediately shouted, thinking they were thieves. Heads turned and Will swore savagely.

"Harry!" cried Arabella, and plunged across the road. They were back in the faint illumination of Cheapside and her eyes had become more used to darkness. There was no mistaking the figure she had glimpsed, set of shoulder and back more familiar than she realised.

He had been leaning against the conduit, now he turned and straightened. "Arabella," he said in astonishment. "What the devil are you doing here?"

"Looking for you," she replied simply.

"Alone?"

She flipped a hand at Will across the street, engaged in furious altercation with the merchant, and Harry laughed, holding her closely. "You always have some dupe well tied to your strings, don't you, Bella? But since you are here . . ." He kissed her with fierce hunger, kindling her as he had before, blood rising, until she was kissing him as passionately. Jostling crowds were forgotten and only the dark remained, a soft and lovely darkness for themselves alone.

He drew back at last and laid his cheek to hers. "Ah, Bella, my love. There is surely no harder trial for a man than living in the same house with your indifference. Did you truly worry a little, or was I your excuse to climb the wall for once?"

"I worried," she said with dignity, wanting him to kiss her again. "Although I'm sure you will believe exactly what you please. You aren't hurt?" His clothes reeked of smoke.

"A trifle scorched, but well enough. Come, we'd better rescue Will before he is taken up by the watch. Keep your hood over your face and languish on me just as instinct bids for once. I doubt you need instruction."

He kept his arm about her while he vouched for Will to Mr. Pellyn, a fellow goldsmith who recognised Harry Cornish and was easily distracted by glimpses of as brazen a strumpet as he had ever seen. She looked expensive too, he thought with envy; a fine tale he would have to tell Alderman Cornish in the morning.

Arabella took Harry at his word and slid her hand between his coat and linen shirt, what point in playing doxy if she could not pleasure herself as well? She was inexperienced but not innocent in the way most girls of her upbringing were. She felt Harry tense to her touch although his voice remained courteous, exchanging pleasantries with Mr. Pellyn, and she was seized by mischievous desire to break his composure before the eyes of others. As she could feel it already lost under her caress.

She snuggled closer and began to move her fingers languorously up his ribs, wanting to giggle as outrage fought lust on Mr. Pellyn's face. As if he sensed some duel between them,

Harry stood like Cheapside conduit: still and stagnant after long journeying, sweating heavily. He was slippery with it to her touch...he leaped sharply and exclaimed, mumbling some apology and dragging her with him down Cheapside, so fast she nearly fell, Will trailing apologetically behind.

They did not stop until they reached Furnival Alley. "I'm sorry," said Arabella clearly. She felt thoroughly ashamed of herself. "I was happy and played a game only. You're hurt, aren't you?"

He dropped her arm and stood staring at her, expression taut. "I don't know what the devil I'm going to do about you, Bella. I can't imagine a more unsuitable wife nor one who will make my life more uncomfortable, when one moment you are all grace and love, and the next behaving like a trollop born, not made. Yet you came into the dark of Cheapside looking for me, and when you apologise you scorn excuses as if you were a soldier facing battle." He kissed her lightly, not at all the way she wanted. "Up with you then, on Will's back, poor fool, and then my shoulders, an even more abject fool. Wait on the top of the wall for Will."

"No," said Arabella, not taking much notice. "You're hurt. I won't climb on your shoulders until you tell me where."

He grunted, it might have been with exasperation or amusement. "Keep to my left then. I took a spray of oil down my right arm and ribs."

He had indeed, as she saw when he thumped on the front door a few minutes later, and was admitted with many exclamations of relief and distress. The night had hidden his state before, but now she saw that his sleeve was burned, hand red and polishy-swollen, the right side of face and neck blistered. Arabella had stripped off her cloak and returned to the parlour before he came in, amazed to find she had been gone so short a time that Mr. Cornish still dozed by the hearth.

While the others pelted Harry with questions, she remained in the background, studying him through narrowed eyes and hugging newfound knowledge of what she could rouse in him when she chose. She grew impatient after a while, when questions were all of oil and warehouses, realising as she had not before that even when he kissed her, he had done so one-handed.

They all turned when she brought a knife and goose salve. "Ah, yes, Arabella," said Alderman Cornish, surprised. "Attend to Henry if you will. You say all the oil is lost?"

"We saved some from the ground floor at Greely's, as for the rest—Queenhithe is burning with such great heat there is no going near it." Harry looked exhausted, sweating badly as she had felt before; when she cut and peeled off cloth, she saw why. From knuckles to neck and down upper ribs, where her hand had first felt rawness, he was flayed by scorching oil. He looked at himself and grimaced. "It was lucky my hand was wrapped in sacking at the time, handling hot kegs."

During the plague, Arabella had become accustomed to more unpleasant sights than an arm like butchered beef, and crisis brought out the best in her. She enjoyed touching Harry's body too, felt satisfaction in her own deft skills, and was taken aback when something in his expression told her not just of pain, but how very much he disliked her tending him.

"My thanks," he said curtly, and stood unsteadily as soon as she had fastened the last strip of linen. He looked directly at his father. "Unless the wind drops, the fire will burn into the City tomorrow."

"There will be time by then to pull down houses in its track, fires seldom spread far in the better streets." Alderman Cornish blinked rapidly, he had not recovered from Henry's news that most of the oil was gone, was upset too by the state the boy was in. As a working goldsmith before he turned banker, he had seen enough melting-shed accidents to know how such burns could fester.

"You would do well to prepare yourself, sir," persisted Harry. "Send apprentices to hire carts before they become scarce, unlock the vault and pack both coin and plate for a move in case it should become necessary."

Mrs. Cornish gave a little scream. "A riverside fire will never reach as far as here!"

"Of course not," said her husband irritably. "There is plenty of water in the conduit and the mayor will organise fire fighting better tomorrow." That old woman Bludworth, he thought in dismay, he lacks courage even to pick a cinder off the floor.

"Unless the wind drops, the fire will be on our doorstep by tomorrow night," said Harry flatly. They heard his feet stumbling on the stairs and the slam of his door while they still stared in disbelief. A fire along the river could not possibly reach Cheapside, for that would mean . . . that meant the whole City would be consumed.

Arabella slept without stirring all night, exhausted by unaccustomed excitement. She woke feeling pleasurably relaxed, glad to find it still dark so she could lie a while longer. She stretched and sneezed unexpectedly: the smell of smoke was very strong. Recollection flooded back and she leaped out of bed, no longer sleepy. It wasn't night as she had thought; instead black smoke hid the sky, boiling angrily in a cauldron of heat. She opened her window and immediately wind swept into the room, setting hangings swaying, pressing her shift against her body. Shouts and scurrying feet were everywhere, and in the background a roar like no sound she had ever heard.

If the wind does not drop, the fire will be here tomorrow, Harry had said. It had not dropped but strengthened, and Arabella no longer thought that Harry's experiences the day before had led him into exaggeration. She dressed hastily and ran downstairs to find the house in uproar.

Clerks and serving maids were running in every direction, falling over each other, spilling loads on the floor, close to blows over every mishap. The vault trap was open, the counting room glittering with gold and silver, packing cloths slipping underfoot.

Mrs. Cornish pounced on her as she entered the parlour. "Wherever have you been? Go and start carrying pots from the kitchen in case . . . in case—" Her face puckered as she looked around at polished oak and familiar furnishings. She was very fearful but could not really believe the fire would come here.

Arabella nodded, but as soon as Mrs. Cornish rushed off to scold a weeping maid, she went into the counting room instead. Alderman Cornish was there, checking lists while clerks packed, and turned as she entered. "Go into the vault and tell Henry the lists don't tally with the plate he is sending up."

She went where she was told this time, descending into cool, brick-lined earth. Harry was at the far end while apprentices scurried plate up the single ladder.

She set a pile of silver tumbling as she squeezed past and Harry looked up. "Oh, it's you," he said, and smiled. He looked white and underslept, but was carefully dressed apart from one sleeve loose.

"Your father sent me to say your lists don't tally." She saw he had paper wedged on some shelves while trying to write left-handed. "Let me help. If you dictate the description, I'll write more quickly than you. Don't be obstinate," she added impatiently as he hesitated. "My dowry as well as your wealth will melt if we don't hurry."

He laughed and handed over the sheet. "And I suppose you

write a fairer hand than I, as well as your other accomplishments?"

"Than you left-handed, certainly." She was soon into the flow of it. She was long familiar with goldsmith's terms, and the sheets went smoothly up with the right loads. She had never been in the vault before and was impressed by the quantity of bullion and plate; for all her father's skills, Alderman Cornish could have bought his entire stock and scarcely noticed the cost. Her contempt for goldsmiths who abandoned their craft for dealing in balances withered as she reckoned the wealth brought by usury.

They worked so fast together that at length they were forced to wait for the packers to catch up. "You'd best sit down," said Arabella practically. "It's going to be a long day."

"Whether the fire comes or not," he agreed. "If it does, we shall have to fight the mob off carts full of more wealth than they have ever seen; if it doesn't, I can't see my father sleeping before everything is checked back in the vault again."

"But you think it will come?"

"Don't you?"

She nodded. Surrounded by cool earth, thought of fire was unreal but the roaring she had heard stayed in her mind. Oil and resin and God knew what else had given the fire a molten heart beyond the control of men wielding buckets and fire hooks. She looked round the vault, surprisingly large now it was nearly empty. "I had no idea you were so rich."

Harry sat on the floor with a grunt, back against the wall. "Has nobody ever told you what outrageous things you say?"

"Only you, and that too often." She sat beside him. "Don't you find it mortal dull to mind each word you speak?"

"Often, which perhaps is why I enjoy forgetting to mind myself with you. And yes, we were rich yesterday. We are less so today, and it is my guess that we shall be in some difficulty by tomorrow."

"The oil?"

"As you say, the oil. And a few other things as well, warehoused along the river and now cinders with the rest. The royal customs will suffer too, and tax to repay loans be delayed a year or more. Most of what you have seen this morning will be owed to creditors whose balances we have lent and now lost."

"Have you enough to repay the balances left with you?"

"Just about, but with very little to spare. And if we have to rebuild as well—"

"My lawsuit," said Arabella flatly. "Bevil will win by default."

He shrugged and winced. "We'll see. We shall do what we can, you may be sure."

The rest of the day passed in a haze of smoke and panic-stricken haste. Carts which could have been hired for a few pence the day before cost twenty pounds apiece, and the price continued to rise: forty pounds by dusk, fifty a few hours later if any could be found. The noise had become immense; the thunder of falling buildings, the roar of flames, screams and shouts of frantic people struggling to save something from the wreckage of their lives, all confined by choking heat and smoke. As the afternoon wore on they saw the first flames, slashing sparks above the roofs of Bucklersbury and Walbrook, but still a fair way off.

Harry had bought three carts outright and completely blocked off Furnival Alley with them, so they could load directly from the side door without fear of theft while the heftiest apprentices stood guard with cudgels. Everyone sweated under the weight of cased gilt and silver, bundles of coin and bales of ledgered records, cursing the need to leave the strongest on guard. Even little Sing-to-the-Lord and Hephzibah staggered under the lighter household treasures though Alderman Cornish was adamant: all the plate and bullion went first, domestic goods awaited a very unlikely second journey, except for a few bales and pots to disguise the nature of their load.

The air became steadily hotter and more fume-laden, until it became an effort to breathe. Arabella took off her stays but still felt close to collapse, back aching and lungs rasping. Mrs. Cornish was breeding and forced to rest, the alderman grey-faced, for he had done little except sit in his counting room for years. Harry, too, looked ill. He had stripped to shirt and breeches and normally spent long hours tramping the City, but his scorching of the day before had weakened him more than he would admit.

By late afternoon all other sounds were swamped by the close and deadly crackle of flames. Hastily, the alderman began issuing the few swords and knives they possessed, distributing the strongest clerks amongst the three carts. "We stay together if we can. Up the alley to Cateaton Street and east from there. If we are separated, wait if you can." Such precious loads were a temptation to clerks and apprentices as well as looters, and he put himself in the first cart with his wife and younger children, those of his employees whom he most trusted in the second, and Harry at the back to keep the vulnerable second cart firmly held.

Arabella scrambled up with Harry and Will followed her. "You drive, Will," said Harry briefly. He knew he had not the strength to beat the wretched cart nag, and even left-handed he would be more skilled than Will with a sword. Arabella grasped a carving knife and stared back at the House of the Golden Spurs as they lurched away. She would probably never see it again, although Mr. Cornish had left a guard on his own house to keep looters away, hoping for time to make a second journey.

Furnival Alley was no more than a dim tunnel, and Cateaton Street little better, although less crowded than Cheapside, as if its citizens believed the extra distance made them safe, as those in Cheapside had thought the night before. The hideous sky was everywhere, though, a furnace glow reflected off smeared black, which grew ever fiercer as darkness fell. Once, an explosion tore the air and a spurt of flame shot clear over the roofs still separating them from the fire, followed by a long, rumbling crash. "St. Clement, Eastcheap," said Harry, staring over his shoulder. "Something stored there which should not have been and has brought the spire down in one."

"Eastcheap! Sweet Jesus, it will be into Lombard and Cannon streets soon!" They were bound for the Tower and needed to keep to safer main thoroughfares if they could.

"Cannon Street is alight already, so far as I can judge," said Harry grimly. "Try Lothbury, Will, for I'm none too sure of Cornhill."

"T'alderman said stay together, an' un is trying Cornhill."

Harry hesitated, then told one of the clerks to push his way through with a message. Their carts were strung out by now and where the first might well get through the third could be in serious trouble. The clerk did not return; there was no way of telling whether he was trampled underfoot or had run off for his own safety. When the turning came at the end of Cateaton, the carts in front swung right, against the flow of people streaming uphill from Walbrook and the solid front of flame they could now clearly see.

"What'll I do, Mr. Henry?" asked Will.

"You'd best follow," said Harry reluctantly. "We can't leave them when they may stick fast, but—" He stopped, but they could see what he meant. The Tower was beyond the fire and at the back of the wind, safe behind its massive open moats and fifteen-foot walls; in between lay either a maze of streets where looting was a certainty or the few wider thoroughfares threatened by advancing fire. They could see the gleaming sickle of it curving inward, between them and the direct route along Lombard and Fenchurch streets. Harry had thought to circle north and chance a longer journey, now they were committed to racing the fire along Cornhill at least, since turning in such crowds was impossible.

Their cart swayed and jolted under the pressure of bodies surging past. People doubled under bundles, people with yelling babies, the sick and old jostled ruthlessly aside; faces gaping and screaming, women wailing for lost children, children jellied with terror in this vast and merciless pack. From several directions they heard shouts that Dutch or papists had started the fire, and once they saw a respectable, middle-aged merchant seized and trampled by the mob.

"A foreigner," said Harry briefly. "Down on the wharfs yesterday the word 'papist' was enough to send everyone crazed. The fire started in a baker's oven and to save himself he swears that papists tossed fireballs into his sheds while he slept, and fools believe him. Or want to believe him and gain a little pleasure from their fear," he added, staring at the swirl where the merchant had disappeared from sight. There was no possibility of aiding him.

Fortunately, most of the fleeing throng were too immersed in their private tragedies to spare much thought for laden carts, but once a black-browed fellow seized the horse's trace. Harry sliced at his hand and he was whirled out of sight while he stared at his own blood. Then they heard a scuffle from the back as a gang of boys tried to cut a bale loose, and Harry had to clamber perilously back, clinging to rope and holding his sword in his bad hand. Arabella sat tensely beside Will while he was gone, fingers slippery on her knife. She would not be afraid to use it if someone attacked horse or cart but a knife was not much against so many. She did slash once at a carter who tried to unseat Will, and felt savage satisfaction when he recoiled, hands clapped to blood spurting from his cheek. She looked round, lips parted, almost hoping that someone would try the same again.

"God's bones," said Will. "Look at Lombard Street."

They were back at the main crossroads of the City, Cheapside behind and still untouched, the steep tracks leading to the river all ending in a wall of fire, while ahead Lombard Street was ablaze from end to end. The richest merchants lived there, the finest shops of all London clustered alongside to serve them: all flamed at once in glare brighter than struck lightning.

Harry clambered back over their delicate, awkward load and slid into his place beside her. He was breathing heavily and looked ghastly in the dreadful light, but then they all did. "Those chicken-gutted clerks, they could have bested the whole pack without any help from me."

"We can't turn, Mr. Henry," said Will. "The alderman is trying Cornhill."

"Nothing else he can do now," said Harry shortly. Cornhill was dangerously close to the fire but clearing for that reason, everywhere else jammed too tight with people for their carts to turn.

It took so long. It took so long. Arabella sat tensely while the carts wound in and out of wreckage lying in the street. The fire had seemed to hesitate while it gulped up Lombard Street, now it regained force and direction and was driving faster than a man could walk through the alleys and courtyards which separated it from Cornhill.

The Royal Exchange was deserted and alight at one end, the bust of Sir Thomas Gresham looking out over the destruction of the city he had dreamed would one day rule the commerce of the world. Arabella touched Harry. "It seems a long time since we were there together."

His face was grim and sad, streaming sweat in the fearful heat. "And a longer time before we go again." He loved the City, and had not known how much until it was lost. "Hurry, Will. Once into Cornhill, the flame will flash from house to house faster than a cart can move."

Will lashed mercilessly at the wretched animal between the shafts until it lurched into a broken trot, throwing them against boards and bundles like spice in a mortar. Harry cried out once when his arm struck wood and Arabella tried to shield him, but he cursed and pushed her away.

Timbers were crashing all around, ahead the spire of St. Peter's, Cornhill, blazed fiercely, set alight by sparks ahead of the main fire. Debris littered the cobbles where an attempt had been made to pull down houses as a firebreak ahead of the flames. Sweating gangs holding fire hooks stood silently as the wind drove great bursts of sparks high over their heads, starting a score of fresh fires between one breath and the next.

Arabella saw a tongue of flame lick out of an alley ahead, between them and the other carts, hesitate, then leap the height of a wall and into timbering above. Triumphant banners of fire streamed into the sky while Cornhill waited, then the flames dipped to the wind and bit into the houses lining the street, flickering from roof to roof. They had to go on. Will lashed at the nag again, now mad enough with fear to be half bolting, and they plunged into the scorching tunnel, faces seared, ears deadened by the roaring blast on either side. The glare was unspeakable, unbearable, eyes screwed up, breath held against crackling dryness in nostrils and lungs.

Then, unbelievably, they were out again, back amongst people running and screaming, into breathable air and a place where fear did not master thought. Arabella became aware that she was tightly held, and holding tightly. Harry's bad arm was across her shoulder and face, his other hand grasping hers, the scrape of unshaven chin against her cheek. He turned his head and kissed her, somewhere between nose and cheekbone as the cart jolted. "I could not ask for a steadier knife hand by my side in danger."

"I thought we were dead. Do you know the only thing in my mind besides fear? How I was to explain my wickedness since he died to my father."

"And now you have time for amendment of life," he said gravely. "What a very fortunate circumstance."

"Oh yes." Arabella blithely set aside recollection of gabbled promises to God in the furnace of Cornhill. "I'm ashamed really of being so frightened, when such a great fire is exactly the sort of adventure I've wanted all my life."

Harry's face set; they lived, but Arabella's adventure was the death of London and it had not finished dying yet. What a selfish chit she was, after all.

And how very long he had known himself a fool to love her.

Behind them, one by one, the busts of the Kings of England exploded like bombards as the Royal Exchange burned.

Chapter Eight

The fire burned into Threadneedle Street, Lothbury and Throgmorton Street, before turning to converge on Cheapside. There was time for Harry and his father to return for a load of household goods, a struggling circuitous journey as street after street was consumed around them. Four flame flows met in Poultry early on Tuesday morning and within minutes the south side of Cheapside was ablaze: gilded Goldsmith's Row with its carved escutcheons, St. Mary-le-Bow, the Mermaid Tavern. At their foot the conduit boiled, heat alone charring the north side. Then the curtain of sparks which swept everywhere ahead of the fire poured down on dry timbers and the north side lit. Harry stood beside his father, watching it burn. The two houses where the Signs of the Corncrake and Golden Spurs had hung burned together, and in minutes they were gone, flames already leaping north towards Goldsmiths' Hall and Guildhall. Of the Lord Mayor and his fire-fighting teams there was no sign, although King Charles had rallied to his capital in its extremity and was handling buckets like a workman.

"St. Paul's next," said Alderman Cornish flatly. "There's nothing to stop it short of Fleet ditch."

Harry nodded. "If I go there, will you be able to take the cart back? I would like to do what I can for London now."

"Aye, I'll manage well enough. If I was a younger man I'd be with you. Alderman Sickert told me at the Tower that the King has drawn out gunpowder and intends to blow up houses to make a firebreak worth having if the flames leap the Fleet."

They did leap the Fleet ditch. Guildhall burned like a great golden bowl, and so fierce was the wind that fragments of charred silks from mercers' warehouses in Cateaton Street were picked up thirty miles away. Cellars of spices burned, so for a while the air smelled of incense instead of soot; St. Paul's burned and sent a lava flow of lead down Ludgate Hill, the precious stocks of the booksellers and stationers which were kept in its chapter house white-hot long after tottering walls were all that was left of the cathedral. Newgate burned, and by Tuesday night the City within its old tracery of walls had ceased to exist except for a small area around Leadenhall and another by the Tower. Now the fire was set to consume the rest of London: Holborn, Fleet Street and the Temple directly in its path.

Frantic teams had pulled down houses along the line of the Fleet, using gunpowder, anything, to widen the natural barrier of marsh and drains around the ditch. Then when the flames came, their efforts went for nothing when sparks started a dozen fires in the time it took to set up a bucket chain to the first.

Fleet Street burned.

Bridewell, Whitefriars and Fetter Lane burned, flushing swarms of thieves and lawyers from their lodging with even-handed justice.

The Inner Temple began to burn.

The fire was half a mile from Whitehall when at last the wind veered and then dropped, so men with their puny water carts, hooks and blasting powder could face it with some hope of success, and by Thursday it was out. A quarter of a million Londoners were homeless, rich and poor jumbled amongst bundles and boxes in the fields north of the city. Ruin was complete, fortunes and employment destroyed, the dream of commercial supremacy vanished.

The Cornishes stayed as close to their city as seemed prudent and were camped in Moorfields; one cart had collapsed, the other two were backed together and covered with cloth to form a crude shelter. Harry returned, filthy and reeling with exhaustion; although he was feverish and his arm infected, they had neither drugs nor salves to relieve him. Mrs. Cornish miscarried and was also ill, the three children shocked and fretful, shivering in lengthening September nights. Soon it would rain and Moorfields turn into its usual swamp; at least thirty thousand people were living there, most without shelter, more crowding in every day as those who had fled further returned. The King produced military tents and issued a proclamation for compulsory subscription throughout the country to the relief of London, while Lord Mayor Bludworth launched his own appeal to other corporations.

"All he's good for," snorted Alderman Cornish when he heard. "At least he has only one more month of office to run. Sir William Bolton is to follow him, and he has doubled his fortune in five years, or so men say. There'll be no fambling nonsense about him."

The Corporation of the City was meeting at Gresham College in Bishopsgate, organising supplies for refugees and already discussing rebuilding, so he was often away; consequently Arabella found herself responsible for the Cornish household, with both Harry and Mrs. Cornish ill. Between the efforts of the Corporation and the charity of villagers around London, there was sufficient food, so she sent their remaining apprentices to haul fuel from the ruins and cooked as best as she could in a single pot. Marauders were a constant danger, and she never dared have fewer than half a dozen apprentices or clerks around, which would become another problem as they drifted off, seeking work.

For everyone knew that Alderman Cornish had suffered badly. Other goldsmiths had envied his profits from lending on goods, but themselves stayed with traditional lendings to the Exchequer and to those possessing land or plate: they should recover, especially when not a single goldsmith had lost the contents of his vault. Every one had acted with the prudence expected of their profession and saved their assets, even if now they froze in a field under a scrap of cloth. But London's trade was dead: ships could not unload; craftsmen went unpaid, nor was anyone able to buy their goods if they should start work again; contracts were lost, markets gone. Those who still possessed gold and silver, and there were plenty, could not sell or find anything to buy, so they began to leave. The prospect of a winter in Moorfields or on Islington Heights was not attractive. They went to Liverpool to found the sugar industry, to Bristol to finance slaving, to Manchester, Bradford and Colchester, bringing prosperity and new ideas wherever they went. They settled as far away as St. Helena, India and the American colonies, and usually prospered there, leaving behind them a forlorn and desolate London, stinking in its ruins and with such wealth as had been salvaged relentlessly haemorrhaging away.

One by one the Cornish clerks and apprentices slipped away too. They were well trained and more experienced than most and so received tempting offers from those who planned to establish themselves elsewhere. Cornish's was bankrupt, and their employees saved themselves while they could. It was natural, and made Arabella very angry. She still intended to go to Bevil but scorned to run for the comfort of an unburned house in the Strand.

"Will you leave London when you are stronger?" she asked Harry one day. He was recovering, being determined to do so in the shortest possible time, but slowly in such wretched conditions.

He stared at her, astounded. "Of course not."

"There's plenty who are," she pointed out.

"Well, I'm not. Nor will my father. Bludworth may be an old fool but at least he hasn't run, and every one of the aldermen has stayed, too. Five years, and we'll have it rebuilt better than before." It'll have to be quick, he reflected grimly, or all the London skills will have gone elsewhere and we shall be left to face a starving rabble in the place where once the nation's wealth was forged.

Arabella stared across the squalid slope of Moorfields at a smoking plain of rubble; walls and gutted church towers stood out like bones on a rotted corpse. "Will you return to your craft once your debts are paid, since you cannot be a banker with an empty vault?"

Harry stood carefully, he exercised doggedly to recover his strength and fetched their water every day, too dangerous a journey for a woman through the half-starved roughs infesting Moorfields. "I intend to rebuild everything we had and more, like London itself. The Sign of the Corncrake will be better wrought this time, in iron as yours was and well gilded besides." His eyes were the bleak ice-grey she had seen before when he was angry. "There will be plenty seeking credit in London during the coming years, and profit for those brave enough to offer it. Cornish's will reopen in Cheapside, you have my word on it."

Two days later, he announced that he was fit enough to go into the City and Arabella went with him, tired of mud and whining children. It had rained during the night, the first heavy downpour of autumn, and everything was wet, her skirts sodden to the knee.

"My father is at the Tower," said Harry after long silence. The ruins of London did not induce light chatter. "He has passed word to his depositors that they can come and be paid in full;

a show of boldness may persuade some to trust us and not withdraw. Your dowry will be kept separate of course, but as you feared, there will be nothing to spare for fighting legal causes."

"I'm going to see Bevil. No—don't interrupt, nothing you say will stop me. I shall stay here so long as your family needs me since I owe a return on your kindness, but must strike a bargain with him before he knows himself safe."

She expected furious argument, instead Harry walked beside her frowning heavily, eyes on cracked and blackened cobbles underfoot. He looked much older than before; pallid, sunken face and grimed clothes quite different from his former elegance. She supposed he must be nearly nineteen, but he seemed more, and held himself awkwardly too. The original burn had worsened under the strain and filth of fire fighting and taking their goods to safety; his arm was no longer infected but the muscles seemed to have shrunk. He said nothing to her but she had several times seen him attempting to use his right hand with very little success, an unfortunate handicap for a banker who could no longer afford clerks to keep his ledgers.

Guildhall with its splendid three-hundred-year-old roof was no more than walls, familiar streets unrecognisable, the ground steaming in light rain. Arabella stared about her, fascinated. Surely there had never before been destruction on so grand a scale. At least her feet felt pleasantly warm, where they had been icy in soggy, disintegrating shoes.

Harry stopped sometimes to help her over rubble, his silence disconcerting though she refused to be the one to break it. She had stated her intention and nothing would change her now. "Last Christmas I reckoned we needed time to see whether my temper and your tongue bedded well together," he said at last. "But prudence no longer seems important. I desire very much to wed you if the notion pleases you. I have nothing to offer at present, but intend to prosper again if you will have brief patience with me." He looked away and added in a cold, dry voice, "I believe my arm will heal and not offend you in the future."

"Oh, don't be a fool, Harry!" exclaimed Arabella, exasperated. "If you could give what I wanted, a flayed arm would be nothing to me. But you can't, and no amount of prospering would change it. I've lived enough of my life mewed up inside four walls and a courtyard; if I wed you I'd be trapped there until the day I died, breeding a brat a year."

"And I mean nothing to you, except as jailer to turn the lock on life?"

"Of course you do! I'm . . . I'm fond of you, you know that. I'd like to come and visit—"

"No," he said flatly. "I have my life too and the day you go, you go forever. So think well on it, Bella, for it's my belief we could find great happiness together and I would do what I could about walls and courtyard: the fire has swept away the old City life and the new will certainly be freer for a woman. My offer stands so long as you stay with us, it is withdrawn forever on the day you leave."

"It sounds like a six-month loan on your ledger," snapped Arabella. If he would only hold and kiss her, how different it might be.

"An open-ended loan where the client holds all the options, which is the most dangerous transaction a banker could consider." He had refused to look at her before, now he did and smiled faintly. "I know what else you're thinking, Bella, and the answer is no. We know already that our bodies deal very hotly and pleasantly together, it is the rest which stands between us."

"So you'll wait and let your chances slip, just as you have before," said Arabella spitefully. "When I wed it will be to a man who finds patience as tedious as I do."

"And the blessing of God rest on it," he said sarcastically, "since assuredly all else will be lacking. Come, I've said what I wanted and am not minded to bicker any longer. We'll need all our strength to face the shocks of Cheapside."

They certainly did. A winding track had been cleared, otherwise it was difficult to tell where the street ended and houses had once begun. Only the gutted tower of St. Mary-le-Bow acted as a landmark, after that it was a matter of pacing and seeking out any familiarity which might show which of the piles of rubbish represented their property.

"Look!" cried Arabella. "I'd know this slate anywhere." She gabbled out about how her mother always kept herbs steeping on cool slate, as if by knowing for certain where she stood, the House of the Spurs already lived again.

"So this must be . . ." Harry paced carefully, slipping on cinders. "These timbers must be our roof fallen outward over the wall."

Arabella followed him into a maze of heavy timbers, like iron from age and only charred on the outside. Now they knew where they were it became possible to find split stones from the hearth, solidified pools of iron where the melting shed had been, fix both boundaries with cairns of calcined brick. Arabella poked about amongst filthy rubbish but found nothing of value. The chimney still stood to half its height, ground plan clear to the eye of knowledge, nothing else remained. Rain was falling more heavily now, wind unchecked from the sea making her shiver. However would they last a winter through without shelter, how could they or the City rise again from such ruin?

The thought returned that she could go to Bevil now, while she felt annoyed with Harry. But she put it aside; so long as Mrs. Cornish was ill the family needed her, she could not walk out while they faced so many and such great disasters. She felt a conscious glow of virtue and went in search of Harry, to find him peering into the black hole which led down to the vault. The trapdoor and ladder were burned and rubbish almost blocked the entry, otherwise it seemed undamaged except the shelves were charred, bricks powdery from heat.

"Perhaps we need not have slaved so hard over moving all that gold," said Arabella, looking down.

"Except it would have melted and looters scraped the remains off the floor," retorted Harry. "Have you a vault like this next door?"

Arabella flushed. "No, we were less wealthy than you . . . then."

"Then, as you say. A pity though, I was thinking we could live through the winter more comfortably on our own property than in Moorfields, and two well-lined holes would give us more space than one."

She promptly felt ashamed of herself for taunting him, and then was annoyed by her shame. All the same, it was a good idea. She hated the squalid discomfort of Moorfields, which would worsen through the endless winter ahead, and longed to restore some order to daily living. "You could dig down from the hearth and extend the chimney for cooking, and once there is timber to buy Will could put in sleeping boards, perhaps build a shelter over the entry," she said enthusiastically. "How marvellous to be warm and dry again!"

"I can go downriver to the naval yard at Deptford for timber. My mother and the children won't survive a winter under flapping cloth."

"How about me? I suppose I can camp in a field forever, like a mare at pasture?"

"I doubt it, my dear," he answered carelessly. "You'd jump the hedge and be off to find a snug stable whatever the price you paid for it."

"I've stayed, haven't I?" she said in a shaking voice. "I could be off tomorrow to silk gowns and a warm house, yet stayed for the debt I owe your family. When it is paid I'll go, and not before."

He stood, staring at her, then bent and kissed her fingers. "You owe us nothing. Stay of your own will and be welcome, but I refuse to be regarded as a burden you must carry."

"Harry, for God's sake, will you stop talking like a fool! Of course I couldn't just leave while your mother is ill and all your affairs like sweepings in the melting spoon!" She was delighted by a chance to point out her rectitude, and without any contrivance on her part, either.

He laughed instead of being impressed, though, no wonder she found him so infuriating. "Well done, Bella. I haven't offered you such a splendid chance for years, have I?"

They moved into the vault within days. Harry and Will cleared a space above the entry and built a shed to keep out the weather and to work in; the vault itself was well drained and warm once the chimney was extended, even if intolerably crowded. Scraps of cloth were hung to give some privacy, their belongings stacked and reckoned. They had a bolt of linen, so Mrs. Cornish was able to occupy herself with sewing and try to forget her sorrows, the rest Arabella organised with brusque efficiency. She disliked cleaning and cooking, lacked patience to deal with sneezing children underfoot, but dealt with whatever must be done to free herself for matters which interested her more. Pots shone, the children learned to take their whines elsewhere and Mrs. Cornish showed such pathetic gratitude that Arabella found it impossible to hide her irritation. She could not imagine herself sick or snivelling, so was intolerant of life's defeated.

The alderman she respected more than before, he looked unwell and wheezed dismally in the icy shed where he and Harry struggled to bring order into their affairs, but he never complained or attempted to compromise on his debts, although besieged by creditors; City government also took up a great deal of time he could ill afford. Within days of the fire the Court of Aldermen was issuing instructions for the relief of the poor, for the preservation of the remains of Guildhall, for clearing the streets. The gardens of Gresham College were staked out to serve traders in place of the Royal Exchange, the safer ruins set aside for artisans and shopkeepers to build shelters and reopen business. This brought a sharp rebuke from court and church, since the most substantial ruins were undoubtedly the gutted shells of churches, and the City authorities turned a blind eye to taverns, smithies and builders' yards springing up in naves and chapels until their attention was firmly drawn to the necessary distinction between God and Mammon.

For speed was vital.

If it was to recover at all London must be rebuilt before the poor starved, the rich departed and craftsmen lost their markets for good. There were plenty at court who rejoiced that a bastion of opposition to Stuart ambitions was no more, sympathetic messages by no means always sincere. London's supremacy was resented elsewhere in the nation; Amsterdam saw its losses recouped, Versailles a dangerous opponent of absolutism humbled.

The war still continued, though the King lacked money to send the fleet to sea, and under the triple blows of plague, fire and Dutch naval supremacy, London's ruin seemed sealed for a generation. Unless, somehow, the flow of trade could be maintained on nonexistent credit and wharfage, customers satisfied by merchants without stocks, premises or records, the wealth of the City re-established by staggering sleight of hand before anyone grasped that it was gone. Charles might talk of redesigning London, the leisured gossip of court and coffee-house be of splendid streets and squares; harassed City officials knew there was neither money for such luxury nor time for discussion. The first, indeed the only, priority was to keep the complex of trade and finance alive, rebuilding must be squeezed from what was left after earning their right to live.

Arabella drifted into the habit of helping with the ledgers; however uncomfortable it might be, the shed was an escape from cramped boredom below. Most of the detailed work fell on Harry since his father was often away, and though his arm was improving, he could only write clumsily. Also, he must help Will to clear their site of debris.

The Court of Aldermen had issued orders that property was to be ready for survey before the spring; bricks piled and boundary markers placed. Each householder must also clear the street along his frontage; if he failed to do either then his lease would lapse and the landlord free to bargain with another tenant. No exceptions were allowed, and vacant property went to those who cleared it.

"It is harsh, and not in our favour, but I could not disagree," said Alderman Cornish when he told them of it. "Those who can afford to clear and rebuild have rent remitted until it is done, and will be well placed. Those too ruined to start again must be forced out so others may take their place." There would be no help for anyone from the Corporation, itself close to bankruptcy when a million pounds was needed to restore the public buildings necessary to trade.

"Where will we go?" cried Mrs. Cornish in dismay.

"Go? What makes you think we'll go anywhere?" demanded her husband. The only time he and Harry looked alike was when they were angry.

"What choice have we? How can we clear both street and land with only Will to serve us?" Arabella smiled to herself. Will had consulted the shades of Robert Sperling and decided that his duty required him to stay to protect her, free of wages.

"My arm is healed and I have a deal of strength," broke in Harry. "Nick is ten now, so will be able to help. Everyone must do whatever they can since we are certainly going to clear within the time, even if we work by moonlight."

Alderman Cornish poked peevishly at the fire. "We can spare a little to hire a man to help with the heavy beams, but everything must be well prepared so we don't waste a moment of his time. We shall lose frontage too, the new streets are to be wider and no overlying storeys or signs allowed. Everything is to be constructed of brick and tile and slate, gutters and downpipes made compulsory, kennels for rubbish removed from the centre of the street."

"It will be the finest city in Europe when we've done." Harry kindled with enthusiasm as he thought of it. "Then the Dutch and a few others will discover how they crowed over us too soon."

"Do you suppose Bevil will clear the Golden Spurs?" Arabella had wondered several times whether the fire gave her a chance to claim her own again, although no one else seemed to spare thought for her inheritance.

"He need not do it himself, he can pay another," pointed out Alderman Cornish. "So long as it's done by the set date at no charge to the City. I put your name on the register as householder when I swore to our holding, but he had already claimed it. There is to be a court to decide disputed claims which will be cheap and swift, freed from lawyers' quibbles and corruption. I do not hold out much hope of success, though, he has the documents and Richard Goodenough's word, who will certainly swear to anything for profit."

Arabella thanked him grudgingly for remembering her affairs in the midst of so much else, but brooded on how she might clear the site before Bevil heard of the new regulations, although it was a blow to discover that he had already entered his claim.

When she broached the idea of selling part of her dowry to pay for clearance, Harry was brusquely discouraging. "Wages are high for good men since there is so much to be done, and most of us unused to doing it. Until the claims court has decided your dispute, any expenditure might simply add to Bevil's gain."

"But if I had cleared it first—"

Harry rubbed his face wearily. "I don't know, Bella. Rebuilding is to be on a time limit too, you'd need seven or eight hundred pounds for the kind of house agreed for Cheapside. Your dowry is not worth so much, and you know we can't help you with credit at the moment. You refuse to wed me because you fear confinement, you need to keep your silver if you are to preserve your choice."

"You should urge me to do it, since you don't want choices in my future."

"I should, shouldn't I?" He stood and stretched. It was bitterly cold in the hut and they were both working wrapped in thick frieze cloth, only a breath of warmth drifting from the open trap to the vault.

Arabella stared gloomily at the ledger on her knees, she had tucked her hands into her skirts while they talked and feeling was just returning to her fingers. She tried to add a column in her head so she could keep her hand in warmth a moment longer, and failed. It was difficult to concentrate in such cold; she sneezed violently and began to shiver.

"Oh, Bella—" Harry put his arms round her; without passion, to offer and receive comfort, holding her into such warmth as he possessed. "I suppose one day we shall look back on this winter and laugh."

"You may, I shan't." She sneezed again.

"Yes, we shall," he said firmly. "I'll be a portly old alderman and introduce a new fashion in fur-lined robes, for surely my bones will never warm again. You will be terrorising the fashionable world by moneylending on their gaming debts, all calculated to the nearest percentage point per minute of loan, while they're too fuddled to know whether you talk of pounds or pence."

"It's an idea," said Arabella thoughtfully. "There must be plenty of gulls at court for those who deal in cash and good security."

He gave a shout of laughter. "And not too many women there who know the banker's trade."

Arabella did not reply, staring out through a hole in tacked canvas. "Harry . . . look, it's Bevil!"

He turned, his arms still about her, and they both watched as a group in the street paced and gesticulated.

"I'm going to speak to him." Arabella twisted out of his grasp and made for the door.

"Have a care. Your dispute comes up for decision soon, and he has witnesses with him willing to twist anything you say."

But Arabella was tired of care, of leaving her affairs to those who only sometimes remembered to tell her what they did. Anyway, she had more than property to discuss with Bevil. She ran her fingers through her hair and bit her lips to make them red and full, wishing she did not look so shabby. Bevil would have no interest in extending charity to a wench with neither looks nor dowry to profit him, however closely related.

He turned to her greeting, and eyed her narrowly. "Who might you be?"

She smiled prettily at him. "Don't you remember me, sir?"

"Aye," he said slowly. "I remember now. 'Twas only you left out of all poor Robert's family. I grieve for you, niece." He wiped his eyes carefully where the wind made them water.

"I'm sure you do," said Arabella cordially. "I thank you for your thought of me. I had intended to call before, but now you're here will you spare a moment to discuss matters of importance to us both?"

His eyes flickered; he was uncertain whether she was making a game of him or, against all expectation, genuinely anxious to be friendly. "If you wish, but it's devilish cold for business in the street."

Arabella laid her hand on his arm and looked up at him

beseechingly. "Just a moment of your time, for my father's sake."

"Well, just a few moments then." He squeezed her hand indulgently; damme, she was a devilish attractive little thing, so sweet and delicate.

"Not out of my sight," cut in Harry. "So don't think you can forget she's your niece behind some snug corner of ruins. We're all used to striking bargains in the rain this winter."

"No, no, of course not." Bevil looked faintly gratified that he should be thought capable of seducing a pretty girl behind ruins in the rain, but with Harry showing no disposition to retire, prudently led her to the cleared space in front of St. Mary-le-Bow. "Is that the Cornish boy? What boors these City merchants are, to be sure. Dealing with gentlemen at court every day, I had become unused to rough manners."

"You are still familiar with the court, sir?"

"Familiar! My dear Arabella, I do not hesitate to say that I am one of its best-known figures! Not as a great lord would be, of course," he added regretfully, "but more . . . more *essential* if you take my meaning. Who would notice if a dozen lords were away for a month? But should Attorney Sperling absent himself—well, a great many things would be quite in disarray! You would not believe the quantity of commissions piled on my shoulders, sometimes I quite stagger with the burden."

"It must be very profitable," said Arabella enviously.

"Well . . . as to that . . . the pleasure of feeling that one fulfils a need is beyond everything satisfying." He patted her hand and found himself regarded with the same wide-eyed stare as before, this time politely sceptical. "Well, yes, of course it is profitable, but—"

"Do you intend to live in Cheapside, sir?"

"Live in Cheapside? Indeed, no. I have lodgings in the piazza of Covent Garden, convenient for my clients and the court. My wife died at Christmas, you know." He dabbed his eyes again and thought of the plump widow he was wooing, a distant relative of my lord of Southampton. Very distant of course, and poverty-stricken, but connections were more important than a dowry. More immediately important, that is, and if the widow had possessed money then she would not have considered marrying an attorney.

"Then, sir, I have a proposition for you." Arabella regarded him levelly, no longer looking sweetly delicate. "I cannot live in the House of the Spurs either, so I suggest we reach a settlement in our dispute, and divide the profit."

He eyed her in astonishment. "Why should I do that? The documents are in my hands and Robert's codicil also, leaving the lease to me."

"Which was forged, so you will lose your claim."

"What a gull you must think me! No, no, my dear, Attorney Sperling does not lose such disputes. Why else should I be so invaluable about the court?" He remembered how Robert had cursed him the night before the plague struck, and would not have given up his revenge for a dozen pleading chits, pretty or no.

"You certainly cannot afford to risk losing such a case or your trade would be gone," agreed Arabella cordially. "Did you know that Richard Goodenough was to have his indentures cancelled before the Court of the Goldsmiths' Company the day after our house was shut up because of the plague?"

"What of it?"

"For theft, dear uncle. And the Goldsmiths' records survived the fire, I asked the First Master." She had not asked, since no case was pending against Richard, but thought Bevil would not ask either; and however fiercely Richard denied the accusation, he had stolen and Bevil would expect him to lie.

Bevil laughed heartily. "Do you know, you are a lass after my own heart? But you shouldn't have warned me, I shall arrange my case differently now and find other witnesses. No one beats Attorney Sperling before the judges of Westminster Hall."

"You won't be pleading in Westminster Hall. All disputes in the City are referred to a panel of judges at Serjeant's Inn, where the Lord Mayor and aldermen can watch their doings. They are instructed to haste their business and hear cases free of great charges, so they won't be anxious to linger. Who do you think has more influence in the City, Uncle Sperling, you or Alderman Cornish?"

"This cause was begun before the fire!"

"It is a dispute of possession which may hold up rebuilding, so will be heard in Serjeant's Inn. You do see my advantage, don't you, when my guardian brings information hot from the Court of Aldermen?"

"My God, it's infamous! Only City men will find justice in such a court, for all that their precious mayor and aldermen rule no more than a midden of rubbish now! You should have heard how Westminster laughed at the mean, poor show Mr. Mayor made when he came to swear his oath in borrowed robes. Men said he should have strung cinders round his neck in place of gold."

Arabella was shaken by unexpected fury at such casual derision for a place she had thought meant little to her, but this was not the time to be overset by anger. "You measure City justice by your own, for surely we would find King's Bench in Westminster Hall partial against us. Still, you may have the right of it, so should we divide, as I suggested?"

Bevil took an agitated turn across the cobbles, flapping his hands and muttering. Arabella stole a glance at Harry; even at a distance she could see the scowl on his face. She turned back to Bevil, smiling. "Well, sir? Thus you avoid risking a humiliation your trade cannot afford, and I save my dowry for a profitable marriage. You remember my father's plate chest? I have it, well filled with gilt and silver, which may benefit us both so long as it isn't wasted in lawyers' disputes." It would do no harm for him to think her better dowered than was in fact the case.

He nodded slowly. Bevil Sperling hounded the weak, he prospered by coming to terms with the strong. "What is your proposition?"

Her heart leaped. She had no real case at all, relying on a well-baited hook and generous terms to do her work for her. If she seemed greedy, he would fight; later she might yet strip him of his gains. "We register our dispute as settled, then divide the benefit of the lease. I remember my father saying it had some fifty years to run?"

"Fifty-two, at a rent below its value before the fire."

"Under the new regulations, rent is remitted during rebuilding, provided it's finished within the limit set." She had listened carefully to Harry and his father discussing the Corporation's plans to force their city out of its ashes in the shortest possible time. "I suggest we hold the property jointly, and sublet to Alderman Cornish free of rent for five years, providing he bears the costs of rebuilding. After five years he pays double the market value, no doubt you can discover a figure. By then he will be prosperous again, or already bankrupt so we can look elsewhere for a tenant."

"Yes," Bevil agreed in a dazed way. "How old are you?"

"Fifteen," said Arabella untruthfully. She lacked a month to her birthday.

God rot me, he thought, fifteen. Whatever kind of Medusa will she be in a few years' time?

"So shall we have a rebuilt property at no cost to ourselves," continued Arabella cheerfully. "And after five years as much in rent each as we would have had if one alone inherited. Once all is secure, I shall pay you a visit and you may introduce me to the court."

"God's bones, no! Fifteen, and Alderman Cornish your guardian, I have no mind to be in Newgate for . . . for—"

Arabella slipped her hand under his arm and squeezed, warmly. "Dear Uncle Sperling! Of course you would not be clapped up when you intended only to honour our kinship. Mr. Cornish is not precisely my guardian, you know, just—just my father trusted me to his care." For the first time her voice faltered. However would she eventually explain her dealings with Bevil to her father? She put the thought firmly from her mind, fear of death alone made such reflections urgent.

"No matter what the legal niceties may be, he would not allow a girl of fifteen into a bachelor's care, to frequent the byways of the court. And very right too," Bevil added virtuously, feeling quite harried by the prospect of Arabella let loose in his previously carefree existence.

She laughed and stood on tiptoe to kiss mottled flesh at his cheek. "I did not mean this instant. I need to stay here, for their sake and also watch over my—our—interests. But one day I will come, by which time no doubt you will have married again, very favourably, I expect. Then we shall deal together very profitably, you'll see. Unless you are executing commissions for simple pleasure still, instead of profit," she added mischievously.

Bevil watched with fascinated horror as she left him and walked back to where Harry was waiting, assurance in every step. If it hadn't been papist nonsense, he would have crossed himself.

Chapter Nine

Spring came at last. Those who survived emerged from cellars and improvised shelters, often shaking with London ague, which that year raged through whole families, cold, wet and half starving as they were. Few babies survived, nor many elderly, personal tragedies adding to the burden of those who remained. Mrs. Cornish lived into April but was coughing blood, and without daylight or fresh air in the vaults, died as birds sang and weeds sprouted under the warmth of another year. Nicodemus fell playing with some friends amongst the rubble, and although at first they thought it was not serious, his ribs swelled and nothing doctors could do in the way of bleeding and clysters could relieve him. Before the end, his agony became so dreadful that Harry bought half a hogshead of rum and stupefied him, so at least if they could not save him, he died knowing very little about it.

Arabella started by nursing him with the same impersonal efficiency as she cooked and cleaned, but as she sat through the last night by his side, she wept. He had been a merry, uncomplicated child, and life seemed very unjust. Nick's broken body cried out for skilled help, yet all she could do was bathe his face and hold him still while Harry forced rum between his lips.

She found Harry weeping too, alone in the cleared yard with its cracked and blackened flagstones after Nick was buried. He turned away instinctively, then changed his mind and faced her, hands locked behind his back. "Laugh if you will, I should not feel ashamed of grieving for my brother."

"I wept too," said Arabella, nettled that he expected her to jeer.

His expression relaxed. "Poor little Nick; how difficult sometimes not to question God's will."

Arabella sniffed, she had not forgiven God for the deaths of all her family, nor did she hold a high opinion of His will. "We shall lose Hephzibah too, unless we find better shelter by next winter."

"I know, and hope to have building started soon. With the survey done, we lack only bricks and timber and cash to start." His tone was sour, since however fast the Corporation hastened, their citizens were desperately short of means and help from outside was minimal. The city of York sent to condole with London's losses and apologise for the mean sum they contributed; most towns complained of hard times and sent even less. The Speaker of the House of Commons had to be sweetened with a hundred pounds in gold to expedite the City's bills through Parliament, and the King, for all his proclamations and aid at the time of the fire, refused the Lord Mayor permission to quarry stone at Portland, on the ground that all production was needed for extensions to his palace. His Majesty offered no finance from royal sources either; the ruined City must pay for its own resurrection, the only concession a shilling tax on each cauldron of coal imported into London. Paid by the citizens, of course.

Harry absently ran his hand over blackened brick. "Half a day to bury Nick, then back to the treadmill again. I must leave tomorrow for the West, and shall be away two weeks or more. But for his illness I would have gone before."

Arabella stared at him in surprise, trade had never taken him out of the City before. "Why?"

"Because times have changed, or hadn't you noticed? We cannot warehouse goods, nor have we means to offer credit yet, especially to those as ruined as ourselves. We must buy on our own account, and ship direct from wagons on the waterfront when the time is right. Bear all the risk ourselves and trust in God that not one single part of what we do goes wrong, for this is our last reserve."

"You would risk the little you have left on a trade you don't know? How will you rebuild at all without a penny piece?"

"We won't, since a house of the design approved for Cheapside costs eight hundred pounds and we haven't the half of that. My father is unable to leave the City, so I am entrusted with it all. If I fail, then our only resource will be my wage as another man's journeyman silversmith, hammering the trade you so much admire. We have no choice but to gamble with what remains, but I intend to win. Now your site is cleared, my father asked me to enquire after your pleasure with the House of the Spurs, and Bevil's too of course," he added ironically. He had held himself very much aloof since her bargain with Bevil, expressing polite incredulity when she told him that Bevil had agreed to divide in a fit of conscience. Yet when she offered Cornish's the site if he could clear it, somehow he had done so. Harry was a hard and efficient worker as well as a gambler, and she could not help admiring him for it.

"I intend to sell a piece of worth from my chest and establish Will hammering silver, as you put it," replied Arabella immediately. "The hearth is intact and a shed cheap to build. I know enough to help him where four hands are essential, and he has sufficient skill to prosper. I mean to learn gilding too from Mistress Spencer, since she tells me that care rather than experience makes for quality there. Do you think Bevil would act as my agent and place my wares at court?" She was teasing, and had no intention of telling Bevil anything about Will working for her by private arrangement with Cornish's.

"You would sell more than one vessel for such a purpose and still have no profit: Will is a careful worker, but not an exceptional one." His voice was expressionless, anger close to the surface again. "Bella, you must not think of gilding."

"Oh, rubbish! It is fiddling work, but light enough for a woman. Silver is doubled in value by good gilding, I remember my father saying so."

"Yet he never gilded; haven't you perhaps wondered why?"

She shrugged, of course she had heard tales of gilding sickness; who had not in the goldsmith's trade? But she was healthy, even plague could not kill her. "You are risking all you have on a new trade since only through risk will you ever be re-established. If Will's skill is only commonplace then there's all the more need for gilding to give his wares worth."

Harry seized her shoulders and shook her, hard. "You little fool! Your heart may be solid rock, but your lungs are so soft as were my mother's and she died of gilding fumes. What of Alderman Smythe, the richest man in Goldsmith's Row before the fire, whose five wives died of the sickness and eight daughters, too? He prospered on this worth as you call it, and the devil take his prosperity. I'll not let you do it, and so I warn you. Hammer silver if you will. God knows anyone with a skill is needed in the City now, but the day you gild, I'll—"

"Yes, Harry? What will you do? Borrow money from my profits if your trade should fail?"

His hands were like wire on her shoulders, so it was an effort not to wince; she knew his rages now, and intended to provoke him. Instead his grip loosened and he stared at her, eyes narrowed. "No," he said at last. "I'll not do that, I promise you. Ever. For the rest you'll have to wait and see, but if you value your investment then do not gild."

"Listen," said Arabella suddenly, attention diverted. Whatever he said, she intended to gild her silver, and that was that.

At first he thought she was simply confusing the issue, so she could claim he had not made his meaning clear, then he heard it too. A deep booming drifting upriver on the wind.

"It's like the battle we heard last year," said Arabella, "but it can't be, can it? The fleet is laid up."

The King and his council had decided that there was insufficient in the treasury to commission the fleet that year, and over the protests of both Parliament and City, it had been laid up behind great booms along the Thames and Medway. "No," said Harry slowly. "It can't be, but it sounds uncommonly like it. God send it isn't some convoy of East Indiamen caught by the Dutch; we can't afford another disaster now. I'll go to the waterfront and find out whether there is any news."

"Take me with you! Please, Harry. I'm weary of so much today." Of the empty place where Nick had been, she wanted to say, of ledgers, of bargaining for the cheapest food and living hugger-mugger in a hole. But none of it was his fault and he must be as weary of it all as she, when each day brought bankruptcy closer.

His face softened as he looked at her; she was thin as they all were, her hands red and split from heavy work. Yet she was more beautiful than before, fine bones giving her an appealing quality, over-large eyes clear and unafraid. Above all, she carried eagerness into all she did, a zest for life which nothing had so far touched. So he took her with him, and thought it as well he was going away for a while. He scarcely noticed the discomforts of their vault when each day he had to contend with the harshness of living there with only a thickness of cloth between himself and Arabella.

Amongst other upheavals, plague and fire had freed women from a life within their walls. Some were widowed and must carry on their husband's trade to keep their family from starving, most had no walls to stay inside nor their husbands an income to provide for them if they did. Everyone had to do what they could, and with the men labouring to clear ruins, women emerged to peddle goods, chaffer for bargains and set up in any craft they knew. The streets were full of them and no one thought it strange any longer; London had many odder sights to offer in the summer of 1667. It was indeed extraordinary to walk down Cheapside, thread their way through the Stocks Market and turn down Walbrook seeing only a flat plain in every direction, far stranger than when ruins had provided perspective in the wasteland. Now there was nothing. With infinite toil and not much more than muscle power, often by men long unaccustomed to such labour, everything was cleared, tottering walls dismantled, the vast quantities of rubbish carted to embank the slope which led to the river. Here and there fresh foundations were already laid, the ring of trowels and rattle of carts a busy chorus, smoke rising from brick and lime kilns where houses once had stood. The streets were pegged out, the web of them clearly marked when only wind sliced over spaces in between.

"My father has ordered bricks and timber," said Harry suddenly. He was staring about him as she was, as everyone did no matter how often they walked the open streets. "Unless I fail, we start building as soon as I return."

"Just the Corncrake or the Golden Spurs as well?" The Corporation had decided that a new street must be driven through from Guildhall to Cheapside and south again to the river; consequently Furnival Alley had disappeared in the reshuffle, and Cornish and Sperling property now adjoined. The new street was to be called King Street as far as Cheapside, and Queen Street beyond: the royal bounty, as it was ironically known in Cheapside, since everyone there lost frontage and had to contribute to the cost, the result of their sacrifice then passing under Their Majesties' names.

"Both together, even if we can only timber one as yet. The outer walls will be cheaper, and give each other strength. We'll keep them separate, never fear."

"I didn't fear it," said Arabella with dignity. "Only, like you, how I will pay."

"Get Bevil to contribute," said Harry flippantly.

She pulled a face, and then smiled. "I told him you would pay, and we'd get double rent once you had done it."

"And he fell for such a tale? Westminster touts are so used

to running to us when their coffers are dry, perhaps he thinks we can coin money out of plague pits dug into ruins."

"He fell for it, and so will you. You want my house, if not now, then later. You'll find I drive as hard a bargain as you."

Harry looked sceptical, as he always did when she made extravagant promises, but at that moment a man rushed past them, shouting, and then another. All about, people had been gathered in groups listening to sound rolling on the wind, muttering in uncertain speculation. Now these groups burst open like shaken pollen, and men began chasing aimlessly back and forth across the street. People came pounding up the slope, boots ringing on cobbles, the river shining peacefully at their backs. Harry drew Arabella behind him as they rushed past, not caring who they overturned, shouts clearer now. "The Dutch! The Dutch are coming!"

Immediately Walbrook dissolved into panic as everyone ran, where to they did not know, shouting about the Dutch. London had lived with disaster for so long that the first whiff of calamity was believed. Harry seized an elderly merchant as he hastened past, purple from exertion. "Pray, sir, tell me. Where are the Dutch? Have they caught some Indiamen coming in?"

He pulled away indignantly. "Indiamen be damned! They've taken the fleet."

"The fleet?" said Harry blankly.

"Aye, cut the boom on the Medway and occupied the dockyard. They'll fire or tow them all out now, God curse their poxy hides." He hurried off.

"God curse Charles Stuart," said Harry slowly. "The navy which our enemies have feared since King Henry's time burned in its harbour, while crews starved and sails rotted because Stuarts cannot be trusted with money or their nation's honour."

Arabella stared at the jostling throng. "Will the Dutch come here, do you suppose?"

He gave a lopsided smile. "You would confound them if they did, I'm sure. I must take you home at once, before the trained bands are called out, with such steel and powder as we still possess. I don't know whether they will come but one thing is certain, there is nothing to stop them but ourselves.

He saw her to the end of Cheapside and by then alarm drums were rolling from the space where Guildhall had stood. Then Harry went and Arabella had to thread her way through jabbering throngs, some people already pushing handcarts of possessions, determined not to lose the little they had left, others shouldering their way purposefully in the other direction, buckling soot-blackened armour, often carrying no more than knives.

Confusion multiplied in the following days. The King came to review the City trained bands at Tower Hill and told them they were to be disbanded because the Dutch had gone; only to be recalled within hours when it was discovered that they had not. The City Corporation itself forced merchants to scuttle ships to block the lower reaches of the river, and eventually the Dutch simply lost the advantage of surprise as makeshift defences were built against them. They came as close as Tilbury and Deptford, then retired, black smoke from burning ships and irreplaceable cargoes staining the sky in their wake.

Harry returned three days after they withdrew, he had ridden to Chatham with an advance guard of London volunteers which had helped the tough old Duke of Albemarle to haste the Dutch away.

They were picnicking where the parlour once had been when he came back; the weather was cloudlessly hot and no one wanted to spend a minute in the vault which could be passed elsewhere. He was exhausted and filthy, sprawling thankfully on straw Arabella had bought when she grew tired of sitting on stones.

"They've gone?" demanded Alderman Cornish.

Harry nodded, gulping hungrily at broth and bread. "Too late for us to feel much thankfulness for it, though. They towed off the flagship and burned the rest; the *London* we saw launched last year is no more than charred planks. What men were muttering against the King would bear shouting to his face."

"I beg you will not try," said his father drily. "We can do without a hanging in the family to add to all the rest. At least they stayed downriver, I hear they menace Harwich now."

Harry shrugged. "Why not? There's nothing to stop them."

"There are to be fortifications built. The King has asked the City to raise ten thousand pounds for defences along the Kentish shore."

"The King has asked the City?" demanded Harry incredulously. "He has the gall to ask us for money now, not for our own defence but for works he has allowed to decay?"

Alderman Cornish sighed. "What can we do? The King has no money and defences must be built. As usual we are forced to find the means."

"What is so usual about it, when no one here has so much as a roof over his head? Ten thousand pounds! A fine pass we have come to when the King cannot find even so small a charge to defend his realm."

"Hold your tongue, Henry, or one day it will lead you into trouble. We attended the King at his council yesterday and agreed to raise this sum for the desperate need the realm has of it. The Lord Mayor will allocate contributions; officially it is a loan but few would feel inclined to lend if they had the choice, and the common coffer is empty. Our share is likely to be fifty pounds."

There was a long silence.

"Shall I have to pay as well?" asked Arabella at last.

"Aye, a half share with Bevil. Perhaps not quite so much since we have a trade partly re-established and you will be paying only on your site."

"Even twenty pounds—why, I could buy enough silver for Will to work a month with that!" she exclaimed indignantly.

Harry gave a sharp bark of laughter. "Welcome to the ranks of over-taxed citizens, Bella, and remember who pays the reckoning if ever you prance around court with backstairs gossip as your only occupation.".

At least the King had no choice except to make peace, and as the year went on the first walls began rising in the City. In the aftermath of the Dutch attack, Arabella thought seriously again of going to Bevil, but in the end she stayed. Harry's trip to the West brought enough profit to pay for a first consignment of bricks and timber, but she knew that Cornish's could not afford to rebuild both properties and each difficulty made her more determined not to forfeit her inheritance. She was also gripped by the sheer excitement and challenge of it all, as was nearly everyone who had survived the brutal past two years. They all faced such enormous tasks, means were so slender, time totally lacking when everyone was struggling to carry on their affairs on draughty street corners while new premises rose behind them, each brick financed by such profit as they could squeeze.

Yet the new Lord Mayor was as exacting as the last, and the aldermen backed him although they were often themselves the losers. You rebuilt, or forfeited your occupation without compensation. And so, somehow, it was done. In the summer of 1668 whole streets were going up, and by the following year those merchants who had preserved most of their assets were moving into fine, brick-built, square-faced houses, a standard pattern laid down for each type of street. Cornish's lagged behind because of their great losses, and for several anxious months in 1669 they were heavily in debt to rival goldsmith-bankers.

It was then that Harry began a new venture; taking delivery of monies in the West, using it to pay other merchants' debts there and then refunding the original creditor in bills in London, since many country landlords did their spending in London yet feared to carry coin from their rents on dangerous roads. It was chancy business, depending on contriving a coincidence of debtors and creditors, and sometimes Harry simply took commission on running coin successfully to London. A single loss would have ruined them, and highwaymen were not particular over whether they killed or not when such sums were at stake, but in spite of some narrow escapes, gradually Cornish's began to prosper again. Success was sealed when Colonel Rumsey, the King's collector of customs at Bristol, allowed them to handle his accounting with the Exchequer, a protracted business which left thousands of pounds in their hands while it was settled. This was lent out meanwhile, and Cornish's profited from interest on money not their own.

Nearly six years after the fire the Corncrake sign was gilded and fastened to the wall again, a few pounds spared from bare necessity to invite acquaintance to toast success. Guests flowed into new, airy rooms, high-corniced and large-windowed, quite different from the old beams begrudging light. Outside, St. Mary-le-Bow was rebuilding too, the Royal Exchange and Guildhall nearly finished, although an accounting of the City's finances revealed a colossal deficit. Even so, the Court of Aldermen refused to change their policy: build, build, build. Regardless of cost, of risk, of hardship. Somehow they would pay when it was done, no purpose would be served by losing their nerve now. Meanwhile, those who had re-established themselves lent what was necessary.

Fresh immigrants were flowing in to replace those who had left, the multitude of back-streets trades more skilled for the years of improvisation. The goldsmiths were financing government again, the days past when ten thousand pounds was an intolerable burden to be distributed by force. Since the King seemed permanently bankrupt, he had no choice but to agree to his bankers' terms, so they appropriated his revenues to repay themselves in strict rotation, confidence only slightly shaken when the country plunged into another ill-conceived war against the Dutch as an ally of hated France.

Only Arabella was dissatisfied with the passage of events.

She had established Will, although it cost her far more of her dowry than she expected. He took a long time to recover his skills too, blunted as they were by years of heaving rubble. He was uncertain away from a master's eye, and Arabella could not supply the lack: she could curse and drive him, none better, but did not have the knowledge to supplement his shortcomings.

So she had decided to gild. She waited until Harry was away, then visited a gilding goldsmith of her father's acquaintance and watched his wife and daughters at work.

It was a horrible job: no wonder the women did it, Arabella thought viciously. Fumes curled visibly in the air, strangling breath as mercury and gold seethed together in a chamois bag. The mixture had to be squeezed and hammered through soft leather, then rubbed on prepared silver: arms ached with the effort of squeezing the tiniest scrap of gold through soggy chamois, eyes watered and lungs laboured for air.

But it was not difficult.

By the end of a week she had mastered such tricks as there were for easing the task, and sold another cup to pay for gold and mercury. She sold it with a pang, remembering her father making it and resenting the image of poverty brought by her emptying chest. Next day she set to work, away from sight in one of the skeleton-brick rooms of the House of the Spurs, where Cornish's had simply put up outer walls to conform with the letter of the law. She hammered the bag with a wooden mallet to make the gold flow, stooped and rubbed until sweat dripped off her nose, somehow forcing gilt into each joint and curl of Will's ornamentation. By midday she was gasping, blood pounding in her ears and behind her eyes. She ate her meal in a daze, thankful Harry was away; Alderman Cornish remarked on her flush but was too harassed to enquire into what ailed her, although probably he would not have cared even if he knew since the risks of gilding were deeply woven into the goldsmith's trade. By dusk Arabella felt very strange, and when she put down her bag was caught by a wash of dizziness. I will get used to it, she thought grimly. I must; it won't be for long. Harry was right in this at least, I don't intend to rot away my life over a gilding bag. Half a dozen salvers to set me on the road to profit, and perhaps some—she vomited painfully in the dust and thought reeled.

Will found her sitting on some bricks in the yard, her head in her hands. "Be you all right, mistress? Gilding isn't something to fly upon, but to take gradual-like until you're used to it."

"I'm all right," she said firmly, and indeed after a while she felt much better and was inclined to laugh at her weakness. Tomorrow would find her more accustomed to the work.

She ate her evening meal with a good appetite and vomited immediately afterwards; but she slept heavily and woke feeling better, wondering whether perhaps she should give herself a day free from gilding to recover completely. She decided against it, Harry would be home soon and also she was afraid that gold powder and mercury might set if left in its bag.

I will be more used to it today, she told herself, and at first she thought she was. The work went more swiftly and she did not have to stoop so low into fumes to be sure she covered each curl of silver. She pressed and hammered, humming cheerfully, thinking how beautiful gilded silver looked, no wonder it was a profitable trade. By evening, the bag seemed stiffer and she decided she must finish that night, although her head ached and her muscles trembled with exhaustion. She sent to tell Hephzibah to cook the supper and stayed at her improvised bench by a single candle.

After what seemed a long time, she looked up to gauge the hour and as she did so the room swam before her eyes; but for the bench under her hands she would have fallen. She was going to vomit again.

She had a horror of vomiting since the plague, hated the fact of it far more than any illness she might feel. She stood very still, muscles clenched on her swimming belly. Air, she needed air, and dared not move. I'll finish tomorrow, she thought dazedly. Just let me not vomit and I'll finish tomorrow.

She was on her knees when she felt herself jerked, then roughly spilled on stone. She was fearfully, rendingly sick.

"You cheating little jade," said Harry coldly.

Chapter Ten

"*I didn't cheat,*" *said Arabella much later.* "I never promised not to gild."

"You waited until you thought me safely away. Then would have lied no doubt, hammered silver while I was home and waited for me to go again. You little fool, don't you believe me now?"

They were sitting in the yard; the moon had not risen, so his voice came disembodied from the dark. She sighed and leaned her forehead against cool brick; she felt sore from eyeball to stomach. "I believe you and do not intend to kill myself gilding, but I need money now; not next year or the one after. I lasted better today than yesterday. You can't stop me, Harry."

"I can and will. A few pieces may not kill, I don't know enough to say; my mother was dead thirteen months after her marriage and she only gilded sometimes. And even if you live, do you want your beauty shrivelled and breath wheezing before you are twenty?"

"You can't stop me," she repeated obstinately.

He grunted, and stood. "I'll finish the salver you were doing, it can't be left three-quarters gilded and unsaleable."

She sat on in soft darkness, gulping air as if she could never have enough, half comatose in soothing sounds all around: wind brushing over brick, the hum of voices and tramp of feet in Cheapside, once a child's clear laugh. She slept and woke shivering as the moon came up. Harry was sitting close by with his head in his hands. She cleared her throat, it felt as dry as a gilding bag and as full of fumes. "You haven't finished already?"

He nodded. "Folk will be stirring soon. You slept a long while." His voice sounded strange too, and she wondered whether he had the same band-tight headache which had grasped her senses earlier. Another half-dozen pieces, she thought, and then no more. To show him he cannot run my life and also for the profit I must have.

That had been two years ago and still she had not gilded another piece. As more guests crowded into the Cornishes' brand-new parlour, Arabella laughed and chatted, enjoying admiration and her first sempstress-made gown since the fire, aware of Harry laughing too, lighthearted as he had not been in years, for he was a winner while she was not.

Cornish's were living on the tightest of margins, but they had survived, their house was rebuilt and within another year it would be furnished too. They had clients and credit again, the respect of those who had likewise survived. It was the eighth night after Christmas, the streets white with snow, so everyone consciously relished the comfort of solid walls, of warmth and spiced punch and good fellowship again.

The roar of voices and chink of goblets battered Arabella's ears, normally she would have delighted in the novelty of a party. Instead she wanted to shout and stamp her foot; when a nobble-nosed merchant pinched her cheek and jested slyly about women silversmiths, she nearly did. "Time you were wed to Harry, eh, my girl, and forgot about gilding, don't you think?" He stamped off roaring with laughter before she could tell him exactly what she thought of Harry Cornish.

For he had exactly stopped her as he said he would: every goldsmith in Cheapside was warned not to sell her gilding or mercury on pain of Cornish enmity forever, and with the family plainly recovering fast, no one felt tempted to outface his threat for the sake of Robert Sperling's orphan. So she laid her plans and eventually found a goldsmith in Lombard Street willing to sell to her. When she returned in triumph with mercury and gold hidden under her skirts, she found Harry waiting, and he showed no embarrassment at all when he had to unhook petticoats in order to confiscate her purchases. He then worked his way through every goldsmith in the City, delivering the same warning he had given to those of Cheapside.

So the House of the Spurs was not nearly finished, and Arabella had to content herself with such profits as there were from middling-quality silverware. Bevil had introduced her to a reliable dealer in Covent Garden who marketed her wares at not too exorbitant a commission, otherwise he was a disappointment. I must go to him and make him pay his share, she brooded. At court there must be a dozen ways to make quick money. Suddenly, she was tired of the drudgery of silver, bored by a return to normal living. The City was alive again, the novelty and drama of recovery almost over; she eyed the throng disparagingly, how dull they all were, to be sure, talking of nothing but cargoes and balances and the iniquities of the Dutch.

"You show a very mopish face amongst so much cheer," said Harry in her ear.

"So would you if you faced a room full of crowing cocks, and had lost your squawk," snapped Arabella. "You can just take your hands off me, too."

His hands stilled on her waist, but he turned her to face him. "Bella, you must have noticed how these past few years I've said no more of wedding you?"

She nodded, faintly intrigued.

"I've been afraid," he said simply. "You refused me when you were young and alone, and you're twice as self-willed at twenty as you were then. I knew there was no changing what you said now, so I have waited and cursed myself as a fool a dozen times a day."

Warm pleasure spread through her. Henry Cornish, at twenty-four already a substantial man of affairs and so depressingly often right, was giving her the chance to deliver a truly splendid snub. He must be mad; she looked more closely and saw that he was at least bewitched into an uncharacteristically false position. His face had thinned and hardened over the past few years, lined already from exposure to all weathers on the tracks of the West, grey eyes level. But she sensed also the longing which had lowered his guard, the desire which belied the image of strength. He wanted her so much, had waited so long that when resolve hardened, suddenly he could not wait another minute, however unsuitable the time.

"Well," she said, dropping her eyes demurely. "How you have surprised me, Harry."

"Have I, my dear? In truth, I surprise myself. I did not mean to become the target for jesting before a room full of acquaintance. But since I have—"

"Yes, Harry? Since you have what?"

His hands tightened at her waist and a rueful gleam came to his eyes. "Since I have been so long a fool over you, there's no choice but to chance my fortune, to win or lose it all. It isn't as if I don't know what you are, a devilish, scheming, obstinate little shrew." He touched her face gently, as if they were alone, then held her hand in his. "But gallant withal, and mistress of your soul. Bella, sweeting, I love you very much, will you say yes when I ask you this time and make me the happiest of men?"

"You have not asked me your question yet," said Arabella, thinking of how long he had kept her dependent on his whim. "I fear I cannot reply until you have."

His face had flushed, now it paled abruptly, as if he read his answer from her flippancy. "I ask you to wed me, as you well know."

"And you will be desperately unhappy if I refuse?"

"Desperately? My dear, I would not insult my manhood by such a phrase." He tossed her hand aside, as if it was some rubbish he had been holding, and made to turn away. Abruptly, he changed his mind and looked at her directly again. "I will only say with what very great happiness I would hear you accept my offer. I believe I could give you much contentment too, if only you would let me try."

Arabella tapped her foot on the floor, watching him with satisfaction, saying nothing. After the years of mastery he had come begging to her at last. "No," she said pensively. "I don't think I want you to attempt it. How mortifying for you to have your suit rejected, and how unwise a place to present it."

His mouth tightened, the flush of temper on his face now. "You gave no thought to it at all, nor intended to! I could have asked you a dozen times by moonlight, or set my father to bargain gold on my behalf, and you would still have brushed me aside as if I was a beetle in the copper."

She gave a swift gurgle of laughter. "Oh, Harry, a black one in a scaly coat. It was you who said it and not I." She sobered suddenly. "I was thinking this evening that the time has come for me to ask your father to make the necessary arrangements. After this, I am sure he will agree that his son is best rid of so grave a temptation to the flesh. Just think of it, Harry. Near seven years in your house, two of them behind no more than a thickness of curtain, and you are still free of sin. Do you think they will be so scrupulous—or so dull—at court?"

"No, I am sure they will not," he said curtly, and left her.

She looked around, trying to seem unconcerned but very conscious that everyone in the room must know what had happened. She was disappointed. Certainly they had been watching, for she had sensed elbows nudged into ribs, and amusement too, when Harry had been so clearly pleading with her, but not one person was looking in her direction any more.

Locked in their own duel, neither she nor Harry had noticed a stir by the door, the flurry of respect greeting one of the two greatest goldsmith-bankers of the City, Alderman Backwell, financier to most men in the room, to the City Corporation and the King as well. The men hastened to bow, all faces except Harry's and Arabella's turned in his direction, then everyone froze, petrified by the look on his face. As Arabella looked up she saw him stumble, and grope his way to a settle: someone offered wine and he gulped it thirstily.

Alderman Cornish touched his shoulder. "Edward, are you ill?"

Everyone seemed to stop breathing while waiting for an answer. Many businesses would suffer if Backwell became sick. He glanced up, the flesh of his face looking squeezed off his bones. "I still live, for how long I cannot say. The Exchequer is stopped up."

"Stopped up?"

"Aye. By command of the King. All payment of interest and principal is stopped, all assets held."

There was an audible gasp, as if every jaw in the room dropped simultaneously. "What of our balances and plate held at the Tower in safekeeping?"

"What of my loan to the King?"

"What of the interest due . . . ?" The women watched each other uncertainly, while the men crowded round Backwell, shouting, shaking his shoulder, clamouring for answers when five minutes before they would not have addressed him without a bow.

"Enough." Alderman Cornish elbowed them aside, although his face was sweating with the rest. "Henry, give our guests more wine. Then Mr. Backwell will answer such questions as he can, I'm sure."

Harry handed wine, his face unreadable. Arabella could not tell whether he no longer thought of her, or was so mastered by fury and disappointment as scarcely to heed this new crisis.

Backwell roused himself at last, and stood, studying them almost with compassion. Since he was a ruthless and grasping man, this frightened them even more that his moment of distress. "I apologise, but I had come direct from the Exchequer. No past debts are to be honoured, nor interest paid on loans already made to His Majesty. If you have balances or assets at the King's disposal, either in the Exchequer or in safe deposit at the Tower, then you cannot withdraw them."

"But... but... but..." stuttered a man over by the door, wig askew as if lifted by the pressure of his mind. "How can I honour my debts if the King will not repay my lendings?"

"You can't," said Backwell calmly. "Neither can I."

They all stared at the man whose credit had been unquestioned even on the morrow of the fire, who held balances from every trade and cargo as well as from half the landlords of the realm; on whom the City's own finances depended.

"I loaned the King twelve thousand, secured against the customs," said a dazed voice. "Surely he has not stopped repayment of secured loans?"

A chorus broke out then, of voices naming sums lent, until Backwell held up his hand. "All repayment is stopped, no matter how great or small the loan. All interest suspended and your personal assets seized, pending fresh negotiation at the King's pleasure."

"What am I to tell my clients tomorrow when they come to withdraw their balances? When this news spreads, a hundred will be beating on my door and even money I have not lent the King be lost, when every trader finds his banker ruined."

Backwell smiled, a travesty like a death mask. "So you will be bankrupt like the rest. And in good company too, for the King owes me a quarter of a million pounds."

A quarter of a million. Arabella was smitten like the rest, goggling wordlessly at so great a sum, nearly a quarter as much as the whole tax granted to the King for this present war.

If the disaster had been less they would have shouted or railed against the perfidy of Kings, talked of petitions or the good old cause against the Stuarts. As it was, when Backwell left they filed out in his wake, forgetting cloaks and wives, minds and tongues completely numb.

Arabella went too, through to the kitchen since they employed only a single servant, Harry and his father already pushing goblets aside to start figuring on paper. Cornish's lent as little as possible directly to the King, since Harry was so hot against the Stuarts, but would be hard hit just the same, as the scarcely greased wheels of credit seized up overnight.

Arabella swore one of Harry's oaths as she clattered the poker amongst embers. She had thought to go next week, but could hardly expect Alderman Cornish to give attention to her affairs at such a time. She felt surprising compassion for her

City too. An hour earlier they had been rejoicing that the iron years were over, rebirth complete. Now, without warning, fresh ruin had come and turned effort into dust. Those who lent to Kings had long been used to fraud and devised their own protection; they had been taken unaware by open robbery.

She hauled the pot down on its chain so water would heat during the night, stacked soiled goblets and drained the last of the punch. It was cold but lay pleasantly in her stomach; she would set Hephzibah to finish clearing in the morning.

Arabella's candle blew out in the draught on the stairs: the unfurnished house was bitterly cold in January frost. She did not bother to relight it, preferring the dark to more delay.

She had her hand on her door latch when she heard an unexpected sound, and stood straining her ears. Breathing, very quiet and close.

A creak, a rub of cloth, then a hand over hers on the latch, another on her mouth.

"So you despise restraint," said Harry softly. "Nor will you put two thoughts together on my affections. Well, we'll see whether a pattern of your own choosing suits you any better." He kicked open the door and pushed her inside, hand still over her mouth.

Arabella was no salon miss, and hammering silver had given her a wiry toughness of hand and arm, but it made no difference. He was possessed by one of the molten rages she had only glimpsed before, his fingers cruelly tight on her mouth and nose.

He flung her on the bed and held her with knee and thigh while unlacing her bodice, no word spoken, no pretence at softness or any pleasure but his own. Skirts and petticoats, ribbons tearing in his hand, and when she jerked free he used his mouth to silence her with all the weight of head and strength of shoulder he possessed. It was not a kiss, nor intended to be; he forced open her jaws and seized her senses with his own, so she would not cry out. Breath lost, she was scarcely conscious of the rest. Of Harry, whom she had known so long and not known at all, turned into pain in the dark; nor the moment when pain became sharpest pleasure. She whirled into darkness, lungs labouring like a foundered coal horse. When sense returned she was clinging to what she had fought before, fingers digging into Harry's back as his grip slackened. He lay quiet at last, weight heavy on her, but his mouth was tender and no longer a ferocious gag.

He moved slightly, but only to give her pleasure, hands caressing, stirring passion to meet his. Still neither spoke, and this second time it was quite different from the first, letting love come slowly until she kindled to meet him, then quickly and strongly as if in celebration. And laughter at the end.

"You were right," he said, still holding her. "How dull to wait so long, my love."

Arabella lay drowsily in his arms, mastered by physical delight. She rubbed her face on his, stubble of his cheek and cropped head without a wig vaguely exciting again. "Mmmmm?"

He laughed and kissed her throat. "As you say, mmm. But I must not let the night pass in grunts, however pleasant. I'm sorry, Bella, and yet not sorry at all. I wish it had been twice in love and tenderness, yet without the first I think perhaps the other would have passed us by."

"Do you enjoy riddles?" she said sleepily, and felt him laugh again. Felt the comfort of no more loneliness in the night, the longing which solitude at night would bring her from this time on. "Don't go."

"I must, sweeting. My father will stir before dawn when all the affairs of the Exchequer must be seen to."

"Not yet. See, it is still moonlight." Londoners never became used to a city without church bells to tell them the time; they were rebuilding too, but no tower was yet complete.

He lay back, though she was wrong. Light was thicker than mere moonlight and he could see her faintly lined against it. She was lovely. Even tousled and her face marked where his hand had been, she was lovely. Lovelier than before, since he had never known her soft towards him as she was in that dawn. Her colours were tints of the night, he thought vaguely. Hair midnight, eyes the clear darkness which yet holds the faintest glimmer of setting sun, skin as soft as the moon itself. He would tell her one day how she was the night. Not now, in case words broke the spell.

And suddenly, as he lay with his head against her breast, tomorrow was upon him. The scuttling streets filled with bankruptcy-stricken panic, everyone facing loss again, the disaster of debts they could not pay. He would be forced to spend more months riding roads and escorting coin, his business now well known and becoming more dangerous with every journey.

He shivered slightly and felt Arabella tauten against him. He had her now, the rest would somehow be resolved. He left soon after, she might be detached from censure by the heedlessness of love, but he could not bear others to hold her in contempt, or think he wed her because he had no choice. "I will speak to my father about us, I may be forced to wait another day for the shock of the Exchequer to fade." He bent and kissed her. "But I think no one minds hearing of good fortune, and also doubt whether I shall be able to keep from boasting of your love for more than a few hours."

Arabella held his wrist. "Wait one day but come again tonight."

He hesitated. "Sweeting, I can wait the short time of our betrothal now, and so make some amends. It was just—just that I had waited so long when you refused me, and then it wasn't so much the waiting as refusal I could not accept."

"Come tonight," repeated Arabella obstinately. "Then we will see."

He yielded and came, tired and harassed after a frantic day in the unfinished Royal Exchange, where at least five great bankers were reputed to be ruined, and scores of lesser merchants, too. There had been no moment to tell his father, and when he might have done so after supper, Arabella stopped him with a shake of the head and lively chatter.

Consequently, when he came he was neither violent nor passionately tender as he had been the night before, but somewhat dissatisfied with both himself and her. Arabella showed no sign of noticing his changed mood, and eventually he responded to lighthearted happiness, only returning to grievance when the time came for him to leave again.

"Nothing will stop me today, Bella, so it's no good shaking your head and clacking like a magpie to stave me off. Anyone would have thought last evening that you didn't want me to call you my affianced bride."

"I don't," said Arabella calmly. She was lying with the coverlet turned back, hair curling over shadowed breasts. "I needed a day to think but nothing has changed: my answer is still no. What made you believe it would be different? I swear I gave no promise."

He stared at her, astounded, partly dressed. "Of course everything is different."

"How?" She stretched and ran her hands over ribs and stomach in an unconsciously sensual gesture. "You loved me before, and I loved you a little but did not intend to marry you. I still do not, for all that we have found a deal of pleasure together."

He jerked the coverlet off her, so she lay completely naked

119

in frosty moonlight. "I'll tell you how it is different. I took you, knowing what I did. You had no choice then, I grant, but later came to me gladly. This is the bond between us, now and always. I pay my debts and this one with all my heart, because I desired it above all else. You have not the right to deny yourself and so defraud us both." He leaned over and held her, shoulders pinned against the bed, eyes tight-locking hers. "Look at me and say you do not love me."

Arabella stared at his face, only inches from hers, and felt words dry on her tongue. "I think we should not deal well together," she said at last.

"That was not what you had to say, if you were to be free."

She stiffened then, her body icy uncovered. "I do not love you, Henry Cornish. Leave me alone and marry some heiress who will rescue your trade from debt, and agree with everything you say. I have other plans for my life."

He did not move, arms rigid, face beaten silver in the strange light.

She wriggled, trying to reach the cover. "Let me go, I'm cold."

He straightened and went over to the window, looking out on the stillness of Cheapside. "I thought I could never regret what I did these two nights, except for my harshness. Now I do."

Arabella sat on the edge of the bed, wrapped in the coverlet. "Why? Didn't you enjoy it?"

"I would not have described it so simply, no. I committed myself and you. Forever, as I thought."

"And were mistaken," she said maliciously. "Oh, Harry, don't make such a great business of it! At court such affairs as ours are gone between one night and the next."

"I don't think so," he said drily. "Go to your life, Bella, I have run out of ways to stop you. But I shall own myself surprised if either of us is able to say in ten years' time that we found again what we have lost tonight."

Chapter Eleven

*A*rabella sat by her mirror, painting her face with long, practised strokes. She did not paint thickly as other women did, but cleverly, to accentuate the tantalising tilt of eyes and bones. She regarded herself critically, head on one side. It was important to look her best tonight. One more flick with the rabbit's foot, a careful smoothing of lip pomade and she would do.

She stood while Catlin climbed on a chair and lowered a paniered dress over her shoulders, a skilled operation when no hair must be displaced nor speck of powder smeared on fine fabric. When it was done, and the neckline pulled low enough to show most of her breasts, she walked slowly across the room, very conscious of rich cloth stirring with every moment. It had been her own idea to have a gown made of silver tissue, ruched so it looked like etching, and she considered that her art looked finer on a gown than ever it had on metal.

"Holy Jesus, mam," said Catlin. "Ye'll outshine them all."

"I'd better, I've not much time left," said Arabella sourly.

The maid nodded sympathetically. "Nothing shows yet, and the sempstress left good tucks in the waist as ye asked."

Arabella stared in the mirror, gritting her teeth on anger while Catlin ran around finding her cloak and fan, offering scented gloves and handkerchief. For she was with child. All her plans scattered because Harry had lain two nights with her and made her pregnant. "God damn him," she said aloud, and Catlin looked at her nervously: her mistress's temper had been uncertain of late.

Bevil had remarried and was prospering; Arabella had overborne his protests easily and was soon installed in his house,

Catlin ordered out of the scullery to serve her, and her dowry chest laid in a corner of her room. She kept it locked since Bevil believed it full instead of two-thirds empty from the costs of rebuilding and buying clothes suited to her new circumstances, and thought herself well set for a leisurely investigation of fashionable life. She was shrewd enough to realise that Bevil's friends were like herself, hangers-on at the fringes of court who knew the great but were not known by them, but she was young and self-confident enough to believe that time would bring her to better things. There was one young attorney, for instance, called George Jeffries, who might help her if he would. He was as fiercely ambitious as she, and when sober possessed a delicacy of manner quite unlike the other lawyers who frequented Bevil's house. She had been sitting in his lap, whispering about how they might both achieve their dreams of court favour, when Harry came one last time to persuade her to change her mind.

There had been a fierce quarrel which ended in Harry punching him on the nose before walking out. She hid her giggles, but Jeffries had cooled to her since and she had not seen Harry again. She sighed; it hadn't mattered, none of it mattered when she thought she had plenty of time. If not George Jeffries, then another would do; but she was over two months pregnant and must find someone willing to wed her almost within days.

"Mam, ye're beautiful." Catlin bobbed a curtsey when she was ready. "Ye'll have yer choice tonight."

Arabella laughed. Catlin had found her sick and instantly diagnosed her trouble, when it simply had not occurred to her. "I wish I knew a few men besides attorneys."

"Ye will, ye'll see. Stand so, and smile, and ye'll have them about ye like bees to pollen."

And Catlin was quite right, Arabella discovered with delight. The silver cloth was a sensation, her unmarked skin and the warm enticement which lay at the core of her appeal an instant lure to men searching for the titillation of something different. She also drank in admiration with frank enjoyment, which was another change from bored court beauties, this being the first time she had entered one of the great houses backing on Pall Mall even if it was only for a musical evening. Bevil had married the elderly widow who was distantly connected with the Earl of Southampton; her grand relations felt obligated to invite her sometimes, but could not be expected to exhibit her vulgar husband at a formal gathering.

Arabella soon had several gallants gathered about her chair, waving their fans and annoying the musicians with their chatter. She blossomed under their compliments, quick retorts coming like magic to her lips so she began to think herself very clever. The evening had half slipped by before she realised her error; she wanted to be famous, accepted everywhere, desired, and had decided that as no one of good standing would marry obscure Arabella Sperling, then she needed a patron. The life of a sought-after court beauty would answer very pleasantly to her purpose.

This wretched child had spoiled all that. A courtesan who did not even know enough to keep herself free of children was likely to be cast aside before her career was fairly begun.

She needed to wed a complaisant man closer to the court than Bevil, and gain herself time. None of these boys would do: she was wasting her efforts with them.

She murmured an excuse when the musicians next stopped their fiddling and went over to join her aunt, the picture of demure obedience.

Mistress Sperling was gaming and not interested in Arabella, whether the wench chose to stay or go it was all the same to her. She was aggressively frumpish and had bred too many brats to consider looks important; she enjoyed snuff and gaming and being invited to finer houses than her own, otherwise she slept most of the day. She fidgeted peevishly when Arabella stood at her elbows. "Out of my light, girl. Can't you see I am engaged?"

Arabella curtsied. "Yes, indeed, ma'am, but perhaps I might stay awhile—out of your light of course! I am too unaccustomed to London to survive a whole evening of gallantry alone."

There was a faint titter, and one or two gentlemen looked at her more closely while she stood with her eyes becomingly lowered. For these were the elderly gathered by the fire, and quite a few widowers amongst them, I'll be bound, she thought optimistically. The hazards of childbirth meant that most men were widowed several times.

The grandest of them wore diamond buttons on his green coat and green plumes in his hat. He was old, sixty at least, she judged, with spindly legs and sharp green eyes to match his cloth. He also kept giving her darting glances although she was unable to catch his eye on her. The musicians squealed to an end at last, sulky at having to play too loud in order to drown chatter, and servants carried in tables with refreshments.

"What will you have, mistress—Arabella, is it not?"

She found the green-eyed gentleman by her side and gave him a ravishing smile. It was all very well to be demure, but once a fish bit, he needed to be encouraged. "Oh, sir, I should have to ask you to choose for me, since I am not familiar with such delicacies!"

"You come from far?" he enquired, offering his arm.

"Not very far," she replied evasively. "I am staying with my aunt to enjoy a taste of London life."

"A dangerous matter when your guardian is so lax," he observed. "Or is your father keeping watch if you do not come from far?"

"Oh no! I was orphaned by the plague and am quite of an age to look after myself, I assure you, sir."

He raised an eyebrow. "What unusual sentiments in a young, a very young lady, to be sure. And quite refreshing, I declare." He flicked his fingers at some menials in a way Arabella much admired, and chairs were brought so they could sit while he made a leisurely selection for her.

He continued to scrutinise her while she ate, as if measuring her against some private yardstick, listened courteously to whatever she said and even occasionally smiled. Once excitement at her catch faded, Arabella found he set her teeth on edge. He was so old and simply playing with her, his breath and teeth were bad, his eyes impersonal, so it was difficult to imagine why he bothered with her at all. But it was too late to change her choice for this evening at least; he was obviously important, she could not simply leave him when everyone else was gossiping in groups and quite unknown to her. Arabella reflected that if she had even a few weeks at her disposal she would say something outrageous and drive this dried-up old dummy away. She was aware that she ought not to blame the child she carried for her predicament but blamed it all the same, frustration and panic stifling any lingering softness towards Harry.

At last, at last, the musicians started scraping their strings again and in the general movement Arabella made her escape. She needed air, but could not open the window in her room where ladies eased themselves. Driven out by stench, she turned away from the brightly lit saloons and hesitated in the hall. A footman stood by the door; certainly she could not go out, but felt reluctant to go back amongst assessing faces. I ought to, she thought, and work my way through some more of those old men.

"You find a crowd distasteful?"

She turned to find her green-clad gentleman watching her, hand swinging a beribboned cane. "I—well, yes sir . . . my lord?" she stammered, ending on a note of interrogation. Surely he must be a lord. He was too unpleasant to bother with if he was less, she decided.

He laughed soundlessly. "Poor Arabella, haven't you found out yet? Wexford, and yes, a lord even if only an Irish one." He ran the polished knob of his cane down her bare arm. "Don't wince, sweetheart, I'm a good judge of flesh. For His Majesty as well as myself."

Arabella made herself stand still, refusing to flinch from his touch or words. This was the chance she had wanted, a man close to the King. He might be lying, but she did not think so. "A compliment from your lordship must have double value then, since it brings an echo from the King."

He looked at her musingly. "You are either uncommonly bold or uncommonly simple. I told Mistress Sperling she should guard you more carefully, but she assured me that you were none of her affair and able to look to yourself. What say you?"

Arabella curtsied. "I say it is time to rejoin Mistress Sperling by the fire, my lord."

Catlin was awed when Arabella recounted this passage to her in the dawn. A close partnership had sprung up between the two, for Catlin had been a scullery maid, given to Arabella because Bevil refused to waste money on providing a trained servant for her; to Catlin this was her chance of realising her dizzy ambition to rise out of the kitchen and marry a tavern-keeper. "'Tis a matter of marvel for ye to be so fortunate at yer first fine evening. Will yer take 'im?"

Arabella scowled. "He's not thinking of marriage. Surely I could do better if I must be hired." In spite of herself, she thought of Harry's long, muscular back and sweet breath.

"Aye," said Catlin thoughtfully. "'Tis the child who'll not wait. But if this lord be grand enough 'e'll give her money for the lying-in and never know the date; an 'usband now . . ." She shook her head. "Ye could be sent to rot in the country when 'e does 'is sums."

Arabella did not reply; whatever Catlin said, repugnance held her from Lord Wexford. He seemed mild enough and a man of such great age ought not to be too demanding, but she felt a shudder even when he kissed her hand. She refused to think of him lying where Harry once had been.

Soon, she thrust him out of her mind completely. After the musical evening at the Southamptons' several young men called and invited her to the sort of entertainment she longed to sample: Bevil's friends were almost as dull as City merchants. She went to masked routs, which were thought very fast, and music breakfasts; to the kind of supper parties where no lady of breeding should be seen. George Jeffries took her once and tried to rape her in the coach he hired to take her home: she fought him with cold determination since she had not come so far to risk future blackmail by some petty attorney. Although very drunk, he desisted, not quite enough of a rogue to take her against such opposition. "I'll have you one day, my dear," he said thickly. "Unless you become poxed by Wexford and his like first."

"Is it true that Wexford is close to the King?" demanded Arabella, ignoring what else he said.

"Aye, King's pander like some others I could name, but don't set your aim too high. You'll find Barbara Palmer and a dozen others waiting to cut your throat in the royal bedchamber."

"I have no intention of entering the King's bedchamber," said Arabella coldly, and it was true; she had enough of the City in her blood to bear a grudge against Charles II. Courtiers laughed at the spectacle of merchants struggling under mountainous debts while their credit was locked up in the Exchequer, and ministers bragged of their cleverness in thinking up such a scheme; often Arabella had to bite her tongue, wishing she was powerful enough to say what she thought of such chicanery.

For if she did not like Wexford, she did not like most of the other men she met either. She was moving only on the outer shoals of the court and found painted foppery unattractive, the older men more interesting but so obviously grimed by years of lechery it was hard to do more than assess their value and hope revulsion would not show.

She received plenty of offers, but so far had refused them all.

These men held virtue in contempt but would not value her if she was too easily gained, and no one had yet offered what she wanted. She was quite clear what that was: a marriage or liaison fine enough to give her the right to be acccepted wherever she wished to go.

126

If only she had time she was sure she would succeed. But the weeks were slipping by, and she was now four months pregnant. However much she starved and laced herself, soon Catlin would have to let out the tucks in her dresses. She had received two offers of marriage, one from an impecunious boy younger than herself, the other from George Jeffries, recently widowed and looking for a wife to take charge of six children. Really, he wanted to marry money, and she thought he was relieved when she refused him. Soon, very soon, she must accept someone.

Or go to Harry and tell him of his child.

When she heard that the child's father wanted to wed her Catlin said frankly that she ought to go to him, but Arabella could not bear it. She could not crawl back from more failure after her fine dreams, having spoiled such love as they might once have possessed, since Harry would know she accepted him only because she had nowhere else to turn.

She still paid Will as a journeyman, and met him once a month at Miles Prance's shop in Covent Garden, squeezing small profits from his wares to pay for more building at the House of the Spurs. A few pounds squeezed out of Bevil too, but for all his boasting Arabella found him disappointing. He was paunchy, disreputable and often drunk, his commissions mostly errands of the most discreditable kind: nor was he the kind of man willing to stint himself of funds for uncertain gains in a place like Cheapside.

Prance was a good silversmith and respected her father's name; he bowed when she came as if she were a client and not a dependant. He also paid her less than Will's craft was worth. In May, when she met Will there, Prance was more obsequious than usual, so Arabella knew that Will had been well beaten down in price. "Well?" she asked sharply. "What have you offered Mr. Prance today?"

Will scratched his chin, looking at her clothes in admiration. "You be looking mortal fine, Mistress Arabella."

He's too stupid to notice a thickening waist, she thought crossly, but there's plenty of others with sharper eyes, and soft summer styles would not be in her favour. "I'd seem a poor booby around Whitehall if I did not. What have you brought today, Will?"

He showed her some salvers and a set of goblets. "I sold a ewer to Mr. Glover down Cheapside, I'll account separately for that."

"Yes, do," said Arabella cordially. "You see, Mr. Prance, if your prices are not right we can place our plate elsewhere. I sold a pair of salts myself last week." This had been a lucky break and saved her finances from disaster, since fashionable clothes were staggeringly expensive. She had pretended she needed to sell them to pay gaming debts and one of her admirers bought them, although in debt himself.

Prance flicked a shrewd glance from her to Will. "I won't say that your wares aren't welcome, since I have too good a trade to make all I need myself, but they aren't so finely crafted as my own. I must sell them cheap or devalue mine."

Will flushed. "No one else finds fault with my skills."

"Apprenticed to Robert Sperling, weren't you? This lady's good father?"

"Aye, and the finest master in London. I defy you to say different."

"I don't," said Prance placidly. "If you were bringing me his work, I'd sell it at higher prices than my own. A year of your apprenticeship to run when he died, yet how many pieces had you designed and finished then, without any aid from him?"

Will looked at the floor. "None of value."

Prance bowed to Arabella, washing his hands against his belly. "You see, mistress, you cannot advise him on design, and Mr. Cornish, who took over his apprenticeship, no longer works in silver. Will is a sound craftsman, but his pieces do not catch the eye."

"I don't agree." She did, though, and Harry had warned her of it, but she would gain nothing by admitting inferiority.

Before they parted she handed Will his wages and money to buy silver. "How much more must I pay to complete the roof?"

He pulled at his lips. "Ten pounds, and another five needed soon to keep the joiners working."

God's breath, thought Arabella, dismayed. Not more to the joiners. She had been extravagant over woodwork, wanting only the best, and it had swallowed an alarming amount of money. "You'll have to tell them to plaster the stairwell and panel only the rooms downstairs."

He agreed gloomily. "Mr. Henry offered to take over the contract."

"You never took money from him!"

"You pay me, mistress, so I carry out your orders. No, I didn't, but think you mistaken. He wouldn't cheat you."

She flushed. "I never feared he would, but this I mean to do myself. How—how is he?"

Will shrugged. "Tired. Awkward-tempered. Sharp on a bargain. He was set on last week carrying coin from Reading, and has most of the business to carry besides. Alderman Cornish married the other day since he needed a woman for his childer, but he's far from well. I doubt he'll see the year out."

"Was he hurt?"

"Who? The alderman's—"

"Harry," she said impatiently. Fancy the alderman marrying again; men did not grieve their women long, after all.

"Nay, he had a man with him as escort and they beat 'em off. Bruised and shook up, that's all. They saved the coin, too. Cornish's be doing better than most these days; you heard Mr. Backwell had to flee to Holland to escape clapped up for debt?"

"I heard," she said briefly. She had kept silent when gallants laughed at the great merchant's ruin, but only just. She walked back to Bevil's house sunk in gloom. Why couldn't her enterprise yield success as Harry's did? Why in God's name were women lumbered with unwanted babies after two nights of pleasuring?

Then, quite suddenly, her luck changed.

Wexford, whose scrutiny she had felt even while she ignored it, invited her to Grey's, a fashionable tavern in Leicester Fields, a newly built area surrounded by hedgerows and rutted lanes. Bevil escorted her to the coach himself, squeezing her arm and muttering about how she must make the best of her chances. "For I don't mind telling you, Arabella, you've not looked yourself lately, and young Gaunt who swore he'd die for love of you is quite gone off. George Jeffries told me he'd found a wench with expectations, too."

Very encouraging, thought Arabella, sinking into green-squabbed cushions. But true. She gave Wexford a dazzling smile. "Indeed I thank you, sir. An excursion out of town just suits my mood at the present."

"I would not describe it as out of town, but the air is pleasant enough." He sat back, watching her in the way she found so irritating.

He was right about the distance. Arabella was only familiar with the Strand, St. James's Fields and Pall Mall apart from the City, and was surprised to find herself in open country so quickly. She sneered as they passed through bundled hay and straw in the Hay Market, and exclaimed with pleasure when she saw a creaking windmill on the slope above, grinding corn for bakeries clustered all around. Scattered across derelict pasture was a gunpowder store, placed in space for security, Mr. Panton's ill-reputed gaming house, some taverns and brewers' yards. Beyond, cows grazed as if brick courts were a hundred miles instead of a hundred yards away, where a new square was building in Leicester Fields.

Arabella breathed sweet air and remembered a picnic on Islington Heights as a child. "It's beautiful, sir! Next time I am asked where I want to go, I shall know the answer, a picnic north of Leicester Fields!"

"That will depend on the outcome of our talk today," he replied enigmatically.

She stared at him doubtfully, but allowed herself to be shown into a private room by a bowing landlord. Whatever happened, she could not visualise Wexford picnicking.

The food was well cooked and Arabella was ravenously hungry, for she had been systematically starving herself in an attempt to delay her pregnancy showing. She had resolved to relax and enjoy herself today, but found it surprisingly difficult when her whole future might depend on whatever plans Wexford cherished for her.

He sat across the table, speaking very little, watching, watching. At first she was angry that he should make so small an effort to entertain her, then she became nervous, clattering her fork and unable to think of anything to say which would not sound ridiculous.

He moved over to the window seat once the cloth was drawn, and took snuff. "You look anxious, mistress. Pray do not disturb yourself, or you will make me uneasy, too. I am not in the mood for rape this afternoon."

Arabella set her teeth, determined not to show herself a green goose, although enough of her principled rearing survived for her to feel shocked. "I am not anxious, except that your lordship might find me dull company."

"Not at all," he replied courteously. "I detest women who chatter."

"Why did you bring me here, then?" she asked bluntly, since nothing would be gained by finesse.

"I had a reason, but you must wait to discover it. I conclude that you are for hire, since your uncle handed you into my coach himself and you come goggle-eyed for profit?"

Arabella gulped at the crude frankness of it. She had been

considering his value for weeks, and the value of others like him, yet still was not stripped of all illusion. "I—I scarcely know how—"

"I am disappointed in you, Arabella." His green eyes widened derisively. "If you cannot do better than that, I am wasting my time."

She took a deep breath, hands gripped tight on her lap. "What is your proposition?"

"That's much better. Refusal should always come after, not before, an offer. Or acceptance, of course. Listen then, and say nothing until I have done. If you refuse, I will take you home and that will be the end of the matter." His eyes flicked over her. "I can buy a dozen women with more skill than you at half what you will cost."

Arabella felt blood burn in her cheeks at the contempt in his tone. Why is he bothering then, she wondered confusedly, if I do not interest him at all? For she did not, or only slightly as all women did, she was sure of that at least.

"I am offering you marriage." He held up his hand when she exclaimed. "Wait, swoon after if you wish. My third wife died a year ago and I have no desire to complicate my household with women again. If I marry you it will be for a purpose. Women learn strange secrets in bed with the King's ministers, and my value to His Majesty comes from the gossip I bring him. In such a trade I have many rivals and find myself beset, likely to be disgraced unless I retain His Majesty's confidence. This grows more difficult when so many younger men press up behind me. You understand what I am offering? I have wealth and position now, but you will have to work to my instruction if I am to preserve them."

"Yes," said Arabella baldly. The King's pander, George Jeffries had called him, so it was no great change of habit to lease out his wife for profit.

There was a gleam of amusement in his eyes now, the first she had seen in him. "Good. Do you accept or refuse?"

Arabella was astonished, shocked, disgusted; swamped by fierce loathing for this corrupt and deadly little man. She sat plaiting her fingers in her lap, thinking quite coldly: I can't afford to refuse. For the sake of his schemings he will introduce me to the greatest men at court, and someone must soon tattle about my figure. This way the child will be born in wedlock;

131

I will meet his anger later, when he discovers the trick I played on him. Perhaps he will not mind at all, used as he is to such cold-blooded dealing.

She looked up. "I accept," she said clearly.

Chapter Twelve

Arabella married within a week.

She was aware that the new Lady Wexford aroused as much mirth at court as she did awe amongst Bevil's acquaintance. George Jeffries congratulated her as one suppliant of fortune to another temporarily more successful. "I am laying siege to the City and am appointed its Common Serjeant already, but Westminster Hall attracts me. Perhaps you will be able to whisper my name on the right pillow."

"I'm sure I don't know why I should," Arabella said tartly. "My lord of Wexford does not concern himself with the law."

He roared with laughter. "Come now, sweetheart. No girl of twenty weds a tainted old lecher and expects to stay long in his bed. He must be sixty-five if he's a day."

"He's fifty-nine." Arabella had no idea of his age, but fifty-nine sounded better than sixty. "You worm your way into the City's confidence, and leave me to my affairs. Take my word for it, there's more money east of Ludgate than in all the corridors of Whitehall." She had been taken aback by Wexford House, a barn of a place in Pall Mall, and disconcerted to discover that Wexford had sixteen children living from his earlier marriages. However, there was nothing to be done about it now, and Bevil tied up her marriage contract as tight as his experience in such matters allowed.

Arabella was determined to retain a shred of independence by continuing secretly to sell silver, but hoped she would soon be able to filch sufficient means from Wexford to finish the House of the Spurs. Cornish's had paid for the exterior long ago or she would have been dispossessed, the rest dragged on endlessly and if the relationship between herself and Harry had

133

been less painful, certainly they would have enforced their rights against her. Beholden again, she thought viciously.

Then she enquired of Bevil about the law on wives' property, and received an unpleasant shock, for she did not intend Wexford to know anything about her house in Cheapside. He must receive what remained of her dowry, that was only fair. Her father's house, never.

"You can't keep it from him," said Bevil at once. "No married woman can hold her own property, and sooner or later he is bound to find out."

Arabella shook her head decisively. "He shan't have it. How would you like him as your co-owner?"

Bevil had not reflected on that aspect of affairs, and at once decided he would not like it at all. A man like Wexford could corrupt any proceeding he cared to take, and help himself to the whole. "What is to be done?"

"I could convey my share to you," said Arabella slowly.

He brightened. "You could, indeed."

"Not so fast, uncle. I would need safeguards."

"There are none which would hold at law for a married woman."

"But if he doesn't know it was ever mine . . . no, that will not do." She could not trust Bevil either. Then she knew what she must do, the only person who would not cheat her when nothing was set on paper. "We will lease the whole to Cornish's as we thought to do before, but on quite different terms. The alderman will agree and Harry, who might not, is often away. You could sell out completely if you wished."

So it was arranged. Bevil went to the City when Will told them Harry was away, and offered to deal, take it or leave it this very moment. Alderman Cornish was in bed and very frail; he demurred at such haste but had traded too long not to re-cognise a good bargain when he saw one. Bevil sold his interest outright. Arabella conveyed hers on what looked like the same terms but for a quarter of the sum, with Cornish's word alone to say that the whole property would be returned to her in fifteen years' time.

The next day Arabella married Wexford, whose name she discovered during the ceremony to be Justin, but as he did not seem to expect her to call him by it, it scarcely mattered. The only witnesses were a selection of his children, the oldest splayed with middle age, so Arabella could not avoid the conclusion that George Jeffries' guess of her husband's age was closer than her own.

At least he was not gross or obviously infirm. He looked trim and alert beside his baggy son, suavely turning aside malice in a way which displayed his breeding while exposing that of others to ridicule. She liked him no better but was relieved he would not shame her.

They lingered together over a meal by candlelight afterwards, alone since Wexford tersely dismissed his children immediately after the ceremony.

"Don't you care for them at all?" asked Arabella curiously. She had never considered that parents might not even like their children, when she had been surrounded by affection so long as hers lived. Nor did she reflect on her own intense aversion from the distorting lump in her belly.

"Should I, do you think?" He swirled wine pensively in his goblet. "Perhaps I should. I really know little about them, except that they wonder how much longer it will be before I die and leave them my possessions. I find Alice quite congenial, and good to look upon. Not beautiful like you, of course."

The compliment was offered in a completely neutral tone but Arabella coloured absurdly. She had been trying not to think about what must follow this meal, which was strange when an end to empty nights had seemed one advantage of marriage. "I—I thank you, sir."

"Not at all. I spoke a self-evident truth; if it were otherwise I should not have chosen you for my purposes."

Arabella nearly burst into tears at such wanton unkindness, tight-wrought as she already was with strain. "We made a bargain, sir. There is no need to remind me of it always."

"I think there is, today at least. I do not cheat, whatever my other faults may be. You entered on this contract knowingly, with everything clearly explained. I wished to serve warning that tears, or pleadings that you did not understand my meaning, will be wasted."

I cheated, she thought in panic. Suddenly it seemed absurd to imagine that he would not mind when he discovered she was several months with child. If she conceived as a result of his plottings, then she thought him sufficiently just not to blame her; he would react very differently when faced by deliberate fraud.

He stood up and bowed. "Now, if you are ready, we will retire to bed."

She nodded, tongue frozen, and was lighted up wide, polished stairs by a footman. The hall was brightly lit, but galleries on either side were black, unwelcoming caverns, draughts blowing smoke from sconced candles. Catlin was waiting in her bedroom, as overawed as herself. "I've counted thirty rooms so far, mam," she whispered, "and as many servants. Every one of 'em as 'aughty as 'is lordship." She clapped her hand to her mouth, but Arabella giggled and felt better for it.

She waited for Wexford sitting up, shoulders chilled in her thin shift. He kept her waiting nearly two hours, so when eventually he came, only pride remained to sustain her. For two hours she had fought off thought of Harry, for two hours tried to think only of her purpose gained by this marriage.

It was not too bad.

She lay in the morning and reflected that it might have been much worse. Wexford was quick and sparing in effort as in all he did, and showed no sign of expecting anything from her. As if he expected nothing from anyone any more. He stayed only minutes and went elsewhere to sleep; Arabella laughed a little at her own astonishment when he left. No caresses or whisperings in the dark with him.

He was waiting in the hall when she came down at noon, newly gowned in velvet slashed and panniered to reveal silk below, a *grande toilette* paid for with money which was now his. She had kept twenty pounds from the sale of her lease and hidden it amongst her clothes, the rest went in her dowry chest because without it there would be far less than Bevil had led Wexford to expect. She would not be surprised if Wexford ordered her effects searched as a matter of routine, and must find a safer hide for her last reserve.

He bowed over her hand. "As always, you look exquisite, my dear. I trust you slept well?"

She agreed that she had, although she had lain awake for hours. She had avoided thought of Harry before, afterwards had not been so easy.

"I stayed to ask whether you would care to walk in St. James's Park with me. There are a great many people you must meet as my bride." His tone showed no sign of sarcasm.

She accepted; eager for the part she had agreed to play. She would belong to the court at last, understand its jests, arouse jealousy with her beauty. And since Wexford had planned it so, surely she would be able to find a man who would offer warmth as well as convenience, and not slither in and out of her bed in a matter of minutes.

During the next two weeks she learned voraciously. Wexford did not present her to the King, saying there was still too much she did not understand, otherwise she went everywhere. She met stout, fiery Henry Clifford, the Lord Treasurer, who men said was a secret Catholic; gloomy Arlington and the ungovernable Duke of Buckingham. She rather liked him at first, he was so dashing and unpredictable, but after she saw him in a near-homicidal rage because his coach was late, her admiration cooled.

"He is not worth any contriving on our part," said Wexford judiciously. "He intrigues so much he deceives himself, and is a loose-mouthed fool besides. You would disport yourself for him and then find the confidences he blabbed were known to half the court."

Wexford increasingly rubbed at Arabella's nerves. He refused to hide the purpose of her training, and continued to help himself to her body as if it were distasteful physic: necessary, but to be swallowed with his nose held. At least he came so seldom and stayed so short a time he had noticed nothing yet, though her waist was thickening daily.

She ate almost nothing as fear grew of what he would do when he did notice, and Catlin scolded her. "The child will suffer if ye're so foolish. My sister were sick the whole time, so fancied only scraps, an' her child were so thin and puling it only lived a sen-night."

"Perhaps it would be best if it did die," replied Arabella wearily. Her back ached from long standing and strolling around Whitehall, enjoyment spoiled by apprehension.

"Now, there's a thing to say! Ye should send it to the father rather than think such wicked thoughts."

"He's married, Will told me yesterday. The daughter of a rich mercer, nothing could be more suitable." It had been a dreadful shock, although she ought to have expected it once Harry knew she was wed; she never intended to see him again but the sensation of the past slammed in her face was almost physical. She often felt very lonely with only a stranger of a husband for companionship, surrounded by palace life she did not yet fully understand. But she was where she had wanted to be and delighted by her achievement: she would fit in, given time. She enjoyed the quick, allusive conversation, the deadly competition for favour thinly veneered by sophisticated manners, the sense of living where events were shaped, instead of being their ignorant victim.

Then Wexford introduced her to Anthony Ashley Cooper, newly created Earl of Shaftesbury and a member of the Cabal, the King's inner council of five. He was in his fifties and looked every year of it, eyelids drooping in jaded indifference, everything about him honed by malice and self-interest. He was also entertaining and enormously knowledgeable; for the first time Arabella discovered the intellectual pleasure of a man in whose company it was impossible to be bored.

He was standing by her when news broke of a naval battle in Dutch waters, hailed as an English victory, and told her not to believe a word of it. "No one wins victories against the Dutch in their own waters. All they have to do is pretend to run away across sandbanks they know, and we don't. In minutes every enemy ship is fast in mud and dismasted."

"Everyone says we won, even the messenger from the fleet," said Arabella doubtfully.

"Of course. We don't behead harbingers of doom any longer, but nor do we reward them. He will be gone before doubts harden." He nodded at the officer who had come with the news, preening himself and clutching a gold box given by the King as a memento of his day of fame.

"Never mind," said Arabella cheerfully. "The box is very poor workmanship and the gilt will not outlast two polishings."

"I hope you are right, lies deserve poor gilding. As those who make false treaties deserve unruly Parliaments, and if they do not get them, then the matter can be arranged."

Arabella's eyes rested on the athletic figure of the King playing pell-mell outside. "There are many whispers about this treaty. You feel bitterly about it, sir?"

"Very bitterly. Nor are my feelings any secret from His Majesty," he added kindly. "I would not like you to waste your time."

She laughed. "Never a waste in talk with you, I assure you, sir."

He bowed ironically. "I thank you, but your husband may expect you to recount something more valuable than stale gossip of my grudges. I suggest you try your wiles on the Duke of York, he is indiscreet enough for six. But no, on reflection I daresay you would be wasting your time there as well; to judge by his choice so far, he prefers his women ugly."

Arabella found the compliment unexpectedly agreeable, for

in truth her looks had faded. She often felt tired, she who scarcely knew the meaning of fatigue, and while her body thickened relentlessly, inadequate diet thinned her face so she was forced to use more paint. "I am afraid I am not yet on terms with the Duke of York, my lord."

"Nevertheless I can safely predict that Wexford will walk off and leave you by his side one day, in the same way he did with me."

Her eyes narrowed. "You are very acute, my lord."

"I have that reputation," he agreed. "I also have eyes to see that you should not stand any longer in your condition. Shall we go in search of your estimable husband and bribe him with promises of state secrets if he will take you home?"

Arabella was completely taken by surprise, long immunity from detection had made her forget that she might not be able to choose her own moment for discovery. "I—I don't know what you mean."

"You are with child, are you not, and find standing a weary business?"

She bit her lip, wondering what to say. Dare she ask him to hold his tongue, or would that be enough to spur him into congratulating Wexford on still siring children approaching his seventieth year? "I haven't told my husband yet," she said lamely. "There is still plenty of time."

"Not much for standing about courts, if I'm any judge." She could see his mind clicking with the very sum she had wanted to avoid. "I can see why you delay telling him, of course. Or is it his?"

Of all men, Shaftesbury was the most unsafe to trust with any titbit of gossip. "Of course," she said stiffly. Wexford would know she lied, but might not in pride admit it.

He smiled maliciously. "I hope, for your sake, that could be true. It isn't of course, as a look at your face would tell, but there's no fool like an old fool; perhaps he has forgotten. Now, I may be old, but I am not a fool, nor do I forget anything which might profit me."

Wexford questioned her closely that night on everything Shaftesbury had said, until Arabella found difficulty in remembering what she must leave out for her own safety, she was so tired.

"Only the treaty, he spoke about the treaty," she said wretchedly. "The rest was idle gossip."

"Gossip is often valuable information."

139

My God, yes, she thought; I must tell him tonight. "He is bitter against the King about the treaty and I think intends to teach Parliament how to harass the royal government."

"Unless the King rewards him sufficiently to buy off his anger. Shaftesbury is for sale to the highest bidder."

"What is this treaty? I have heard so many rumours of it."

"Only a few men know exactly what was in it, and I think Shaftesbury is now one of them. His Majesty signed a treaty with King Louis of France two years ago at Dover, open for all the world to see. But there were secret clauses, and it seems likely that King Charles undertook to become a Catholic and force England to accept Catholicism when the time was ripe. In exchange, he received money from Louis, became his pensioner in fact, in policy as well as soul."

"You can't be serious!" Arabella had been brought up to regard Catholicism as synonymous with slavery in this world and eternal damnation in the next, the French as England's eternal enemy.

"I do not jest."

No, he never did. She could not remember a single light remark he had made in all the time she had known him. "If it's true, no wonder Shaftesbury intends to stir up Parliament against such treachery."

Wexford shrugged. "As to that, Shaftesbury would hold his hand if he was sufficiently bribed, but his price is high and the King poor. Which is one reason why His Majesty took the risk of signing such clauses. I don't suppose he seriously intends to confess himself a Catholic and tear his realm apart, but having signed, he is in pawn to France. The threat of publishing such an agreement will serve Louis well for years, at the cost of a paltry few hundred thousand crowns."

Arabella clenched her hands; Wexford seemed as agreeable as she had ever known him, now was the moment. "I have a secret to tell you too, my lord. I hope you will be pleased."

The green stare hardened. "But you are not sure?"

"I—well, I am pleased but you have sixteen already, my lord."

"Is that your way of telling me you are with child?"

She nodded.

"When?"

"I—I don't know exactly. Being unskilled in these matters, I gave it no thought."

"Ah, then we must do our calculations together. I must

140

confess I thought you changed recently but, like you, gave that particular eventuality no thought. Stand up, Arabella. I have a fair experience in these matters and perhaps may assist your lack of skill."

She thought of protest, of bantering at his brusqueness, but realised it would do no good. He was quite capable of ordering a footman to haul her to her feet. She stood, but spread out her skirt as if in coquetry. He stared at her, still seated, hand to the stem of his goblet, eyes like emeralds in candlelight and as hard. "Put your hands behind your back and take off that shawl."

She did as she was bid and stood quietly, panic stilled. Remember, her father had once said, I know what you are and will be, and love you still. It helped a little now.

"You cheating little bitch," Wexford said quietly at last, and she flinched. "You're six months gone at least."

"Five." The second of January, Arabella remembered painfully, the night the Exchequer was stopped; yes, it was nearly six. She had been lucky with high-waisted fashions."

"So that was why you wed me?"

She nodded. "Although I mean to keep our bargain."

"What bargain? Since I explained exactly my proposal and you did not, any bargain between us must be void."

"I am your wife, my lord, and yet you intend to use me as—"

"As you deserve, and as I never tried to hide from you. Whose child is it?"

She shook her head. "No one you would know, nor anyone at court who might taunt you with his knowledge."

"Then I lay this choice before you. My eldest son lives in our ancestral castle, surrounded by the furthest bog in Ireland. You may go there and rot on his charity if you wish, or you may stay here and not go out until the child is born nor for six months thereafter. No one then will know the date of your confinement."

Arabella sagged with relief. "Oh, thank you! You are very generous, truly I was ashamed to deceive you."

"Let us not add hypocrisy to the rest. You stay here then?"

She nodded; she would be more dutiful, try to love him a little. Surely even Wexford might find pleasure in a little softness sometimes?

"Go to your room now. You may walk in the garden when

I am out, otherwise I wish to see you only when I ask for your presence. Do I make myself clear?"

She curtsied. "Yes, my lord."

He called her back when she reached the door. "If it lives, the child goes to a wet nurse and we tell our acquaintance it was stillborn."

She felt her heart change beat, heavy hammer strokes against her ribs. "Wexford . . . I beg of you! In a year no one will recall its age to the nearest month! I shall never claim a penny of your inheritance for it, I swear!"

"I intend to ensure that you will not. The child will be entered on the parish register as illegitimate."

"But—but I'm your wife! You can't—"

"I assure you that I can and will. Officially the brat will be born dead, and twenty pounds double the amount needed to silence the parish clerk, I fancy; in Ireland a few shillings would do it. It is your choice, but either way you do not keep the child; I have no intention of making myself absurd by housing another man's bastard. You may give it what name you please," he added pleasantly.

Refuge was her first instinct, racing up the stair as if pursued by demons, or one demon more terrible than the rest, with gleaming green-faceted eyes. She had to stop halfway, gasping for breath, only vaguely conscious of hands helping her, of Catlin hovering on the edge of vision.

He meant it, she thought, he meant every word.

She understood Wexford's reaction when she herself regarded her swelling belly as a detested impediment to her plans, but instinct recoiled from Harry's child being cast out to snuffle with pigs in the gutter.

When the footman who helped her the last few steps was gone, she poured out the whole story to Catlin, and found her briskly practical. "Ye've no need to fret so, mam. Ye've told him at last and are rid of a burden for all that the old meanshanks plans to keep ye nine months confined. Mebbe he'll make it less when ye've regained yer looks. As for the child, there's naught ye can do and it'll be best put to a wet nurse out of town. D'ye know how many children born in this house the old lord's buried?"

Arabella shook her head, sipping hot milk and allowing herself to be comforted.

"Twelve! Four wives and twenty-eight childer he's had, the steward were telling me. 'Tis nothing unusual in the back alleys, but if yer asks me, this barn is no place for babbies. You let me find a nice healthy wet nurse and ye can rest happy it's the best thing for the mite, so long as ye've money to pay her."

Arabella's eyes strayed to the wainscot where they concealed her twenty pounds; Wexford would not pay a penny, hoping that the child would die in some filthy stew where women took unwanted babies for the price their swaddling would fetch. "I've not much, as you know, but Will is making better wares each month. You'll have to slip out when you won't be missed, and tell him he'll not be seeing me for a while." She grasped Catlin's sleeve. "Don't tell Will I'm increasing for a few months yet." She could not bear Harry to know, could not possibly dump a child on Harry's new-made marriage.

"I'd not be saying anything ye don't want, mam, but be well pleased ye won't need to starve yerself any longer. Ye want the babe born straight and well."

"So long as it is born and done with," said Arabella wearily. "Lord, what a to-do over two nights' pleasure!"

Chapter Thirteen

*Arabella's son was born early in Oc-*tober 1672, an easy birth although she did not think so at the time. She called him Adam in mockery at the restless urgings of man, and Furnival after the alley which once both separated and joined Cornish to Sperling, and now had disappeared to make room for fine new King Street.

He was a puny, squalling baby, bright pink and ugly at birth, yellow with jaundice and uglier still soon after. She did not know whether her starvation diet during her early months of pregnancy had anything to do with it, but Adam was little more than bone and felt as repulsive as an unfledged bird.

Arabella was relieved that she could not find her son attractive; he did not look like Harry at all, while his ugliness seemed an insult to her own beauty. Catlin told her that most newborn babies had heads which lolled and stick-like limbs flopping at the touch, but Arabella remembered little Tam and did not believe her. After the yellow faded, Adam's skin scaled and he caught some fever from the wet nurse: when she came Arabella thought her rosy with health but almost at once she sickened and her milk dried. Arabella's own breasts were bound and aching, but by then Adam was too sick to suck when she tried to feed him herself, so the painful business of bandaging had to be done afresh with nothing gained.

She felt guilty at being so exasperated by him. Why couldn't he be healthy, why must he scream and infuriate Wexford further; why didn't he live or die instead of hovering between the two, making everything worse, when she had thought his birth would at least free her from one burden?

For she wanted desperately to get on with her own life, leave the past and set out again at last.

Inaction bored her to the point of frenzy, and lay in wait for her every hour as wasted time dragged past. The weeks of her confinement had been endless, and by her agreement with Wexford she still had another six months to endure. This wretched, puling brat was the image of her despair and brought no reminder of the happier time before, nor pride for his future.

Once Arabella made a bargain or formed an ambition she stuck to it, letter and spirit, jot and tittle. It did not occur to her to plead with Wexford, nor did she attempt to leave the house when he was away. She simply wanted time to pass, and Adam was holding it up.

She held him when he cried, and he continued to cry. She tempted him with milk-soaked rags and he was sick. She ordered another wet nurse and he refused her breast like a drunkard offered water.

He infuriated her. She knew it was unwomanly to feel so towards her son but could not help it. At least he did not die, so she need not feel guilty about that, too. Heaven alone knew why he did not, but somehow he struggled through day after day of illness, breath gasping, bones mere bundled twigs wrapped in pithless skin.

"He must be strong to live through so much," said Catlin; she had become quite fond of Adam as he obstinately held to life. "'Twas as I told ye, ye starved him eating nothing all those months."

Arabella felt another throb of guilt, and took refuge in anger. "Rubbish! Babes take what they want, or half the poor would never have children born alive!" She was dressed, delighted to find fashionable gowns fitting again. "We'll have to take in all those tucks I asked the dressmaker to allow. I swear I hardly feel lacing any more after so long a time spent squeezing a belly like a pumpkin into a maiden's stays."

Catlin pursed her lips disapprovingly. "And never a thought for yer poor babe gasping for breath, I daresay."

"For the love of God, Catlin! I did the best I could for him and he has only to see my face to screech like a barn owl. I might as well think of myself a little, since no one else cares at all."

Catlin flounced out of the room without answering, leaving Arabella feeling very ill-used. She regarded her face mournfully in the mirror: another six months shut up in Wexford House, it didn't bear thinking of. She called out to a footman scratching at the door and unexpectedly discovered it to be Wexford. She was astounded to see him, but curtsied with all the grace she had been practising during long weeks when she had nothing better to do. "My lord, I bid you welcome."

She had scarcely seen him for three crawling months, and was thankful she had put on her silver-etched dress for amusement, it had always suited her the best of all her gowns.

He studied her thoughtfully. "You are fully recovered?"

"Oh yes, my lord! And mightily pleased to find myself in health again, I can tell you. I cannot imagine why so many ladies find moping in bed half the day so agreeable!"

"It depends on whom they are moping in bed with, no doubt," he replied suavely, and watched her flush with his usual detached interest. "I hear your son is not similarly recovered?"

"Oh, he is much better today," said Arabella blithely. Indeed Adam seemed slightly less ill and children revived swiftly from ailments. "The new wet nurse suits him better, and says she will take him with her when he is well, and so avoid another change. I hope you have not been too much disturbed?"

"Do you know, Arabella, you surprise me? You wanted this child, or presumably would have been rid of him before you came to sell yourself at Whitehall. Yet now you have him, he means as little to you as I do."

Arabella was taken aback. Could Wexford mean that he did desire affection, something more than a commercial relationship? If so, she was in luck. She went and put her hand on his arm. "My lord, how can you speak so? Of course I have regard for you—respect too, when you have treated me so fairly."

He removed her hand immediately and smoothed his sleeve, "Well done, Arabella. Even when you lie, you achieve a certain ring of sincerity which should make all but the most experienced pause. But I am very experienced, and most women would not consider that fairness entered into our dealings. Only generosity might be worth a little affection and I have not been generous. The boy leaves as soon as he is well." He went out, leaving her with the strangest impression that she had played her cards badly, that he had come prepared to be generous in some undisclosed way. She puzzled at it awhile, wondering where she had gone wrong, but without success, so gave up quite quickly. It was infuriating to think that if she had been more subtle he might not have insisted on the full six months of further incarceration.

A week later, Adam left for his new home in the village of St. Mary-le-Bon, two miles away across May Fair Fields, where Moll Dempster, his newest wet nurse, worked as a laundress. She was to be paid by results, four shillings for every month she kept Adam alive. Paying a lump sum to women who took in children was tantamount to signing their death entry in the parish register.

Wexford did not come near Arabella again and enforced his bargain to the day: it was the beginning of April the following year before she went out at last, determined to make up for so much time lost, a new invulnerable edge set on her character.

She flung herself into court amusements with a gusto which captivated men jaded by excess, and diverted statesmen grappling with a major political crisis. Shaftesbury had carried out his threat and mobilised all the long-festering resentments against the mismanagement and doubtful ambitions of Charles II, which before had run to waste in spiteful wrangling. When Arabella emerged from seclusion, Parliament had just been prorogued, but before the King rid himself of it he had had to agree to a Test Bill, which forced those who accepted official positions to take communion according to the rite of the Church of England and swear oaths which no sincere Roman Catholic could accept. Amidst a wash of gossip, well mixed with political fury at suspicion confirmed, the Duke of York, King's brother and heir to the throne so long as Charles remained without legitimate children, and Clifford, the Lord Treasurer, both resigned their offices. The King alone was exempt from the act, and opinion was divided between those who said he would not have been able to take the test and those who asserted that Charles cared not at all what he swore since neither his word nor his coronation oath bound him.

The King's council broke into fragments: Clifford disgraced, Arlington suspect although he took the test, Buckingham quarreling with everyone as usual, Lauderdale disliked by everyone, also as usual, Shaftesbury dismissed for the destroyer's role he had played.

Arabella understood it all superficially, and grasped well enough the duel for power hidden beneath events. She was presented to the King and formed the impression of a man who, for all his indolence, did not intend to abate one scrap of what he believed to be his inheritance. She could have slept with him, and was tempted since it was something after all to have been bedded by a King; but it was no achievement since Charles craved women continually, and might prove dangerous: factions formed, policies fell or were put forward in the course of ruthless campaigns fought by the King's mistresses and their sponsors. Also, something in her blood restrained her, even when the challenge of it enticed. Her father had been maimed fighting oppressive Stuarts; she remembered Alderman Backwell's despair when the King's fraud ruined him, the disgrace of the fleet burned at anchor by the Dutch. So she flirted with Charles and as a woman liked him very well: in bone and spirit she was bred his enemy and nothing changed it.

Arabella and Shaftesbury met often, not at court, where he was temporarily unwelcome, but nearly everywhere else, although almost the only strong emotion she had so far detected in her husband was an acute aversion from Shaftesbury.

Shaftesbury laughed when she challenged him with taunting Wexford as cuckold during her long confinement. "Fair Arabella, how could I be so ungallant? No, I quite surprised myself and said nothing, which leaves only one explanation for it. My lord of Wexford is jealous of his wife in my arms."

"Oh no," said Arabella seriously. "He would regard that as success for his schemes. He has no affection for me, you know."

They were standing by an open window above a courtyard off Whitehall, salt sea tang off the river welcome after frenzy at the gaming tables, and he picked a briar rose for her hair before replying. "I wonder. Not that it is of moment, since emotion is the last consideration Wexford would allow to influence his conduct. His anger is well stoked because he is at present my debtor."

"Your debtor? He is rich enough to pay whatever he owes. To be sure, I am stark in debt to you myself since I hold such wretched cards, but he expects me to pay my losses from my allowance."

"Money he, not you, owes me. I have said nothing of how it was another man's son stillborn in his house, but he does not account me chivalrous and believed me when I told him my silence would be expensive. It is saddening to reflect how well ill-repute often serves, when he could have called my bluff without cost."

"You mean you—"

"Let us say he contributes to the funds we need to oppose His Majesty, and resents it, not being of our mind himself."

Arabella gave a gurgle of laughter. "Oh, Shaftesbury, I haven't heard anything so droll this twelvemonth! And he a staunch King and court man, no wonder he treats you like an overflowing kennel." She saw no reason to tell him that Adam lived, and give him another weapon to use against Wexford; she had some loyalties, although fewer as time passed.

He stared at her, almost curiously, and saw a vivid face alive with laughter, full breasts almost uncovered by low-cut gown, and a tiny, tight-laced waist. "Do you know, I wasn't sure whether you would be angry? There is relief in finding another as untroubled by hiding behind fine sentiments as oneself."

"Meaning that all are unscrupulous, and only words differ? Fie, Shaftesbury, when men call you our Protestant champion and guardian of England's liberty."

He bent to kiss her. "I have few scruples, as the King and your husband already know, and others will find out. Only a purpose. And that, God willing, I shall accomplish."

He would say no more and allowed himself to be enchanted as she intended, and part achieved already through weeks of stalking him through salons and gaming rooms. He chose his moments as well as she, and time was ripe for them both. She never learned to whose rooms he took her, or whether he kept them for his needs, but they were admirably suited to their purpose. There was a four-poster bed hung with tasseled draperies, a multitude of candles, and windows open to the river. Even so, there was the faintest shade of disappointment in a night when she had expected his lovemaking to complement the satisfaction she felt in being known as the conqueror of so great a man. He was, of course, enormously experienced, and unlike Wexford would have felt his pride diminished had he not given as much pleasure as he obtained himself, yet there was something missing. She could not name it, and by morning came to think herself absurd. Perhaps it was simply that he, too, was old, even if years younger than Wexford. At least there was all the difference in the world between being a man's wife and his mistress, she reflected, and in every way the change was for the better. She did not have to face Shaftesbury when either found the other tiresome, although she was aware that when their parting came it was important that she should read the signs correctly. She must quit him first rather than be jilted, even if afterwards she must run the gauntlet of his spite.

The months began to pass quickly for Arabella; however much the King might hate him, Shaftesbury was too considerable a man to be ostracised, too powerful not to be at the centre of most events, and her connection with him gave Arabella a consequence she had never known before. She was busy from first light until the following dawn if it was a night he fancied her, and thought herself very famous. She was accepted as Wexford's countess at court, for the King did not hold a woman's amours against her, enjoyed herself vastly and refused all other offers. Casual affairs would lower her value, and Shaftesbury was an ill man to cross so long as she was his.

More naval skirmishes were lost against the Dutch; New Amsterdam gained in America and renamed New York, providing fresh cause for grousing since the Duke was more suspect every day. Men said openly that there was a conspiracy between the royal brothers and the Pope, through his mercenaries the Jesuits, to take over England and put true Protestants to stake and sword again. Louis of France would pay the cost, indeed was already paying under the secret clauses of Dover, and seize all England's trade in recompense. Since there were a surprising number of indiscreet tongues blabbing of French payments to Charles, the tale was easy to believe: England had grown accustomed to winning naval wars, and mutterings of treachery in high places grew.

Peace came in February 1674. The King had gained nothing from a war undertaken to please his French paymaster, and was more completely beggared with debts than ever.

"Further payments from Louis will appear to answer the problem best, no doubt," observed Shaftesbury. He should have sounded shocked, but was pleased instead. "Charles will deliver himself bound to his opposition one day, through debts he dare not have uncovered.

"So will we all," said Arabella tartly. She was losing heavily at the gaming tables, and Wexford had informed her that he would send her to Ireland unless she paid for her keep with better information. So far, Shaftesbury had been so anxious to gain popular support that there seemed little to discover, since he told the wildest supposition to any chance crowd under his window. It never occurred to Arabella that he was more than capable of keeping his own counsel on such matters as suited him, while appearing unusually indiscreet.

"My dear, you should not play with men who were gaming before you were born. You are a quick learner, but too anxious and your mind is often on other things. Me, for instance, or how to trap that handsome Aston boy."

She turned her head swiftly and kissed his hand where it fondled in her curls. "Lord Aston means nothing to me, my lord!"

His hand stilled. "As well, if he does not. He is thirty years the younger, but I can still ruin him if I care to try."

Arabella felt her lips dry. She liked Lord Aston and wanted to know him better; just sometimes, she tired of old men and their intrigues but knew she dared not ignore Shaftesbury's warning. She had seen him destroy others too often to doubt his ruthlessness; he schemed to ruin the King too, and might succeed, which made him doubly dangerous to cross. Also, she was pregnant again.

She hesitated several weeks, then told Wexford on one of the few nights they were alone for supper. He raised his eyebrows in the way she detested. "How unfortunate. I should have thought you skilled enough in harlotry to avoid embarrassment a second time."

"Well, I'm not!" she snapped. "And you are an ill one to think I might be. What do you suggest, my lord, since apparently you know more of these matters than I do?"

"Is it Shaftesbury's?"

She nodded, it could not be Wexford's, since he had kept away from her since Adam was born.

"You're sure?"

"Of course I'm sure! What do you think I am? There's no one else."

He smiled unpleasantly. "You cannot be surprised that I should think the question necessary. He will not acknowledge it, you know, he is not a gentleman in such matters. Are you willing to act out scenes and throw hysterics at court to force him?"

"Good God, no! I would be ruined for life; the women hate me now and that would frighten off every man in his senses."

"As always, my dear, you never lack for sense. I will furnish you with a direction where you may be rid of your trouble. Go at once, it is worse if you wait."

She had always known that Wexford would not countenance

Shaftesbury's child, and was relieved he took it in so practical a spirit. She went two days later to Mistress Dawkins, who lived close by King's Conduit Springs; as she drove there through the scents of the Hay Market, she could not help thinking of the time she had come this way before, nearly three years before to hear Wexford's proposition. During the time between, Lord Southampton had nearly finished his speculative building in Leicester Fields and now the area between Wexford House and old Pickadil Bob's crumbling mansion was covered with brick and lime kilns as Leicester Fields had been before. Arabella had her mask, but this was a rough area while in the building and she kept leather curtains drawn until after the coach crossed Pickadil Bob's track, where houses sprouted in his weed-strewn gardens. He was long dead, but folk memory survived in the name: it is not often a man prospers sufficiently to build himself a mansion on the profits of manufacturing pickadils, or ruffs.

Once across his tumbledown boundary, she leaned out gratefully although it was bitter weather, and iced ruts jolted her so badly that she wondered whether she would need Mistress Dawkins' potions. She shivered, and leaned her cheek on Wexford-green squabs, tears slipping on rough cloth. Why must women have babies? She hated babies.

After the sharp turn into Conduit Lane, an area reserved to royal ownership as the source of water for Whitehall, the surface became even worse as the track crossed frozen bog, so apprehension was lost in relief when the journey ended. Mistress Dawkins was brisk; bit each coin she was given, then served her with a foul decoction of herbs, followed by a horn of neat brandy. Arabella had expected to stay—did not know what she expected—instead she was bundled back into the coach feeling deathly sick, an extra pair of horses hitched to the coach and Wexford's impassive lackeys instructed to drive her home across the roughest parts of May Fair Fields.

Humiliation, nausea and pain banished awareness of her surroundings long before they turned back into St. James's, which was fortunate, mind and stomach swinging and tearing in obscene unison until her only wish was to hide in dark stillness.

She swam sickly back to consciousness to find Catlin scolding, distraught by fear and rage. "Mam, don't ye ever be visiting that old witch again! The women she've killed, I could tell ye stories to make ye run screaming from the sight of her.

I couldn't believe it when the coachman told me where ye'd been."

Arabella sighed, and ran her hands over her belly. Nothing had showed before, but she remembered enough of the past nightmare hours to be sure she was rid of the child. "Mistress Dawkins profits because of those who have need of her. When they have built over May Fair Fields she will move across another set of ruts, and still not lack for trade."

"Who told ye of her? For sure, I'd give 'em a piece of my mind; ye have yer babies and be thankful!" Catlin had not found a tavernkeeper willing to wed her, and though she slept with the second footman, remained childless. "Why not ask his lordship whether he'll let ye have little Adam home? If he don't know what ails you, perhaps he'll soften when he sees ye ill and pale."

Arabella smiled sourly. "I doubt it, he gave me the witch's name." She must send Moll money again soon, when she had been late once before Catlin had found Adam a mass of sores from neglect.

Money.

Arabella twisted over and suppressed a groan. Her back hurt savagely. I won't do this again, she thought, and resolved to discover more of the skills of harlotry Wexford had expected her to know. Money. She lost too often gaming, and once when she pledged some of Wexford's rubies he ordered her thrashed by his valet, dispassionately as he did everything, but enforcing sufficient strokes to leave no doubt in her mind that his heirlooms were not for casual losing. Shaftesbury gave her odd amounts, but maintained a huge establishment and with many political supporters dependent on his bounty was often embarrassed himself. Wexford paid dressmaker's bills but had no interest in making her independent of the need to repeat gossip to him; without the little which came from Prance, Arabella could not have maintained Adam, and continued to gamble believing she would win.

Arabella was unwell longer than she expected. She was used to health and found weakness infuriating, especially when no one sympathised with her. Catlin was sulking, Wexford enquired formally after her each morning; Shaftesbury certainly would not come to Wexford's house, even if he felt it necessary to enquire after her indisposition.

The delivery of a new gown from Madame Bouchard's dressmaking establishment helped revive her, and the day after

153

it came Arabella felt well enough to saunter along the gravel walks of Pall Mall, greeting acquaintance and enjoying spring sunshine. Enjoying barbed envy too, for it was a daring outfit. Between them, she and Madame Bouchard had overset fashion and the result made other women look dowdy, each line severe yet curved to reveal her figure, the skirt gathered at waist and thigh, shifting pattern with every step.

She was so pleased with herself that she walked farther than she intended, accompanied by an admiring group of young men on their way to view some new addition to the King's horse-flesh. Then, quite suddenly, their jests and flattery became more than she could bear. Her back still ached, it was only a day since she came downstairs and had been beguiled outside by sun and a new gown. She did not want to admit weakness, though, when her greatest asset at court was the zest she brought to all she did, so refused an invitation to Ranelagh by pleading a romantic assignation, wondering as she did so whether she could get away before she vomited.

Even then, they would not let her go until she gave an address for the sedan chair, the matter becoming a joke as one held her off with his sword, swearing he would fling himself on it in jealousy.

"Prance," she said at random, handkerchief to her lips while faces and buildings blurred. "Miles Prance, the silversmith in Covent Garden." She did not know why she said it, except she or Catlin must go there soon and surely he would let her sit quietly and ask no questions. She could not be carried up the steps of Wexford House twice in a fortnight.

The chair almost finished her. Chairmen were of two kinds: those who kept in step and those who didn't. These didn't, and the resulting motion brought back recollection of her recent journey across May Fair Fields, where once she and Harry had thought to go on a day's diversion. Ah, Harry, what kind of wife is your Elizabeth?

Arabella had to pay the chairmen double their worth before they would let her down, although she was three parts fainting. A woman alone was fair game and lucky to be left unrobbed. At least Prance received her with remembered courtesy, hands washing against his belly, face inscrutable. Two men in his shop looked up at her entry, one she had seen somewhere about the court, and her heart sank. She had not come here since she married Wexford, to ensure that no one suspected her of com-

154

merce when she wagered silver to pay her debts, and a moment's carelessness today might ruin everything.

But she could not worry about it now and forgot him instantly, for the other man was Will.

Chapter Fourteen

*A*rabella *realised afterwards that she* must have given herself away completely to the man she recognised, but at the time he simply lacked significance for her. She hugged Will as if she was a child again, except she had never hugged him then, and tumbled out questions even while Prance hustled them into his workshop, mouthing excuses.

When the door shut behind them, Will and Arabella stared at each other, sheepish after unguarded emotion. "You don't look well, mistress," said Will with the devastating candour found only in the friends of youth.

Arabella gulped, part sob, part laughter. "Winter is a bad time to live on the swamps of Westminster, and the palace mortal cold. Oh, Will, it's good to see you again." She could not reckon how long it was since they had met.

"Aye, and you, mistress. Or my lady, I should say, I suppose." He grinned. "I doubt I'll ever think of you as such."

"Nor I," said Arabella frankly. "How are things, Will?"

He shrugged. "Well enough."

She wanted to shake him, why must he be so dense when there was so much she wanted to know? "Trade is good, then?"

"Aye, and peace very welcome."

"And the City?"

He stared at her, unable to grasp an abstract like the City, or her yearning to hear of things she knew. Of Cheapside scuttling with footsteps and merchants gravely pacing in the rebuilt Royal Exchange, each able to produce more coin in an hour than most courtiers in a year; of tradesmen richer than peers and not thinking it strange to work sixteen hours a day; of streets and churches, markets and warehouses risen out of cinder and surely completed during the years she had left. Arabella felt a desperate ache; she wanted to see it all again, and had not known her own desire. "The House of the Spurs," she said at last. "How does it look?"

He thought, wrinkling his brow. "Much like the rest. There is one pattern of house for all the great streets, as you know."

"It is complete?" Before, she had felt only triumph at keeping it from Wexford, now there was loss where her inheritance should be, which she had planned to build up for herself.

"Oh aye, 'tis finished long since and nothing used but the best; Cornish's be mighty prosperous these days. Clerks overflowing every door, 'tis all ledgers and balances now."

"But you are undisturbed in the melting shed?"

He stared at her, surprised. "Of course. They promised, didn't they? The Sperling sign is on the wall too, for all to see; just the Corncrake on the other house, but Corncrake and Spurs both on ours."

Arabella felt tears gather in her throat. Dear Harry. She had never thought that her father's proud sign would look down on Cheapside again. "And Harry?" she said with difficulty, sitting blindly on Prance's stool, fingers moving amongst familiar tools.

"He's like to be an alderman in his father's place. You know the old man died two years back?"

She shook her head. Damn him, who cared whether Harry was Lord Mayor; how did he look?

"Well, he did." Will lapsed into silence, unwrapping some silver he had brought, whistling beneath his breath.

Arabella stared at a punch she had picked up, its shape flickering through tears. No good asking; no good going, seeing, thinking. It was all over, long ago. One day we will look back and laugh. Harry had said, when I'm a portly alderman and you are terrorising half the fashionable world. She was sure that, alderman though he might become, he would never be portly. She thought of her hands on the muscle of his back, of . . . she shuddered slightly and looked up. "The City is quite rebuilt?" She had meant to ask how Harry looked, and did not.

"Aye, the foundation of Paul's is laid at last, Guildhall complete. We've done it all, just about."

And that summed it up, she supposed. They'd done it all, with precious little help from anyone; the past was cleared away, the future beckoning.

Arabella sighed, none of it was her affair any more. "What have you brought?"

Will showed her candelabra and pledge cups, as well as trinkets he made especially because they were easy to wager without arousing comment. She looked at them carefully and recognised an improvement in workmanship. She ought to pay Will more or he would set up on his own; Robert Sperling's memory would not hold him forever. "We must divide; it is time you were your own master, Will. My premises, your skill; half the profit each after buying such silver as you need."

He coloured with pleasure, but she knew from his expression that she was only just in time. "Do you want to go on using Prance?"

"Unless you can sell better elsewhere; with Cornish's using the house we have no outlet of our own, and at least Prance seems honest." She looked around her curiously. Silver was locked away of course, but shelves were loaded with objects she had never seen before. She stood and fingered one idly, then snatched back her hand. "They're popish images!"

Will nodded, he seemed quite placid about it. "Aye, I've been in here before. Prance supplies most of London's papists, a profitable trade since it's illegal. The Duke of York buys for his chapel here, and the Queen too, he told me, so I daresay he's safe enough from the parish constable."

Arabella regarded statuettes and rosaries with horrified fascination. Papists were close to cannibals since they believed they ate the very flesh of Christ; papists were slaves of a foreign tyrant; papists were sorcerers and plotters, shackled by bigotry to eternal hell. She had never met one until she came to court and still regarded them as she would a two-headed freak in a booth.

It was a shock to discover that Miles Prance was papist, a man she knew as an honest trader and skilled craftsman; even more startling to find soon after that Lord Aston was one too, a man whose bed she would very much have liked to share.

She could not resist asking Wexford what he thought of rampant popery at court next time she ate alone with him.

He looked at her in mild interest. "I wonder what made you ask? They are men and women as we are. I agreed with His Majesty when he issued his declaration of indulgence to their faith, and regretted that bigots in the Commons' House forced him to withdraw it."

"Bigots? They are Protestants, aren't they?"

"My dear Arabella, what is that to the matter? The Duke of York is Catholic and a bigot, Lauderdale Protestant and a bigot. Shaftesbury—" His lips tightened. "Well, we will not speak of him, since he uses all emotion for his own ends."

Arabella gulped her wine, she had seldom seen him look so grim. "He means to approach the King again."

"What makes you think so?"

"He said something yesterday which made me think it likely. I cannot remember his words precisely."

"Yesterday," repeated Wexford thoughtfully. "Could it be yesternight you meant? It would make your inability to remember detail more understandable."

Arabella found herself blushing, and was immediately annoyed. "Yes, in the night," she said deliberately. "As is likely with the task you set me to, my lord."

There was a long silence while she watched her fingers rather than his face. Perhaps he will call his valet in to beat me again, she thought bleakly. It was not the beating which rankled, but the fact that his valet had delivered it.

"Shaftesbury came today to seek audience with His Majesty," he said at last, sounding tired rather than angry. "Do you know what he said? Some pleasantry was needed to ease the moment when so much enmity lies between them, and the King bantered him with being the greatest whoremaster in England. He laughed, and said perhaps, if we count only Your Majesty's subjects in the reckoning."

"You told me once he was no gentleman," said Arabella dully. "It applies to his women as well as bastards, I suppose." The glamour of being Shaftesbury's mistress had somehow not survived her experience with Mistress Dawkins, although he knew nothing of it; at the same time, his drive towards political power left her aside. She could have found the issues interesting when the core of dispute was how and for what purposes England should be governed, but Shaftesbury discussed nothing of interest with her. So she betrayed such confidences as she learned, when she might have stayed silent if he had considered her at all.

She heard Wexford's chair scrape, but did not look up; a call for his valet or chill leave-taking so she was abandoned to sit out the meal alone, he was capable of either and she was uninterested which he chose. Was this the life which had recently seemed so splendid?

He came to stand beside her chair. "Look at me, Arabella."

159

She looked up obediently and he smiled faintly. "Well done, my wife. I disliked very much standing beside the King today, knowing you were the object of his jest, especially when others knew it too. I wished I was able to withdraw the condition on which I wed you, and earn myself the right to play the jealous husband. I ask you to allow me to do so now."

"I?"

"We made a bargain, if you remember. I keep my word, yet this contract I would like to set aside; the first time in all my life I changed my mind about such a matter."

Arabella regarded him dazedly. Was he intending to turn her into the street, then? He was leaning slightly on the ebony-tipped cane he affected lately but was self-possessed as always, green eyes uncomfortably intent. She shifted under his stare, pain in her back a reminder that she would manage very ill if left to fend for herself as she felt at present. "What is your meaning, my lord? In honour you cannot set me aside penniless."

There was little a powerful man could not do to an erring wife if he chose, as she very well knew.

"It's strange, isn't it? I am old enough to be your grandfather, but I should like to make a fresh bargain. A true marriage this time; the right to be jealous and the devil take politics, the King and Shaftesbury. Laugh if you will."

She did not laugh, instead regarded him with a dropped jaw. He meant it. This ancient furniture of courts really meant her to become his alone, offered to clatter petrified passion as if it could become real again. She nearly did laugh then.

But as she moved, her back flashed its warning again. Arabella dropped her eyes and stared at her hands, tight in her lap now. Her time with Shaftesbury was nearly done, whether she wanted it so or not. There were plenty of others to take his place of course, and she craved love with a young, strong man, not thinking of intrigue at all. But she was frightened. Apparently she conceived easily, and had learned nothing she judged of value to save her from childbearing.

She needed time to recover her health, to learn and choose and find her place again. Wexford surely was too old to be importunate or give her children, too old for such an unnatural contract to endure long. Exactly fifty years older than herself, she had discovered.

Arabella looked up. "Very well, my lord. I agree to remake our bargain. What is it you wish?"

"There is a crude directness about you, Arabella, which suited our original contract better than it does this moment. A younger man than I might be disconcerted to confront eyes and mouth more suited to the duelling field than promises of eternal love."

"It is still a bargain, is it not, my lord?" His breath was still sour and she still disliked him, she thought crossly. Eternal love; in the name of God, what next?

"As you say, it is still a bargain and one I shall enforce as I enforced the one before. I do not cheat, nor accept short change either. You are my wife from this night onward, until death do us part. It may not be for long, and I am too old to fight my own duels, but do not imagine I am incapable of ensuring that you keep your word."

Each syllable was laid in place beyond any possibility of doubting that he would do exactly as he said. Arabella took a deep breath; now he had admitted to some feeling for her, perhaps she could will herself into response, bring some shadow of grace to a relationship which neither should ever have contemplated. "I must see Shaftesbury alone once more, in decency if nothing else, and to avert his malice. I promise to speak with him only."

"Very well. So shall we go to bed, my dear?"

The same bald statement as on their wedding night; how little changed, after all.

I wish I could share the joke, she thought sardonically as she went before him up the staircase. She could have held her tightly boned sides with laughter at the sight they made, at Wexford's notion of how to retain his dignity while admitting infatuation. She wanted to scream and stamp and taunt at fate, which came to her in the guise of a proud old man, seeking lost youth. She wept instead, in the cold dawn after he left her.

Still, Arabella was not one to repine. She had agreed to her life being wrenched into a different course in full knowledge of what it entailed, and must make the best of it. She expected little good to follow, and so far as Wexford was concerned her expectations were fulfilled. He had been so unemotionally swift before that she scarcely thought of his visits as more than ceremony, now he came frequently but there was no pattern to it: he might come each night for a week, then not for a month or more. Sometimes he sent Catlin from the room when she was dressing Arabella, and stripped her naked again; occasionally he parted formally in the hall and woke her in the

161

middle of the night. She found herself on edge, because she needed a man yet hated him. Her body cried out for passion and was left desolate by slack-muscled pawing, responses she had hoped for out of reach.

In other ways, it was better than she expected. She was amused to discover that she created more gossip by living with her husband than ever she had by becoming Shaftesbury's mistress; at first she had to endure ill-natured jesting, even wagers followed by efforts to waylay her. But she was becoming more experienced in court habits, and Wexford proved himself as ruthless and omniscient as she expected. After two gallants more importunate than the rest were found beaten bloody by the watch, and another ruined at the gaming table, Arabella was left to find such diversion as she could with those who understood a man of Wexford's stamp.

He was also well read, knowledgeable and politically shrewd; a drily entertaining companion when the chance arose. He took her to Newmarket races and she found surprising delight in it. The countryside was beautiful, and she had never seen more than the fields clinging to London's skirts before. Cattle stood knee-deep in meadows thick with buttercups, slow rivers wound between undulating hills, which changed to wide-skied plain as they travelled north, the emptiness of it all very strange after London crowds. At Newmarket, Wexford hired a quiet mare for her, whose fine breeding and red-tassled saddlery added to her consequence, and Arabella's pleasure in mastering a new skill made her view him more kindly the whole time they were there. Long after, she remembered the joy of galloping in the wind of Newmarket heath, and considered it a gift given for good behaviour.

She no longer always lost gaming either, partly because Wexford chose her opponents, and also because he schooled her in matters of technique and profit once there was more time which they must spend together. She went to balls in gowns of lace and gauze; arms, neck and bosom flashing with jewels: Wexford did not dance, so she enjoyed these evenings best of all, even if she must change partners frequently to avert his suspicion.

For a while Arabella had been wretched over her appearance, every time she looked in the mirror she bewailed her drawn face and the lost gloss to her hair. As strain faded her old vitality returned, only a firm line to her lips and faint air of reserve betraying a change within herself. Both added to her loveliness; men still argued over whether there really were chestnut lights in her eyes and hair, now they also disputed over the contradictions of her nature. Above all, how one who promised passion with every curve of bone and laughing glance could shackle herself to a wrinkled gnome leaning on his cane by the ballroom door.

Catlin scolded her about Adam. Since Arabella won more often at the tables she sent money to Moll regularly, but had only once taken it herself. Wexford never mentioned Adam, and she was unsure what his reaction would be if she asked to visit St. Mary-le-Bon; she had freedom to come and go as she wished, but never escaped his vigilance. He took himself so seriously, it defeated imagination. Arabella dimly grasped that he knew he was incapable of satisfying or arousing her, yet his reaction was to double-lock her prison and refuse to accept defeat.

To be honest, she did not particularly want to see Adam.

"He is all right," she said crossly when Catlin nagged her one morning while dressing her hair. "If he is to live in St. Mary's, then it is best for him not to have visitors in coaches. You grew up in Whitefriars and I in the City, you know how cruel boys can be to one who appears different."

"He is different and might as well have some good of it. He hasn't had much joy from his life so far." She jerked angrily at Arabella's hair.

"Stop tugging this instant! How is he different? What do they know of him in St. Mary's?"

"Go and see for yerself, like I said. Why should I tell ye anything when all ye'll do is twitch yer pretty shoulders and go off to yer whisperings in Whitehall without giving him another thought?"

"I do think of him," said Arabella defensively. "I gave you money to take there last week and it can't be a full month since you took the last."

"Aye, money. He's not starving, but he's not well either. He's fair enough treated too, for I beat Moll with her own washing paddle when I found him too lame to walk one month, though some boys did it. But—"

"You scratched her face when she neglected him too," said Arabella sullenly. "He's better left to fend for himself, since I can't bring him here to live. Otherwise he'll grow up a weakling."

"Why can't ye bring him here?"

"Why can't . . . are you mad? What do you think Wexford would say if I brought my bastard to live here now? How old is he?"

Catlin shot her a venomous glance. "Ye should know, since he's yours."

Five, thought Arabella with a distinct feeling of shock. She had visualized Adam as whining on hands and knees as he had been on the only occasion she had seen him, as unappealing as when he was a babe. He must be standing, talking, now. She met Catlin's eyes in the mirror. "Can you imagine Wexford allowing himself to be the joke of the court if some slum brat from St. Mary's were acknowledged as his wife's bastard? He might have passed Adam off as his five years ago, but refused; he would throw him in the street and say he was serving wench's get if I brought him here now."

Catlin sighed. "Ye ought to see him, mam. 'Tisn't right how he is. Whatever else ye can't do, ye can at least visit him once in a while."

Arabella refused to answer, and left the room with something like a flounce. The boy was kept secure, otherwise she would have gone; the past was past, and must not live again.

All the same, she was unable to forget Adam as completely as before. Catlin continued to tug at her hair, fastened ribbons with unsympathetic hands, sighed often and snapped pots and brushes on her dressing top with disapproving cracks. Arabella boxed her ears, but eventually began to consider how she could reach St. Mary's.

In the end, she ordered the coach to take her on the fashionable drive to the hamlet at Knight's Bridge; as roads dried in spring ladies often drove there to pick primroses and stroll along pleasant walks by the stream. It was a haunt of footpads in the dark but safe enough by day, though Wexford provided her with four outriders for the journey. The coachman would certainly tell his master that she had gone to St. Mary's instead of Knight's Bridge, but she could not help it. She would face that when it came.

Arabella thrust away knowledge that this was the first time she had deceived Wexford in the three years since they agreed to their fresh contract, and he would not take deception lightly, whatever might be her reasons.

She looked out of the coach windows, glazed in the newly fashionable style in place of the old leather curtains, and wondered how much longer he could possibly live.

Chapter Fifteen

Arabella had forgotten how tumble-
down Moll's cottage was; reed thatch and daub looked attractive
when seen from a coach on the way to Newmarket, in reality
wind drove straight through flimsy walls and feet sank into
mud on the floor.

Moll was straining at a vast tub of washing, and did not
recognise her. "Who'll ye be, my fine lady? If 'tis potions ye
want, ye've come to the wrong place."

Arabella shuddered, she had never outlived her memories
of Mistress Dawkins. "No, not potions. I've brought you money
and wanted to see Adam myself this time."

Moll peered at her uncertainly; her face was running with
sweat from the fire needed to boil so much laundry, her hair
straggling limply into her eyes. She looked drained of everything but enough sinew to work her paddle, although she had
been buxom when she came as Adam's wet nurse. "My lady
of Wexford. Come to take yer whelp off, 'ave yer?"

"No . . . that is, I wanted to see him." Arabella was taken
aback by the offhand disrespect of her tone. Wexford's servants
were perfectly drilled, even when his valet beat her he had
done so with complete impassivity.

Moll jerked her head. "'Elp yerself."

There was a pack of children squalling in one corner, a girl
picking ruffles at the table, another coughing savagely on straw
underneath. Arabella had no idea which of the many was Adam,
and was ashamed to ask.

Moll slapped down her paddle and regarded her derisively.
"Don't know yer own, do yer? 'E'll be the one on 'is own, ye
can be sure."

Arabella picked her way across the littered floor, there was plenty of food but of the coarsest and least appetising kind. A pitcher of congealed gruel, a baby playing with a cartwheel loaf in the dust, home-brewed ale in a jug giving off an aggressively potent smell. There was no indication that a man lived here but Moll was heavily pregnant, belly thrusting from skin and bone.

The children were like a nest of snakes, coiled in and out of each other, some crying, the rest apparently content to fondle their fellows. One sat slightly apart, legs drawn up, face on his knees.

"Adam?" said Arabella tentatively, and then louder when he gave no sign of hearing her. Her throat felt tight, for this was the child of Harry's love, tenderness possible at last. She would be patient, admit her mistakes and be forgiven; then they could start afresh.

"Ye'll 'ave to give 'im a kick afore 'e takes notice," said Moll. She sounded exhausted rather than unkind. "I never met a more blockish child, begging yer pardon of course, mam."

Her child blockish. Stupider than the sweepings of St. Mary's. Arabella was humiliated by the thought of it, and shook Adam's shoulder more roughly than she intended. He scrambled to his feet with a swift, defensive leap and stood looking at her in stupefaction. She never thought what an apparition she must appear in her red velvet and rakish bonnet, feathers bobbing in the draught; instead his open-mouthed alarm annoyed her. "Well, sirrah, can you speak or are you dumb as well?"

He closed his mouth and nodded.

Arabella tapped her foot. "Well, which is it?"

He shot a harried glance at Moll but did not answer.

Arabella studied him, dismayed. A moment before she had wanted to kiss and hold him, grovel with repentance, explain away neglect and make amends; remorse shrivelled when she found herself confronted by an ungainly simpleton. He was as ugly as she remembered, or more so, since memory softened most things. His hair was coarsely dark and stuck out where ringworm patched his skull. He was quite warmly clad, since Moll was honest over money, but his face was unhealthy white, hands a coarse, peasant red. Nothing about him seemed to fit; legs and arms loose-jointed; dark hair and pale eyes, no longer the baby blue she remembered but ice-grey; head over-large for his frail body; defensive fear in place of the drive and courage she expected from Harry's son.

Moll came over and hauled him out from behind the rest. "Ye'd be staring at each other all day at that rate. Bow to the lady, Adam." She shoved hard enough for his nose to touch his knees in the parody of a bow. "Taught 'im fine manners, I 'ave, never say Moll don't give value for money, eh, Adam?" She shifted her grip to the scruff of his neck and shook him with a kind of rough affection. "It's yer ma come to see ye, boy. Ain't ye lucky, then? I told 'im about 'is grand ma."

He wept. Hanging from her hand, mouth open and nose slobbering, he wept in long, desolate wails.

"In the name of God, what ails the boy? Can he speak?" Arabella had never fainted in her life but felt close to it as revulsion swept softness aside. Adam was not Harry's love but retribution from an unforgiving God.

"Aye, 'e can speak, but 'e don't that often bother. I tell ye straight, mam, I can't reach 'im. 'E don't give much trouble, does what 'e's told like, but 'e don't mix with the rest, and the big boys set on 'im if 'e goes out. 'E's neat with lace, though," she added judiciously. "'Elps Meg, don't 'e, love?"

"Aye, 'e do." The child at the table ducked her head and gave a gap-toothed grin.

Even that gutter get has more manners and address than mine, thought Arabella bitterly. Suddenly she regretted very much that she had not birthed Shaftesbury's child, had others in whom she might feel some pride. Now feeling had been slaughtered Arabella sensed the immensity of her loss, the void where love for her son had been only moments before.

Moll dropped Adam in a heap on the floor and shuffled back to her washtub. "Are ye thinking of taking 'im?"

"I suppose I'll have to soon," said Arabella reluctantly. "God knows how. Is there nowhere here where he might do better?"

Moll shook her head. "I'm 'onest, see? I'd do better if I wasn't. I take some o' yer money for my living but the rest I spends on Adam, though little good it does 'im. There's not many 'ereabouts'd do the same."

And Moll has not much longer to live, thought Arabella, looking at her. She could not be much over thirty but looked as old as Wexford. "I'll let you know," she said aloud. "Catlin must search around St. James and find lodgings where we can keep an eye on him. Now he's not a baby, he should survive as well there as here."

"Can't 'e live with thee, mam?" asked Moll bluntly. "'Tis what 'e needs, 'e's not like any child I ever 'andled."

"No," said Arabella shortly. "I see you and Catlin have put your heads together."

And no again, she thought, driving home. She could manage to care a little about Adam when she did not see him, but detested the idea of that feeble snivelling creature underfoot every day, destroying the last vestige of Harry in her mind. When she left Moll's hut Adam had still been lying where he was dropped, face hidden in his hands again.

Wexford was out when she returned, and they were bidden to a masque at the Duke of York's in the evening, so there was only the short coach ride to Whitehall to endure his company. He talked impersonally of events, which were indeed startling enough to absorb attention. Shaftesbury was recently released from the Tower after more than a year's imprisonment for an intemperate attack on Parliament, which he alleged to be illegally constituted since eighteen years had passed without elections. The King had judged his moment, arrested him while the Commons smarted from his insults, and exacted an apology before and, so men whispered, his nature less restrained after months of brooding on his wrongs.

Yet Arabella could not keep her mind on what Wexford said, only the tone of his voice. She was certain that he knew she had not been to Knight's Bridge, for he did not once ask about it.

The Duke of York's galleries were crowded. Gambling tables were laid ready, candles burned by the thousand, music sounded softly beyond the shifting crowd. The ostensible reason for the gathering was a masque acted by ladies of the court, but no one imagined that such insipid entertainment would be sufficient to beguile a whole evening, nor were many likely to stop talking long enough to grasp the gist of its scenes. Satin-gowned ladies flirted over spread fans, brocade-suited gentlemen used feathered hats and precisely calculated bows to indicate the social standing of those they greeted in relation to themselves.

Young gallants watched new arrivals and boasted of which women they had bedded, while the ladies whispered of the latest scandal; the Duke of Monmouth, the King's bastard son, was appointed Captain General of all the armed forces of England and Scotland, and had bedded three wenches in one night as celebration. Or so he said.

168

Arabella and Wexford parted when she was asked to join a galliard by a fop whose coat was so stiffly boned he creaked at every move. She sighed and accepted, she enjoyed such evenings as a rule but had not shaken off the gloom Adam induced in her.

"Lady Wexford, your humble servant." A man bowed over her hand immediately the galliard ended, lips brushing her hand closer than etiquette demanded.

"Why . . . why . . ." She stared at him as he straightened. "George! George Jeffries! What are you doing here?" He was as richly dressed as most and less foolishly than many.

He looked around, and laughed. "Why, I am where I said I would be, my lady. Matching your luck and beauty with my wits so we both achieve our ends."

She forgot the fop at once, drawing Jeffries aside and pelting him with questions. It was good to see someone—anyone—with whom she need not pretend. He was flushed by heavy drinking and garrulous in consequence, eager for admiration. "You realise I've only two more steps to go: Lord Chief Justice and Lord Chancellor. Now I've reached so far, I'll have these last within five years."

Arabella laughed. "It's more than just a couple of paces to two of the highest offices in the land. I wager you a silver casket you're not Lord Chancellor in five years, nor ten either."

"Done," he said instantly. "And I will give you a gold brooch if I fail. I'm recorder of the City already, Sir George Jeffries and Solicitor General to the Duke of York. I told you I'd practise in Westminster Hall one day." He had only just begun to bloat with prosperity, but his manner was louder than she remembered, as if he was well used to bellowing at prisoners; or perhaps she had become more elegant during the gulf of time since leaving Bevil's house.

"How is Bevil?" she asked. "I have not called in years, but—"

He laughed, a grating whinny which made her feel as if everyone must be watching them. "Too vulgar for my lady, eh? I don't blame you. He's not dead, but I don't keep such company myself nowadays." He contemplated the silken crowd surrounding them complacently.

"I must go," said Arabella, without reluctance. Had he really coarsened, or would she find all her old friends rough now? Was Adam a distorted mirror of Harry after all, and he only

169

so splendid in her mind? "You said you were recorder of the City," she added, despite herself. "What does that mean?"

"You are chosen by the Corporation, preside at the Old Bailey and the Lord Mayor's court quite often, the senior law officer of the City. It's an honour and a step to greater things."

"Lord Chancellor for instance," said Arabella drily. "You know the City aldermen well, then?"

"I know most men I need to know by now. Women too, and still more for pleasure." He bowed in mock gallantry.

"Do you know Henry Cornish? Someone told me he was to be alderman, and he used to be a neighbor of mine."

His expression darkened. "I know him. He is alderman for Bassishaw ward, a goddamned overbearing swine of a man. You are fortunate not to be still his neighbour."

Arabella's heart hammered; he knew Harry, had spoken to him only a few days past, perhaps. It must surely be a recommendation that Jeffries disliked him. Her thoughts rebounded from depression; Harry returned to his pedestal again and she immediately forgot Adam. "Does . . . does he prosper?"

"Aye, as merchants and bankers with their percentages always do. Yet now the King is trying to raise a loan in the City, he is one who speaks against it."

I'm not surprised, thought Arabella, but was uninterested in loans. She wanted to know whether Harry's wife was beautiful and how many children he had. Other children, who would look and act as he did instead of like a spineless dolt. She looked blindly at the throng, hearing nothing of Jeffries' babbling about his successes as recorder, and found her gaze crossed by another. Across the gallery a man was watching her intently, with no trace of admiration in his stare. He was vaguely familiar and she fumbled with recollection, then stilled abruptly. She had last seen him as a customer in Miles Prance's shop.

She tugged at Jeffries' sleeve. "George, who is that man over there by the fireplace?"

He looked annoyed, since he was in the middle of describing some dispute in which his judgment had been much commended. "Who? Oh, Edward Coleman, the Duke of York's secretary. At least, he's dismissed for popery but still mighty intimate with the Duke's affairs. He's below your touch nowadays, although he looks well struck with you, I'll own. Shall I fetch him?" He plunged into the crowd before she could stop him.

He towed Coleman over almost by force; George Jeffries

had taken to court intrigue like a runaway horse to its stall, and enjoyed the embarrassment of others. "My lady, may I introduce a sincere admirer, your humble servant, Edward Coleman?"

Coleman bowed and mumbled something, he looked as alarmed as Arabella felt. "I did not intend to presume, my lady. I admired from a distance only."

She did not believe him. He had been interested, speculative, not admiring. She decided to take a risk, since she was only interested in what use he might make of the strangely intimate scene he had witnessed when she met Will. "We have met before, sir, but for the life of me I cannot recall where. Can you, pray?"

He looked at her squarely. "No, my lady. Our paths are not often likely to cross."

She sighed with relief, how pleasant to meet a man of honour for once. He must be curious but would not probe. "I fancy it was some while ago when I was less familiar with the court. Sir George tells me you serve the Duke, as he does."

Coleman looked uncomfortable. "In some ways, my lady, but the Duchess more. I cannot hold an official position."

"A papist," said Jeffries bluntly. "And so unable to take the test. There are always alarms in Parliament about papists and their treasons."

"I am sure Mr. Coleman is no traitor," said Arabella warmly. The images Prance sells, she thought, enlightened. Coleman must have gone to purchase for the papists of York's household, no wonder he will not speak of seeing me there.

"My dear Arabella," said Wexford at her elbow. "I wish to present you to the Duchess of York. I believe your acquaintance will accept your apologies."

In common politeness she attempted to introduce Jeffries and Coleman to him, but Wexford stared at them as if she was presenting a pair of footmen and bore her off without waiting for her to finish. "You should judge your company better," he said when she protested. "York's household is a mixture of the dangerous, the unsavoury and the stupid. Jeffries is not stupid although he lacks ordinary sense, otherwise those two combine all these undesirable qualities to admiration. It would not surprise me if both ended on the scaffold, and I would prefer that you did not accompany them."

She looked at him in astonishment. "Two of York's own

household? Surely not, my lord. And I assure you, we spoke only of trifles."

"Indeed? You looked intent enough to me, even if your interest was not theirs." He would say no more, and appeared asleep in the coach when they clattered home through empty streets.

He summoned her to the library in the morning.

She shut the door behind her, knowing he was likely to be at his most insufferable and not anxious for the servants to hear. He was seated by the fire, feet on a stool, ankles crossed, fingers steepled. Although he must have been tired after standing through the night in York's galleries, nothing about his appearance suggested it, each hair of his wig in place, aigrettes of his silver-laced coat precisely aligned. You had to admire his sheer durability, reflected Arabella as she seated herself opposite. She was not going to stand like an errant footman.

"You wished to speak to me, my lord?"

"Don't pretend to me, Arabella. You expected this interview and are relieved you were not forced to wait longer."

She laughed. "As usual, my lord, you are right. I went yesterday to see Adam."

"Why not tell me first instead of after? You knew I would discover it, and merely forced me to beat my coachman for a fault he could not help."

"I was afraid you would forbid me, and knew you well enough to know that once you had done so, I would be prevented from ever going." She recognised that he respected honesty and probably very little else except her beauty. "I did not want to go, but felt I ought."

"Why?"

"It's hard to explain . . ." She stopped, her feelings towards Adam impossible to explain. "I don't love the child, although yesterday I went hoping . . . thinking that perhaps I could. Instead, he aroused the worst in me. I am ashamed to say it, but cannot help myself. Even so, I can't simply abandon him."

"Why not?"

She stared at him, such a simple solution had never occurred to her.

"There are a good few bastard gentry roaming the streets of London, nobles too. One more will make no difference and he is as likely to make a life for himself without your interest as with it. Is he worth your trouble?"

The question was jerked out while she still fumbled with

what else he said, and she answered without reflection. "In truth he seems half-witted. That is . . . with care, I daresay . . ." Her voice trailed away and he smiled sourly.

"The truth suits you best, Arabella, so let us set aside hypocrisy. The answer is no, is it not?"

She hesitated, unable to dismiss Harry's son like unwanted offal. "The answer is, I don't know. Moll doesn't understand him and I could not tell which one he was yesterday. Catlin is fond of him, I think."

"Very well. Let us delay any decision until he has developed sufficiently for you to be certain of his worth. As you expected, I have given orders that you are not to go to St. Mary's again, but I will also instruct the parish constable to inform me when the woman Moll dies; I understand she is sick. Then the boy will be fetched for me to see and judge where he may best go in his own interests."

Arabella stammered some kind of thanks, all the while aware that she would be deeply ashamed for Wexford to see Adam. "He—he is not used to great houses, he may seem—would seem a trifle clumsy to you, my lord."

"Well, we shall see. You already called him half-witted, and if he is also uncouth then he's best apprenticed in the slums. If he shows some promise I will find a better trade, it is up to him. Seven is the usual age for orphans to be set with a master, and we must hope that Moll lives until then."

He would say no more, nor did he punish her, so on the whole Arabella felt she had been fortunate. Catlin was philosophical too, with the fatalism of the poor who are used to chance shaping their destiny. A pattern had been set for Adam although he was unaware of it, and a term to his stay with Moll; it would simply have to do for the moment. Arabella hid a hope that Moll would outlive Wexford: she shrank more than she would have believed possible from exhibiting Harry's son as an object for her husband's scorn.

In the event, both died within weeks of each other.

Wexford suffered an apoplexy in July 1678 after a long night in attendance on the King, but with the toughness characteristic of him lingered several weeks without quite losing his grip on the world around. He was hazed in his mind but by no means devoid of understanding. Arabella sat beside him sometimes, surprising in herself a faint stir of tenderness. They had been married six years and she had disliked and feared him most of that time, but he was not a negligible man and refused to die except on his own terms. In a strange way, she would miss him even while her heart lightened at the thought of gaining her freedom again.

She turned from the window and went over to the bed as he stirred. It was breathlessly hot, London empty of company, the King at Newmarket with his closest cronies.

"Is . . . there anyone in the room?"

His words were so faint, she had to bend to hear them. "No, my lord. Do you desire your valet?"

His head moved slightly in denial. "The estate is . . . entailed, and my will not . . . generous to you."

She stared at him. "Why tell me when it is too late to change your mind?"

He gave a faint choke of laughter, only about the second sign of genuine amusement she could remember in all their years together. "I did . . . not intend you . . . to keep others in my bed . . . at my expense. Let them pay for themselves. You'll find the payers a more honourable sort."

It was her turn to laugh. "I thank you for your continuing care of me, my lord."

His lips twisted. "I loved you, Arabella. I fought it . . . and called myself dolt . . . and lost. I never admitted it, did I? But you knew."

She wished she could say she had loved him even a little, but she never had and he understood her too well for pretence to serve. Instead, she bent and kissed him gently on the lips, the only gesture of true affection she had ever given him, and a few hours later, he died. By then, the room had filled with his children and she was pushed to one side, but he was unconscious and knew nothing of it.

The new Lord Wexford gave her the will to read in privacy, which was considerate since she inherited nothing except her clothes, the furniture of her private apartments and a thousand pounds a year. She encountered scant consideration otherwise: Wexford's children detested her for making their father appear ridiculous and had spent the years since her marriage in the expectation that she would succeed in making away with most of their rights. When they discovered that she had not, their attitude was too set for change and she was given a month to take what was her due and vacate Wexford House.

So news of Moll's death could not have been more unwelcome; Arabella did not remember how much she had dreaded exhibiting Adam to Wexford and merely wished he was still alive to settle the boy's affairs as he had promised.

"You must find somewhere for him quickly," she told Catlin. "Somewhere near and we'll think about him later."

"Why not take him yerself, then? The old lord can't stop ye now."

"My God, no! I owe it to Wexford not to bring my bastard into his house before his bones are cold." And I've my way to make, she thought bleakly. She had been excited by the thought of freedom at last, but at the moment its problems were more obvious than its benefits.

Catlin found a sempstress off St. James's who was willing to take Adam for a few shillings a month. It was a strange area as stews were tumbled down and new rows built around the Palace; some parts were as rich as any in London and then around the next corner would be filthy hovels awaiting demolition. It suited Arabella's purpose very well, parts being respectable enough for her to visit without remark, others sufficiently rough for a stray boy to pass unnoticed.

Arabella promptly forgot Adam again in the hurly-burly of getting herself settled. She enlisted Bevil's aid, since he showed not the slightest ill-will over her long neglect providing she paid him well, although he was too stout and gout-ridden to move from his own hearth.

He listened to her plans to set herself up in lodgings, much shocked by the paltry provision made for her. "I know a man who will find you something. I sit at home and let others do the walking now, but I've both hands on my affairs, never fear."

"I shall want three rooms and an attic for Catlin. I can't manage on less," Arabella said ruefully. "Not if I'm to establish myself again. A good address, but I can't afford more than fifty pounds a year in rent. I shall need money to spare for clothes and hiring a coach."

Bevil nodded. "No good scamping the edges and catching a baron instead of an earl again. At fifty pounds the address cannot be of the best."

"It must be good, though. And this time, earl or no earl, I'm not taking an old man. I wish it wasn't another nine years before the House of the Spurs becomes mine again to rent at a profit."

Bevil chuckled. "Aye, you'd make Cornish's pay then. Henry's a devilish warm man from all I hear, but might be handsomely held to ransom for space he cannot manage without."

Her lips parted. "Have you seen him?"

"A couple of years back, him and his goodwife. Pretty little thing. He's in bad odour with the King, though, for opposing a loan from the City. You'd skin him right enough if you could haul him up before royal judges."

"No," said Arabella hastily. "I wouldn't want to do that. You'll send me a message as soon as your man discovers good lodgings?" Trust Harry to choose a pretty wife.

An anxious time followed while she packed boxes and bags, waiting for Bevil to send her word. She could have taken a hackney and looked herself, but was confident that Bevil's creatures would manage better on their own. She had offered him a hundred guineas if he found exactly what she wanted, and thought that for such a bait he would squeeze someone into bankruptcy if necessary, simply to take his rooms.

At last a footman announced that an attorney was asking to see her and she flew down the long staircase, forgetful of dignity in her excitement. She was weary of Wexford House behind its mourning blinds, weary of suspense, and wanted to start her life again. Jesus, she thought, I'll soon be as old as Wexford.

"You are very welcome," she said frankly to the sober-suited figure waiting for her in the hall. "Have you found just the place I need?"

"Why, I think so, my lady." He sounded amused, and she looked at him sharply, eyes narrowed.

"Do I know you? You are Mr. Sperling's man of affairs, aren't you?"

"Aye, my lady. And yes, Miss Arabella, I do know you. Richard Goodenough, if you remember." He flourished his hat in a parody of court fashion.

"I remember," she said flatly. "Cheat, forger and coward. Does my father's spirit visit you at night?"

He grinned. "No, never. Does he visit you? Shaftesbury's strumpet and wife to a lecher half a century older, I should think he might grieve over you before he worries overmuch with me."

"Get out!" said Arabella in a shaking voice. "Get out this instant! Whatever made Bevil think I'd take anything from you?"

"He's old and forgetful. I daresay he doesn't remember a

fraud twelve years cold, there've been so many since. I have served him, but now chiefly serve myself and prosper very well. This time, though, I thought it might be amusing to carry out his orders. You'd be a fool to turn down the rooms I've found."

Arabella hesitated. She wanted to order a footman to kick him down the steps, but with ten days to go before she lost possession of Wexford House she could not afford to be self-indulgent. "Where are they?"

"Come now, Arabella. You'll have to do better than that. Ask me nicely, with the smile I admired as an apprentice. You still tap your foot when you are in a rage, I see."

She stared at him, mouth a hard, tight line. "Tell me and go, or don't tell me and go. I'll neither smile nor beg from you, when I'd sooner see you branded for the thief you are."

"Strange, isn't it? Harry Cornish told me the same when I offered to pack a jury for him. So the case was tried by George Jeffries, and Cornish lost. And I am still unbranded." He drew a paper out of his pocket and put it in her hand. "For old times' sake, Arabella; three good rooms at fifty pounds a year in Bear Street, Leicester Fields. It's just by Leicester House, you won't do better at the price." He sauntered out, fingering furniture and looking at pictures as if they were his own possessions.

After a visit to Bear Street, she was forced to admit that he was right. Leicester Fields was not St. James's, of course, but development there was prettily laid out, the rooms in an end house so she could glimpse fresh-laid turf in Leicester Square from the salon window. Everything was in the latest fashion, the salon hung with straw-coloured damask, the dining room freshly plastered, bedroom papered with the new Chinese wall-paper which was all the rage. She wondered a trifle uneasily what had happened to the last occupants, but put the thought aside: it was too late to do anything about them, so she might as well relish her good fortune.

Chapter Sixteen

Arabella enjoyed herself enormously settling into her new home. She had never regarded Wexford House as a home, although she came to appreciate its austere spaces as memory faded of the cramped City houses to which she had been accustomed. The last time she had been called on to make a home, it was in the Cornish vault; so it was pure pleasure to place the elegant furniture Wexford had left her, to change her mind and hesitate over hangings. Without realising it, her judgment had been moulded by six years of contact with court tastes and when she was satisfied at last, her salon was uncluttered, swagged curtains supplying richness, her best pieces of furniture shown off by space. The dining room was less as she liked it; money seemed to melt away now she must pay for everything herself, so better furnishing there would have to await the time when she found a rich protector.

For she had no wish to remarry. She wanted a man for enjoyment and profit, to live as she had never done before, for the sheer delight of it. Husbands meant intolerable restraints, quarrels, duty. Children, too. After the exertion of moving into Bear Street her back hurt again and the faint wish she had once felt for a child she could feel pride in disappeared completely.

She was determined not to spoil everything by haste. She was not rich and had overspent disgracefully, but with care and luck at the gaming table could afford to wait and take her choice. There was never any shortage of men anxious to bed a beautiful widow, but few were likely to reach the exacting standard she set for herself. She had no intention of becoming a pox-ridden courtesan hanging on the fringes of court, which meant extreme care if she was to avoid marriage yet remain fashionable.

Wexford died on the last day of August, and had been ill for a month before. It was mid-October before Arabella felt ready to take on the world again, and went to a morning party at Lady St. Albans' house in St. James's Square; they were friends of Wexford's, and would be of use in reintroducing her into court society. Henry Jermyn, Lord St. Albans, had leased all the fields between Pall Mall and Pickadil Bob's just after the Restoration and had almost completed twenty years of profitable development. St. James's Square was his, his own house in one corner, Jermyn Street named for him as was St. Albans Street, while King Street and Duke of York Street commemorated a lifetime of ultimately profitable loyalty. St. James's Street was growing before he started his planned grid of streets, May Fair Fields encroached upon, the political history of a decade petrifying in bricks and mortar as this part of London expanded year by year; the defunct Cabal commemorated by Arlington, Bennet and Clifford streets; a royal bastard in Grafton Street; indomitable old Monck, Duke of Albemarle, who had fought on both sides in the Civil War, engineered the Restoration and stayed in his house there, carrying on government throughout the plague when the court fled, fitly remembered in Albemarle Street.

It gave Arabella a pleasant feeling of immortality to see men she knew and events through fields only years or months before. She wondered how much more London would have grown before the same time passed again, and what would have happened to her.

Lord St. Albans normally carried an air of settled confidence with him, which she could well understand, when everywhere he looked he could see his mark set for posterity. That morning, however, it was different, nor were the people gathered in his salon indulging in the decorous chitchat of morning gatherings. Groups mumbled in corners, furtively watched by the rest; loud argument came from people usually urbanely mannered, while lackeys fingered pistols, apparently more than ready for a fight.

Arabella looked at it all in astonishment, the atmosphere of panic unmistakable.

"It's Godfrey, you know," a languid youth said, fluttering his fan. "He hasn't been seen in nearly a week."

"Godfrey?" Arabella racked her brains hastily, not wanting to commit some gaffe.

"Oates swore depositions to him, if you remember. Now Parliament is due to reassemble and the rumour is that papists have murdered Godfrey."

She could make no sense of it, although she did remember talk of some recanted Jesuit called Oates spilling stories of Catholic plots against the King's life. For the benefit of York, presumably. "Titus Oates accused Godfrey?" she asked cautiously, those unversed in the latest gossip were regarded with contempt.

Fortunately, he was only too glad to tell her, and launched into a long explanation she found excessively difficult to follow. In essence, it appeared that a City parson called Tonge and the informer, Oates, who both seemed to Arabella more than a little mad, had sworn before King and council that there was a vast Catholic conspiracy to overset the nation. Assassins would kill the King (swords, staves and poison all mentioned), thousands of Catholics fall on their Protestant neighbours in bloody massacre; French money would flow, the Jesuits direct the whole business and place the Duke of York on the throne as their tool. This statement Oates had sworn by solemn oath before Sir Edmund Berry Godfrey, a Westminster JP, who was now missing.

Arabella shared the popular horror of Catholicism as something aggressively un-English, the threat it represented made worse by her ignorance of its teachings, but she possessed a practical mind and had unconsciously absorbed some of Wexford's attitudes. When the young man finished, she observed lightly, "It sounds like miming death to the Pope on Christmas Eve. If Oates swore to the Privy Council, then any deposition he made to a magistrate cannot be vital; Godfrey has probably gone into the country on business. What does his wife say?"

The boy gave a knowing grin. "He's not married, nor the man to be so, so 'tis whispered. Oates the same, beyond doubt. Perhaps 'tis why he chose Godfrey for his swearings, that and their families come from near the same place. A strange coincidence of taste and past, as you might say." He giggled. "Celibate Jesuits draw such to them."

Arabella felt blood come to her face. She was not shocked, but knew he would never have ventured such a remark if Wexford had been alive. She left him with a cold nod and went over to some acquaintance, conscious of how well black taffeta suited her skin. Nobody even noticed her. They were not deliberately rude, but so preoccupied with papists conspiring behind every bush they could think of nothing else. French money...Jesuits...murder...Shaftesbury was right about rot in high places. Shall we all be murdered in our beds before Parliament can meet? Oh, la la, thought Arabella in disgust. They are as bad as the mob in the City during the fire, killing foreigners because of talk about fireballs thrown by French or Dutch.

As if in tune with her thoughts, Lord Southampton's obese lady turned to her. "Do you know, my dear, they say 'tis all part of the same? The papists burned down the City intending to destroy us all, but the flames died before they reached Whitehall. Now they try again in a more cunning way, but there have been a dozen fires these past few days, started by Jesuits, I don't doubt. We shall be burned in our beds unless they are clapped up directly." Her watery eyes peered anxiously from rolls of fat.

"The great fire was investigated." Arabella felt herself expert on the fire if nothing else. "It was caused by a great wind and a fool of a baker, who tried to blame his carelessness on others for fear he would be torn apart by the rabble."

"No, no, no! That shows how cunning papists are! They can make people believe anything with their arts." She lowered her voice. "Do you know how Jesuits send good Protestants out of their wits with a secret spell they chant?"

There was more, much more of the same; bored, Arabella decided on the spur of the moment to visit Adam. She had been too busy to see him in the six months since she visited St. Mary's, but he was only a short hackney drive away—what luxury to decide and go, accountable to no one.

The sempstress with whom he lodged lived in a tumbledown block between the disreputable Catherine Wheel Inn, renowned for its whores and conveniently placed for the palace, and St. James's Place, a modern row tumbling into half-built brick at one end. Although Londoners were accustomed to the new sprawl of their city, it was still difficult to avoid shock at stepping from hedgerow to town square, from stews to gentlemen's lodging and back again within a dozen paces, and nowhere was this easier to do than in the half-finished streets off St. James's.

Bricklayers jeered at Arabella's gown, and ragged urchins pelted her with mud as she stepped from the hackney. "Wait," she said to the jervey. "Don't drive off and leave me here. There's sixpence for you now, and double if you wait."

He swore he'd be gutswoggled if he'd leave her, and slashed his whip at the boys, who ran off streaming blood.

Arabella had to hold her skirts out of wet rubbish, provoking more derision, but took no notice. The thin-skinned did not survive in London. The house leaned crazily and clearly awaited demolition, its stairs and passages filthy, although Mistress Temple curtsied with the grace of one accustomed to serving the wealthy.

"Waiting woman to Lady Buckingham I was, mam, and highly thought of. Milady used to tease her friends with half-promises when they begged her to loan me to them, but she never did. I had a way with flounces and ruffles no one else could match, until my eyesight faded and milady hired another in my place. I iron and set by touch now, and do the best work this side of St. James's." She beamed with simple pride and launched into more tales of Lady Buckingham, for whom she seemed to have remarkable respect, considering she had been turned out of her place as soon as her fingers slowed.

"Is Adam in?" Arabella cut her short at last.

She looked surprised. "Of course. Seldom goes out, he don't, although once we walked together to look at Wexford House. Before you left, that was."

Arabella was touched by Adam wanting to see where she lived; perhaps he had improved. Mistress Temple was certainly more genteel than Moll and must be a better influence on the boy. "Does he talk much now?" she asked as they toiled upstairs. The poorer you were, the higher you lived unless the cellar was particularly unsavoury, when the poorest of all burrowed in darkness there.

"Talk? I dunno as he talks much, milady." She seemed puzzled by the idea of anyone interrupting her flow of words. "He's no trouble, though. Catlin persuaded me to take him, but now I like having him around."

Oh God, thought Arabella, heart sinking, he's just the same.

At first, hope flared when she saw him. When they reached Mistress Temple's tiny attic he was standing on a chair, head poked through a skylight, and as he scrambled down she saw a likeness to Harry. It was fleeting, the set of his head and the way he stood, a tight line of mouth she had only seen gaping before, then it was gone. He shuffled and looked away, hands twitching as if he wanted to cover his face as he had last time she came.

"Here's milady Wexford come to see you, Adam dear. Aren't

you a lucky boy? Come here and let me tidy you, then perhaps she'll let you bow over her hand and show the manners I've taught you." Mrs. Temple chattered on, dusting him off and twitching clothes as if he was a dummy, at least bridging intolerable silence between them.

This time, I'll make him say something and not go until he does, thought Arabella grimly. He came over reluctantly, urged by scolding pushes, eyes on the floor.

"Aren't you going to look at me, Adam?" she asked as gently as she was able.

He shook his head. She looked down at him in exasperation, wondering what to do next.

"Come on, Adam," said Mrs. Temple briskly. "My lady Wexford takes the trouble to climb all them dratted stairs to see you, and you stand like a booby. Bow like a good boy, or it'll be two days of water without bread for you, and I'm sure she'll not trouble to come again."

He looked up. "I climb the stairs at least twenty times a day."

"Well!" gasped Mrs. Temple. "Of all the rude boys! I'm sure you don't deserve a roof over your head when you behave no better than a gutter urchin to milady." She cuffed him, hard.

"No, don't scold him," said Arabella, relieved he had at least spoken. "Are you going to bow or not, Adam?"

He hesitated and then took the hand she extended to him and bowed clumsily, before scuttling off to the far corner of the room. He still seemed as awkwardly loose-jointed as a puppet, and very small for his age. Tam had been younger when he died of plague, but far taller and more robustly built. Arabella had a vague feeling that she ought to talk to him but had no idea what might interest this strange child who was her son, and Mrs. Temple's chatter distracted her. "Do you want to stay here, Adam?" she asked abruptly.

Mrs. Temple stopped in mid-flow. "Why, are you thinking of taking him, milady?"

"I don't know. I asked Adam what he wanted, perhaps it is for him to choose." He was looking at her now, body tense, face bone-white.

"You don't want to go, do you, lovey? Leave what you know again when you've just settled in nicely?" There was fear as well as persuasion in Mrs. Temple's voice, she could ill afford to lose the shillings Arabella gave her, or Adam's help either.

There was a long silence while Adam's glance darted from one to the other, tongue licking his lips. He shook his head.

"Which is it to be, Adam? Come with me now, or stay here?" Arabella fought down irritation: she did not want to take him, he would be an enormous complication in her new, and by no means easy, life in Bear Street. It was provoking all the same, to find he did not leap at the chance when she offered it.

He turned abruptly and put his face in the corner, so all she could see were roughened hands tight-locked behind his back. He's weeping again, she thought in disgust. Ye gods, what a milksop.

"That would seem to be my answer," she said coolly to Mrs. Temple. "I will come again in six months to see whether he has changed his mind. Goodbye, Adam."

She waited a moment but he did not move. At least he spoke once, she reflected bitterly, so I suppose there was some improvement on last time.

Outside it was raining and she was relieved to find the hackney still waiting for her. The jervey was in a bad humour, though, over the length of time she had been gone, and demanded a shilling before he would move.

"Certainly not," said Arabella; she could not afford to be fleeced by every driver and chairman who thought her easy game. "We agreed on another sixpence, and I'll pay your fare when we arrive at Bear Street."

"Then just perhaps I'll drive off 'n' leave ye, mam. 'Tis a likely day for walking." Puddles and ruts were everywhere, made worse by dumped bricks and timber.

"Then you wouldn't see the sixpence either." After Adam, Arabella felt ripe for a quarrel.

"Mebbe, mebbe not." The jervey started to peel off layers of canvas covering, preparatory to descending. "I reckon I'm owing a shilling, mebbe more as I'm still waiting like."

"May I offer my services, madame?" said a drawling voice behind her. "It sounds as if this lout is intent on rooking you."

She turned in relief and saw a tall, broad-shouldered young man in the uniform of the King's Guards, hand on the military sword at his side. "Oh, sir, would you? I could pay, but don't see why I should."

He laughed, displaying excellent teeth. "Neither do I, madame. Back to your box, you greasy swine, and drive where the lady wants. I believe my sword will prick your miserable buttocks as easily through canvas as through cloth." He poked at the jervey disdainfully. "I'll drive with the lady and you can be sure of feeling it if you mistake your way." He handed Arabella in and demonstrated his meaning: the driving perch was separated from the interior only by flimsy, tarred canvas.

The hackney creaked under his weight when he climbed in after her, although he had not an ounce of fat on him; he was the most splendid-looking man Arabella had ever seen. Without thought or will, her blood flowed faster as he looked at her in frank admiration. "May I introduce myself? Giles Albury, captain, late of His Majesty's garrison in Tangier."

"Tangier? That's Africa, isn't it?" His skin was bronzed and he wore a small moustache in imitation of the King, as many of the military did.

He nodded. "Aye, and pleasant in many ways, but I'm not sorry to be back. In time a man wearies of wilderness and women wrapped in cloth from head to heels."

"I'm—I'm the dowager Lady Wexford, I—"

He burst into a loud crack of laughter. "You, a dowager! My God, I never saw a more fetching example of the species, or one more unexpected! I always thought of them as on two sticks and wearing mittens."

Arabella dimpled. "I have a pair of mittens in my press."

"You'll have to show me before I'd believe anything so unlikely, my lady dowager. Is that what I must call you?"

"Oh, no . . . no. My friends call me Arabella, and I'm sure you will be one, sir." She stole a glance at him out of the corners of her eyes. It was years since she had enjoyed such easy banter, completely free from strain. When he moved, he touched her and she could not tell whether it was deliberate or not. "I expect you wonder what I was doing in such a place," she went on hurriedly. "My sempstress—"

He held up his hand. "I never allow myself to wonder about things like that. Keep your sempstress, Arabella, and I won't tell you where I had been either."

"Oh, I know that. You must have visited the Catherine Wheel, it is well known as a haunt of the King's Guards." If she had hoped to disconcert him, since few went to such an inn for ale alone, she was disappointed.

"*Touché*, my dear. Guarding suspects is weary work and, as you say, the Catherine Wheel well placed to the palace. Is the jervey following the quickest route, or shall I jab him for you?"

She assured him that he was, alarmed by his readiness to sink his sword in a man whose range he could not judge through canvas. "What suspects were you guarding, sir?"

"Since I have managed Arabella already, do you think you could put your pretty tongue to Giles?" He kissed her hand carelessly, but his eyes were on her mouth, his meaning unmistakable. I must be careful, she thought wildly, or all my plans will blow away.

"I've been bringing Coleman for questioning by the Privy Council, and a gaggle of priests and informers, too. The whole pack of 'em have run mad, in my opinion," he added.

"That's what I thought too. Such a tarradiddle as I heard today." She explained how her husband had recently died, and she had remained almost completely ignorant of the Papist Plot until it had run several weeks of its course and ramified beyond easy comprehension. "Now this stupid magistrate, Godfrey, has run off somewhere and thrown everyone in a fresh panic! Even the lackeys had pistols, it was ridiculous."

"They've put chains across the streets in places, don't ask me why. Godfrey has been found dead this very day, you know."

"Dead? Set on by footpads, do you mean? Magistrates pile up grudges against themselves."

He shrugged. "Set on by Jesuits in terror of their lives, or so the tale runs."

Arabella wrinkled her brow, wondering whether his closeness made her miss some obvious deduction. "If the Privy Council already knows all Oates has to tell, then such a murder wouldn't save papist necks but rouse all London against them, surely?"

"Why, so I think, but it's none of my affair. You wouldn't believe the brisk trade in informing around Whitehall these days: every chance Bedlamite is sure of his hearing and reward. They haven't been so merry since the day they were weaned, though Coleman's papers had treason enough in them without need to invent more."

"Coleman? Edward Coleman, the Duke of York's secretary, he's been arrested?"

"Where did you say you'd been hiding these past weeks?" He kissed her hand again and did not let go afterwards. "He was arrested a fortnight ago on Oates's accusation, and will certainly hang; I stood guard during his cross-examination by the council. The man is a vain fool, who had his wainscot stuffed with treasonable letters to Louis of France begging money for the Duke. I was hard put to keep my face straight when they read 'em out in full council, King Charles presiding, with half the letters saying that subsidies Louis now paid to His Majesty would be better sent to the Duke, since Charles was too idle and immoral to be a worthwhile investment. You couldn't hear so much as whalebone creak, I can tell you, as councillors stared at their papers with red ears, and the King looked fit to cut Coleman's throat. Louis's too, I daresay," he added reflectively. "Such matters cannot be kept secret any longer now, and will be through Parliament like a summer flux when it meets."

Arabella chuckled, but for all her sophistication could still be shocked by the discovery that the King of England and his heir had been competing in abject begging from the realm's hereditary enemy. Their hackney reached Bear Street soon after, and in common courtesy she asked Captain Albury up. Courtesy, and a great deal more besides.

Of course, she would keep emotion tightly reined and remember she had sworn to take her time, but his heedless high spirits were enormously attractive when so much life had passed her by, and great longings run to waste. He was uncomplicated. He was fun. He radiated vigour to match her own, and set starved senses crackling with anticipation.

He insisted on searching for the mittens, and made it seem a harmless game for him to be in her bedroom uninvited. He stayed to supper and they drank too much, laughing louder at easier jokes as wine sank in the flagon. He roused her with careless touches, lips brushing her neck and bosom when they laughed. Then he abruptly left, while she was still halfheartedly fighting her own emotions.

Arabella was relieved, and at the same time very angry. She needed time to consider whether all her designs should be changed for the sake of a Tangier captain, but he had no right to treat her so casually. She would not let him in if he came again.

He came again, and she let him in.

He took her to places she had never been before, where ladies did not go, and she found them more amusing than the court, with its mixture of etiquette, lechery and boredom edged by malice. They went to the theatre and flicked derisive coins on the stage when an actor fluffed his lines; Arabella was startled to see women on the stage, three-parts undressed and

187

such drapery as they wore transparent. They packed hampers and rode out in warm October noonday, Arabella delighted to show off her skills on horseback—in truth she was not skilled but incapable of doing anything without grace. He took her to rough ordinaries, where women solicited openly and a cinder eater gulped red-hot coals and breathed out smoke.

Very soon, she forgot design and felt her body tingle whenever he was near, knowing he would take her soon and needing all her pride to refrain from begging him to wait no longer. She wondered why he waited, hated him for waiting, and only discovered the reason on an expedition to the isolated village of Chelsea, sculling up the Thames on the flow of the tide. It was a glorious late autumn day, sunlight flat-planed on the river and the air droning with insects.

They landed where a great oak trapped dry leaves between its roots and Arabella started to unpack the hamper Giles had brought: pressed pheasant and salad made from a dozen different greens; fruits of all kinds and two bottles of Burgundy, since Giles drank wine by the pint with only an extra quickness of eye and temper to show for it.

He knelt beside her, hands on her shoulders. "Later, Arabella. We shall be devilish hungry later." His hands went from shoulder to neck and he kissed her with a great deal more than the careless ardour he had shown before. Then his hands moved again, to the fastenings of her dress, and even while she drowned in passion she felt a flicker of amusement for his skill: ribbons, sprung metal and fastenings, he never hesitated over their complexity nor did his mouth cease in its quest, rousing each part of her as clothes were loosed. This he had waited for and intended. He could buy women whenever he desired them, and certainly had done so even while he met her. This must be different, something neither would forget, or it was wasted.

They were a match, as he had seen from the beginning. Both possessed enormous vitality and healthy bodies which rejoiced in passion, Arabella's had been long repressed and desired everything he could give, and more; he knew only such restraints as yielded greater pleasure and revelled in the challenge her craving brought him.

There was no time, no feeling but themselves, nothing but ecstasy in all the world. The sun was low, wind sharp, when they stirred to recollection and laughed to find the meal untouched, their skin goose-pimpled by chill they had not felt. They dressed hastily and bundled food back in its hamper, their

188

teeth chattering, breath still caught on the ratchet of desire. The ebb tide was nearly over, so Giles had a hard scull back to Charing steps, and all the way they hardly spoke, each aware only of the other, although Giles watched the tide and Arabella the rough line of London growing on the riverbank.

He came back with her to Bear Street and both were young enough to find even greater pleasures in the night after such a day. Arabella completely forgot plans and calculation in the sunburst joy of physical passion at last requited; this was not what she schemed for but it was everything she wanted.

Her beauty was intensified by something no art could give, and just occasionally she wished she could go to court and show them what they were missing. But, of course, she couldn't. She had not been anywhere fashionable with Giles, but they had certainly been seen together: courtiers would not be shocked by her taking a lover, but they would despise a penniless Tangier captain of modest birth. A nobody herself, Arabella had abandoned her protective Wexford shield and without it had nothing but her looks to carry off her position, and while looks alone might find her a richer or politically more important protector, they would not bring acceptance into court society. Only the King openly brought actresses and orange girls there, and hatred made their position unenviable.

She didn't care. The life she had with Giles was worth it, worth everything.

December came and Coleman was executed, making her remember Wexford's shrewd judgment of him, although George Jeffries was riding high, his name a household word as he harried papists from the judge's bench. There were no acquittals from his court, however contradictory the evidence.

"Not one has confessed, though," remarked Arabella one evening. She was sitting on Giles's knee, her cheek to his chest, his heart beating in her ear. "Surely if there was anything in this plot at all, some would have admitted to more than simply being priests."

"There's no doubt of Coleman's guilt, even if he dabbled in the kind of conspiracy which runs on gold, not blood or the holy spirit. The real trouble is that the King himself is guilty, and no one dares say it, does not wish to say it for fear of civil war. So they put everything on the Duke, who is guilty too, and Shaftesbury plans a bill to exclude him from inheriting the throne."

Arabella considered his words with a flicker of re-aroused

interest. She had thought about little but him lately. "You mean the King is guilty because he took bribes from Louis?"

"There is a conspiracy," he pointed out. "Nothing like what Oates is saying of Jesuits and plots to burn down London, but men use his words to cover things they dare not speak. Oates is a perjured trickster, stirring a devil's brew of hatred for his own glory and excitement, but there's no hiding the fact that for the past nine years the King himself has been Louis's tool, not England's servant, probably a believing Catholic long before he swore his coronation oath to the Church of England. I'm not a religious man myself, but that is treason, perjury and fraud. More important, if Charles is Catholic, then both Louis and York know. What better lever for blackmail can there be than that? So men remember our defeats those recent years, the fires, the ships lost and money drained away God knows where, and ask themselves just when the cheating began. Oates's allegations are too convenient to be exposed as the fraud they are, Shaftesbury particularly whips them on for his own purposes."

Arabella shivered. "So for men's policy, the Catholics hang, and not for any plot at all. If you are right, then this has precious little to do with them."

"They've behaved like fools too," he said frankly, stretching a hand for a bottle. "You should hear them brag of their numbers when they should be keeping quiet, toasting the succession of York when he's pelted if he rides abroad. Now today someone's been arrested for Godfrey's murder. The first clear lead in six weeks of investigation, and he's a Catholic too."

"Who is it?" asked Arabella idly, tracing the line of his jaw with her finger.

"A silversmith called Prance. He trades in forbidden relics, knew Coleman, and is accused by a lodger. He refused to confess and has been sent to little-ease in Newgate, I commanded the escort which took him there. A few December days stripped naked in a cell so small he cannot stand or sit will prise something out of him, true or false. And who is to care which, after all?"

Arabella stared at him in horror. "Prance? Miles Prance, who has his shop off Covent Garden?"

"Aye." He drank again, then saw her face. "My God, you don't know him, do you?"

She nodded, heart fluttering in fright. She knew Lord Aston too, who was soon to be on trial for his life. Prance's ledgers would be seized, her name there for all to see against amounts of money which would be difficult to explain. Some silver she had sold, some he had sold for her, some of his she took on commission and some of hers she did not; and as a married woman she would not have had any such transactions at all. Sweet Jesus, what would it all look like to a Privy Council searching for scapegoats?

Giles lifted her off his knee and stood up. "Tell me. Everything. You're not a papist, are you?"

She shook her head. "I suppose, like you, I'd say I wasn't religious, although—although my family were Dissenters." I'll go to meeting every Sunday for the rest of my life if I get out of this, she thought feverishly. I'll give to the poor, I'll listen to sermons, I'll—I'll have Adam to live here with me. Just sometimes, she thought of Adam and her conscience twitched.

Giles shook her. "Tell me. We haven't much time."

She stared at him, at the mat of hair where his shirt was open to the waist, at wine stains on his breeches and heavy muscles at thigh and shoulder. They had been about to go to bed. She told him clearly and from the beginning, voice expressionless, except about Harry, of whom she said nothing.

Giles frowned heavily and then without comment went into the bedroom and dipped his head in a pitcher of cold water. He came back, towelling vigorously. "Let me be certain of this. Your name will be in Prance's records?"

She nodded. "I've seen it there, and signed the ledger as correct several times."

"The council might believe you since you have a sensible explanation, could bring as witnesses those to whom you lost gaming. It must have been remarked on that you so often wagered silver even though they were only trinkets. Think carefully now, do you have enemies at court? Real, spiteful enemies who might have an interest in seeing that you weren't believed?"

"Yes," she said unhappily. "The Wexfords would be delighted to show me worthless as they always thought, Shaftesbury too . . . I was his mistress once; I walked out on him, which hurt his pride, and only my husband knew the reason."

Giles pulled his nose reflectively. "Which church do you attend?"

"The Chapel Royal sometimes. Not very often. Nowhere since Wexford died."

"God," he said quietly. "You are in trouble, aren't you?

Anyone could say you went to papist mass and you wouldn't be able to disprove it. Shaftesbury heads the committee of investigation."

"They couldn't prove it either!"

He began lacing his shirt and pulled on his coat. "They could, and quite possibly would. I don't know how many people have disproved most of what Oates says a dozen times over. It suits no one to listen to them, so he still struts in adulation and the papists hang. Women burn alive for treason, did you know? Put on clothes for the street, nothing splendid, we're going for a walk."

Arabella felt as if she was physically choking while she tied ribbons and tapes. Burned alive, like the martyrs of Smithfield a hundred years before. No one who had gone as she had to meeting house all through their childhood could be ignorant of the horrors of burning, when most sermons referred to Protestant sufferings under Catholic oppression in ghoulish detail. She grasped Giles's arm. "You meant it? Women burn?"

"For treason, yes. Though you wouldn't do much better if we could persuade a judge that you were male, which God forbid."

She shivered: cut down before you were dead, disembowelled alive and entrails burned before your eyes. Skilled hangmen boasted they could do it while the victim lived. "Where are we going?"

He covered her hand with his. "That's better. We'll walk past Prance's house, it's not far. Just to see what guard there is, and whether his papers have been taken yet. They'll look for secret hidden places first and not bother overmuch with ledgers: he was only arrested this afternoon and royal officials are not renowned for their speed."

They appeared to have been efficient enough over Prance: a real suspect six weeks after Godfrey's murder was not to be treated lightly. A crowd had gathered in the street, eddying aimlessly and talking of papist outrage, a few bolder or more drunken than the rest throwing cobbles. Some troopers were on guard and slashed at anyone who came too near, but most windows in the street were broken, the front of Prance's house running with filth.

"No good," said Giles, looking at the scene appraisingly. He was enjoying himself, she could tell. He found guard duty in London tame and several times had told Arabella that he hoped popular fury would break out into civil war again. "We'll go around the back, I'd hoped I might know the guard, but these must be from the Tower."

Back-streets London was unfamiliar to Arabella. She became confused by winding alleys when roofs almost met overhead, and Giles put his arm round her waist to prevent her falling in unlit rubbish. "This must be it," he whispered at last.

Not far ahead Arabella could hear the shouts and jeers of the crowd. "To the right?"

She felt him nod. "There'll be a guard even at the back, though the mob's only enjoying itself, not planning anything. If anyone challenges, I'm taking you to Blue Lil's. Cling to my arm and keep quiet."

Arabella wondered who Blue Lil was, this looked too run-down a district for the kind of whorehouse Giles would patronise. Carefully he led the way, he could touch both sides of the alley easily. Crowd noises were much nearer when he stopped, listening. Then she heard what he had, voices muttering quite close. She felt his hand on her arm, pulling her aside, the breath of a whisper telling her to stand.

She stood a long time, imagining horrors. Surely he would not kill guards? Yet she had become aware that Giles's nature was set in a violent mould: violent in desire, in hatred and in action. She rejoiced in it, sometimes detested it and then rejoiced again; recently she had come to fear it a little. Now, she feared it very much. She could hear her heart beating, the guards must be deaf not to hear it too. Her eyes had adjusted and she realised she was standing in a derelict yard, irregular, leaning buildings at her back. One of them must be Prance's, impossible to tell which since all seemed to be empty: occupants presumably fled for fear of the mob.

A shadow moved and Giles was back, holding her arm, his fingers on her face to impress even more caution. She felt for each step, annoyed he should think she might be clumsy, hands on timber and then plaster, a sharp corner she must grope her way past, before she heard a click and he led her inside a building. "It's empty," he said softly. "We're safe so long as we don't show any light. It's two down the row from Prance, any closer was too near the guard."

"How are we going to break through? The attics?" She felt satisfaction that he did not have to tell her, and sensed his chagrin too. Good. She thought he had taken pleasure in telling her that women traitors burned; there is an aspect of desire,

193

not love, which enjoys fear in another and this was not the first time she had detected it in him.

He led the way upstairs, treading close to the wall but even so, rotting timbers creaked. Up and up again. Stale smells of cooking, old cloth, other less pleasant odours; stench strengthened as they climbed. The roof space at last. A clutter of straw bedding and bare boards, plaster crumbling at the touch. Old roofs were seldom securely blocked off from each other and Arabella remembered crawling through their neighbours' attics as a child.

It was difficult fumbling skirts through tangled darkness, only just space enough to crawl between beams and trusses; she was thankful when Giles stopped and began picking out plaster so they could wiggle back into attics.

"I don't think there are guards inside, the searchers have made a start and will return in daylight," he said softly. "What are we looking for exactly, and where?"

Arabella described Prance's workroom and tiny shop. "He keeps a daybook on the counter and two ledgers by his bench for goods bought and sold. My name is in all three, although the daybook is less deadly, being all signs and scribbles."

As they crept down the last few treads, light from flaring cressets outside grew brighter, figures casting gigantic shadows into dimness within. At least the shouting would drown any sound they made. Her feet crunched unexpectedly and Arabella stopped, astounded. The floor was covered with broken plaster and chipped wood; every one of Prance's images had been split, looking for secret messages presumably. She thought of Prance, and standing amid the ruins of his life was swept by disbelief. Disbelief that she should be in his workroom in the dark, a mob baying for blood outside; that he could possibly have deserved such ill fortune. Prance was surely not the stuff of traitors, yet he was naked in a four-foot Newgate cell until such time as he confessed to whatever the government wanted. Including her name, if anyone thought to ask the question.

Very cautiously, they began sifting through wreckage. There was no silver, which must be looted or safely in government coffers already, but almost everything else one could imagine: clothes, pots, tools, stale food and wrecked shelves adding to the confusion. Giles found a ledger, but when she studied it in faint light, the entries referred to sheet silver bought. Then under trampled plaster she found his book of designs, delicate, beautiful drawings torn and filthied. Her spirits rose, the search-

194

ers had sought letters and papers such as Coleman hid in his wainscot; it had not yet occurred to them the ledgers might have a tale to tell. They found both the ledgers soon after, but not the daybook, although Giles crawled into the shop itself, a soldier on guard only the thickness of lath away.

It was infuriating.

Almost certainly, it was here somewhere but search as they would they could not find it. "We shall have to go," whispered Giles at last. "You said it wasn't so important."

Arabella shrugged. There was no point and great danger in staying longer. Prance used his own abbreviations in the daybook and wrote up his ledgers after: with luck no one would ask him to interpret hundreds of scrawled pages so long as he confessed to whatever he was asked.

The journey back was a nightmare of suspense. If they were caught the ledgers would be impossible to explain, and Arabella felt close to collapse. Her back ached as it did when she was tired, her stays were banded with iron which cut off breath and blood, the finicking caution which was necessary almost beyond endurance.

They were out at last and sauntering arm-twined together when a patrol relieving the guard saw them, and shouted. Giles turned and swore good-naturedly. "What's to do?" The ledgers were heavy between their arms.

The soldiers had no tinder and peered uncertainly in darkness. "It's for us to ask the likes of you. Don't you know a papist traitor's house lies yonder?"

"What of it? I've more pressing business than throwing cobbles at an empty house."

"What business?" asked one suspiciously.

Giles laughed. "You should know, with Blue Lil around the corner. I've a reluctant wench here and not long before morning."

The men sniggered but stood aside and Arabella added colour to his story by hanging back. Giles laughed when they were clear. "Well done, sweetheart. I had a notion I might have need of you before the night was out."

"Who is Blue Lil?" asked Arabella curiously.

"No place I'd take you, you may be sure. She offers a night's lying-in to free women of unwanted children, but her methods are so foul that most never leave. So she is paid, and sells clothes from the corpse as well. It's known as a place to rid yourself of inconvenient women as well as bastards."

All Arabella's horror of Mistress Dawkins returned, and she shuddered. At least Wexford had not sent her to a place where the proprietor set out to kill.

Back in Bear Street they examined the ledgers. Giles gulping wine while he flicked over pages. "No wonder a silversmith suspect appealed to the government. A prosperous man, Miles Prance. He'll lose everything, of course, whether he confesses or not."

Arabella looked over his shoulder and her own name leaped at her, and again two pages later. She sank back on the settle; sweet Jesus, I thank you, she thought drowsily.

Giles began tearing out pages and blowing on sparks in the grate; the ledgers took a great deal of burning, flames shimmering before Arabella's eyes. Surely no one would bother to decipher the daybook, if they found it.

Giles turned and smiled at her. "All done." He bent and kissed her, his mouth warmly demanding.

She pushed him away. "Not now, Giles, I'm too tired."

His eyes narrowed, they were bloodshot from wine, his face flushed with excitement and the heat of the fire. He felt stimulated by the dangers of the night, the release of a woman exactly what he needed. "What poor thanks for the risk of my neck. You should show more gratitude than that. Arabella, even though you do not feel it."

"Giles, I do!" She put her arms around his neck and kissed him. "I'm so very grateful I cannot say it all! But just tonight—"

"Just tonight is the time I want my thanks," he interrupted, and held her without waiting for an answer. Eagerness in a woman was all very well, but he had enjoyed months of ardent responses from Arabella; reluctance was a pleasant change, and his need imperative.

Chapter Seventeen

Despite the discovery that Prance was denounced by lodgers who owed him rent, the only evidence against him their word that he had been out on the evening Godfrey disappeared, he was held in little-ease cell until he confessed to organising the magistrate's murder on behalf of the Jesuits. Giles said that when he was brought out and taken to Whitehall, he retracted his admission to the King personally, and so was returned to little-ease. After the second time he did the same, but half dead with cold thereafter held to his confession, and named three accomplices who had done the killing.

These were menials from the Queen's official residence, so presumably Shaftesbury rather than the King was responsible for the choice, but it made no difference: protesting innocence, they hanged just the same while Prance was given a pardon for informing.

"Christ," said Giles in disgust. "If ever I saw murder done, I have seen it in the royal courts of justice these past few weeks. I don't know who killed Godfrey, and Prance looks and behaves like a five-day maggot, but he had the brains to leave no doubt with men of sense that his confession was worthless."

Arabella was standing by the window staring into the street; she still felt frightened sometimes, it could easily have been she who was made a scapegoat. "Will they see it, do you think?"

He drank deeply and made a face. "They'd be very stupid if they didn't, although most men are fools, so, perhaps only a few will waste thought on such a matter. I doubt whether Green, Berry or Hill could see the joke."

For when Prance confessed, the names of those he called his accomplices tallied exactly with the place where Godfrey's body was found: Greenbury Hill.* The government did not care who hanged so long as culprits were demonstrably punished, and Prance had surely shown the random nature of his choice by a coincidence no judge should have allowed to go unchallenged. But a full bench had made no comment.

"Why won't you marry me?" asked Giles abruptly, watching her by the window.

"Oh, Giles, we've been over this before! I don't want to marry again." Arabella leaned her forehead against cold glass; she was beginning to feel trapped again.

"There must be some other reason, every woman wants to marry."

"Well, I don't! What's a wife, pray? A thing to keep for breeding, while a mistress has all the pleasures. No one will catch me that way again, not even you, Giles Albury."

"There's no one else?" he asked suspiciously. "I never met the woman who did not leap at marriage before."

She went over and kissed him, aware of impatience when he at once began to fumble with her clothes. They had been together so long it was becoming as dull as a marriage. He wanted a child, too, while she used the less respectable company in which she found herself to discover how to prevent one.

"Of course there's no one else," she said a shade regretfully. She did not like Giles's friends except for an evening's entertainment, and missed the choice offered by court life. "As if I would; I'm not one of your common drabs, you know."

He went elsewhere, she thought. Often, too. But once the excitement of his lust staled she had to whip herself into fury before she minded very much.

He picked her up and carried her to the bed and words were lost; when he slept afterwards she stared at the ceiling and wondered how to set her life in motion again. Giles fired her desire and she missed him when duty kept him away, chiefly because she was bored. He bored her, too. She felt dissatisfied when all dispute was stilled by his body, her life as dependent on his whim as it had been on Wexford and with less interest, since Giles brought gossip secondhand. As my lady Wexford she had heard a variety of opinions, while Giles was knowledgeable on the interrogation of witnesses and not much else.

*Now Primrose Hill.

She had not even her trade in silver any more, nor could she contact Will without visiting Cheapside.

She must get back to court, but how?

Her problem was unexpectedly and most unpleasantly solved a few weeks later. Catlin showed a lackey into the salon, disapproval clear in the downturn of her mouth. "He says he has a writ for ye."

Arabella recognised the ash-grey livery Anthony Ashley Cooper, Earl of Shaftesbury, used for his servants, and her heart began to thump. "What kind of writ?"

The man bowed and handed her a paper. He had no look of constable or jailer. "From my lord of Shaftesbury, madame."

Arabella took it to the window and tore open the seal, Shaftesbury's writing unexpectedly difficult to read. *I suggest you come with him if you wish to avoid the enclosed being served on you.* There was no superscription or signature, and the paper enclosed with his note was an unexecuted writ for her attendance on the Parliamentary Committee investigating the present dangerous condition of the realm due to the fiendish contrivances of papists.

She couldn't believe it; it had been so long, months since Prance was arrested, weeks since Green, Berry and Hill had been executed, the worst fury of the plot apparently spent.

Really, she had no choice. If they had discovered anything, then Shaftesbury as chairman of the committee was her only chance, and she had enough self-confidence to feel a flicker of excitement at the prospect. Whatever grudge he held against her and no matter how devious his politics, Shaftesbury was a man and with men she felt secure.

"It's not a writ," she told Catlin as coolly as she was able. "There's been some mistake. It is a summons from my lord of Shaftesbury to hear evidence I can give."

"What evidence?" demanded Catlin suspiciously. "What can ye know? 'Tis his revenge more like for—" Her voice trailed away when Arabella jerked her head at the lackey. She was probably right, though. Shaftesbury was quite capable of blackmail and still serve the writ afterwards.

Arabella experienced a surprising thrill when she stepped into Shaftesbury's coach. It made her somebody again, however great the threat she faced. She had taken time to change her gown and paint her face, conscious that her beauty was the only weapon she possessed; she laughed aloud, at least those who must rely on their wits to keep out of prison did not suffer boredom.

Shaftesbury had moved his residence to the City, where much of his support lay, but as she expected, Arabella was driven to Whitehall. She remembered Shaftesbury as a man of so many purposes requiring privacy, which perhaps exaggerated his reputation for lechery, that it seemed almost tame when the lackey guided her to a gallery overlooking the Thames. Several men waiting there regarded her curiously, but there was no attempt at secrecy and Arabella's spirits rose still further; Shaftesbury would never interview her under the eyes of court gossips if he expected her to be arrested within hours.

She sat a long time, agog with interest. She ought to feel apprehensive, instead she found the constant comings and goings fascinating, tried to guess who all these people were. Recently, Arabella had sometimes wished that she had listened more carefully to Wexford and his cronies, regretted she had been so dazzled by the idea of bedding Shaftesbury that she had cared little for his affairs. She remembered his wit, but could have learned so much from a man who had stood for years at the centre of so many and such bitter disputes, who was also regarded as one of the finest minds of his time: philosopher, politician of genius, an opponent even Charles Stuart feared. Instead, he had been no more than a prize to be exhibited, a small, wiry man with a bad back and poor health of whom she tired quite soon.

She recognized the Marquess of Halifax when he came out of the inner room: Shaftesbury's nephew and one of the few men he considered his equal in intellect.

He recognized her too, and came to bow over her hand. "My lady Wexford."

Arabella smiled roguishly. She might need allies, and George Savile was a personable man. "I am not sure whether you are safe to be seen with me, my lord."

"Indeed? It is of course difficult to know whom one will meet next to Shaftesbury's anteroom, a peasant labouring under heavenly instruction or a royal bastard who desires to be King are quite commonplace nowadays. A friend's widow too dangerous to acknowledge is at least a fresh experience." He apparently regarded it as beneath his dignity to lower his voice.

Arabella unfolded her fan. "Fie, my lord. I have been a year from court, but I hear words are dangerous things these days."

200

"Words are certainly unsatisfactory things. The ones you don't hear are so much more informative than those you do; as chance acquaintance is invariably more pleasant than full knowledge with the disillusion it must bring. Your servant, madame."

Well, she thought, eyeing his back as he conversed further down the gallery, the King's government is run by the strangest people these days, if their only hope of agreement is to know as little as possible of each other's activities.

A footman came up to her. "If you would come this way, madame."

She did feel frightened now but refused to show it, every eye on her as she walked the length of the gallery. Head held high, skirt caught in one hand so it murmured as she moved, she looked at no one as she passed.

Shaftesbury's room was quite small, a single window open to sun glinting off the river. He stood as she was shown in. "My lady Wexford. You have not changed during the three years since we last conversed."

She could not say the same of him; he looked worn and ill, prominent nose and bones of his face starkly framed by the luxury of his wig. "We met, if you remember, my lord, in the King's presence shortly before my husband died."

He smiled. "Some meetings are less interesting than others. Sit down, Arabella."

She sat, shaking out her skirts around her, sun hot on the bare skin of her shoulders. She was conscious of looking her best; pale green silk over darker green underskirt enhanced her vivid colouring and strong light exactly what was needed to strike chestnut flecks from her hair and eyes. No matter what the sunlight, he will see no pock or blemish on my skin, she thought complacently. She smiled at him, but uncertainly; no man softened easiest to female arrogance.

"You do not appear as apprehensive as you ought." His tone was neutral, he might easily be thinking of the grudge he owed her.

"No, my lord, since I think you have less public places for the kind of interview I would do well to fear." Too late, she thought of the opening he had given for tears and pleading.

His eyes flickered with what might have been amusement, then he held up Prance's daybook. "You recognise this?"

She had expected it, but suffered a shock all the same. "No, my lord."

201

"Don't lie, Arabella. You will do better with me if you keep to the truth."

"No, my lord. I do not recognise it." She was not admitting anything to do with papists.

He shuffled through some pages. "Then it is strange indeed how often your name appears."

"Very strange," she agreed politely.

He sat back, wincing slightly. It was rumored that he was so malicious a man that his evil humours needed to discharge through a pipe set in his side. The story was sufficiently intriguing for Arabella to have been disappointed to find a cloth patch on his ribs when she slept with him, annoyed she must profess ignorance to spiteful courtiers who called him Tapski behind his back. "You are not a good liar, Arabella. Which is surprising, considering the practise you must have had. I, on the other hand, am about the most difficult man to deceive in the kingdom, for I learned my trade at the hands of Charles Stuart and his father. I am not tricking you into admission, merely stating fact. You were a frequent and long-term customer of Miles Prance. I want to know why."

"Or you will send me to little-ease, as he was?" She bit her lip and wished the words recalled. As Lord President of the King's council, he had the power to do exactly that.

He shut the book with a snap. "I doubt whether you are important enough for such a course. But I intend to know, so you will save us both a deal of trouble if you would tell me plainly."

Arabella thought fast. She had intended not to admit anything, but instinct told her that some confessions are best made at once and Shaftesbury facing her alone was more likely to be generous than Shaftesbury with a part to play in front of his supporters. "What made you think my name was there, since it cannot be true?" She allowed her voice to hesitate, denial less certain than before.

He was watching her steadily, he would indeed be a difficult and vengeful man to fool. "You were not surprised to see this book here, only that you had been connected with it. Which is understandable, when you look at Prance's scrawls. He was not asked to interpret them since he confessed anything we wanted, but I looked through it lest there was something more we ought to ask him. I noticed one frequent abbreviation: ARSP. It was unique for a maker's mark to appear for commission as well as payment, on sale as well as purchase, and I intended to ask him to explain when I remembered gaming with you four years ago. Then I thought perhaps it was a question better left unasked before a committee of both Houses."

"Gaming? What did you remember, my lord?" She was bewildered by how he had managed to connect her with such a cryptic reference.

"It is your turn now. Then I will tell you."

So she told him everything, there was nothing to hide providing he would believe her. He nodded when she had finished and went over to a cupboard; when he turned he was holding one of her father's exquisitely wrought flagons. "I won this, if you remember, when you lost so heavily you had to pay the whole table. I redeemed it with coin since it could not be broken up, and paid the guineas you owed. The workmanship is some of the finest I have seen and I enquired who the smith was." His finger touched the maker's mark. "Robert Sperling, RSP, dead of the plague leaving only a daughter to inherit. Then I find Prance buying pieces, a few very expensive marked RSP, many more of ordinary quality marked $W\frac{s}{p}$, yet all being sold through the mark of ARSP, the best of which came to me through you. So I set my secretary to enquire for your father's name."

There was a long silence while Arabella stared at the flagon, tears unexpectedly close. She no longer possessed anything of her father's making, her expenses had been so great and Giles one of the non-payers against whom Wexford had warned her. She was not thinking of danger or Shaftesbury at all, but of her father saying he would love her whatever she became. "What are you going to do?" she asked at last.

"Why, nothing. There is no treason and I did not expect there would be, although I confess I was curious. No one else will make the connection."

They certainly wouldn't; even with Robert Sperling's work in his cupboard Shaftesbury had been exceptionally astute to do so. She stared at him, thinking of the innocent men he had helped hound to the scaffold these past months. "Guilt has nothing to do with it, though, has it? What of Green, Berry and Hill? If you are clever enough to link me to a craftsman's mark on silver, then you must know that they were picked by Prance off a list presented for his choice, for no better reason than because their names would show he lied. You say you are a difficult man to deceive; what then of Oates, do you believe him?"

"You headstrong little fool," he said softly. "You escape with your attractive hide untouched and then deliberately provoke me before you are safe out of the room. The King is ill, did you know?"

She shook her head, taken aback by the change of subject.

"Yesterday he was like to die, but this time he will live. The Duke of York was sent for so he would be at hand if His Majesty died. I summoned Monmouth, the King's bastard, since I and many others do not trust a Catholic on the throne, and certainly not York. Last night this realm was as close to civil war as it has been these thirty years, and only a dozen people knew it. Today the spectre fades again, but we cannot go on like this. The succession must be settled to safeguard England's future, and this I intend to accomplish. By any means."

Arabella gaped at him; he was utterly certain of himself and speaking treason as if he was addressing a public meeting. "My lord, you talk of untouched hides, I think yours is more at risk than mine."

His expression relaxed and he sat again; the same involuntary wince as he did so, and an almost greenish tinge to his skin.

She touched his hand, unexpectedly concerned when she remembered no feeling for him before. "Take care, or you will join the King on a sickbed. Perhaps that would be best, and common affliction settle what a struggle for power never can."

He threw his head and laughed. "Very likely. Strangely enough, there is a deal of common fellowship between us; were we not on opposite sides His Majesty and I could have been excellent friends. You are good for me, Arabella; I have a room full of people to see and a meeting of supporters afterwards, will you return to sup privately? It will be very late."

She accepted at once.

It was very late, so Arabella had plenty of time to think about Giles. He had not come by the time Shaftesbury's coach called for her at Bear Street, but she expected him and told Catlin to spin a tale of her being summoned over Prance's daybook. "Tell him all is well. He must not worry or say anything to anyone." It would be disastrous if Giles stirred up an ant's nest of accusation when Shaftesbury had no intention of calling her for examination.

"Aye, I'll tell him," said Catlin dourly. "He'll believe ye

this time, but he's jealous enough for six. Ye'll have to think of a better tale if ye intend to make a habit of it."

Catlin liked Giles, indeed few women remained indifferent to his splendid physique, although duty in London was thickening his body and puffing his face. I can't worry about him now, thought Arabella as the coach rumbled through dark streets. After all it may just be tonight and then Shaftesbury will never ask me to sup with him again. He certainly did not look well enough to bed a woman.

He did not behave as if he intended to, either.

They ate alone, with only a valet waiting on them, windows open to the air. It was quiet enough to hear the slop of waves on Westminster steps below, and so dark there was a glow downriver from torches lighting Southwark's brothels, bear pits and taverns. "It's a wild area," said Shaftesbury, sipping wine, although he ate and drank very little. "I used to go there as a young man sometimes. Being outside City jurisdiction, it has never been tamed even by Cromwell and his like. I expect it would please you, Arabella."

"Considering it is known to hold more whorehouses than the rest of London put together, I do not thank you for the compliment," retorted Arabella, stung.

"But then you should not know such a thing, should you? No, I meant that it holds an excitement found only in the untamed, a lack of restriction which would appeal to you. Not to live there, of course, for it is the filthiest place on God's earth and in London that is no idle boast."

"You live in the City now, don't you?" The old, familiar pang. How long, how long before she dared go there again?

"Yes, in Aldersgate Street. I find my strongest support amongst merchants struggling to remedy the great damage wrought upon their livelihood, and that of the nation, by royal policies. And one day when the King decides to try me for my life it may not be quite so easy there."

"You think he would?"

"Yes, of course. Don't you?"

"I—I hardly know," she stammered. "I have been long from court. Surely—why are you Lord President of his council if you feel your neck at risk?"

"Because these past five years I have so wrought with Parliament that His Majesty is unable to conduct his business without my contrivance. Opposition is organised now, where it used to consist of individuals angered by injustice. I have

205

welded them together with whatever came to hand, I have no choice but to use events not of my contriving. I do not yet completely command this opposition, and probably never shall, but no one else remotely understands its nature or how to use it for their purposes. The King needs me while he nerves himself to try whether he can destroy what I have made."

"How have you made it, then?" asked Arabella curiously. "By money?"

"Shaftesbury's pensioners, as men call them? Yes, quite often. But the King's minister, Danby, tried the same and failed; he's impeached, as you know. There is more to it than money or self-interest, although I have many interests. Also, as I think I told you once, I have a purpose. Men are tempted by money, held by common gain; they persevere through all changes and dangers for a purpose they believe in. England's well-being and just government, for instance."

"And you do not care how you gain your purpose, so long as it is gained?" He had nearly admitted to her in the afternoon that he sacrificed victims to anti-popish frenzy to further his designs, and she sensed that tonight he was exhausted beyond caution. He had asked her here because for a brief space he needed not to watch himself.

He stood and walked over to the window. "Let me answer one question with another. Have you heard of the Habeas Corpus Act?"

Fortunately, she had. Passed in the confusion before the King dissolved Parliament the year before, Giles had remarked that if it could be enforced then the days when English governments could imprison subjects without trial were over. She nodded, mystified.

"I passed that act. Without me it would have failed, and shall I tell you how I did it? Not by mouthing principles, although I did that too, but by hearing the teller of votes count one fat member as five in jest and keeping the House talking so no one else noticed. So we carried it by three votes. Not glorious, was it? But it was done, and another English liberty secured. In the future governments may ignore the law, they cannot pretend it doesn't exist."

"So you don't care how," she said flatly. "There is a difference, though, between innocent men hanged so you can whip up the mob against York's succession, and a fat man counted as five."

He shrugged. "Perhaps. Perhaps not. The purpose remains.

You will see one day who was right. My grandfather was clerk to Elizabeth's privy council and sailed with Drake; I have served Cromwell, Commonwealth, Republic, the whole pack of them as well as two Stuarts, so perhaps have some right to judge affairs, however imperfectly. England has a natural balance if left alone, and law is to preserve it; all our rulers in my lifetime have sought to upset it, and much ill has resulted. Glib promises from a man unfit to rule offer scant protection against tyranny."

Arabella thought of Monmouth, the King's bastard son; so the whispers were true, Shaftesbury would not accept York's pledge to limit his powers but meant to place Monmouth in the succession if he could. She looked at him speculatively. "Will you succeed in your intentions?"

"I shall be worth knowing if I do, will I not? Since we are being honest tonight, I am not sure. But I have concerted an opposition and forced it to think; with or without me it will not remain an opposition long, but become part of the balance. These things take time, and what must be destroyed on the way I cannot tell. No one wants another civil war, so the struggle will be fought out here, in London, with words and the headsman's axe. Who wins London, wins the realm."

"No one wins London," said Arabella indignantly. "It stands of itself."

He came over and kissed her. "There speaks a daughter of Cheapside. You are probably right, and that being so, the matter is resolved. If London stands of itself, then England will stand too. That is another reason why I live in Aldersgate now."

She felt him flinch the moment she responded to his touch, and slid her hands to his shoulders. His ribs seemed tender to the slightest pressure, and she was not surprised when he sent her home soon after. Shaftesbury was not a man who would willingly accept the humiliation of extreme care in his love-making, and without it he would be helpless.

He kissed her hand as his valet waited to take her to his coach. "You have grown, Arabella. You were beautiful before, but the court is full of beautiful women. Now there is more than beauty to it, and more still to come if I am any judge." He laughed suddenly. "And I am, of women. Will you come again when I am in need of cheer? These few hours have been poor entertainment for you, but eased me beyond measure."

"With great pleasure, my lord, and I assure you I have been very well diverted." Which was true, she reflected. After months of Giles and his demands it mattered not at all that her evening had been spent talking over the supper table. The reverse in fact, since she had not been for an instant bored as she almost immediately was when she found Giles waiting for her in Bear Street.

He hugged her hungrily. "My God, Arabella, I was about to search Whitehall for you! What happened? Was it Prance's daybook?"

Since he knew nothing of silversmith's hieroglyphics, he did not find it odd that she had been questioned once the book was found, nor was he curious as to why she was released. He bore her off immediately to the bedroom, anxiety and the pints of wine he had drunk while waiting for her kindling such need that he did not notice her lack of response, although usually sensitive in such matters.

Arabella took intense interest in events during the following months, although her own life still drifted. She went twice more to sup with Shaftesbury, on both occasions it was very late and neither time did she stay the night. On her second visit he was in so much discomfort he could not bear his back so much as to touch his chair: he made no reference to his state, however, and since she reckoned he asked her to take his mind off affairs and pain, Arabella did not either.

He was finally dismissed from his position as Lord President in October 1679 but the King found him even more of a nuisance away from his council than in it, and almost immediately tried to persuade him back. But a fateful shift in the balance was taking place, for the King was pensioned with French money again and so able to avoid meeting Parliament, where the core of Shaftesbury's power lay, thus forcing him to re-exert pressure through the mob, which frightened his more sober supporters. Then he presented the Duke of York as a popish recusant and the King's mistress as a common nuisance before the court of King's Bench. The jury were dismissed before the cases could be heard, but the whole of London laughed at his impudence.

Arabella could not help laughing too, although she scolded him when she supped with him again. "The King will never forget you! What revenge will he plan now, pray?"

Shaftesbury grinned, he seemed more relaxed and was leaning back in his chair. "He will be as busy as a coat full of fleas searching out a warrant of treason against me. You must watch yourself, or his eye might light on you."

Her heart bumped. "You think he might—"

"Of course not. The Duchess of Portsmouth is far from an innocent party, and a damned meddling woman. She deserved all the ridicule I gave her; His Majesty was angry I had done it, not displeased she was humbled. No, the trial between us will come in Parliament as it was always bound to come. At least I have brought him by one means or another to the point where he must call one again, to find out who is master. French pensions are no longer enough."

"Can't you accuse him openly of taking French money?" demanded Arabella, it all seemed too tortuous to her.

"I don't want to ruin the King, I intend to force him to rule as his forebears ruled and set the pattern straight for his successors. A pattern of justice and duty a ruler owes to his realm which was broken by his father and grandfather, and the Republic could not mend. And I take French money, too."

She stared at him, her mouth a round *O* of astonishment. "I don't believe it!"

He smiled wryly. "Thank you. George Savile said the same, and you are both probably right to consider it reprehensible. I cannot finance opposition without it and that is what matters, but I can scarcely attack the King on such an issue."

"Good God, I should think not," Arabella said fervently. She had thought she understood Shaftesbury, and realised now that there were layers of deviousness in him she had not even seen.

He came round the table and folded her hands in his, pulling her to her feet. "I am honest in some ways, though. I wanted you to know from me, not discover for yourself the tricks men stoop to. My secretary—" He broke off and poured them both wine. "I have a most unusual secretary called John Locke. One day he intends to write a book and men will read him long after they have forgotten me. It will all sound more splendid written, tidy and full of principles . . . John is very hot for principles. It is men like me who dirty their hands and are executed for their pains." He handed her a goblet and toasted her. "Long life to beauty, plenty of paper and ink for principles, and time gained by my like to enjoy them in."

He had already set down his goblet when she finished drinking, and took her in his arms at once. "My dear, you have been confidante and encouragement to me these past months, a rest on a weary way. You have also been very understanding. You know I am not a fit man, nor one who is likely to give you much pleasure, but tonight I should like to try if you are willing."

He had never asked before. Four years ago—nearly five now—she had offered and he had taken; it had meant very little to either. Now, she could hurt him either by refusal or by too easy acceptance. As he had said, she had grown recently and although she neither loved nor completely understood him, this time she thought only of him as she yielded to his touch.

There was no easy way to fulfillment either, in fact that part of the night was far from simple, as she discovered.

"You know I have a wound draining in my side," he said with detachment once, refusing sympathy. "Have a care if you value my senses, but I will take it as a compliment if I help you to forget."

He was bandaged from armpit to waist and preferred the candles doused, otherwise he was a subtle and amusing lover who did not take himself too seriously. Arabella was surprised by how much she enjoyed him, having thought that perhaps his age would remind her unpleasantly of Wexford. There was little of the urgent physical excitement she found with Giles but instead skilled playing on her senses, a range of pleasure she had not felt before.

She kissed his side before he rose in the dawn, and smelled the whiff of corruption. "I would not have known."

He stood carefully, he looked drawn and skeleton-thin in grey dawn light. "And you made me forget awhile, which is not easy." He kissed her hand, she thought he could not bend sufficiently to kiss her lips. "Wait at your leisure, Arabella, and ring when you are ready. Wheelock will see you home. My dear..." He hesitated. "I do not know whether we will have any more suppers together, the real struggle is about to begin. You have given me much happiness these past months. I loved my first wife and never found her equal; your grace and honesty supplied a lack often felt in the years since. I wanted you to know."

He went without waiting for a reply, and she lay a long time while the light strengthened, thinking of him.

She left it very late before she rang, the alleys and courtyards of Whitehall were bustling, voices calling outside; Shaftesbury had probably been at work a couple of hours or more. His valet, Wheelock, was nearly a foot taller than his master and Arabella reflected that a lesser man might well have disliked being dwarfed by his servant. But in his own household Shaf-

210

tesbury apparently commanded real affection, and Wheelock regarded her with benign approval, where he had merely been respectful before.

He bowed and handed her a cloth-wrapped package. "His lordship wished to give you this, my lady."

"I don't want—" began Arabella, angry that Shaftesbury should think her a paid trull.

"It is a personal gift, madame, which his lordship thought would have a particular meaning for your ladyship."

She took it reluctantly and from the feel instantly realised what it must be. Her father's flagon. There was also a note in Shaftesbury's cramped hand. *One mark is no greater than another, and value comes from the whole, not part. I hope you will accept this in memory of many things.* It was unsigned.

She unwrapped the packet carefully and stood looking at the fourfold assay mark; her father's proud craft sign RSP; the leopard head of London; the letter identifying a single year in England's life; the lion of realm and King. All the same size and the flagon itself a thing of beauty. "Yes," she said at last. "I should like to accept this, and shall keep it always. Will you tell his lordship?"

Wheelock inclined his head. "Yes, my lady. Allow me." He deftly wrapped it again and cast an expert eye around the room and at her appearance. "Would your ladyship prefer to travel in his lordship's coach or a hackney, as Whitehall is astir?"

She chose the hackney thankfully, not having dared protest before at Shaftesbury's habit of sending his coach to Bear Street. It was only a matter of time before someone told Giles, even though her visits had been infrequent. "Can nothing be done for his lordship's health?" she asked Wheelock abruptly while they were rattling over cobbles.

He looked distressed. "Your ladyship finds him worse?" She nodded; in spite of the night each time she came he seemed more frail, although as active or more so than before. "We care for him as best we may, but he will not rest. If he has a moment's ease, he takes up some fresh interest."

Such as me, thought Arabella wryly. "What exactly ails him, or would you prefer not to say?"

His face darkened. "I would sooner say, since at court men whisper all manner of filth and lampoons show—well, I will not say what they show. His lordship has suffered pain since he was a boy, and Mr. Locke, his secretary, diagnosed an ulcer

211

on the liver when no one else would venture an opinion. Mr. Locke cut him for it when he was like to die if nothing was done. At last resort, you understand; he was strapped down and cut, conscious all the while. He lived, but the wound continued to discharge and Mr. Locke thought it might be dangerous to let it close. So he put in a silver pipe to drain it, and two years ago when his lordship was ill again, replaced it by a longer one of gold. Thirteen years his lordship has endured this torment while men laugh and call him Tapski." He clenched his hands. "I'd gut the lot gladly and give them silver pipes where their bowels were. Don't listen to the malice of his enemies, my lady; there never was a sweeter-tempered master, and a man in my position can judge what others can't."

Lord, thought Arabella, what riddles men were. Wexford loving her in his way, for all his pander's practices and jailer's habits; Shaftesbury, who took French money and whipped the mob after innocent victims for his high purposes, who suffered years of agony without complaint but would not lift a hand to save elderly priests cramped in cold cells for no fault beyond that of being priests. Giles . . . Giles, who was waiting on her doorstep in a fury of jealousy despite having spent the night in a whorehouse.

Chapter Eighteen

"*Where the hell have you been all* night? Although I suppose I need not ask." He wrenched open the hackney door, face ugly with drink and rage.

Wheelock surprised her, turning his back and holding her hand. "Would you like to drive away again, my lady?"

"No...no, of course not," said Arabella wretchedly. She did not intend to be kept from her rooms simply because Giles insisted on behaving like the husband he was not. "Giles, for God's sake don't brawl in the street. Come upstairs if you must, but I am tired and would prefer to see you this evening."

He looked from her to Wheelock, eyes narrowed. "Come mighty low, haven't you, bedding with some common tradesman? My lady Wexford," he added contemptuously. "Your title gave this fellow spice after his own fishwife, I daresay."

Wheelock knocked him down. Arabella stared astounded at Giles sprawling on the cobbles in all his height and strength while Wheelock held his knuckles complacently. She laughed involuntarily. "My lord said he had an unusual secretary, but methinks he has an unexpected valet too! You'd best be gone before he rouses, I can't afford to have bystanders start laying wagers on the outcome of a fight between you."

Wheelock bowed. "As you wish, my lady. If you need his lordship's support, he will—"

"No," said Arabella swiftly. "Leave Giles to think it was you, it's better so."

Wheelock insisted on seeing her inside and then enquired Giles's name, he had recognised him as a soldier from his clothes. "Lock your door, my lady, and do not let him in until time has done its work. His Majesty has personal troops at

213

Windsor, I will suggest to his lordship that Captain Albury is transferred to duties there."

"Thank you," said Arabella with relief. The sooner Giles went before he became even worse than a husband, the better.

Catlin greeted her with her usual censure. "The captain's been like a wild thing since dawn. I had to change my tale, since ye've never been at Whitehall all night before. I told him ye'd been to the theatre with the Grimshaws and ye'd no doubt supped overwell with them. A likely tale when ye come home in the morning, ye'll have to think of a better by tonight."

Arabella giggled, she felt stupidly lighthearted as the pleasures of the night reacted on the absurdity of Giles knocked dizzy by a valet. "I refuse to think of a better. Why should I? He has no rights beyond those I give him and so I have always said."

Catlin shook her head. "Ye'll go a long way and not find a finer man than the captain. What will ye do, pray, when he finds a less troublesome wench?"

"He finds them every day," retorted Arabella, and boxed her ears for impudence.

All the same she dreaded seeing Giles again, too much heat of body lay between them for heedless parting without hurt. She did not feel she could take Wheelock's advice and keep him out for days; he was capable of bursting the door and would be easier to handle if his temper was not freshly inflamed, nor was she minded to cower indoors, waiting for him to cool.

It was very late the following evening before he came, and he had been drinking again. Arabella was in bed but not asleep and let him in herself, calling to Catlin to stay in her attic. She would do best on her own.

She did not kiss him but left her nightrail unlaced, his eyes drawn to her body as they always were, whether he wanted it or not. "I should have expected this," he said jerkily. "But I didn't, although my acquaintance were laughing behind my back no doubt. Who was the swine? He had enough courage to take me unaware, but not to be with you tonight, I see."

"I warned you, Giles. Many times, but you wouldn't listen. I'm not yours, nor ever pretended to be."

"No? There was some fine playacting on Chelsea riverbank then, as well as since. I gave you everything, and offered more. What do you want, for God's sake?"

"I don't know," said Arabella honestly. "Entertainment.

Life. Not to be bored. Not to be trapped so I cannot find myself."

Giles scowled. "I wouldn't expect your fastidious ladyship to discover much to amuse you in a greasy shopkeeper."

"He was neither greasy nor a shopkeeper, and I find my own amusement as I told you. Giles, I beg of you, let us part in amity for the sake of all we have had together."

"No." He grabbed her arm, holding her so her shoulder creaked in its socket. "I'm not in need of friendship or sweet reason. Willing or unwilling, I want you."

"Let go of me, you sot!" His wine-soaked breath was sour on her face, the pain in her arm savage. "I can't give what you want, don't you understand? I never pretended that I could. Once given, my word binds me and I will not be bound."

"Pox on you, then!" He shook her and threw her hard against the wall. She struck one of Wexford's delicately shaped tables, and it splintered under the impact. He laughed and came towards her again.

She scrambled to her feet, arm aflame, above all furiously angry. "Get out! What makes you think a beating will change my mind? Or did women in Tangier enjoy it?"

He slapped her hard, palm and knuckles, first one side then the other of her face. Light exploded and her mouth filled with blood before she felt herself picked up, senses spinning so she scarcely grasped his words. "I am posted to Windsor for some real soldiering at last, thank God. But I will be back, and mean to make sure you will not go whoring after others while I am away." His grip tightened viciously and through waves of pain she felt the bone of her arm snap. Then she was thrown and knew nothing else at all.

There was pain all around when she woke. Sometimes it faded, but was waiting to advance out of the dark again as sense returned.

Catlin kept forcing her to drink and Arabella couldn't explain how the worst pain lodged in her mouth, words blocked by swelling. Another face swam in and out of sight, a doctor heaving at her arm until she screamed.

"Don't tell," she said when she could speak. "Don't tell anyone what happened." A fine fool she would look with a face like a tavern tough; nor did she want Shaftesbury to hear. He had so many burdens, was so driven by events, yet had acted instantly over Giles. Unless word spread of what had happened he would not expect anything to be amiss.

"Don't worry," said Catlin grimly. "No one but the doctor knows and he won't blab. I've no wish for us to be turned out by a landlord anxious for his repute." In the slums it was the victim who suffered and was left for law and landlord to find, not the attacker.

Arabella sat up three days later and called for a mirror. She had a tooth missing, fortunately where it would not show; for the rest she looked like a drab after a difficult night in the stews, but supposed she would mend. Her ribs hurt and her arm dragged uncomfortably under heavy splints; God's blood, she thought, all this for a single night's bedding. Yet she did not regret it; she was furious with Giles but conscious that she had had more than just a night's bedding with Shaftesbury. He had talked to her as an equal, one of the most intelligent men in England eased by her wit as well as by her body. She stared across the room where the flagon he gave her stood on the mantel; her thoughts drifted and she dreamed she heard hammer strokes again, the hiss of annealing and tap of punch strokes which had been the accompaniment of her childhood.

When she woke again, it was dark. I must have Adam here: resolution was framed the instant she stirred, as if her dream of past happiness made her realise for the first time the bleakness of his life. She had not returned to Mrs. Temple's crumbling house, but would go as soon as she was well. This time her own feelings were of no account; she might find him unattractive, a gall on memories best forgotten, but he had a heritage and must be given the chance to grasp it if he could.

Her arm was slow to heal, during which time she stayed indoors, missing the excitements of Shaftesbury's campaign to exclude the Duke of York from succeeding to the throne. Pamphlets poured off the press arguing both sides with varying degrees of scurrility, and Arabella read these avidly, having nothing better to do.

It soon became clear that the exclusionists had lost.

Perhaps the only man able to match Shaftesbury in Parliament had turned against him. George Savile, Marquess of Halifax, held to the hereditary right of succession although he detested York, and Shaftesbury was bested in debate, since exclusion of an undoubted heir was too radical a course to attract propertied men. They might recognize York as a threat but after half a century of unrest recoiled from the revolutionary notion of putting a bastard in his place. Shaftesbury's English balance had told against him once he seemed to be preaching insurrection.

Arabella read Halifax's speech in smudged broadsheets and smiled wryly, remembering his words in Shaftesbury's gallery. It was obvious that as soon as George Savile had defended the cause of legitimacy and won, then closer knowledge of his new friends made him dislike them as heartily as he had come to dislike the old.

She pitied Shaftesbury. He had organised such torrents of petitions for the right to have a Parliament that the issue of whether Parliament should meet or not obscured the bleak fact that the King no longer needed to call one now his pockets were full of French gold. Charles had been provoked into a trial of strength when he would have been content to let time pass, knowing himself the master at last. But once a Parliament was forced on him he moved to rid himself of opposition; without the need to beg money from the English taxpayer and with exclusion appearing a wildly inflammatory notion, there never would be a better time to rally moderates to his side. The country was frightened of another civil war and the squires disliked Shaftesbury's habit of rousing mobs to dramatise his campaigns. They did not agree that York's word would not bind him and were exasperated when Shaftesbury refused to accept pledges on how his power would be exercised.

Only the City of London did not waver in its support. Perhaps merchants were more used to taking a man's word alone as security for their dealings and recognised a bad risk when they saw one. The Lord Mayor and alderman passed a resolution backing Shaftesbury and resolved to deliver it to the King personally: a fearsome quarrel erupted when George Jeffries, their recorder, refused to present it. So the City dismissed him and sent their sheriffs to present it instead although the King refused to receive them.

Arabella stopped dead in her reading; the two sheriffs who presented the petition on behalf of the City were Slingsby Bethel and Henry Cornish.

Suddenly, she was raging with impatience. I must get out of here, out of this God-rotted alley in my life, she thought feverishly. I want to see him again, mark how he looks; eight years since I left Cheapside, surely for past times' sake I could see him now, visit the House of the Spurs, go to the City, my city, the true London, again? Her impatience lasted through the three more weeks she was forced to wait before the splints came off her arm, then through miserable winter weather while she exercised doggedly, regaining its use. Parliament was dissolved, nothing more happening until a fresh one met at Oxford the following month. Oxford . . . away from London mobs and Shaftesbury's base of power; in Oxford the King might triumph as he did not yet dare triumph in his capital.

Who wins London, wins the realm, Shaftesbury had said, and no one had won it yet.

Impatience dried when she went about once more. Away from solitary imaginings, reality settled again. Of course she could not break into Harry's life now; he was a great man in the City with wife and children of his own, perhaps exposed to the King's anger if Shaftesbury lost again in Oxford. Arabella stared at the crowds in Leicester Fields, at chariots and chaises roaring across the cobbles of Whitehall: she didn't seem to belong anywhere any more.

She fetched Adam next day.

Mrs. Temple was completely blind and became tearful over losing him, Adam himself utterly silent as usual. He had grown slightly but was rail-thin, only his eyes alive in a blank, expressionless face. He had no possessions to bring with him and Arabella felt guilt accuse her again when she had never once thought to take him a hobbyhorse or hornbook to learn his letters, the kind of trifle she had taken for granted at his age.

She chattered brightly all the way to Bear Street in the hackney, tongue sticking in her mouth. She was seldom at a loss for words, but had had nothing to do with children since Tam died, and Adam did not so much as nod in answer. Despite all her resolutions, Arabella had to clench her teeth against irritation again.

"Here we are, Adam," she said with relief when they arrived. "I must buy you a trundle bed so you can sleep in the dining room except when I have visitors." He would be much in the way when she did have visitors, she reflected.

He followed her upstairs hesitantly, eyes showing white like a balky horse; wide, polished staircase, fresh paint and airy rooms like nothing he had seen before. Arabella went up with her usual impetuous grace, and had to wait for him at the top. "Good gracious, Adam, can you not move faster than that? I'd have thought you'd be well used to stairs in St. James's."

He muttered something which might have been apology and she tried to feel encouraged. All he needed was a firm hand

and some town polish, perhaps instruction in reading and lettering, and he would improve.

"Look who I've brought you!" She opened the door and called out gaily to Catlin, then stopped dead.

Giles was there; she had forgotten how tall he was until he stood to greet her.

Catlin bustled in. "Why, Adam love! What a surprise!" She jerked her head at Giles. "I didn't know who it was until the door was open, and he promised—"

"I've promised to apologise and go, if that's what you want." Giles's voice was unexpectedly rough. He stared at her as if it was years instead of months since they had parted.

"Very well," said Arabella, stripping off her gloves. She gave Adam a little push. "Go with Catlin, Adam. I'll see you later."

Giles and Arabella stared at each other, silenced by awkwardness, after Catlin and Adam went. I'll be rotted if I'll help him, thought Arabella, and seated herself by the window. She hoped she looked cooler than she felt. She was not afraid of him since he was sober and had come to beg, but anger which had faded slightly with the passing weeks returned in all its starkness.

He tugged at his neckband. "I couldn't stay away any longer. Jesus, Arabella, I was mad with jealousy that night. Will you forgive me?"

"No," said Arabella calmly. "Why should I?"

"Because . . . because I love you! You are enough to drive any man mad, or didn't you know it? I could not bear another finding what I have had from you, and from no other."

She looked at him objectively. His stay at Windsor had thinned bloat from his face and body, given his skin the same tan as when she first met him newly returned from Africa. His eyes were bloodshot, though, and she guessed he still drank heavily. "Why have you come here today?"

He looked disconcerted by her brusque approach, having clearly expected rage or hot-blooded reconciliation. "To ask forgiveness and to start again." He flushed when she laughed derisively. "No, Arabella, I mean it. I swear I won't touch you unless you want me to."

"Nor beat me unless I want that, too? No, Giles, I don't think you sufficiently master of yourself to take the risk. Why should I, after all?"

His eyes moved from her face to her body until she felt her

senses stir under the caress of his gaze, bringing with it so many memories of the ecstasies they had shared. "I think you know why. We deal very well together, you and I. I came here today not only to ask forgiveness but with a proposition. I am ordered to Oxford with a troop of King's Guards. Come with me and I swear that on our return I'll accept what you decide: marriage or parting. No half measures, since I cannot answer for my temper."

She was sorely tempted. Her journey to Newmarket with Wexford was the only time she had left London and she would like the excitement of going to Oxford, now all the world was going there. She wanted to know what happened, to be in the centre of affairs she had briefly touched with Shaftesbury. It was a risk, though. Having lost his temper once yet by his reckoning won her back, Giles would not guard himself in the future, whatever he said now. Still, what was life but risk? "All right," she said abruptly. "If those are your terms, I agree. I'd like to come to Oxford with you."

He came across with a rush and swung her off her feet. "Arabella darling! I knew you loved me!" He kissed her hungrily, hands running over her back, down her thighs. She just had time to feel resentment that he could take her again so easily, before she was borne away on the tide of passion he seemed able to summon out of nowhere.

She had forgotten all about Adam again. When she and Giles were supping together hours later, Catlin pushed him into the room, freshly scrubbed but still wearing the threadbare clothes which were all he possessed.

"Hullo, I remember you were here earlier." Giles put down his fork and turned to Arabella. "Who the devil is he?"

She flushed, wishing Adam did not look like a half-fledged gowk. "My son."

"Your son! Not Wexford's for sure, or he'd be served by a row of lackeys in Pall Mall. Come here, boy, and let's have a look at you."

Adam stayed by the door, his face tight. "Of course he's not Wexford's," said Arabella irritably. "God's blood, he was nearly seventy when I wed him. It's no business of yours whose he is, but he lives here now and you'd best not forget it."

He gave a hoot of derisive laughter. "Don't let him find us twining on a settle d'you mean? My invitation to Oxford doesn't extend to him, you know."

"He can stay here with Catlin." She wished she had been

less impetuous over fetching him today, it would be horribly inconvenient to travel without her maid.

"Come here, brat," said Giles again, not unkindly but his tone putting disobedience beyond possibility.

Adam came, and stood staring vacantly at the table. When Arabella touched him she felt every muscle tense, as if he was straining at some great weight. "Are you ill?" she demanded, she had been a fool not to ask Mrs. Temple about sickness in the district.

His hands twisted, breath heaved. "No," he whispered, and looked up to meet Giles's stare. His face was wet with sweat, the single word an effort beyond imagining.

Giles slopped wine into his glass. "You can't travel without your maid, Arabella, since I must ride with my men. Set him with friends to share a tutor, one more won't make any difference in most schoolrooms, and he looks in need of company. Feeding, too," he added, poking Adam so he leaped and scuttled back to the door.

"Yes, of course," said Arabella, relieved. "I daresay the Grimshaws would have him, they keep a tutor. I'll call there tomorrow." Since she revelled in company and craved change, she never thought of how Adam might find another upheaval of his world terrifying.

Three days later Arabella set out for Oxford in eager anticipation. It was March, and harsh, blustery weather. The countryside did not look beautiful as she remembered it, but desolate, the road full of potholes. When she had travelled to Newmarket she had gone by easy stages in Wexford's coach, this time she jolted hour after hour in the unsprung public stage. By the time she arrived in Oxford she was exhausted, and although she expected to recover quickly once the journey ended, she did not. Giles had hired a room for her near the river; it was damp and dark but she was lucky to have one to herself, accommodation was so scarce.

She shared a single, sloping bed with Catlin when Giles was not there; when he was, Catlin slept in the passage. Arabella tried to make Giles welcome since her company was his payment for bringing her, but felt too unwell to respond as he expected. She was still sick occasionally, as she had been on the stage, and needed to send him scuttling for a basin one morning when he stayed late after coming off duty.

"Ye're breeding," said Catlin bluntly when he had gone.

"And no nonsense about stage sickness, though ye wouldn't have come here if ye'd known."

"Breeding?" said Arabella blankly. "I can't be, not after the remedies I learned have kept me safe so long."

Catlin shrugged. "Are ye sure ye're not?"

Arabella thought back feverishly and realised her convalescence had made her lose count of time; she had vaguely reckoned herself late and put it down to shock after Giles's beating, then forgotten the matter completely. Sweet Jesus, she thought desperately, it's months. Her back hurt too; what she had thought of as discomfort after the journey were niggling pains which reminded her of that dreadful time at Conduit Springs. She lay back, staring at the dirty ceiling, a prey to helpless rage. Another pregnancy when she thought herself safe. She fumbled through memory trying to remember whether she had forgotten her wiles and specifics since she lay with Giles again, and then tensed, recollection clear. Shaftesbury. She had bred with him before and her monthly issue—yes, it had failed before she lay with Giles again. All this time when she had thought herself so clever, perhaps it was handsome, virile Giles who could not breed and she was caught like any country bumpkin the first night she bedded elsewhere. Harry too, only two nights, and she had Adam round her skirts for life. She could have screamed at the unfairness of it all.

There was one small comfort. Once she admitted to herself that she carried a child, she preferred Shaftesbury to be the father rather than Giles, and since there was nothing to be gained by moping in bed now she understood what was the matter with her, she went out next day and felt better for the effort.

Oxford was full of swaggering gangs. Shaftesbury's followers sported green ribbons and waved paper to recall the petition campaign which had helped force Charles to call a Parliament; nobles were attended by retinues they had not thought necessary since the wars; students from the university gathered in shouting groups, while townsmen resentful of the mob which had descended on them robbed the unwary as darkness fell. King's men were everywhere too, swept by the same hysteria Shaftesbury had earlier kindled against papists; this time it went under the name of loyalty to the throne and they set on anyone who refused to shout their slogans. There were also more soldiers than Arabella had ever seen, shoving everyone out of their path, spewing drunk in gutters and almost openly raping Oxford girls. Hurrying messengers were upended into horse troughs by those who thought they served the other side, or for pure sport as violence spread. Bewildered country squires huddled together for security and began to fight out private feuds with rivals from the next county doing likewise. Soldiers, and more soldiers. Men had muttered discontent at how King Charles was building an army in time of peace as English Kings had not done for centuries; here was the evidence of it, kept out of sight until the crucial moment.

Shaftesbury lodged at Balliol College and Arabella saw him once as he drove to a meeting of the Lords. He looked grim, acknowledged cheers and disregarded jostling hostility which threatened to overset his coach. Giles was with her, since it was not safe to walk the streets alone, and observed cheerfully, "Old Tapski's done for and the King will have such guts as the devil left him. He's gone too far in his hammerings to exclude York: the Duke is disliked but men hold to known ways and he has right of inheritance on his side."

"Such known ways as soldiers ruling at their whim, I suppose," retorted Arabella, infuriated by the cheap sneer at Shaftesbury's affliction. "If he loses, we will all regret the consequences."

"For God's sake, mind your tongue! Do you want to join him in the Tower?"

Arabella looked round at frolicking, disorderly crowds. "I think I might prefer my company there." Her belly griped queasily as she thought of Shaftesbury facing defeat alone, and she wished she could have been with him in his coach. It would be more comfortable too, she reflected, and grasped Giles's arm as she was nearly knocked flying by shouting King's men. Tories they were nicknamed by their enemies, after Irish ruffians of that name, and Shaftesbury's opposition became Whigs in riposte, since these were an even bloodier pack of desperadoes causing trouble in Scotland at the time.

"Are you all right, Arabella?" Giles looked down at her white face, this time in Oxford was a disappointment to him since she was so unlike herself, although his duties were amusing enough.

She swallowed, she had not told him what ailed her yet. "It is the crowds and jostling. I think I would be better quiet if you would take me back."

He agreed instantly. "I'm on duty this afternoon, as we all are. Something is brewing, take my word on it."

Even before she was back in her room, the pains started. She lay with the curtains pulled, willing them to stop, scarcely knowing whether she wanted this child or whether her memories of Mistress Dawkins made a miscarriage seem unreasonably terrifying. Women had them all the time, she told herself; it would be better than another child underfoot for years.

All the same, she wept when the pain came. I don't want to lose this baby, she thought wildly, nails digging into rotten wicker at the bedhead. She relaxed as the pain faded, it was going to be all right. But after a few minutes another started, tightening into cramp. These were the spaced pains she had suffered during Adam's birth. She moaned and twisted; she was quite alone, Catlin out somewhere gaping at the crowds.

Alone, with only shadows moving slowly across the ceiling and fleas in the bedstraw for company.

She could hear shouts drifting over the grey walls of Magdalen, yells, clattering hooves of horses. Sound blended with her moans, time lost all meaning. A tear of agony worse than the rest and warmth drenched her thighs.

She had lost the child, which this time she had very nearly wanted.

She was staring dry-eyed at the dark when Catlin returned, chattering with news which instantly turned to concern when she discovered what had happened.

"I've feared it since ye've felt unwell, and wondered how ye'd manage the journey home. If 'twas to happen, 'twas best done at once," she said practically, bustling about with fresh coverings and water. "Ye'll not even have to tell the captain, he won't be back for a day or so, I'm thinking. The King has dissolved Parliament again, and the military are out of town. Men say they're under arms in case there's resistance."

Arabella's eyes filled with the easy tears of weakness. She and Shaftesbury had both lost more than either knew on the same day. "The opposition...the Whigs...Lord Shaftesbury?"

"They're milling around the streets but there's no disorder. No one wants war again and they know the soldiers aren't far, hands itching on their swords."

"Shaftesbury?" she repeated.

"Gone. The King was set to arrest him, or so they say."

She shrugged. "I dunno. He's slipped the noose for the moment anyway."

He had not escaped but returned to London, so forcing one last encounter with the King, in the city where he had said their duel would be decided. He had lost command of Parliament by attempting to place a bastard son in place of legitimate succession; now he set the law itself at issue. Would the King dare try Shaftesbury himself for treason, and use his judges to carry out the murder he would then require, when Shaftesbury was the man who had taught them how easily evidence could be twisted? When he had also put laws like Habeas Corpus on the statute book?

Arabella did not return to London until the end of April, and found it in almost as great a turmoil as Oxford had been. One-sided turmoil, though. King's men were everywhere, extravagant loyalty the rage. Exclusion had failed, Charles was victorious, and York one day would rule if he outlived his brother. Men were looking to their interests and in the foreseeable future these were royal. Shaftesbury lived openly in Aldersgate Street, waiting for the King to strike, and Charles hesitated until July; then arrested him on a charge of high treason, and placed him in the Tower.

He immediately petitioned under Habeas Corpus for a writ to bring him to trial or allow bail. After consulting the King, his judges ruled that the Tower was out of their jurisdiction and therefore exempt from the act, and in revenge Shaftesbury's confinement was made harsher. From this at least his poor health soon released him. He became seriously ill and since the King could not afford to have him die on his hands, he was given better quarters.

Arabella drove to the City. This time she could not keep away and ordered her hackney to go to Aldersgate Street by way of Cheapside. St. Paul's was a mass of builders' scaffolding, outer walls rising in glittering grey stone, otherwise there were no ruins left. Everything was rebuilt and bustling: a few churches still lacked spires, otherwise the splendid, elegant streets made her blink. Raised pavements where she used to walk in the dirt, richly dressed merchants strolling where these same men had struggled to re-establish their trade from hovels and holes in the ground a handful of years ago; women taking the air in safety when before the fire they seldom ventured into filthy, teeming streets. Pipes of drilled and jointed sycamore bringing water right into new houses, a glimpse of

225

rebuilt Guildhall glinting with gold and paint, everywhere the red and white sign of George's Cross and sword, the City shield in place of the royal arms she had grown used to elsewhere in London. Her breath tightened as the hackney clattered past King Street where Furnival Alley once had been. The House of the Golden Spurs. A splendid wrought-iron sign gilded as in her father's day but fastened to the wall instead of swinging, since City streets must be kept clear of obstruction since the fire. Fresh brick, large windows, a painted board by the door with Harry's name and corncake sign, a much larger one on the house adjoining. Then they were past.

Arabella leaned back against leather, sweat prickling her body. It did not look as she expected at all. Of course, she had watched Cheapside rebuilding, but when she left it remained a confusion of bricks and scaffolding, the roadway bottomless mud. The vigorous bustle of the City touched a responsive nerve too; she was part of this and no amount of politicking at Whitehall or ease in St. James's could change it. Here, crammed together, fortunes were made and lost, colonies founded, ships sent to Cathay or the Indies laden with English goods, and exotic luxuries resold. Here silver was hammered and gilt applied amid the deadly fumes; fish, skins, metals, clocks, a thousand other things made and shipped, coins minted, dealings settled on men's word alone in the rebuilt Royal Exchange.

There was a token guard outside Thanet House, where Shaftesbury had lived, and the shutters were up. She told the hackney to drive to the rear and then dismissed him. She had dressed in her shabbiest clothes, but even the back door of such a mansion was difficult to pass, a footman in a well-frilled shirt telling her curtly to begone.

"I want to see Mr. Wheelock, and will stay here until I have," said Arabella flatly. She lowered her mask and smiled at him. "I know he tends his lordship in the Tower but if you will let me in I won't give any trouble until he comes again."

He hesitated, not proof against her unblemished skin and brilliant eyes, a trifle overawed by her style. She was a beauty, and not at all the usual type of back-door caller. "Stay here then, it's as much as my position's worth to let you in, but as luck will have it, Mr. Wheelock's here. If he vouches for you—what name shall I give?"

"No name. When no one else is by, bid him remember the

cobblestones of Bear Street and ask whether his knuckles healed."

He looked at her doubtfully and shut the door in her face. If he'd been made a fool of by a pretty face then Mr. Wheelock would have him cleaning grates for a month.

Arabella shivered a long time on the doorstep. An autumn breeze was blowing, full of London damp, the day unsuited to waiting about kitchen yards.

The door opened at last, Wheelock bowing as if he entered a royal salon. "Madame, if you would come this way?" He did not call her "my lady" in front of listeners, and led her to a basement office. He smiled faintly. "The steward is out about his accountings, with all his lordship's papers seized nothing is simple these days."

Arabella tugged at her gloves, fingers trembling. "How is he? I—I had to come but don't want to add any further burdens—" Her voice trailed away; she had no idea of Shaftesbury's domestic situation beyond his one comment about his first wife.

"Won't you sit down?" Wheelock pulled out a chair and helped her with cloak and mask. "His lordship has been very ill, but is recovering. He is determined to stand trial and will live to face it, since his spirit has always been stronger than his body."

"How—where is he kept?"

"He was kept in a stifling hole of a place, like an oven under the sun and slime wet on the walls at night. He is better lodged now, since he would have died else." His lips tightened. "You know how it is with him, and conditions like that would infect a whole man."

Arabella looked down at her hands, plaiting and replaiting the fingers of her gloves. "What will happen, do you think?"

Wheelock smiled unexpectedly. "Why, we shall see such a trial as England has never seen before. His lordship has not long to live, madame, and will enjoy it, I think. He hates losing and will try to win so long as he has life, but is in too much pain for death itself to worry him unduly."

"Yes," said Arabella thoughtfully. "I can imagine him like that very easily. Will you tell him I came, and have not forgotten him? The marks must still be equal for a balance even if the punch has slipped a little at the moment."

"I will tell his lordship, madame, and give you now the greeting I know he would desire you to have." He bent and

227

kissed her hand, before helping with her cloak again. As she had thought before, Wheelock was a very unexpected valet, and testimony for a Shaftesbury his political opponents would not recognise.

Shaftesbury was brought before a grand jury a month later, on a charge of high treason. Since both the Tower and his home were in the City, the jury was chosen by its sheriffs, no longer Harry since his year of office was ended, but of Whig inclination as might have been expected. Twelve leading citizens sat as jurymen and listened to contradictory, disreputable witnesses allege that Shaftesbury had plotted rebellion, disbelieved the pack of them and threw out the charge without Shaftesbury ever having to plead on his own behalf. The City rang with bells and was lit by bonfires as was customarily done for victory over foreign enemies, while the news stunned the rest of London and the court. It had indeed been such a trial as England had never seen before, although not in the way Wheelock had expected.

Shaftesbury had failed through Parliament, but now the City had come out in insolent defiance of the King's will, and as if to emphasise its independence, when Shaftesbury was released on bail the Lord Mayor held a banquet in his honour at Guildhall.

Who holds London, holds the realm. Who holds the City with its wealth and ancient liberties, its charter and self-government, holds London.

"And that stands of itself," said Arabella to Adam as the sound of bells drifted faintly on the wind; she wished she was in Cheapside to share this moment. "I'll take you there one day and you'll see for yourself."

Chapter Nineteen

Arabella had finally achieved a better relationship with Adam, after several false beginnings and much misunderstanding. She had been so alarmed by his state when she returned from Oxford that in spite of her preoccupations with Shaftesbury and Giles, she forced herself to persevere in attempts to gain his confidence. He had always been small, now he seemed like an old, wizened gnome. He held himself hunched together and was limping.

"Them scaggish Grimshaw boys," said Catlin. "They're not much older but twice his size; they racked him up proper, I reckon."

"Oh, Adam," said Arabella, irritated. "Can't you look after yourself at all? Beat them if they beat you?"

He flushed and as soon as she said it she realised she was being unjust. He was completely defenceless. He had been taught nothing, knew nothing except life in ramshackle hovels filled with dressmaking or washing; he had no words, no strength, no skills.

He had pride, though.

She gradually came to realise that his silence came from fear of disgracing himself, of disappointing her in some way he did not understand. He knew nothing of her except what he had been told: she was infinitely grand and out of his reach, he was fortunate if she condescended to look at him occasionally. If he disgusted her, and fine ladies were easily disgusted, then she would go away and he would be left alone in the slums forever; so far, each time he encountered her she had been repelled by him, and Adam knew it.

He had grown up in a world which offered him nothing, so

229

he literally starved from the lack around him. Not physically, although Moll's unappetising gruels left him with a temperamental digestion, but in every other way. Almost by accident Arabella discovered his craving for books; he admitted that he had not run away from the Grimshaws only because their tutor taught him his letters.

So in the afternoons she read him anything which came to hand, declaimed Shaftesbury's or Halifax's speeches from pamphlets, taught him to read from her father's massive Bible. She had saved it from the fire and left it with Bevil when she married since it had family names from the past hundred years inscribed on the flyleaf and she had not wanted any prying into her past. Now she claimed it back after an acrimonious scene and wrote Adam's name there, impressing him with the splendour of his grandfather's craft.

He fingered the flagon when she told him of the House of the Spurs, and she found him several times in her bedroom looking at it. "Would you like to be a silversmith one day, Adam? I am sure that for my father's sake, I could find someone willing to take you as apprentice and you are of an age when we must be thinking what you want to do."

He rubbed his hands on his breeches, he still hesitated before speaking, searching anxiously for possible offence. "I don't know. I—I shouldn't like to be less than he was, when his name is still remembered with respect.".

She hugged him. He disliked being touched, in his experience the prelude to beating or humiliation, but she had persisted and now he suffered it without running in a corner. Jesus, she thought as he tensed like woven rope, a wife will have a task to force intimacy out of him. "I don't think you need fear it. I have a stupid notion that whatever you do, you will accept no second best. It may not be silver, but I hope one day you'll live in the House of the Spurs and put your name on the wall. It's mine again in a few years' time, you know."

His eyes glowed, although he was rarely stirred to enthusiasm. "Yes, I will. I swear it."

"No, no!" She laughed. "Don't swear things like that, no one can tell what the years bring. You wouldn't believe the stupid scrapes I have fallen into through swearing rashly."

"Well, I will. One day." He hesitated. "Do you—could you speak to me ever of my father? I know..." His voice stumbled. His face was a dull brick-red, over-large hands and feet shuffling. "You tell me of my grandfather, the House of the Spurs. I would like to know . . . one day . . . who my father was."

Arabella was so startled she nearly slapped him for insolence; he had never asked anything about himself before. "What makes you want to know all of a sudden?" Surely he was too young for such matters although his manner was completely adult. Adam was a child who had never known childhood.

He shook his head, tongue-tied again.

She sat down and took him by the shoulders. "Tell me why you want to know."

He avoided her eyes for a long time, when he looked up at last it was with Harry's ice-grey, determined stare. "I've wanted to know ever since I can remember. Wouldn't you if everyone said you were spawned by rats out of the gutter? That even you didn't know who my father was? The Grimshaw boys—" He gulped but his gaze did not waver. "They held me over flame till I admitted it. I—I . . . afterwards I thought I might have been able to hold out against them if I'd known it wasn't true. Or if it was, then I might as well admit it before the flame next time."

"Oh, Adam." She wanted to weep at the desolation in his voice. He had not told her before how he had come by the suppurating sore they found on his ribs after he returned from the Grimshaws'. What unthinking harm she had done him for so long, and there was no easy way to undo it. But this misery must not be left a moment longer; Harry would agree, whatever the consequences. "You have a father to be proud of, a past sheriff of the City. Last year when Parliament was dissolved and the King's men everywhere triumphant, I read that he was one of the five aldermen who went to Windsor to petition the King to call regular Parliaments for the upholding of the realm." Charles had refused to see them, but the petition stood.

"Really? I really have . . . you are not just—"

"I swear, and you know what I think about swearing. One day I'll see that he knows you for his son, but—" She broke off, staring at the flagon across the room but seeing only Harry's face. Harry who had said they would be lucky if either found again what she denied between them. "I love your father, Adam," she said steadily. "I think I always have but did not see it so, was unable to see it until I knew more of life. He loved me, too; never think that you came from anything but love. Perhaps when you are older you'll understand it all a little better and forgive; I don't think now that I understand myself."

231

After that she often found Adam spelling out some of the many broadsheets which were being printed in a pamphlet war raging between court and City. Charles had been incensed by the aldermen's petition coming on top of Shaftesbury's acquittal, and had a stroke of luck the summer following. The Lord Mayor normally served a year in office, and unless he declined to stand or was obviously unsuitable, the next-senior alderman followed him in office. When Whig Sir Patience Ward retired as mayor, the senior alderman was Sir John Moore, one of the few court supporters amongst the aldermen. In spite of protests he was duly installed in office and proceeded to nominate Tory sheriffs. Since the aldermen also claimed the right to nominate, the quarrel raged for months with elections, protests and counter-elections following hard upon each other. Finally the King sent soldiers to throw out the aldermen supervising proceedings since the citizens' choice was consistently Whig. One of those so handled was Henry Cornish, but force prevailed. Tory sheriffs were installed and Shaftesbury, who had been living with impunity in the City all the year, went into exile in the Netherlands since he could expect no mercy from juries which would now be packed in the court interest. He died two months later; after such long struggle an undoubted loser.

The King, whom men thought of as good-natured and easygoing, had almost realised the long Stuart aim of absolute power and moved on his last enemy.

The City of London.

Even before the death of Shaftesbury, the next phase of the struggle opened. Sir John Moore was bad enough as mayor, but the next alderman in seniority was little better than a bought court toady, and his fellow aldermen took the almost unprecedented step of refusing to accept him, the mayoral election contested for the first time in years. Henry Cornish was one of two candidates nominated to stand in the Corporation's interest.

Arabella could not resist telling Adam that this was his father. She ought not, when it was unsafe to give Harry's enemies a single opening for attack at such a time, but she decided that he deserved to know and swore him to secrecy. Whatever his faults, Adam was reliable and certainly no talker. He watched himself less carefully now with her but made no other friends; he loathed Giles, who still came to Bear Street in spite of what he said about not accepting half measures, and spent much of his time reading or wandering on his own through the streets and alleys off the Strand and Whitehall. Arabella made him promise not to go to the City now he knew who his father was, and felt rewarded by the change in him once his yearning for pride was given roots. There was still so much he could not express, and passionate hero worship for a father who did not know him supplied some of the lack.

He nearly always came home with a pocketful of pamphlets, most of them extremely obscure for a boy to grasp. He understood them, though, expressionless face and silence his defences against a hostile world, not signs of stupidity as she had thought. "The Lord Mayor has sold his charge," he said disgustedly after careful perusal of a stack he had brought home. "The aldermen's return of votes puts Cornish and Gold first, but the mayor has declared his court creature, Pritchard, elected and the King's judges accepted it. What do you think my father will do now?"

Arabella smiled at the proprietary way he said it. "There is little he or the Corporation can do surely, without rebellion, and sober merchants are not the men to overset the state."

"They could take the whole matter to the courts and challenge such a falsified election," said Adam hopefully.

"Before George Jeffries and hired Tory juries? They would certainly lose." Since he had been dismissed by the City as their recorder, Jeffries had gone over entirely to the court; his change of loyalty hastened by the indignity of presiding over the court which threw out the charges against Shaftesbury when, for good measure, the jury had also been extremely rude about his judicial malpractices.

Adam sniffed. "Do you know what a man told me in Whitehall today? The King himself said Jeffries had no learning, no sense, no manners and more impudence than ten carted street walkers."

Arabella laughed, as a woman she was no more proof than the rest against Charles Stuart's charm. "I can imagine him saying it, but it hasn't stopped him making Jeffries Lord Chief Justice. Years ago he told me he would be Chief Justice and Lord Chancellor one day; I had forgot until this moment, but he wagered me a brooch that he would have them both within ten years."

"How long ago?"

She thought back carefully to the gathering in the Duke of York's gallery, and Wexford's contempt for both Coleman and

Jeffries. "It must be nearly six now, he has another four to make good the second part of his boast."

"What did you wager in return?"

"A silver casket," she said ruefully, "and you may be sure he'll be on the doorstep the morrow of his appointment. But surely he is too much of a scoundrel for the King to stomach him long as Chief Justice, let alone Lord Chancellor."

"There's no knowing with this King," said Adam darkly, as if he had personal knowledge of His Majesty.

When appealed to, Giles agreed with Arabella. "The fellow's always drunk. The King told him his brain would turn to vapour when he went on circuit in the August sun."

Adam went out of the room, slamming the door so Giles exclaimed angrily. "Wait until I get my hands on that brat of yours! He's lived too long with women and needs a whipping each day to learn respect. When do you intend to be rid of him?"

"Why, never, or so I hope," said Arabella coolly. "My home is his so long as he desires to stay, and anyone who comes had best understand his position here. And no more whippings either, he has endured enough harshness in his life."

"He takes advantage of you and it's more than time he was set to a trade, though God knows what master would take on such an unhandy, insolent whelp. Perhaps you'd best put him to climb chimneys since it is the only task he's fitted for. What manner of monstrosity did you bed, my dear, to birth a misshapen dwarf? No one can say your figure lacks symmetry."

"Get out," said Arabella, voice shaking, bile thick in her throat. "Get out and never come back. Adam's father is five times the man you'll ever be, and Adam too, one day. You are good for one thing only and I've kept you like a tame tomcat because from you I do not breed. Once there was more than lust between us and I owed you a debt because you came to Prance's shop with me, but by my reckoning I have paid your due and more besides these past few years. Can you remember when you last came here to give pleasure as well as take it?"

"My dear Arabella," he drawled. "Since when does a man think of more than habit after four years of the same woman's body? Though you're still beautiful, I'll admit, but unwomanly for all your looks and growing into shrewishness with age." He came over and, despite herself, she flinched. He was not drunk, but not sober either, and his temper lightly held. He laughed. "You do well to fear me, but this time I'll not touch you. I was mad with jealousy before, now you're not worth the trouble of throwing across the room." He grasped her chin brutally between fingers and thumb before clamping his mouth on hers in a hurtful, derisive kiss. When her senses cleared, he had gone.

Her jaw was so stiff she could not eat properly that evening, but when Adam remarked on it, she told him she had a toothache. He possessed a relentless temper when roused, and was capable of subtle revenges since he lacked muscle for the usual tussles between boys. She had discovered by accident that both the Grimshaw boys suffered burns when a roast-chestnut seller upset his charcoal as they were passing. Mrs. Grimshaw bewailed the series of chances which enabled the chestnut man to get clear away when chased by their groom: Arabella agreed politely that the state of the streets was a scandal, but detected her son's planning in his escape. Since he had a six-inch scar on his ribs where he had been held over a lamp while staying with the Grimshaws, she simply startled him by congratulating him on his success, but had no wish for him to devise a similar requitement for a man of Giles's dangerous stamp.

So for the first time since she came from Cheapside, Arabella found herself without an admirer, although she was detached enough to feel wry amusement at her own predicament. She disliked living for any length of time without a man, not only for bodily pleasure, but because women bored her. She was not domestic except that she ran her own establishment, whatever it was, very capably. This stemmed from impatience with inefficiency, however, rather than any concern for housewifery; she enjoyed men's conversation, compliments and affairs, and found that matters which interested them usually interested her, too.

She still had an entrée to the salons of St. James's through her connection with the Wexfords, and after much anxious peering in the mirror decided that her looks had not yet deserted her. Giles's taunts at her age shook her more than she cared to admit, although until then she seldom remembered that her thirtieth birthday lay behind her. Sweet Jesus, thirty! Once past thirty women rotted fast. Skin dried and became infected as cosmetics had to be more thickly applied, muscles sagged, yearly pregnancies dragged down those who had survived the first seven or eight children without serious complication.

Arabella remembered Harry's comment on cosmetics and

used them sparingly: she was confident she did not look thirty, but she did fear childbirth. Once she was back in the salons of St. James's she could have had a dozen liaisons, but no one attracted her enough to make the risks seem worthwhile. Adam was a complication, too. Almost certainly he would loathe Giles's successor as much as he had detested Giles, and as he became more confident so he was more likely to prove an embarrassment.

She still had no wish to marry, yet only a lover from the highest rank of society would give her sufficient standing not to be ostracised: it was all very disheartening and complicated. But if time was slipping by, so too was money. Although she tried to live simply, appearances must be kept up; she also needed to play the tables, but could not afford to lose. Adam ought to have a tutor, and a good one; as his ghosts faded his mind burst out of its constraints, avidly seeking stimulation. It seemed to Arabella that he had become interested in everything and she was annoyed when he left her far behind in swift, intuitive leaps of imagination. He also possessed the kind of application which rejected inadequate or too simple explanation, so was often excessively uncomfortable to live with.

She met George Jeffries once in a gallery of Whitehall and he recognised her instantly. "My lady Wexford! I trust you have not forgot our wager?"

"If I had, I am sure you would be unhandsome enough to remind me," said Arabella tartly. "Providing you won, of course. You aren't Chancellor yet."

He hitched his gown higher on his shoulders. "I am like to be, and Lord Chief Justice is no beggarly office meanwhile."

"Perhaps it depends on who occupies it. To be Lord Mayor of London was a matter for respect until this year, when a man was put in at the point of a sword." Jeffries had been the judge who accepted the falsified poll.

His eyes narrowed; they were deeply pouched and his face patterned with drinker's broken veins, the pale, fastidious young man she had met at Bevil's ten years before almost unrecognisable under jowls and bloat. "That is treason, my fair Arabella, and suffcient to gain you death by burning at this time. As for my office—soon the City will be under the King's hand and his Chief Justice eat mayors and aldermen for breakfast." He roared with laughter, as if he had made the wittiest quip of an evening's jesting.

"Never," said Arabella flatly.

"You think not, eh? Then come to Westminster Hall tomorrow and hear them grovel. Their fine new recorder will be pleading for their charter—the fools," he added contemptuously. "The King issued a writ to demand by what right they choose their own sheriffs when His Majesty appoints all others in his realm, and they thought a chestful of charters proving they had done it for five hundred years would settle the matter."

"And doesn't it? Five hundred years of charters, and of Kings pledged to uphold them, would seem sufficient proof to me."

"This King does not intend subjects to dispute his will, and laws are but words patched over holes. I am not worth my keep as Chief Justice if I cannot find my way through a pack of quibbling charters, and prove whatever I choose. When the City loses its case the penalty will be forfeiture of all rights, not just those of appointing sheriffs."

"When, not if? You would forfeit the City's charter over some trifle of interpretation?"

"Why not? They'll be given another, with privilege struck out and the King in his rightful place. Already our juries have made a start, now opponents of the King face fines for defamation each time they open their mouths. Ten thousand pounds the last Whig Lord Mayor is owing so far."

Harry, thought Arabella. What fines and harassment will he face if the charter goes? "I should like to come tomorrow," she said slowly. "Westminster Hall, you said?"

"Aye, my little rebel. I'll tell my clerk to reserve a seat for you, you'd profit from a lesson in loyalty. Also, I must convince you that my casket will soon be due, so you'll start saving for it." He stamped off, laughing.

Arabella thought wistfully of Wexford's prophecy that Jeffries as well as Coleman would end on the scaffold: God send he was right, but she feared his nature was now well suited to the times.

Westminster Hall was crowded when Arabella arrived the following morning. She knew nothing of law courts and the clamour took her aback. Men strolled and chatted, hawkers peddled pies, the stark stone walls under a splendid roof echoing sound. She attracted curious stares since few women came to such a place, but Jeffries had remembered his promise and a clerk placed a chair for her in what seemed the center of all the blown draughts of the universe. Outside was a brisk winter's day, and in Westminster Hall where only judges sat near a roaring fire, it was icy. Words, often in Latin, floated past distorted by distance: King's Bench court was no more than tiered seats at one end of the hall. Eventually she made out that a knot of men facing the bench represented the City, their spokesman the new recorder, Sir George Treby, while five figures wrapped in fur and rich cloth under painted royal escutcheons were the judges.

The sense of crisis she expected was lacking. After all, the City itself was on trial for its life; there London's beginnings lay and becasue of it these men guarded rights wrested from centuries of reluctant Kings. Yet the proceedings Arabella watched were formal, usually courteous, an endless droning of precedent and clauses. She would have drowsed if it had not been so cold.

Except for one thing. Each time the recorder answered, he prefaced his argument with the flat, clear statement: "That this City is, and time out of mind was, an ancient city and county, its citizens a body politic by right established." No grovelling, such as Jeffries had predicted.

A stir at last as the court adjourned, and Arabella stood on shivering legs; there seemed little point returning when she understood so little of it. She stilled suddenly. One of the men talking to the recorder, stretching stiffly after the hours the City representatives had been made to stand before the judges...

Without thought, she thrust through jostling people, not noticing any of them, and touched his arm. "Harry."

He turned, still saying something, then words died and expression drained from his face so he was almost a lampoon of Adam, a likeness she never expected to see. "Bella." His lips moved, but no sound came.

She nodded, it was ridiculous to be struck dumb after so many years at court, where words were tools to shuffle over any awkwardness.

He recovered himself with an effort and bent over her hand. "It is good to see you after so long, my lady."

Her eyes filled with tears. "Oh, Harry, is that all?"

His face was completely colourless, the light tie wig he wore no shelter. He always disliked heavy wigs, she remembered irrelevantly. "Would that it could be more, but I am not a safe person to know these days. Especially in Westminster Hall."

"Then somewhere else, please, Harry. Just this once, for— for past times. Will you walk part of the way home with me?"

He bent over her hand again. "Farewell, my lady." Then he added, very low, "Take a hackney to St.-Martin-in-the-Fields and wait inside." He turned back to his friends.

She waited a long time, the church even bleaker than Westminster Hall. There flames from the great hearth gave an illusion of comfort as they flickered over mellow walls and ancient timber; here all was new, the stone aggressively bright, clear glass reflecting scudding February sky.

Harry came at last, taking her hand and tucking it deep into warmth between his elbow and ribs. "What a place for an assignation! My wits were scattered or I would surely have thought of a better." He smiled at her, in a way Arabella had forgotten but remembered instantly. "Do you know how much I want to kiss you? For past times' sake, of course."

She chuckled shakily. "Let's find somewhere warmer to do it, then. Harry, it's . . . good to see you again."

He did not reply, but his arm held her tightly against him as they went into the street again.

He hired a private parlour in a tavern nearby, and sent a boy scurrying for punch. "Though in a place like this it will be poor stuff," he remarked, stooping over a sullen fire. "A moment and I'll have this burning for you."

Arabella watched him arrange coals with deft competence, everything about him so familiar they might have been parted a week instead of nearly eleven years. The flat City intonation of his voice, so different from Whitehall drawl or nasal Strand twang, the slope of shoulder and set of head distinct from all others she had known. He had not thickened at all with the years, in fact his face had thinned. New lines either side of his nose and beneath his eyes as if he lacked sleep, otherwise he was exactly as imagination remembered him; and the eyes were Adam's, so needed no recalling.

He stood when the fire was burning to his satisfaction and they stared at each other while a boy came and went with punch, as if they could never look enough. "You're shivering," he said suddenly. "Here—" He slipped off his caped overcoat and wrapped it round her, led her to a settle as if she was a child, and brought over goblets of steaming punch. "Your health, my dear, even if it needs no toasting. You look more beautiful than in my memory, although I thought it faithful enough."

She laughed, sound catching in her throat. "I'm over thirty, Harry. I looked in the mirror the other day and thought—I thought how long it has all been."

He sat beside her, arm tight around her shoulders. "My God, how long. I used to hear news of you from Will; these last few years when you've hardly met he's had little to impart."

"You did, Harry? You did too? And cursed his tongue which never said the things you wanted to hear?"

"Always, although I swore that I only sought word of old acquaintance. Do you know that I once existed for six months on a description of your maid's insolence?"

"And I on how you were like to be chosen alderman."

He sighed. "That might be something I slept easier without."

She turned her head to look at him, a breath away at her shoulder. "You said you might be dangerous to know just now. Tell me, how serious is your position?"

"It's serious for us all, as you must know since you took the trouble to come to Westminster today. We've fought Charles Stuart and his ambitions four years now and he has us in a corner. He means to take the charter whatever our rights may be, and since the judges are his creatures we cannot stop him short of rebellion, and that no one wants."

"And once he has it, the weathercocks will swing in the City too, and be rewarded by licence to sue Whig merchants before judges who will always find against them?"

"That's about it," he said ruefully. "I have a judgment of a thousand marks against me already for inciting riot last year, when the King forced his choice of sheriff on us."

"Did you?"

He laughed. "I counted the liverymen's votes as was my duty, regardless of some jackanapes with a sword who thought he could stop me. He had me thrown down Guildhall steps in the end, and counted them himself."

"Which came to a very different total from your reckoning?"

He nodded. "As you say. Bella, my sweeting, have you noticed how already we might never have parted? We babble of mayors and sheriffs to keep ourselves at bay."

"Yes," she said, smiling. "I had noticed."

He kissed her. "Bella, my love."

"Oh, Harry."

"It seems there are never the right words to speak of love, or years lost, either. Only us, finding ourselves again."

"It's so silly," said Arabella contentedly, much later. "Holding hands and kissing on a hard oak settle like a pair of 'prentices on a Sunday. Nice, though." She put her hand to his face, the line of bone achingly familiar.

He lifted her on his lap, holding her tightly, fiercely almost. "You haven't married again, have you?"

"No, but..." She did not want to hide anything from him, but he cut her short.

"I don't want to know. Whatever there's been, there's been both good and bad. For me, too. Elizabeth...my wife...I would not discuss her with you except I don't want you to think—" His voice trailed away, then he set her down and stood to face her. "I want you, Bella, God knows I always have. Not secretly in a flea-ridden tavern but as mine for everyone to know. But it isn't possible. Elizabeth has been a good wife to me, and is frail after six children in ten years, although only three live. I can't add to her troubles by letting acquaintance see you with me. But...I must keep from her, have done so these past two years, since another child would kill her. I wanted you to know that though I can only offer secrecy, you need not feel it theft as well. She understands I must sometimes go elsewhere. Bella—you always had my love and nothing since has altered it. If it would please you at all, you would only be taking your own again from me." He stopped, breathing heavily.

"Yes," she said simply. "The wrong was mine all those years ago, and Elizabeth my victim more than yours. Nothing will change it, except we may salvage a little happiness on our way. There is something you should know, though. We have a son."

He stared at her, face tight with shock. "That time in Cheapside?"

"Well, there wasn't any other," she said, ruffled.

"Of course not. I meant, my God, you went off and—"

"I didn't know," she pointed out. "Not until later and then...I was stupid and selfish, I admit it. It seemed that I would be locking us both in a trap, you in the oldest one of all, the wench who begs for her child after seduction. Me, well, you know how I felt about living my life within four walls and a courtyard; I wasn't capable of loving you until I'd broken out. So I married Wexford instead."

There was a long silence. "The boy is acknowledged as his?"

"No," she said wretchedly. "Everything went wrong." Stumblingly she explained, tried to explain, found it impossible to explain. Above all how she had left Adam so long alone.

"Why in heaven's name did you not come to me?" he demanded when she had done. "You can't have thought I would refuse to provide for him."

"Somehow it was never possible, although it seems madness now. As if I was possessed by another self, all greed and pride, but at the time I tried to do the best I could. It's just that my best didn't amount to much."

"You say he lives with you now, though?"

She nodded. "And I love him dearly, although I was long realising it." This was not true; neither she nor Adam could forget the past. A better understanding had grown between them but softer emotions failed to strike roots. "Harry, I told him about you, your name and everything. He needed to know, he—he is rather an unusual person. He swore he'd never try to see you until I said he could, but he had suffered so much from not knowing that I thought we both owed him a father he could respect."

Colour came and went under his skin, leaving it almost grey. "God send I may be able to live up to my character, then. I would like to come back with you if I may."

She was taken aback. "Now?"

"Why not?" He looked at her keenly. "What else is there you haven't told me?"

He knew her too well. Eleven years apart and he knew her better than Giles had ever done. Haltingly, she tried to prepare him for seeing Adam. "You see, he has built you into everything he is not. I am not sure whether he cares what most others think, but you could hurt him dreadfully if you showed distaste."

He made some exclamation under his breath and turned his back to lean on the mantel, staring into the fire. "You said he was unusual," he said jerkily. "Is he simple?"

"He has the sharpest brain of any boy I've met, sharper than most men, too. He seems stupid because he fears contempt, I think knew nothing else until he came to me. God help me," she added. "I dream of it sometimes, but it is done. He has a look of you, Harry, the same eyes and tilt of head, but in all else . . . he is smaller than he ought to be and so lacks proportion."

"Why?"

She took a deep breath. "I starved myself while I was increasing, to gain time. Perhaps it was that, perhaps a stomach bred from Cheapside could not take Moll's slops. I don't know, except as always I am the one to blame, not him."

242

She thought he would never turn, when he did he took her in his arms and held her. Not with passion this time but as no other man had ever held her, to give comfort, his cheek to hers. "I cannot believe there is another woman who would have said it so, without shuffling. It's done, as you said. So much is done we both would wish undone; my blame for his birth is clear enough, but there's only more harm in looking backward. Surely we must manage better in the future, however little we can have, since at least we are not fighting each other any more."

She wanted to touch seven black cats and spit in the nearest horse trough, she was so happy. As if she could feel the devil thrash his tail and wait for her undoing, since good fortune never lasted and she could not remember happiness before. She felt real affection for Shaftesbury in spite of all his failings, had experienced physical ecstasy with Giles; even her relationship with Wexford had been lanced of bitterness at the end. With Harry she came home: all reason fled, no calculation in her mind that the half-life which was all she could have with him might not be worth it. She could not imagine how they had lasted until today apart, often scarcely noticing so great a lack.

He laughed when she told him how she had named Adam, then frowned. "I suppose Furnival is better than most names when we know how it binds us together, but I should like to give him mine, were it possible. Though at present he is best without it; any Cornish stands in danger of being fleeced and then thrown into Newgate by the first King's officer who sets eyes on him."

They were walking to Bear Street past the pillory at Charing Cross; some poor wretch sagged there plastered in filth, neck wrenched askew as consciousness faded. Arabella shivered. "Don't jest about it."

"I wasn't jesting," he said grimly. "Once the charter goes, and it will, every Whig in the City is at the mercy of packed courts and bought constables. I am a rich gander for the plucking and will have to tread very warily if I am not to be beggared by fines."

"There is no way to defend the charter?"

"None, before a bench of Tory judges led by Jeffries. I hope we will not yield it, but make the King seize it by force so there's no doubt where the evil lies, but we cannot raise the country for us even if we wished. Rich merchants being robbed rouse little pity and since the King is well pensioned by Louis, Parliament will not be called. So we must wait until the realm needs our wealth and finds it lost, or the King requires our support and falls for the lack of it. And God look mercifully on our ruin meanwhile."

"I never knew you give up before," said Arabella frankly. "Even after the fire you never doubted that both City and Cornish's would be restored, and from what Will told me you've more than recovered your loss since then."

He looked at her quickly, and then away. We shall not be easy until we've lain together, reflected Arabella irrelevantly. We're jabbering like hucksters to drown quite different thoughts; the feel of him beside her, his hand on her arm, the inflection of his voice, all loosed sensations singularly unsuited to the cobbles of Charing Cross. "I haven't given up," he said after a pause. "It's just that I think some time must pass before we win. As the two of us have come to a fresh beginning only after long journeying which is not yet done. Nor is it possible to repair some kinds of damage, as we both know too well. You have a conscience over Adam, I for Elizabeth, with more to add no doubt before we finish."

Adam was sprawled on the floor, reading, when Arabella pushed open the door at Bear Street. She felt ridiculously nervous, knowing how easily a wrong word could ruin months of patient work.

Adam scrambled to his feet at the snap of the lock, then stood glowering. He resented Arabella's guests and thought, correctly, that they sneered at him behind his back.

"Adam, I've brought your father to see you," said Arabella instantly. Shock was better than misunderstanding.

He flinched and ducked his head instinctively, so she was poignantly reminded of her visit to Moll's when he hid behind his hands rather than face the recoil he expected. She could have helped him then and had not, from this encounter she must stand aside.

"Not exactly to see you, Adam," said Harry. "Since it sounds like a courtier taking his turn to hand the King his shirt in the hope of reward. But to make my peace and become of value to each other once we are acquainted, or so I hope. Your mother tells me you are a shrewd pamphleteer."

Adam nodded uncertainly. "Have you ever handed the King his shirt?"

Harry laughed. "Definitely not. I went to Windsor last year

to present the City's petition that Parliament should be recalled, and was kept waiting through a hot August day in a room full of dirty washing before being thrown out, but that is the nearest I have come to His Majesty's shirts."

"Have you requited him since?" demanded Adam.

"Not yet," replied Harry gravely. "Unfortunately trade at the moment is all the other way."

"For heaven's sake, Adam," exclaimed Arabella, half laughing but enormously relieved. "Don't try one of your quittances against the King. Burned boots for the Grimshaws are all very well, but bolting the King's horses with a snapped washing line would be something else again!"

"Not if you don't want me to," said Adam obligingly. "Even if it would be no more than he deserves."

Harry pulled up a chair for Arabella and sat down himself. "Do you always requite those who offend you, Adam? It is a dangerous practise, surely?"

Adam met his eyes squarely for the first time, light grey exactly matched. "I do not mind some kinds of risk."

Harry leaned back, smiling, and answered as if he had said something quite different. "We all mind the other kind, the risk of loss from those we love. We should be less than men if we did not."

Adam flushed vividly, eyes very bright. "Will you come again?"

"As often as I can, which may not be very frequently. You and your mother must believe that I should like to be here even when I am not, and I shall beg you not to requite me for my absence."

"Of course not!" said Adam indignantly. "A fine booby I should look, distracting you from battle with the King!"

"No!" said Harry sharply. "Not battle, for that's high treason. Watch your tongue, Adam, if you value it. Have you any wine, Arabella? Perhaps it's the moment to drink a loyal toast instead."

She brought a bottle, astonished by his ease with a boy as prickly as Adam. Of course, he had children of his own, she thought with a pang; both reprimand and understanding had the confident touch brought by familiarity.

Henry raised his goblet. "To His Majesty, and also his subjects' duty to uphold the right." They drank, and he added, "Your turn, Adam."

"Us," said Adam, as one who did not believe in wasting breath, and spluttered as he downed his wine in a draught.

They laughed and drank and thumped him on the back, and suddenly there was so much happiness each wanted to hold this moment and prevent it sliding past. Adam watched Harry kiss her before he left and did not mind at all, when he had looked ripe to cut Giles's throat each time he touched her.

~ *II* ~

Harry

1683–1685

What confusion & mischief does the avarice, anger and ambition of Princes cause in the world, who might be happier
with halfe they possesse.

JOHN EVELYN'S DIARY

Chapter One

*A*rabella was unprepared for the sheer practical difficulty of becoming Harry's mistress.

He was overwhelmingly busy; he had become one of the most important goldsmith-bankers of the City, and with trade again depressed his affairs demanded unremitting attention. He was the leading member of the alderman's committee of five appointed to defend their charter, and besides had a Crown action enforcing fines against him to fight, and probably another after that when he lost, as he was certain to do. His wife was ailing and compassion reinforced by affection meant that he must spare time to sit with her and oversee his household, make up what he could of his children's lack from her.

Then, there was Adam. Hero worship of a shadowy unknown vanished and in its place grew deep attachment at a level Arabella only partly grasped. Adam had grown up amongst women, except for Giles, whose influence he rejected, and Arabella only realised the loss this represented when she saw him with Harry. Because of his size and reticence she had never thought of it before, but Adam was aggressively male in his reactions; he was passionately interested in matters only Harry could explain and ruthless in his questioning; he was also combative, ambitious, intellectually agile and determined to succeed in spite of, probably because of, all his handicaps. Harry brought out the best in his character, since it was Adam's mind which interested him and there was little chance to do anything together except talk, so physical shortcomings were easily forgotten. Consequently the vengeful, defensive side of Adam's nature never appeared while Harry was there, but he did become extremely possessive.

If either had felt like laughing about it, the problem of finding time alone together would have been farcical. Harry rented one of the new houses being built around St. Paul's for them, but since he could seldom stay the night Arabella often had to meet him elsewhere to avoid Adam, with only minutes squeezed from his affairs.

"You didn't know what you were letting yourself in for," said Harry ruefully. "There's not much grace to loving in an hour snatched between the Old Bailey and Guildhall."

Arabella stretched luxuriously, hands still lingering on his body. "I'm not considering lodging a complaint. An hour with you or a wilderness without—there's no choice left, Harry. I think there's nothing you could do to me which would not be so mixed up with my loving you that I would find pleasure in it."

They were in a sparse attic above the taproom of the Spread Eagle Tavern in Ludgate Hill; although his wife knew he sought relief with other women since she had been so long ill, Harry disliked forcing her into knowledge of when and where, and was too well known in reputable City hostelries to avoid gossip. He turned his head and kissed her with the lingering delight which comes after completely fulfilled love. "Oh, my Bella. So do I love you beyond hope of cure. Beyond right or wrong, or a dozen flea-ridden beds. I'd give a hundred marks for the Court of Aldermen to see me now."

"King Charles on the other hand would probably feel quite reconciled to you," observed Arabella. "Just keep on as you are, and the Court of Aldermen can go to Newgate."

She felt him laugh against her, and suddenly they were both laughing, clinging together and completely happy. "There's not one of them who would not envy me, it is the quality of tavern and bed which would stick in their gullet." He shook his head and pulled his mouth into disapproval like a mocking boy. "Too demeaning for a City father, who should make love in splendour or not at all."

"Wrapped in your robes?" enquired Arabella anxiously. "Or would a miniver coverlet do? I saw one for sale in Leadenhall Market if it would ease your consequence."

He rolled over, still laughing, bodies locked as if they could not bear to part, although partings were woven into the life they lived now. "What wouldn't I give for the rest of the day together, doing nothing particular, in the certain knowledge of a night and tomorrow to come. I must go, sweeting. As always, I must go; I'm late and don't know when I can come again."

She lay and watched him while he dressed with quick, angry jerks, her flesh still glowing from his caresses. Laughter was gone, instead he looked exhausted and depressed.

He bent and kissed her gently on the lips before he left. "I will call a hackney and bid it wait until you are ready. I shall say you'll pay double fare, you have sufficient with you?"

She nodded. Harry was a generous lover and she still found pleasure in paying bills promptly. "Take care, Harry. When is the vote?"

"Tomorrow, and this is one I'll win, never fear."

"That's what I'm afraid of," she said simply. "In all the City there cannot be another man the King now hates as much as you."

He laughed and kissed her again. "There's Patience Ward, our last freely chosen mayor, he's just been fined ten thousand pounds, and Pilkington the sheriff, fifty thousand. I have the King's action to prove I'm only worth a thousand yet."

She leaped out of bed as soon as he closed the door, and stood with her nakedness wrapped in dusty curtains to watch him stride away through stone stacked ready for half-built St. Paul's. Tomorrow the Aldermen and Common Council of the City would vote on whether to surrender their charter to the King, since judgment had been entered against them after long delay while the King waited, hoping for voluntary submission. His Majesty's judges of King's Bench had unanimously found (after one with the courage to disagree was forced to retire from the case) that the City of London did wrongfully exercise its pretended powers and privileges, and in the following months Guildhall had been torn apart by faction, the fellowship of aldermen and Common Council lost, commerce suffering in the tidal wave of recrimination. With Lord Mayor and sheriffs already royal nominees there were plenty who saw their fortunes made if they jumped to the court side before it was too late. The threat of prosecution, of constant financial harassment, deterred others who would have liked to fight.

In June, the discovery of a plot to waylay the King and Duke of York at Rye House in Hertfordshire on their way back from Newmarket sent a wave of patriotic indignation through the country, and the Tories rode higher than ever. The Lord Mayor seized his opportunity and led a delegation from the City in humble submission to the King at Windsor. Harry and other opponents of surrender, while joining in congratulating the King on his escape, refused to accompany them, and when legal instruments were drawn up which empowered the mayor to yield up the charter, they forced a fierce debate in Council. The recorder, Sir George Treby, backed Harry in maintaining that surrender would leave the City without redress, while the mayor argued it would enable a new charter to be gained on better terms from the King. The vote was to be taken on the morrow, after tempers had been given time to cool.

Arabella sighed and turned away from the window; however light he made of it, Henry Cornish was established as leader of Whig opposition in the City. If he won tomorrow and forced the King into open seizure of the charter, there was no telling what might happen. After his massive fine, Sir Patience Ward was now facing charges of perjury and would be forced into ruin and exile if he lost.

Harry won his vote.

He hammered at their door very late the following evening and entered on a gust of autumn leaves and satisfaction. "I can't stay, but wanted you to know. No surrender by one hundred and three to eighty-five. You should have seen mayor and sheriffs standing goggle-eyed and thinking up excuses to tell the King when we forced them to count the votes in open Council. No juggling with figures this time."

"What will happen now?" Adam was hopping from one foot to the other as he caught his father's excitement, while Arabella stood quite still within Harry's embrace, thinking of nothing but the King's vengeance.

"The charter will be forfeit, but by the King's action, not ours. Then our fine Tory mayor will grovel on his knees at Whitehall and accept a new one from His Majesty's grace, where everything is kept in royal control."

"And you, Harry?" asked Arabella quietly, her heart cold.

He shrugged. "I shall be surprised if the King leaves me as alderman in his new Corporation, but since I should not wish to serve it is no great matter. For the rest, we'll have to wait. It's not the end, I promise you. London . . . my God, he's not having the City as a creature about his court."

Adam snatched his grandfather's flagon off the mantel. "A toast, and a pledge you'll not refuse this time." He brought over goblets and wine, smiling at his father as if at an equal. "The City of London, and may God guide us."

"Aye, I'll drink to that," said Harry. "Five years. It'll take a while, but we'll see who is victor then."

Domine dirige nos, the motto of the City.

Arabella drank with them, dread sunk into bone for Adam as well as Harry since neither knew the meaning of compromise.

After all the great drama of the year, the aftermath of London's battle seemed strangely flat. As Harry had prophesied, the old charter was declared forfeit and the King took all appointments into his hands. Mayor, sheriffs, aldermen, all were sworn by royal commission without pretence at election, the Court of Aldermen informed of the King's wishes with no chance for debate, Common Council never called. Sir George Treby was dismissed from his recordership, as were eight aldermen who had been active in defence of the charter, Harry being one. Then the King turned his attention to livery companies, who between them controlled most other City functions. Every one of their charters had to be surrendered, their officials appointed by the King and removable at his whim.

The royal triumph was complete.

George Jeffries went on circuit the following spring and collected in charters by the chestful on his travels: with London fallen no other could stand.

Arabella's life subsided into routine again, this time a tantalising, unsettling routine. She was intensely happy, for nothing could change the contentment of being loved and loving so completely; yet the misery of days when Harry could not come was unavoidable, her old restlessness stirring when few household tasks had the power to distract her for long. She laughed wryly at herself, alone in her small house in Swithin Court, thinking of the bustling household she would have had to occupy her in Cheapside, of clients in and out of the parlour and silver still being hammered in the old workshop of the Golden Spurs. She had thought it all intolerably dull, now it seemed a hive of interest. Also she would be with Harry, see him a dozen times a day even if not to speak to, the turn of his back and the stiff way he held his flayed right arm.

She asked him about it during one of only three or four complete nights he spent with her, sleeping and waking to the incredible pleasure of the other still there.

"It's well enough, for some things anyway." He demonstrated so she laughed against him. "And for the rest I can afford such clerks as I need nowadays, although none I like so well as the one I had the year after the fire. Adam will find his brains of more use than muscle in the City."

"It's what he wants, you know. You can't take him yourself, of course, but—"

"I wish I could," he said with real regret. His other sons, Henry and Roger, although he loved them dearly showed few signs of Adam's intellectual ability. "I must look around and approach a discreet friend who would be willing to take him as apprentice. He tells me he is drawn to banking but I don't want him to feel he must follow in my footsteps, in fact for all our sakes it might be better if he did not. I could place him in a junior clerkship with the East India Company while his ideas settle perhaps."

He had wanted to send Adam to St. Paul's School but they decided eventually that he would be too badly bullied. It would be bitterly unjust to forbid him to name his father when as a nobody without strength to defend himself, yet possessing a mind which outshone boys twice his size, he would be a natural butt for spite. So he continued with tutors, soaking up knowledge with effortless ease, growing a little now in his changed circumstances, yet terrifyingly solitary. He was completely at ease only with Harry; Arabella did not think he bore her a grudge or quite understood the nature of the grudge he ought to bear her, but there was a certain formality in their dealings she could not overcome.

Harry slept towards morning while Arabella lay wakeful, not wanting to waste precious time in sleep. He disliked muffling draperies, so she was able to watch him as light strengthened; he stirred at length, as if roused by the intensity of her gaze, and felt for her, smiling. "The best waking a man could wish for." Nearby the bell of St. Sepulchre's struck the hour. "Seven! I haven't slept so late in years. You ought to have woken me before."

"You were so tired, my love. Now you are turned out of the City's affairs, can't you at least rest a full night?"

"You sound like a wife, my dear." He got out of bed and stood, grunting. He was not far short of forty and looked it in unforgiving winter greyness.

"Perhaps Elizabeth and I should concert our efforts to stop you killing yourself," she retorted, stung.

"Perhaps you should," he agreed. "But His Majesty is likely to save you the trouble, and give me enforced rest in Newgate. I have a great deal of business to arrange before he strikes."

She leaped out of bed and snatched at his arm. "You don't mean it!"

"Yes," he said gently. "I thought you best prepared as I have prepared Elizabeth, but didn't want to spoil our night. I have been served two more writs, alleging duties I failed to carry our while sheriff four years ago. You are not to worry since the King intends to harass only, a warning perhaps to keep my hands off City affairs now I am no longer alderman. But don't be surprised if I'm locked up awhile, the most respectable citizens are behind bars these days."

"Why not accept the warning and keep from meddling now you are dismissed from office? What can you achieve except to infuriate the King and bring anxiety on your family?"

He threaded the lace of his cravat through delicately stitched holes. Elizabeth, supposed Arabella bitterly, although she hated needlework. "There is a certain amount of organization which must be done. One day the King will need a loan again, few last long without recourse to our money. When he does, we must be prepared."

"Rebellion?"

His eyes met hers in the mirror, then he turned and pulled on his coat. "No. Never, or not the way you mean with Englishman killing Englishman. We wait our time and edge out Tories where we may meanwhile."

He left her then, protest dead on her lips. She could not change him, and did harm by persisting when he was already so hard-driven. A few days later, a curt note came for Adam to present himself at East India House and enquire for a Mr. Markyate if he desired to apply to a junior clerkship there.

More evidence of Harry arranging his affairs while there is time, thought Arabella as she watched Adam go, ecstatic at the idea of embarking on the life of commerce.

The same afternoon news spread that the King was ill and not expected to live, the Duke of York sent for while the royal bedchamber slowly filled with ghouls waiting for his brother to die. Adam returned bursting with pride in the evening, his clerkship secured. "Of course, I expect my father spoke to one of the directors for me, but that only brought me the interview. Mr. Markyate was mighty pressing in all his questions and I quite thought he had decided to refuse me."

She tried to show suitable pleasure, and instead felt intensely depressed. What a crazy whirligig life was; here was Adam setting out on his way, and she was pregnant again. She had fought against the knowledge, although in her heart she wanted Harry's child, but could no longer do so.

However much she might want it, though, she could not shake off memory of Oxford and Conduit Springs, and also shrank from thrusting further complications on Harry. She had not told him yet; only Catlin, practical as always, said she'd best rest and get him out of her bed unless she wanted to miscarry again, and had her face slapped as a result.

The King died after four days of illness, and the bells of the City tolled for his passing. Arabella felt a strange mixture of emotion as she listened to them rattle glass in her windows: no one who had spent years around Whitehall, as she had, could fail to be touched by Charles Stuart's charm. Kind, generous, easy with women and his friends, in the end his devious, unscrupulous skill had dragged down and outlasted all his enemies. His subjects had called him idle and a spendthrift cheat, driven by pleasure instead of policy; too late, they discovered that he also possessed an unrelenting memory for past injury and a drive for power astonishing in one who appeared to hold it so lightly. For being the man he was, once his battles were won his interest waned, and he did little with his winnings beyond desultory harassment of those who had opposed him.

James, his brother, was proclaimed King by the grace of God, and few doubted that he was a man of a very different stamp. Better, some said; courageous, active and no dissembler as Charles had been. Far worse, feared many, even though they had felt unable to oppose his right to succeed; a traitor and a Catholic like his brother but set in an infinitely more brutal mould; obstinate, stupid and ill-tempered with it, too.

The City bells tolled as much in foreboding for the future as in sorrow for the passing of a King who had ruled both well and ill, and left his people bitterly divided.

Chapter Two

Week by week, the screw of tension tightened.

Within a month of James coming to the throne, Harry was in Newgate charged with having failed to keep a prisoner close enough confined while he was sheriff. Either the evidence was so perjured that even a packed jury could not accept it, or the King only intended to deliver a warning, but he was released after two weeks' confinement.

He looked wretchedly unwell when he came to Swithin Court and as soon as she had done hugging him Arabella made him sit by the fire. "Rest, and don't even talk unless you want to," she said sternly, and sat at his feet, his hand held against her face.

He gave a gasp of laughter. "Don't worry, I won't leave you in suspense, although there's little to tell. I was fortunate not to be in the common hold and have sufficient funds to pay for a degree of comfort. But next time I'm clapped up I hope it will be warmer, and I find my belly is too delicately bred to accommodate itself to Newgate stenches."

"Next time? Sweet Jesus, Harry, even a Tory jury could not accept such an array of perjurers against you!"

He felt in his pocket and handed her a piece of paper. "This is a draft for five hundred guineas on Sir Robert Vyner. He is a banker in good credit with the court, but an honourable man. He will accept my drafts and wait for settlement if I am held. I think the King warns the City through his handling of me, and the difficulties I face in my trade and person are intended to quiet the waverers. So I don't expect relief until circumstances change, which may take a while."

Arabella stared at the paper signed by Harry's formal gold-smith's signature as if it was a warrant for his arrest. "Couldn't you go abroad for a few months?"

"And be ruined as Patience Ward was? I can't keep up my trade from Amsterdam and would forfeit everything if I ran. Nor is Elizabeth fit to travel." He slid his hand under her chin and bent to kiss her. "Don't imagine things, Bella. I've done nothing but use legal rights and powers to oppose the King. He doesn't like it, so has devised punishment for me, since James is a harsher man than his brother, but I have only dis-comfort and inconvenience to fear. He is not going to panic me into losing more. I think also that I offer my best service yet by letting men see through the King's handling of me just what we yield when we accept injustice." He laid a second paper on the table. "This is a reconveyance of the lease on the House of the Spurs to you. I know it isn't due for two years yet, but would prefer such matters straight between us. The sum at Vyner's can be regarded as an advance of rent and evidence of your title if you should need it."

She did not reply, staring into the fire with her hands locked with his about her shoulders. Men died of diseases no one could name in Newgate; he knew it and was preparing his affairs as best he could, whatever face he put on it to cheer her.

"I'm having your child, Harry," she said at last. She had hesitated over whether to tell him, but decided she had not the right to keep it from him after what had happened with Adam.

He moved sharply against her. "My dear, I hope you're glad."

She laughed and looked round. "I hope you are."

"I suppose I should not be, but yes, I am. Very glad. There's so much misery at the moment, a life between us seems a matter for rejoicing."

"I wasn't sure before, or even whether to tell you. Yes, I'm glad too." She felt the familiar cringe of fear at her words; she might want Harry's child but still disliked the business of child-birth intensely and resented her lost beauty.

They sat together in flickering firelight, handfast and saying very little. Sometimes Harry dozed, a thing she had never known him do however tired he was. He stirred when Adam came clattering in, full of the day's doings at East India House, and by the time he left she thought he looked slightly rested, the strength of love in his kiss her reward for lack of passion.

A week later he was in the Fleet prison on a charge of debt, which, since he was one of the richer men of the City, was simply laughed out of court when it came to trial. Then it was Newgate again, where he was left stewing through weeks of summer heat before being released, on bail this time.

Adam brought the news that he was out again, since the baiting of Henry Cornish was a matter of deep resentment in the City, but over a week passed before he came to see them and he admitted under questioning that he had been both too busy and too unwell to come before. "Things get into the devil of a scramble when I'm not there, and clients are uneasy at leaving their balances with me. Nor can I blame them." He sighed. "I've been changing the direction of my affairs into factoring and trade recently, since I reckoned that few would care to trust a banker more often in jail than out, but dealings are far from simple now I must conduct them from the Upper Side at Newgate. It's a pity you can't act for me, Adam."

"I could if you would let me," said Adam eagerly. "I've learned a lot already."

Harry laughed. "I'm sure you have, and one day I might well take you into partnership in my merchanting, even if the goldsmith-banking must be for Henry and Roger. You keep away from me at the moment, though, and look after your mother; together we'll outlast the King's spite. There are whispers already that he needs a loan; when he does, the bargaining can start in earnest."

"Parliament is solidly Tory," said Adam sourly. "Every corporation in the country is appointed by court faction, so returns the King's creatures. He'll get what he wants from them."

Harry grinned at his son. Although thin to emaciation he seemed in better spirits than before his ordeal had begun. "One day we'll have it solid with Whigs, when even court toadies cannot stomach things this King will do."

His bail was revoked and he was in Newgate again soon after Parliament met. Arabella was almost beside herself with worry; although Harry paid for food to be sent in, disease and stench redoubled in the heat. She was unpleasantly reminded of Adam, stunted for life because he could not digest contaminated, ill-prepared slops, and Newgate was infinitely worse than St. Mary's had ever been.

Harry had made her promise not to bribe her way in to see him, and as she was by now heavy with child, reluctantly she obeyed. Adam went once and by ill-fortune ran slap into Elizabeth Cornish, so he said he was a merchant's runner, which as Harry conducted complicated business from his cell she did not find surprising. Adam said she looked insipid and although relieved she had not queried his identity, he resented bitterly having to call himself a menial while his father did not dispute it. It was the first time he had felt out of charity with Harry, and he refused to go again.

While Harry was still in prison, there came the thunderclap of the Monmouth rebellion. King Charles's bastard son proclaimed himself King in the West and from all over Dorset and Somerset peasants flocked to his banner, for this was Shaftesbury's home country and they did not forget the fight their lord had made, nor that he had championed Monmouth's right to inherit the throne.

The City was quiet and sullen while they waited for news. Soldiers tramped the streets fingering their weapons and shouldering citizens into the muck, for beyond doubt there were many who would back Monmouth if he could reach London.

But between them, Charles and James had built up a regular army of twenty thousand men, and peasants armed with scythes were no match for royal guards. Monmouth fled and was caught, made grovelling submission and was hanged by his uncle two days after vast, silent crowds gathered along the Thames to watch his arrival as a prisoner. No enthusiasm either way, no loyal address, no disturbance; only sulky discontent which anything might spark.

George Jeffries went to the West on circuit, together with half a dozen judges of similar stamp to himself and troops recently returned from Tangier, and therefore accustomed to barbarism. Between them they brought ruin to a swathe of towns and villages in what became known as the Bloody Assize. The Bishop of Bath and Wells protested and was told curtly to hold his tongue; travellers coming to London spoke of how it was impossible to journey half a mile in Somerset or Dorset away from the stench of corpses rotting by the roadside. Arabella thought of Giles, almost certainly there, and enjoying himself.

Harry was released on the same day that Arabella was brought to bed with her child. Perhaps because she was so anxious about him, she had given her confinement little thought, pacing restlessly through the long nights, wandering about the City by day as a woman could safely do since the rebuilding. She was also stubbornly determined to have Harry's child, and almost willed herself to health: when her pains started she felt only satisfaction that she had lasted her full term.

Even so, pain lasted a long time. Once she heard herself curse the child for refusing to be born, and Catlin scolding her for tempting the devil with such words. So she spoke Harry's name instead, chewed her lips to stop herself speaking it, for Harry was in Newgate and could not come.

Her baby was born as the sun rose for another day. "A girl," said Catlin, disappointed. "A girl, I might have guessed from all the trouble."

Arabella roused, the image of Adam unbidden in her mind. "Is she all right?"

"Aye, and no more ugly than most in the first hour of life," said Catlin grudgingly, slopping water. She had never quite forgiven her mistress for not marrying Giles, a fine man if ever she saw one. Who could blame him for an attack of jealousy when his woman came home like a harlot in the dawn?

Arabella drowsed, relieved it was over. She did not truly care for babies except that this one was Harry's, nor could she summon energy to feel more than mild regret it was a girl. She hoped Harry would not mind too much.

She woke with the feeling of lassitude which comes from hours of undisturbed rest. Amber light dappled plaster high on her wall as the sun set; she had slept the whole day through. She stretched and smiled contentedly, feeling her flat belly, instinct turning her head on the pillow. Harry was sitting by her bedside, head in his hands. He jerked upright at her movement, face tense, thoughts obviously scattered.

She put out her hand. "Harry, my love. You and your daughter out into the world the same day."

She saw strain ease, and he smiled. "It must be almost worth a chronicler's note. Sweeting, how is it with you?"

"Well," she said without hesitation. "And better still for finding you in my bedchamber."

He bent and kissed her, she could feel his lips smiling. "I'm sorry not to have been here yesterday. I've worn a track through Newgate flags these past weeks, thinking of where I should be and was not."

Not just here, she thought without bitterness. "Elizabeth?"

He nodded. "She hasn't been strong since Roger's birth and anxiety for me makes matters worse."

"I worry for you too." She could not keep sharpness from her voice. God, how she worried for him, and what a coil of loyalty and disloyalty, love and obligation they had wound round themselves.

His hand tightened on hers. "I know. As I feared for you; the consequences of childbirth hold unhappy memories for me."

She lay back, contented by his hand in hers. "Do you mind?" she asked at last.

"Mind?"

"A girl. I wanted a son for you."

He stood abruptly. "Bella, listen to me! Adam is son enough for any man's pride. He is smaller than average, no more. As he grows to manhood he will be valued for the many qualities he possesses, not condemned by the few he lacks. You mustn't watch him through the eye of guilt, remind him constantly of insufficiency, simply because you cannot forget that if you had acted differently he might have had more. He is as God made him, as is our daughter too. Already I love her, as you do."

The easy tears of weakness pricked Arabella's eyes, his face swimming against plaster walls. She loved Adam too, he need not have been so harsh.

Catlin came in with the child for feeding, and tried to hustle Harry from the room.

"Wait," he said briefly, not looking up.

Slowly the blur faded from her eyes and his face steadied again. He looked less weary after weeks of enforced idleness, but the lines about nose and mouth had deepened and confinement drained his face of colour; but for the expression of his eyes he would have appeared as harsh as his words. "All right, Bella?" he asked quietly.

She wanted to turn from him in rage, to show her fury at the time he chose for a quarrel. Instead, she felt her lips curve because it was Harry after all, and as she had told him, there was nothing he could do to her which was not so mixed up with love that she would find pleasure in it. "What fools love makes of us all," she said, eyes closing.

He threw back his head and laughed. "Ah, Bella, fine foolishness indeed. What shall we call her? Is Adam here?" He disentangled his hand from hers and went out, calling.

"Gentlemen should know their place," said Catlin disapprovingly. "Which isn't at a lying-in, nor souring your milk with hey-go-merry tramplings all round the room." She dumped the baby none too gently in Arabella's arms, still unforgiving of its sex.

Arabella looked at the minute, contented face, fuzz faintly

pulsing on her skull, and was reconciled. She did not scream and showed no signs of sailing or tearing her peace apart as Adam had done, nor did Harry mind. Girls were surely less bother than boys.

Harry came back accompanied by a reluctant, embarrassed Adam trying hard to be polite about his sister, and failing. Harry was carrying wine, and held a goblet to Arabella's lips, his arm about her shoulders. "What shall we call her, love, so it can be a true toast?"

"Jenny," said Arabella for no reason, except the name had the same soft feel to it as Harry did. His face was against hers as he drank from the same goblet, the beat of his heart loud in her ear.

"To Jenny then, and may she know God's blessing and happiness." He held her even while he filled goblets for Adam and Catlin, as if this was a moment which must last them all a long time.

Chapter Three

Arabella recovered swiftly from Jenny's birth. She was naturally healthy and it was as much the ill-fortune which had stalked her previous pregnancies as the inevitable pain which made her view childbearing with such fear and distaste.

Jenny proved a model baby, suckling greedily and sleeping at most other times. Arabella's spirits rose as she viewed herself in the mirror; to be sure her waistline was no longer quite so slim as it had been but the grosgrain gown just delivered became her mightily, her skin was as clear as ever, and the sparkling October weather seemed to bid her welcome after long constraint indoors.

She decided to walk as far as the Stocks Market and perhaps view the rebuilding of St. Paul's; she went quite freely about the City since no one but Harry knew her, and had only once encountered him. Then she had known a surge of triumph when he came and bowed over her hand, incapable of the slight which would deny acquaintance between them.

She never tired of the life in London's streets. The hucksters walking with a swagger when they remembered and in haste from bargain to bargain when they did not. Players, bear wards and monkey minders clearing a circle for their act; hawkers shouting their wares; tallow-fat rascals behind stalls full of doubtful goods; children scampering and thieving, the markets crammed with people and buzzing with gossip, swift London wit badgering the uncertain into purchases they did not want.

It was nearly two months since she had done more than saunter near Swithin Court and she tired quicker than she expected. Reluctant to go home on so beautiful a day, she decided to take a hackney to the Royal Exchange and bid the driver to wait if she felt unable to linger long. Harry still somehow managed his affairs with extraordinary skill; through the long, harassed summer she had never lacked for money or needed to present his draft to Sir Robert Vyner.

And now at last the King seemed to have wearied of him and the future looked more settled, though Harry came only briefly to Swithin Court, for Elizabeth was ill again. Arabella looked at sunlit sky as her hackney jolted up Cheapside and tried, although not very hard, to avoid the thought that when Elizabeth died there would only be a few decent months to pass before she wed Harry.

The new Royal Exchange was more splendid than the old, its courts and arcades overflowing with fashionable strollers, knots of merchants gathered about their own particular pillars doing business with each other. Those outside the inner circle of rich traders approached these pillars at their peril and Adam already dreamed of the day when men would talk of Furnival's pillar on 'Change.

Arabella loitered along the displays of goods and jewellery, suddenly lonely. She had never felt the lack of female companionship before, but now Harry diminished all other men she felt drawn to the homely chatter she had despised in women before. Ah well, everything would change when she wed Harry. She pulled herself up sharply and touched the wood of a counter; she was too realistic to pretend that the wish for Elizabeth to die was not there, but it brought ill-fortune to will the death of another.

Her attention was caught by a display of silver, instinctive judgment recognizing fine quality and inventive design. London spawned splendid craftsmanship in ever-multiplying quantity as its wealth created a market for excellence. There was a row of caskets amongst the rest and she examined them distastefully, although they were pleasing enough to the eye. George Jeffries had been made Lord Chancellor while she was lying in, a hangman to command a crew of jackals as Harry said.

Still, she owed him a casket and would not be in debt to such a man. She bought the least attractive, disappointing the trader with her taste. "This one is superior, mam, and not much more expensive since the weight of silver is less." He put an exquisite box in her hands.

"I know, my father was a silversmith in Cheapside and I can judge fine work when I see it, but I'm only paying a wager to a man I dislike. I would not waste good craft on such as he." Arabella was ashamed to mention Jeffries by name; a pretty pass we have come to, she reflected, when the Lord Chancellor is so much a scoundrel that decent folk are ashamed to claim his acquaintance.

The trader immediately enquired further about her silver-smith father, his manner respectful but quite different once he accepted her as part of the community of the City. When she told him her father was Robert Sperling his face unexpectedly clouded. "A fine craftsman, one of the best. His fellow guilds-men were well pleased when Mr. Cornish kept the Sign of the Spurs in Cheapside, for all that Will Leggatt is no more than a jobbing smith. We pray God that the Cornish sign may not soon be only a memory in the City, as Robert Sperling is."

Arabella stared at him, blood thinned with shock. "Why should it be?"

"You haven't heard?"

"I know how the King persecutes him, yet surely his trade prospers so long as men trust his skill and honesty? And that he has in plenty."

"Aye," he said soberly. "There's no finer man in the City. He was arrested earlier this morning, here in the Royal Ex-change while about his business, this time by the King's own officers."

"Where is he taken?" Her lips felt stiff.

He shrugged. "Newgate again, or so the tale of it goes." He scowled, hand stroking silver without feeling it. "It's time we had men in Guildhall again, instead of rats scavenging on injustice. I was on Common Council, yet since the old charter went we've only met to receive royal orders and disperse again in silence, like brats before their master."

Arabella was not listening. "How long do you think they'll keep him this time?"

"Cornish? God knows, mam. He hasn't been taken by King's officers before."

She scarcely knew how she found the hackney again, re-collected herself only as it passed the achingly familiar houses in Cheapside, a cluster of merchants talking earnestly under the Cornish sign, blinds drawn in the windows above. I wouldn't draw them, thought Arabella viciously, what a milksop the woman must be. I'd be on the steps of Whitehall palace so the whole realm knew King James for the whoreson he is.

The turnkey at Newgate was surly, took the coins she offered and grudgingly agreed to deliver a message, but refused her entry. "'Tis a King's matter, and more'n my position's worth to let ye in. Come back termorrer, 'e's well used to Newgate by now and won't vanish in the night." He slammed the grill in her face.

Adam came in soon after she returned to Swithin Court; he had learned the news in East India House although no one there, except possibly one of the directors, knew he was Harry's son. "Everyone's fit for revolt, I can tell you," he said savagely. "Were they not so frightened for their precious hides. Too few believed my father when he told them how it would be once the charter went; they understand well enough now, when it is too late to help him."

"What is the charge, has anyone heard?"

He shook his head. "They think there will be a charge this time, though, and a fine large enough to ruin his trade. Perhaps months or years in prison while no one hurries to present it. Habeas Corpus is not much help once the judges are bought."

Arabella thought of Shaftesbury. How right he had been in his estimate of James, wherever else he had been wrong. She remembered Wheelock's description of the cell where he had been first held in the Tower, and clenched her hands in despair; Harry was unknown outside the City, James would not care if he died in confinement. She forced herself to rest, for she was still suckling Jenny, but could not sleep. Bells tolled each hour, shadows moved, wind beat gently on the wall; close by, Harry would hear the same sounds, perhaps see through some barred hole how clouds were blowing across sky which had been clear the day before. Arabella tried to convince herself that it was absurd to feel such dread when he had been four times in prison this year already and come out safe, but could not keep fear at bay. King's officers had taken him openly in the Royal Exchange, and half the amount of money she offered the turnkey at Newgate had admitted Adam before.

She went to the towered entry of Newgate prison again the next day and the next: the answer was still the same. Henry Cornish was held close and allowed no liberty or visitors during the King's pleasure.

"Is he able to send out for food?" asked Arabella, when a slightly less disagreeable turnkey returned the same answer on the third day after his arrest.

"Aye, for near its weight in gold. Such well-fleeced prisoners are welcome to the likes of us." He wiped his mouth and spat, eyeing her speculatively.

"Is there no way I could see him?" She no longer cared whether she encountered Elizabeth or not.

"He's a fortunate fellow to have two flesh-morts on the doorstep for him. Not so long as he's held in close ward; be off with ye, I'm tired of saying it!"

George Jeffries, thought Arabella. He could get me in there if he would. She had intended to send the casket by messenger; if Harry was still in solitary confinement tomorrow, she would go to Jeffries herself.

Next day, she decided to wait until the afternoon in the hope of a different turnkey, but as she let herself out of the house Adam came lurching round the corner, puce-faced from running. "Adam! What are you doing here? Why aren't you in Mark Lane?" The East India Company kept its clerks hard at work from seven in the morning until six at night, Saturdays included.

He clung to the railings, gulping breath. "I . . . had to come. My father . . . they've . . . he's charged with treason!"

Light dazzled, lips chilled. She was not aware that she was clutching the railings too. "Treason . . . why, they can't!"

"Well, they have." He levered himself upright and came over to hold her arm, the first gesture of spontaneous affection he had ever shown her, only she was too dazed to notice. "He is to be tried at the Old Bailey on Monday."

"Monday," she said numbly. "That's the day after tomorrow! They can't. Sweet Jesus, they can't. He's been held solitary, he hasn't even seen an attorney far less . . . How can he defend himself without counsel even?"

Adam uncurled her fingers from the railing as if she was a child. "Come inside. We can't talk here, nor think what to do."

She allowed him to guide her to the parlour and seat her in the chair where Harry so often sat. She could not think at all, mind scattering images of how he looked, the patterned veins on his hands, the light in his eyes when he held her close. Adam brought her wine, then stood looking down at her. "The news spread when one of the sheriffs returned from Westminster, where they are bragging of attainder for treason against Henry Cornish. I don't know whether they have even served the charges on him yet, but it's certain they intend to allow him no defence. Somehow, one of us must see him, find out more about the charge and let him name witnesses we must seek out for him. Otherwise he will face his judges without anyone to speak for him at all."

Slowly the daze faded from Arabella's mind under his insistent voice. Later she could allow herself the luxury of tears and disbelief, now was the reality of Harry's life poised on the executioner's block, the handful of hours left in which he might be snatched from Stuart vengeance. "Jeffries," she said. "He could get us into Newgate, give us a copy of the charges if he would."

"He could have the charges dismissed if he would, since he is the King's creature and men say that King James does not move in the law without his advice."

They stared at each other in dawning hope, then Arabella pulled herself from the chair. She seemed to have become an old woman in a few minutes. "I'll go at once and take the casket I owe to help gain admission. The King . . . I was never more than slightly acquainted with him, but he might see my lady Wexford. In any event, he can't leave me all night in his gallery."

"Perhaps," said Adam sceptically. He had no faith in such courtesies as butchers might feel moved to offer. "I'll go to Newgate then. If I can't bribe my way in directly, then I'll try the ordinary. They need a boy to carry food ordered by the prisoners; if you will give me coins I swear I'll find a way in somehow."

Arabella felt steady now but very strange, removed by such an immense distance from emotion that she could look at it and experience mild surprise. She took time to complete a grander toilet than she had found necessary for years, and ordered Catlin to put up a court dress in a box. She could change at Bevil's and go on to Whitehall after she found Jeffries. She ordered Jenny woken and fed her until she dropped off her breasts, completely sated. Heaven knew when she would be able to feed her again. Or what would have happened by then; she shut panic back in its kennel as horror threatened to engulf her again.

She had not considered that Bevil might be dead, and he was not; apparently pickled in the distillation of a lifetime's wrong-doing, he seemed indestructible. He sat before a blazing fire, a shawl over his knees and another around his shoulders, a quart of claret conveniently within reach.

"Arabella! Where've you been all this time, hey?" he said

269

immediately. "No one's heard of you these past two years you've been gone from Bear Street, but I said you'd be back when your lover turned sour. What's your eye on this time, not selling more silver through a Catholic murderer, I trust?"

Arabella bent dutifully and kissed his cheek, determined to leave nothing to chance which might help gain her ends. "Prance wasn't a murderer, as you well know, dear uncle, I want to see George Jeffries immediately and thought you would know my best approach." There was no need for concealment with Bevil, nothing in life could surprise him any more.

"Jeffries? The fellow's always bottled nowadays, and Lord Chancellor besides. You won't reach near him."

"I will. I must. I'll pay whatever you wish, but a man's life depends on my seeing Jeffries tonight."

"A man, hey? I might have known." He chuckled. "Always a bad chooser, weren't you, Arabella? A dried-up corn dolly like Wexford, a brainless adventurer fresh out of Africa, and then Shaftesbury of all men, in and out of the Tower his last five years like a tumbler after coins. Now you pick gallows bait." He drained half a pint of claret and belched.

"It's no concern of yours," said Arabella fiercely. She moved the wine out of reach. "Tell me where to find Jeffries."

Bevil stared wistfully at his claret and took a large pinch of Special Blend snuff. "You're a restless, harebrained chit, Arabella. Always said so. You won't find George at this time of night. Chancellor he may be but he always had a low taste in friends; he'll be drinking in some tavern, a slut on his knee."

"Then I'll find him there. Which one?"

"For God's sake, girl! You can't chase him round the taverns of St. James's!"

"I must if I'll not find him otherwise."

He looked at her in a bemused way. "Give me back my claret, there's a good girl."

She held it just out of his grasp. "When you've told me what I want to know."

He moaned, but his glance was needle-sharp. "Fifty pounds in gold."

She nodded. "It's robbery as I expected, but yes. If I see him tonight, otherwise not."

"I can't guarantee he'll see you. That's up to your pretty face," he said peevishly.

She shrugged and said nothing, so after another goaded look at the claret, he added: "He has rooms in the Upper Courtyard off Birdcage Walk. You might find him there as the courts have only just risen. His footman, Sparrow, is said to be the easiest corrupted. His valet, Smithers, Smithson, some such name, he cuts up dear but is worth it if the matter's vital. He'll tell you where his master is if you make it worth his while. The Blue Bear in Holborn used to be George's favourite haunt, perhaps as Chancellor his taste has improved, but I doubt it. The Cockpit in Whitehall is likely, too."

"The valet's name exactly," said Arabella inexorably.

He groaned and closed his eyes. "Plague on it, Arabella, don't you realise I'm old? Let me see...Smethurst." He opened his eyes. "That's it, Smethurst."

She handed him the bottle. "Not a coin do you see if you're wrong." She went out, closing the door behind her.

There were guards around Whitehall she did not remember from King Charles's day but no one stopped a solitary woman, and cressets were burning outside Jeffries' entry. Arabella's spirits rose; she was worried by the idea of wasting half the night ferreting around taverns, and finding Jeffries sotted at the end of it. Hurry. Hurry. Hurry. Time is whirling past, crumbling away the few hours left before Harry's life is forfeit.

She pulled at the doorbell and waited, hand on the casket inside her muff. The porter was taken aback when she calmly walked past him into the hallway, but she cut expostulation short. "Is Lord Jeffries at home?" He had been created baron earlier in the year.

He hesitated. "It's not my place to say."

She slipped two gold coins into his conveniently poised hand, and he nodded imperceptibly. Jeffries' servants apparently accepted their master's standards when it came to corruption. "I want to speak to Mr. Smethurst, will you send to tell him my lady Wexford is below?" She chinked coins suggestively inside her muff, and gave him another.

He ushered her into a cold parlour and in the distance she could hear male voices, a bray of laughter, the fashionable clink of glass.

Smethurst was unexpected when he appeared. Although dressed like a valet, he had the aspect of a street brawler; Arabella had expected someone like Wheelock, or Wexford's impersonal minion, and took a moment to rearrange her approach.

He did not bow, and stood regarding her with suspicion. "His lordship is occupied."

271

Arabella bit back the retort that he would do well to occupy himself with the manners of his servants, but rudeness stiffened her. "He is here, and I wish to see him."

Smethurst hesitated, apparently estimating her intentions. He was as much bodyguard as valet, Arabella realised, enlightened. George Jeffries must stir up a multitude of enemies as he moved about the country, the grief of his victims' kin making them heedless of risk if only they could wreak revenge. She drew the casket out of her muff and flicked open the lid, showing it filled with coins. "I owe Lord Jeffries this casket in payment of a wager long ago, and have my own reasons for wishing to deliver it personally, tonight. If you can bring him here, I do not owe him the contents." She tipped the coins on a chair seat and covered them with a cushion, seating herself on top. "I can't grovel after coins once he enters, but have a fine scream if you try to take them now."

His calloused face was incapable of showing much emotion, but she thought she detected a certain reluctant respect. He nodded and went out.

She sat, hands clutched coldly on her lap, trying to think what she must say. Steps at last, a loud slurred voice. The door slammed open and Jeffries strode into the room. "What the devil . . . Arabella, I might have known it." He bowed over her hand with mock gallantry. "My lady Wexford. Smethurst told me some farrago of a wager and promised me a fine harlot; I did not connect the two with you, although I should have. How much did you pay him to get me here?"

He was far from sober but did not appear excessively drunk. Arabella smiled, putting all the enticement she knew into it, when she would rather have raked her fingernails across his face. "The casket I owe you full of gold; he must make a profitable living as your valet."

"All servants of great men do, it keeps 'em loyal," he said carelessly. "I enquired of Bevil where you lived when I won our wager with two years to spare, but he said you had vanished. I hope your latest bedding is worthwhile."

"Yes," said Arabella evenly. "Very worthwhile. I have come to plead for his life." She had decided that no hidden approach would serve.

He stilled and blood came into his face; she could imagine how he looked on the bench. He was wearing a full-bottomed wig and despite excess his appearance was formidable: high forehead; thick eyebrows; loud, harsh voice. "Who is this fine gentleman?"

She met his eyes squarely. "Henry Cornish."

He broke into a great crack of laughter, and stamped so the ornaments rattled. "Christ's blood, that's rich! You are the fellow's doxy?"

"Yes," she said clearly.

He spluttered. "God's bones and entrails, it's the best tale I've heard in a twelvemonth. Give me the box and go, woman."

"You have his life in your hands, you could direct his judges—"

"No, no, my dear! This is the King's policy, not mine. It's nothing to me."

"You could direct them if you would, warn the King against angering the City further. You were their recorder, and know their feeling well. This is a case where mercy would serve the King better than blood, I swear it."

"One quarrel more or less between His Majesty and the City makes no difference. So long as the King wins, fear makes the best master. Let them learn their lesson in humility, and Cornish kneel for mercy if he will."

"He never would and you know it, but I will." Arabella knelt swiftly. "I beg you, George, at least to try."

He stared at her, face puckered as if he prepared to spit. "Get up and be done, you trollop. You could crawl into my bed and it would make no difference, this matter is of the King's devising and I'd risk his displeasure to speak against it."

"And nothing I can say or do would make you try?"

"Why should I? I can help myself to Henry Cornish's wealth any time I wish and gain credit, not disfavour, for doing it. And I prefer my women willing, not spreading their legs for carrion better dead. Even you, fair Arabella."

She stood, trembling with fury restrained only by prudence. He refused to help Harry, but a single word from Lord Chancellor Jeffries could certainly kill him. She must not tear at his face or say anything to goad him into speaking that word.

He followed her to the door. "Come again when you've cleared merchanting from your blood. They're greasy fare to gag on."

It was raining outside; cold, wet air had never been more welcome.

Arabella paid Bevil his fifty pounds without explanation, and borrowed a maidservant to help her dress for court.

"There's a reception for King Louis's emissary tonight," he offered, claret firmly grasped for safety. "In the Great Gallery, with all ceremony."

"Good," said Arabella briefly. She felt sick and her legs trembled with exhaustion; as it gathered force, fear was sucking out her strength.

"Here," said Bevil abruptly. "You'd best drink something or you'll be fainting at the King's feet. Not to say he wouldn't enjoy it, mind. Strange tastes, has King James. Will you take a word of advice?"

She nodded, sipping the wine he offered. Bevil's advice was valuable on matters of intrigue.

"Don't rush at him before witnesses, he has a despot's temper. Charles relented to a woman's tears, James would see it as mere weakness. Alone you might have a chance, although he hasn't a yielding temper."

Bevil's words hammered at her as out-of-step chairmen increased her sickness all the way to Whitehall. God knew she did not doubt James Stuart's unyielding way with those who opposed him.

She had her first snatch of good fortune by the flambeaux-lit entry to the Great Gallery. The Earl of Sunderland, a distant connection of Wexford's, was talking to acquaintance there and greeted her with the usual chilly politeness of Wexford relations, so no one dreamed of challenging her right of entry.

The gallery was lit by banked candles, the throng sufficiently familiar for her to feel no uncertainty, yet idle chatter and court splendour were so far removed from her thoughts that she might have been watching a dumbshow behind glass. A few acquaintance greeted her with barbed enquiry and covert speculation over where she had been, but she was unable to respond even with common civilities. It was two o'clock in the morning, Sunday morning, tomorrow ... tomorrow Harry would be on trial for his life.

She edged her way up the long gallery, wide skirts hampering movement in the crush. The King was surrounded by courtiers and a gathering of French, fiddles scraping so she could scarcely think. She remembered the royal withdrawing room behind where James stood: Wexford had often been called there to attend Charles about his backstairs dealings.

She forced herself to talk sensibly to some men Sunderland

introduced, so the footman by the private entry would not doubt her standing, then withdrew to coolness in the passage; the flunkeys did not even eye her as she passed. She went through a small room where giggles came from behind the hangings, and entered a dimly lit passage, followed some stairs down to another long and excessively cold passage. Whitehall Palace was a warren of stone and brick from a dozen reigns; she recalled how Wexford had escorted her this way once and told her of women brought directly to the royal bedchamber by similar convenient routes.

At the end of the passage was a buttery and outer entrance, guarded against stray intruders. A woman was there, two children at her skirts, entreating the guard to let them past. Arabella gave thanks for the distraction and hurried past, for that was the danger point. The woman's voice, broken by tears, came to her as she paused at the bottom of more stairs. "In Christ's mercy, I beg you, sir. My husband is to be tried tomorrow, I do but seek to entreat His Majesty for mercy on his life."

The man returned some rough answer while Arabella stood in the shadows, trembling. This was . . . this must be Elizabeth Cornish on the same mission as herself. She laid her forehead against stone and struggled for thought: James had his Queen with him and a handful of French emissaries. Surely he would find it harder to resist a wife's pleas than those of a mistress of poor repute. A wife, moreover, risen from a bed of illness, the prisoner's children at her skirts.

She nodded to herself, like a child, her decision made; picked up a candlestick and went back into the hallway. She made a fair noise about it too, so the guard turned and saw her come as if from the King's private apartments.

"Is this the woman?" asked Arabella, thinking how odd her own voice sounded.

The guard blinked. "'Tis some City goodwife whining for entry to the King."

Arabella nodded. "His Majesty heard of her pleadings at the other entry and bids that she be admitted."

The guard looked relieved, he had not relished kicking a woman and her brats off the step. "Up with ye, then," he said gruffly. "Good fortune."

Elizabeth had once been a lovely woman, though Arabella wondered whether Harry chose her because in every way she was opposite to herself: she wore her own ash-fair hair in long ringlets, her eyes were blue, expression gentle despite lines scored in her face by illness. Indeed, she looked ready to faint and the boy put her hand on his shoulder in a protective gesture which reminded Arabella unbearably of Harry. The children were about ten and six, she supposed, a boy and a girl. The other boy must be too young to come.

"Wait, mistress," she said abruptly. "There is something I must say to you."

Elizabeth paused on the step above, hand on the wall. "I ask God's blessing on you. Is the King willing to see us now?"

"I don't know. I lied to the guard to get you past. The King knows nothing of you, but this stair does lead to his withdrawing room. You'll have your chance to plead with him, God knows whether to any avail." She gestured to the stair. "It is poor seating but you look ready to drop, and there are a few matters I must explain before we go further."

Elizabeth Cornish smiled with extraordinary sweetness and sat, drawing the children down beside her. "I am in your hands, madame."

Arabella swallowed, she had no intention of facing this frail woman with the truth of who she was, the whole situation intolerable. She understood now how Harry had felt since he became so divided between them. "I am no waiting woman but was on my way to the King's apartments. I heard you pleading with the guard and guessed who you must be since I come from the City too. I help you because I wish you well and pray for your success, but I have no influence with His Majesty, nor has he heard that you wish to petition him."

Elizabeth wrinkled her brow, she looked gentle and pretty but not particularly clever. "If you are no waiting woman, then what are you doing here?"

Well, thought Arabella furiously, what a fool the woman is. Anyone with a particle of sense could make a shrewd guess at what women in royal passages were likely to be doing. To her it had seemed the obvious explanation to offer. "These stairs are convenient to His Majesty's bedchamber," she said drily; and truthfully as it happened.

Elizabeth's cheeks stained crimson behind almost transparent skin and instinctively she gathered her daughter close. "Oh! I—I'm sorry if I embarrassed you!"

"On the contrary, madame. I appear to have embarrassed you," replied Arabella coolly. "Now, if you are pleased to go up, we will see what we can do."

Chapter Four

Elizabeth was plainly distressed by the time they reached the top of the stair, and Arabella eyed her doubtfully; she looked sick enough to move any heart not completely lost to pity. The boy had his mother's delicate build and blue eyes but also an indefinable air of Harry in gesture and stance; the girl was a merry little thing who obviously thought stumbling around palaces in the small hours a great joke.

James was already in his withdrawing room, standing by the fire talking French to Louis's ambassador, and turned at their entry, so Arabella advanced boldly before sinking in a deep curtsey. "Sire, my lady of Wexford offers her humble duty and begs to present Mistress Cornish with a petition clemency for her husband."

James frowned. "These are private apartments, madame."

"Your Majesty, I would not have ventured to intrude but for the urgency of the matter. Mistress Cornish is distraught and begged for my assistance to gain Your Majesty's presence."

James's eyes flickered, he was no naïve innocent and she could see him speculating on her own interest. "Bid her forward then, since she is here."

Elizabeth did it well, Arabella thought critically. Very well, considering she knew nothing of courts and flattery. Only desperate anxiety for her husband and her sincerity showed. Young Henry knelt beside his mother, the girl stared round-eyed at finery and dribbled on the floor.

"Rise up, madame," said James when she had finished. "Your husband has opposed and displeased both the late King and ourself through many years, and pays the penalty for his insolence." He had a long, rather melancholy face, which gave little indication of his thoughts. Or of mercy, either.

"Sire, he stood by what he thought to be his duty as alderman of the City; since he lost office he has traded quietly and stood aside from controversy." She stayed on her knees.

"Such is not our belief, but he will have his chance to speak at his trial."

"Your Majesty, I beg you to grant him time. Whatever he may have done to anger Your Majesty, he is no traitor and so close kept that he can neither name witnesses nor instruct counsel. No one is allowed to see him, not even an attorney."

The Frenchman said something to James and they both laughed; Arabella caught the word "Presbyterian" and so did Elizabeth, for she added hastily, "I assure Your Majesty that my husband attends the Church of England and took all the oaths prescribed for his office."

James was still smiling. "So do half the Nonconformist sweepings of the land, so perjuring themselves as well as endangering their souls. Begone, madame, we will instruct our judges to listen to such complaints as Cornish makes of his treatment and defer the trial if necessary."

"God give you His blessing, sire, as I do!" Henry helped her to her feet and she kissed the King's hand fervently. "He is innocent of treason, Your Majesty. With time to prepare his defence he will have no difficulty in proving any charge baseless."

"We will trust that he may, and so repay our clemency to him. His judges shall be so instructed." James began to talk to the Frenchmen again.

"Thank God . . . thank God . . . thank God," whispered Elizabeth when they were outside. "How can I ever repay you for your help?"

"By forgetting you ever saw me here," said Arabella. "There are always hackneys outside the palace whatever the hour of night, I advise you to begone before you faint."

She smiled. "If I do, it will be for joy. Surely, now the King's word is pledged to mercy, they will let me see him tomorrow."

The King's word given to precisely what mercy? brooded Arabella as she too travelled back towards the City. She and Elizabeth had achieved something, time alone would show whether it was enough.

Adam was waiting for her, looking like a white ghost of

himself. He had left for work at East India House nearly twenty-three hours before and had not rested since: because he always seemed more like a shrunken adult than a child it was easy to forget he was only thirteen years old. He took her cloak and pushed her into a chair with surprising tenderness. "What fortune?"

Arabella lay back, eyes closed, swept by exhaustion. "I don't know. I—we—saw the King and he said he would instruct his judges, whatever that may mean. I think he will allow the trial to be deferred, in fact he promised he would, so we have won time at least." She opened her eyes, encouraged by her own words. She had won time; Harry would not be on trial for his life tomorrow and, however obscurely, James had mentioned clemency.

"The King? What of Jeffries?"

She had forgotten that she had left to see Jeffries, it all seemed so infinitely long ago. She told him everything then, too tired to be guarded, and his face darkened into bitter rage. "Whatever Jeffries says, the King listens to him on matters of law, and two of the judges down for tomorrow's trial were with him on the Bloody Assize."

Arabella shrugged, she could not be bothered with Jeffries now. "How did you—did you get into Newgate?"

He nodded. "I took my father's meal from the Mitre in Cock Lane. The turnkey stayed in the cell the whole while but I told him what I could as if it were gossip. He hasn't seen the charges and knows no detail—" He broke off, face crumpling suddenly. "God, it's unbelievable! On trial for his life tomorrow and he is shut up in the dark without pens or paper, or even a copy of the charge."

"It won't happen now. He'll lodge a complaint with the judges and they will set another date. How was he?"

Adam leaned his head on the mantel; so she would not see tears, she thought. "You know him," he said jerkily at last. "He offered me cheer instead of the other way. He has paid to be lightly chained but the cell is foul. Cold and with one small opening giving neither air nor light. No candles and bug-ridden bedding. Lucky to have that, the turnkey said."

"They'll have to take him out of such a place once delay is granted or risk him pleading the same again." Arabella said it as much to convince herself as him. Draggingly, she pulled herself from her chair. "We must rest or we'll be no use to him at all." Her breasts ached and her busk was wet.

Adam went over to the window. "I must be out as soon as it is light. He gave me some names . . . since he does not know what the charge of treason relates to, all he can do is call witnesses to his character, and God knows there are few in the City who will not swear to that."

Adam had gone when Arabella woke out of the blankness of utter exhaustion. St. Sepulchre's bell was striking nearby: three o'clock. *Three.*

Sweet Jesus, she had slept half the day away. She dressed and fed Jenny, then did not know what to do next. In the end she took a chair to Cheapside to enquire after Elizabeth; when she learned, as she had hoped, that Mistress Cornish was ill in bed she went directly to Newgate.

If she cherished any hope that the King's promise would already have eased Harry's confinement, it was soon dashed. Even the offer of twenty guineas brought only a reluctant shake of the head. "Wait till 'e's condemned, sweet'eart, then we'll see. After the trial 'tis usually easier, but this un's special, see? The keeper took the sheriff in to see 'im but stayed 'imself all the while. Ye'd not want that, would 'ee?" He winked.

"I would accept it, if there was no other way."

It was no good. Newgate turnkeys were usually the most corruptible of mortals but the trial of Henry Cornish within the City's own boundaries was a matter the government did not intend to slide out of control. So their prisoner must be kept away from help and advice, away from any chance of concerting opposition when over the years he had learned a great deal about how to oppose Kings. Without his treason even published, the instinct of those who otherwise might have rallied to him would be to wait and see what the charge was before doing anything.

Arabella returned to Swithin Court deeply depressed: James's promises of the night before seemed insubstantial when viewed in the light of day. Adam was back, haggard with fatigue but holding a list a foot long of those willing to swear to the integrity of Henry Cornish. "God send he won't need them," Arabella said soberly. "Character witnesses, what are they against a charge of treason?"

He shrugged and would not reply; he had been pleased with the success of his efforts and felt deflated by her pessimism.

Another sleepless night, then they dressed in a bleak dawn and joined the throng outside the Sessions House at the Old Bailey. Adam squirmed his way past kicks and cuffs, and secured a seat for her next a stinking fishmonger, while he curled into a corner of windowsill. Arabella was aware of the stares she attracted; she had dressed as unfashionably as she was able but nothing could disguise her beauty, nor breeding which set her apart from street women who were the only females usually to be found at the Old Bailey.

She did not care, could not have stayed away. At least there was no sign of Elizabeth, she realised with relief.

The air was cold but stinking from packed humanity, one end of the court permanently open in an effort to preserve judges from infection by mob and prisoners.

A stir at last as guards filed in, far more than customary in such proceedings. Then the prisoner. Arabella stared at Harry as if she could never look away and eventually the intensity of her gaze caught his attention. She saw colour come into his parchment face as he realised she was there: he tried not to attract attention to her, but his eyes kept straying back after that. He was carefully shaved and dressed although his clothes were crumpled, presumably he had slept in them since he was arrested. He stood without shifting between his guards and was not chained; Arabella thought he looked angry rather than afraid.

Another stir and the judges entered, a considerable array of them, including the Lord Mayor, a court Tory, so no friend of Harry's, and the recorder who replaced Sir George Treby when the charter was forfeited, he would be an enemy too. The Attorney General, the Solicitor General, Lord Chief Justice Jones: all Jeffries' appointees; Judges Levinz and Withins, who had been with Jeffries on the Bloody Assize. If James had not been true to his word, Harry would find no justice from such a crew, the number and importance of them alone was ominous. Arabella's heart changed beat, heavy hammer strokes slamming against her ribs.

The clerk called the court to order and pulled out a sealed paper. "Set Henry Cornish at the bar. Henry Cornish, hold up your hand."

Harry moved forward, but instead of holding up his hand to accept the reading of the charge he immediately addressed the judges. "My lords, I wish to protest against my treatment." His eyes flicked over Lord Mayor and recorder; she had been right, he was furiously angry. "Some of you know me, and can judge whether I am a man whose word is to be trusted. I am set before this bar to plead for my life, yet have been held in close confinement, without light, pens or paper, without

281

access to counsel or knowledge of the charges against me. I ask that I be granted facilities and time to prepare my defence, as is customary in cases of such gravity."

The Lord Mayor and recorder looked uncomfortable and left the Lord Chief Justice to reply. "You must plead, Mr. Cornish. You will have your chance to speak later."

"I cannot plead to charges I do not know. I need time, details of the charges and legal advice."

"No, Mr. Cornish. Such is not customary. You must plead."

Harry's eyes narrowed. "I have been kept in such conditions as would disgrace swine. Then I am told I must plead for my life against charges I do not know."

The judges nodded in unison. "You must obey the rules of the court," interrupted the Lord Mayor anxiously.

"Rules!" said Harry contemptuously. "Your rules are one thing, my innocence quite another."

Crown counsel stood. "You are out of order and out of time, sir. Arraign him, sirrah clerk, whether he will or not."

"I have some knowledge of the law," said Harry deliberately. "Having once been an elected"—he hesitated on the word "elected," staring derisively at the Lord Mayor and recorder, who went scarlet in embarrassment—"sheriff of this City. Although these present judges may deny it, an accused person has a right to appeal against arraignment when injustice has prevented him from preparing his defence. I do so appeal, and have more injustice to plead than perhaps any prisoner who ever stood at this bar."

A gasp was expelled almost simultaneously from every throat in the court. The fishmonger beside Arabella gave a grunt of approval and thumped the woodwork.

The recorder stood. "Do you plead, or do I enter you as refusing?" The law's remedy for those who refused to plead was to order them to be taken hence, stripped, spread-eagled in Newgate Yard next door, and pressed with weights until their mind was changed, or they died.

Harry hesitated and then held up his hand. "I will plead, so help me God. For it is sure that no one else will."

So he was sworn and the charges read. They were immensely long and related to . . . Arabella listened, dumbfounded. They related to King Charles's reign two and a half years previously. Henry Cornish was accused of supporting Monmouth and plotting to raise the City in conjunction with the Rye House conspiracy. That crazy affair which had never sparked, when old parliamentarians and some of the wilder Whigs plotted to capture the King on his way from Newmarket, and were betrayed weeks after their plottings had collapsed.

"How sayest you, Henry Cornish?" asked the clerk when he had done.

"That it is indeed a remarkable charge." Everyone laughed, except for the judges, who fluttered their robes and exchanged angry looks.

Crown counsel stood. "You must answer in due form."

"I am perfectly innocent."

Counsel sighed. "Are you guilty or not guilty? You must use the correct words."

Harry grinned. "Fine things, words, Mr. Counsel. Not guilty."

For God's sake, thought Arabella, they'll tear out his throat in a minute. Have a care, in the mercy of Christ. But she could see from the ominous tightness of his lips, the stiff way he held himself, that after months of self-control these past few days had slipped his formidable temper from its hold at last.

The court was thoroughly flustered by now and confusion was redoubled when Harry used his experience as sheriff and alderman to argue over the composition of the jury, to trip everyone on points of law until eventually he was shouted down by the Attorney General; then he withdrew and left him bellowing like a wherryman into the silence. The court collapsed in laughter again.

While quiet was being restored Harry stood aloof, succeeding to admiration in giving the impression that better order prevailed in courts where he presided. Then he shouldered guards aside and came to stand directly before the Lord Chief Justice. "My lord, I have pleaded as required. Now I have the right to object to this trial going forward at this date, on the grounds of harsh treatment and the impossibility of searching out witnesses on my behalf. The sheriff has informed me that my wife and children petitioned His Majesty, and he was pleased to refer these objections to his judges. I now make my application to you and demand that they be heard in due form."

"Demand, Mr. Cornish?"

"Demand as is my right under the law, and as the King promised that you would hear my representations."

The Lord Chief Justice looked along the bench enquiringly. "I have no instruction from His Majesty." The other judges shook their heads. "Mr. Attorney General?"

"No, my lord. No instruction from His Majesty. Let the case proceed."

He turned back to Harry. "You see, Mr. Cornish?"

"I do indeed," said Harry acidly. He went back to his place.

Arabella closed her eyes. She had harboured grudges against God and Stuart Kings before, but nothing to those she felt now. No prayer or plea to either kindled a spark of mercy. James had probably laughed about how easily he had rid himself of an uncomfortable scene, and prayed to his God before he slept without so much as remembering the name of Henry Cornish.

The Attorney General rose and droned a long monologue about treachery. The court dozed gently until he came to the nub of the matter. ". . . it will appear that there was a meeting at a Mr. Sheppard's house in Eastcheap in connection with the Rye House plot to kidnap His Majesty King Charles, which was attended by the Duke of Monmouth in all secrecy. That the accused, Henry Cornish, did arrive during this meeting and was shown into the room where the conspirators were, that they read to him a paper summarizing their treasonable aims and he assented to them. The Crown will also prove that on another occasion he stated his intention of dividing the City into areas, and raising men therefrom, with the purpose of seizing the Tower of London. I would also remind the court of the part Mr. Cornish has recently played in setting the commonalty of the City against their undoubted King and ruler, and the Crown will maintain that this was all part of the same treasonable mind."

"May I ask that Crown witnesses be kept separate and out of the court until they have given evidence?" Harry looked unmoved, but Arabella chilled with dismay. She had expected vague allegations, not detailed charges.

"They will prove everything against you twice over."

"I don't doubt it, if they are given every opportunity to concert their evidence together."

The Attorney General choked as the court laughed again. "Call Mr. Rumsey." No one gave any orders about the witnesses.

An elderly man went to the witness stand, bobbing his head half apologetically to Harry as he passed. The burden of his evidence was that he had been involved in the Rye House plot, and had gone to Sheppard's house in the City to discuss a rising there if the King's person should be successfully seized. "I had not been at the house long when Mr. Sheppard was called downstairs and came back with Mr. Cornish. Mr. Cornish greeted those present but said he could not stay as there was a meeting he must attend about the City's charter. Immediately, another of our number, Mr. Ferguson, pulled a paper from his bosom which set out our aims and read it to Mr. Cornish while Mr. Sheppard held the candle. Mr. Cornish said he liked it very well."

The Lord Chief Justice looked up. "Was there anything in the paper about an insurrection?"

"I did not hear all of it read, my lord, but it was in the paper."

"Repeat exactly what Mr. Cornish said."

"He said he liked it very well, and with the small interest he had, he would back it. Or words to that effect."

Harry interrupted. "My lord, since he makes so free with my name I desire to state clearly that I never was at such a meeting in my life."

"You deny you were at Mr. Sheppard's that night?"

"I cannot tell. I have many dealings with Mr. Sheppard since he is a vintner, although not a man I care for personally. In fact he owes me money at this time." He smiled slightly. "Which might be of interest to impartial judges. But I never was at any secret meeting of this nature."

"Nor heard any paper read?"

"Never. I also object to this witness."

The Attorney General looked wary, Harry's knowledge of legal procedures had disconcerted the bench, who had moreover expected a man cowed and confused by five days alone in the dark. "On what grounds?"

"He stands charged with high treason over the Rye House plot and admitted his guilt in his evidence. He is a discredited person."

"He has turned King's Evidence, and expects a pardon. He is charged with nothing."

Harry gave a bark of angry laughter. "What is the price of his pardon? False witness against me?"

Rumsey looked ready to burst into tears. "Mr. Cornish . . . I beg of you . . . we have dealt together these fourteen years, do you think I would find pleasure in accusing you?"

Harry looked faintly interested. "I don't know. Do you?"

"No, no, no! I know you for an honest man and—" He turned to the judges. "I collected customs for six years in Bristol and Mr. Cornish accounted for them in London as my agent, and never once was there an error. I suffer from having to give such evidence more than he does."

You hypocritical whoreson, thought Arabella, her fingers crooked like claws, and heard Harry enquire sweetly, "How is it then, Mr. Rumsey, that two and a half years have gone by since my alleged treason, during which time you have accused me of nothing?"

Rumsey's eyes dropped. "I make no doubt that if you also would turn King's Evidence as I have done, you would receive His Majesty's mercy even as I hope to do."

"I thank God I do not stand in need of His Majesty's mercy, since I am innocent in this matter," replied Harry drily. "You have not answered my question."

"You should not question me, but I you." The little man looked sulky and defensive, words learned by rote slipping away under such treatment. "I am a witness and you the accused."

"Well, my lords?" Harry looked at the judges. "What think you of this witness?"

"This is not the place to question Mr. Rumsey's standing. You may make speeches later."

"Later? Why wait when his evidence should not be admitted in any reputable court until such time as he is pardoned of his treason?"

"If you have other questions to ask him, Mr. Cornish, pray ask them."

"Very well." Harry turned back to Rumsey, who cringed visibly. "In all the fourteen years of our acquaintance, do you allege that I ever spoke or acted in a treasonable manner before or since this one occasion?"

"Oh no, Mr. Cornish! Never, upon my word!" He looked delighted by such an easy question.

"Mr. Cornish!" Two or three judges interrupted at once. "This is no time for a dialogue."

"You bade me ask my questions. Does it not strike you as strange that in fourteen years of dealings, the Crown's own principal witness alleges only one occasion when words of treason passed my lips?"

The judges exchanged looks and agreed that it did not seem strange to them, Rumsey ordered to stand down immediately.

"Call Richard Goodenough."

Arabella started, alarm bells ringing in her mind. It couldn't be . . . but it was, she recognized his self-confident swagger immediately.

"Mr. Goodenough, are you acquainted with Mr. Cornish?"

Richard looked across at Harry and smiled maliciously. "Yes, I am."

"My lords," said Harry instantly. "I object. This man was also indicted in connection with the Rye House plot, but fled before his trial, so was declared an outlaw."

The Attorney General nodded. "What of it?"

The Lord Chief Justice turned to Harry. "The prosecution admits outlawry of their witness, but he is pardoned, so therefore admissible."

"Another half-pardoned felon, lying for his life?" said Harry tightly. "He is a man of known bad character; I can produce a dozen witnesses to it."

"Yet he was your undersheriff."

Arabella gasped, she had not known that; surely Harry could not have appointed a man who he knew had defrauded her of her inheritance.

"Much against my will. I can and shall produce witnesses to swear that I objected to him and refused to agree to his nomination as undersheriff. I was overruled by my fellow sheriff after long debate, but never accepted him myself. Nor did I deal with him throughout my year of office since I had long known him as a cheat and thief, and he bore me bitter malice for it. That is why he is a witness against me here today."

The Lord Chief Justice shrugged. "Objection overruled. Proceed, Mr. Attorney General."

Richard bowed mockingly. "We are not in Guildhall now, Mr. Cornish." He turned to the bench. "When I was Cornish's undersheriff, he instructed me to divide London into twenty parts so that out of each part we could raise five hundred men to storm the Tower at a convenient opportunity. Later he asked me how affairs went when we chanced to meet on 'Change, which I understood to relate to this matter, and I told him they went slowly."

"When was this?"

"As I remember it, Easter 1683, during the time when the charter was much at issue."

"My lords," said Harry. "Out of his own mouth he is found false. I was sheriff from midsummer 1680, for one year."

"He did not say that you asked him how it went while you were sheriff."

"He could relate but one conversation we had in four years, both while I was sheriff and after," said Harry drily, "and that one very obscure. Is it likely that I would entrust so delicate and treasonable a business to a man I quarrelled with to the extent of refusing to act with him in any capacity at all?"

The Attorney General returned to his witness. "Relate any other discussions you had with Cornish these past four years."

"Aye, Richard," said Harry derisively. "Relate them. I have character witnesses waiting outside: several certainly can corroborate the long-standing nature of our quarrel and the malice likely to have brought you here today. One of them must also have seen or overheard anything we said together, since the bad feeling between us was too well known for any chance conversation to pass without remark, and you are bold enough to say we met on the floor of the Royal Exchange."

There was a long silence. "There was no other discourse," said Richard sulkily.

"Thank you," said Harry ironically. "My lords, I ask you to exercise your own judgment on this matter. Is it likely that I could be so foolish as to act as this witness has described?"

"It is not for us to cavil at likelihood or improbability," said the recorder sharply. "It is for you to prove that you did not act treasonably."

"I beg your lordships' pardon. I thought it was for the Crown to prove that I had."

The Attorney General bounced to his feet, jerking angrily at his robes. "Is there anything else you wish to ask this witness?"

"Yes. His pardon for earlier outlawry has been accepted by this court. I would ask whether rumour in the City is true, which says he stands yet again indicted for further treason, namely complicity in the late Monmouth rising in the West?"

"What is that to the matter?"

"Everything, I think. Rumsey awaits his pardon, and if Goodenough does too, then I am accused by two men still uncertain of their lives who have turned King's Evidence. We all know that such pardons are customarily granted after certain services have been performed, and I think the nature of these services must be clear to this court in the case of Rumsey and Goodenough. Even though Goodenough at least finds pleasure in what he does."

There was silence you could touch in the Sessions House.

"See you here, Mr. Cornish," said one of the judges. "You cannot object to each witness the Crown produces."

"Why not, if each is objectionable and discredited?"

"You must plead your case, and not urge improbability this and probability that. Mr. Rumsey has said it was compassion for you which made him not accuse you before, and the court accepts his explanation."

"I also ask the court to accept that it is a strange thing if so good a government as we have now, protect not innocent men."

The Lord Chief Justice banged on the table as a shout, half laughter, half of derision, went up. "Have you witnesses of your own to bring?"

"Against Mr. Rumsey?"

"Against any man."

"I have, and beg also that the official record of Lord Russell's trial be admitted to evidence if the court will discover it. As your lordships know, I face difficulties in procuring documents, but if my memory serves, then Mr. Rumsey was also a Crown witness against Lord Russell over the Rye House treason, in which Lord Russell was implicated. Mr. Rumsey deposed then, under oath, that he had related everything he knew against all persons whatsoever. I read his evidence, since I had financial dealings with Mr. Rumsey, as I have admitted. If he spoke truly and discovered all he knew, he cannot now decide to allege my complicity in this plot since he made no mention of it then. If he did not speak truly and held back evidence against me from . . . compassion, or whatever other cause, then he perjured himself on oath and a perjured person cannot be regarded as a reliable witness. Quite apart from the pardon he has not yet obtained, of course," he added sarcastically.

Arabella exhaled a long breath and found herself clutching the fishmonger's arm. "He's done it," she said aloud. "It needs two witnesses for treason and he's torn Rumsey apart."

The fishmonger grunted. "Your man, is he?"

She nodded, uncaring of niceties.

"Good on ye, mistress, and on 'im, too. Lacking counsel and locked up till an hour ago in the dark, yet 'e's tied five judges and the 'Torney General into knots. Not counting the Lord Mayor, who don't deserve counting in nothing."

The judges were consulting feverishly together, then the Lord Chief Justice thumped the table again. "The record of previous criminal proceedings is not evidence."

"I ask that it be admitted."

"Mr. Cornish," he said, exasperated. "I have just ruled that trial proceedings are not evidence."

"An official record is not evidence?"

"It is not. Call your witnesses, Mr. Cornish."

Harry's eyes wandered along the bench of judges. "I am not a lawyer, but a merchant needs a fair memory, as I believe is required of judges also. If mine serves me well, then at least two members of this bench sat on Lord Russell's trial and could recall Mr. Rumsey's evidence there, if they would offer it on my behalf."

Simultaneously, the eyes of every member of the bench dropped as each judge began flicking through the papers in front of him. At that moment Arabella grasped the truth at last: Harry was already condemned. Nothing he said, no inconsistency of evidence or absurdity of accusation would help him. Sentence had been decided elsewhere before ever this trial came on, as Jeffries very well knew. This was simply the morality play, the dramatic presentation which hammered home the will of the King's government.

Everyone in the court was yelling as the judges remained silent, soldiers standing around the walls lashing out with halberds and the flat of their swords. Constables and ushers bellowed for order and eventually a few of the most disorderly were thrown out, the bench plainly torn between a desire to adjourn and clear the court and a realisation that the sooner the case was concluded, the better. Quite apart from the risk of riot if it dragged on, Harry had been forced to stand throughout the proceedings, to improvise his defence from moment to moment as the charges unfolded, any respite would be to his advantage.

Arabella watched his face; her eyes were dry, only her throat tight-shut by tears. He no longer looked angry but sad, very tired, and—she realised—resigned. Probably he had known from the beginning that he played in a farce, which perhaps accounted for his rage. He had still beaten the court at its own lethal game; unlike her, he had not expected it to make any difference.

When a measure of order was restored he called a whole series of witnesses while the judges fidgeted. Witnesses to corroborate that he had refused to accept Richard Goodenough as his undersheriff, witnesses to speak for his repute as a trader, an alderman, a banker; clients who spoke of his probity, fellow merchants who swore to his integrity and the respect in which he was held in the City. Once, he glanced at Adam perched on his windowsill and smiled for him alone: these were the men he had feverishly marshalled the day before.

"What is this to the purpose, Mr. Cornish?" Lord Chief Justice Jones kept asking peevishly. "You are not on trial for fraud. The Crown does not dispute your honesty in trade, but your loyalty to His Majesty. Call witnesses to that, if you can."

"I think it is to the purpose, my lord," Harry replied evenly. "I am on trial as one from the community of this City, so let the City be my witness." And called another half dozen while the judges fumed. He could not have said more clearly that two could stage morality plays. Common Council was no more, the Court of Aldermen a farce, mayor and sheriffs intruded by the King: the City no longer possessed a voice, but survived in its own tight-knit loyalties. Alive and waiting to outlast Kings, though Henry Cornish died.

The bench finally brought it to an end, and the Lord Chief Justice shouted down protests to begin his summing up. No one felt surprised by his bias against the prisoner as he un-critically repeated Rumsey's evidence about the paper and Mr. Cornish's acceptance of it, dwelt with horror on Goodenough's account of how Mr. Cornish had plotted to divide the City and raise armed men. He stated flatly that both witnesses were of good repute and admissible, then went on to sneer at Harry personally and morally, at his religion, his public acts, his absurd insistence that by its nature what the Crown alleged was improbable. He then turned to the jury and bade them find their verdict.

"My lord," said Harry, apparently unmoved, although the tightness of his face told Arabella that his temper had roused again. "I had not finished the presentation of my witnesses. I wish to call Mr. Sheppard."

"For God's sake, how could you call so many and forget one so material?" demanded the Attorney General, glaring at him. "I beg your lordship not to hear him."

"I did not forget, but had no facilities to subpoena him, if the court recalls the conditions of my confinement. I now see, however, that unwise curiosity has brought him to this court." He stared at a man standing somewhere behind Arabella.

"No, no, Mr. Cornish, we cannot allow it now."

"His name was on my paper of witnesses submitted to your lordship. I stand by my right to call him."

The court exploded into yells and catcalls, Sheppard thrust forward bodily by those around him. The judges conferred anxiously and gave way, fearing for their skins if they refused.

"Now Mr. Sheppard," said Harry; the same clipped voice as earlier, the same glint in his eye, as if anger rekindled by the Chief Justices's summing up had dredged strength from exhaustion. "Do you owe me money?"

Sheppard muttered something indistinguishable, eyes flickering to the judges, who in turn resentfully studied the packed mass on the floor of the court and would not meet his gaze.

"Louder, if you please." Harry stared at him as master banker at a fraudulent clerk.

"Aye . . . yes, sir."

"A very great deal of money, namely a hundred and forty pounds for wines recently sold to my clients?"

He gulped. "Yes."

"Thank you, Mr. Sheppard. Mr. Rumsey gave evidence that I came to your house during the spring of 1683, while a meeting was being held which discussed a plot to kill the late King and replace him by the Duke of Monmouth. He alleged that I was invited upstairs and approved a paper which set out the aims of the conspirators. He also said that you held the candle while this paper was read. Do you recall it?"

"Was Mr. Cornish ever at your house?" interrupted the Chief Justice.

"Aye, often, my lord."

"I do not dispute it," snapped Harry, anger showing for once. "I have substantial dealings with Mr. Sheppard. I do dispute that I was ever at this meeting. Mr. Sheppard, do you recall the occasion to which the Crown's evidence refers?"

"Very clearly."

"We have heard that the Duke of Monmouth was there, a Mr. Ferguson and Rumsey. Who else?"

"The . . . the Lord Russell, I think. Perhaps Lord Grey. I am not sure."

"You said you recalled the occasion very clearly. Yet you had three great men in your parlour and do not remember their names. Were you in the habit of entertaining the peerage?"

Sheppard's gaze darted to the bench, his tongue flicking in and out, silently beseeching the judges to intervene, while they sat calculating the chances of riot if they did. "No, Mr. Cornish," he said unwillingly, at last.

"Yet you do not remember names from this single occasion when you did?"

Sheppard cracked his knuckles despairingly. "I am sure the Duke of Monmouth was there. I remember no one else."

"Very well. Did I speak to him?"

"You—you spoke to one of the company."

"Which company, since you do not remember who they were?"

"Mr. Sheppard." The Lord Chief Justice was unable to watch the disintegration of such a key witness any longer. "This is not to the matter. You remember clearly that Mr. Cornish was at your house on the night of this secret meeting?"

"Yes, Mr. Sheppard," said Harry softly. "Do you remember that? And while you think carefully on it, remember also the many witnesses to my name this day." If the Crown could threaten, so could he: if Sheppard lied now, then his trade was ruined. Not one of those who had sworn for Henry Cornish, nor the many others who had been willing to do so, would ever deal with him again.

"I—I . . . truly, my lord . . . I—I cannot say whether it was that night or—or another when the paper was read, but I . . . do positively swear that no paper was read while Mr. Cornish was by, since he was not regarded as one of us."

The howl which broke from the packed court dislodged dust from the rafters.

"Tell me then, Mr. Sheppard," interposed the recorder silkily. "If Mr. Cornish did not come to take part in your meeting, why did he come?"

"I—I think it was . . . he said he could only stay a half of a quarter of an hour, since he was due at a meeting about the charter where he must preside, since no other alderman was in town. He was great in opposing the surrender, you will remember, my lords," he added, anxiously trying to keep himself from destruction by both sides.

"The court well knows it," said the Attorney General. "Did he speak with the Duke of Monmouth?"

"I believe so, my lord."

"Do you positively know so?"

Sheppard hesitated, met Harry's stare and lost himself in a flurry of half-sentences until the Attorney General changed tack in disgust. "How was it you brought him upstairs to so secret a company, if you now allege he was not of it?"

"I believe he wanted to speak to the Duke."

"Did I speak to the Duke?" interrupted Harry.

"I . . . think so. Perhaps it was another."

"Pray remember, sir. It is important. Did I or did I not speak to the Duke of Monmouth on the night of your secret meeting?"

"Have mercy on me, good sirs!" Sheppard was a pitiful sight, had surely never expected such an ordeal when he agreed to easy swearings. "I—I do not remember precisely. I think Mr. Cornish spoke to the Duke. Perhaps it was another night."

"Rumsey swore that you held the candle when I came upstairs—if of course I came at all," added Harry sarcastically.

"Perhaps . . . I do not remember. It is a long time ago."

"It is, isn't it? Yet Rumsey remembered everything perfectly, as you swore you did a few minutes since. Rumsey deposed that you held the candle while Ferguson read a treasonable document, of which I approved."

Sheppard hesitated, staring at Harry like a trapped stoat. Then he inclined his head in a strangely dignified gesture and turned to the judges. "No document was ever read in Mr. Cornish's presence. I would remember that, since he was not of our number. Once at a meeting Mr. Ferguson took a document out of his shoe and read it, but the time Mr. Cornish came he was only there a few minutes, in great haste, and no document was read. He was about the business of the charter."

Harry pounced. "Ferguson kept this document in his shoe?"

"Aye, Mr. Cornish. I remember it well." He seemed quite steady now, almost confident.

"Rumsey said he pulled it out of his bosom."

"Certainly not," said Sheppard, affronted. "He had a very cunning hiding place in his shoe."

"And though I may possibly have spoken to the Duke of Monmouth on some occasion, at a time when he was high in the King's confidence and not known as a traitor, you do positively remember that no document was read from shoe or bosom, nor was your conspiracy discussed in my presence?"

"Yes, sir."

"Indeed it would have been difficult to do so, if I stayed only a half of a quarter of an hour, and greeted the company who were unknown to me within that time, don't you agree?"

"Yes, indeed sir."

Harry looked at the bench and smiled. "Your witness, I think, Mr. Attorney General."

He made the best he could of the shreds left of Sheppard's evidence, but it was not much. Once driven in a corner, the vintner had chosen his future in the City as against the immediate favour of the Crown, and was not shaken again on the crucial admissions Harry had wrung from him. Rumsey was recalled and made an even worse impression than before, repeating his story in a flat monotone without allowing for any of the fresh evidence which had been extracted from Sheppard. Nothing he said was queried by the bench, and Harry declined to examine him again since a perjurer, now double-perjured and working his way to a royal pardon, was a worthless witness.

The jury was out and back in a matter of minutes, hungry and thirsty after more hours' work than they expected. Henry Cornish was brought in guilty by unanimous verdict.

Arabella had known it would happen, but not believed it. The courtroom faded, shouts, stamping and bright judges' robes blurring into one engulfing wave. They could not convict when every witness was discredited, demonstrated as bought, activated by malice or else contradicted the Crown's case. They could not, but they had.

As dazed disbelief faded, the Lord Chief Justice was on his feet, his relish unmistakable. Never before had he been so baited and exposed in his own court. "Mr. Keeper, tie the prisoner for sentence."

Even Richardson, the keeper of Newgate, looked startled at that. Only dangerous criminals were tied in the dock, or madmen offering violence to their warders. He recovered himself almost at once, though, and jerked his head at two sergeants; the crowd were not yelling any more but shuffling with excitement and the unexpected sensation of it all. Harry gave one involuntary jerk when he was seized, then stood unresisting while they twisted his arms brutally behind.

Richardson checked the binding. "He is secure, my lord."

The Lord Chief Justice hooked his thumbs into his robes. "It is now my duty to pronounce the full sentence on Henry Cornish for high treason." He stared directly at Harry. "That you return to the prison from whence you came, from thence you shall be taken to the place of execution, which in this case shall be Cheapside by the corner of King Street, in sight of your own abode. When you come there you must be hanged by the neck, but not until you are dead, for you must be cut down alive, your bowels taken out and burned before your face, your body divided into four portions for the King's disposal, and your head exhibited on Guildhall in this city. And

295

may God have mercy on your soul. Mr. Keeper, take the prisoner from the bar."

Harry did not move, not one person in the court moved, stunned by shock. Treason; men were hanged, drawn and quartered for it. Not usually alive any longer, although it was not unknown, but this was the full, ancient sentence; and such matters, if they happened, happened to unknowns at Tyburn or Tower Hill, where the mob could enjoy its pleasures and the squeamish go about their business undisturbed.

The judges filed out hastily while the court was still quiet, the sergeant at Harry's shoulder turning him roughly so blood already at his wrists could be clearly seen. The first of so much blood still to be shed before he died. Then he was hustled out, surrounded by drawn steel.

Too late, spectators shook fists and jeered, under their fury a sense of anticipatory gloating at the prospect of uncommon butchery. Many would be disappointed if their spectacle was stopped now.

Arabella sat with nerve, mind and movement frozen, until the kindly fishmonger carried her out and dumped her on the steps of Old Bailey to recover. "I daresay 'tis just a threat, to keep t'City frightened," he said awkwardly. "There'll be time for petitions, for mayor and aldermen to do summat, anyways. Appeal to the King's mercy like. Don't upset yerself too much, mistress."

"A pox on the King's mercy," said Arabella, and spat in filth. "That for James Stuart's mercy, and may he hang me for saying it. At least it would be for the truth."

Chapter Five

The same evening the scaffold began to be erected in Cheapside.

No stay of execution, no time for anything but foulest death. Arabella never knew how she returned to Swithin Court, Jenny's screams when she gulped at her mother's breast and found it dry, rousing her briefly before she sank into blankness.

Bells swung and clashed all around. St. Sepulchre, St. Andrew-by-the-Wardrobe, St. Benet, each relentlessly marked hours chipped and falling until the moment came when Harry— She hid her head in her arms as if she crouched inside the womb. The moment when Harry would be led not to the infinite mercy of a rope, but to a butcher's shambles. She muttered and jerked at curses; curses on pitiless Kings and a God who fed on blood. She did not sleep but found that Catlin had undressed her; could not rest with her mind beating against the frail bones of her skull, yet lay unmoving until the room dripped red as the sun rose on the last day of Harry's life. It was less than a week since he had kissed her and promised to return on the morrow. Since he had gone to the Royal Exchange about his affairs and been taken without warning.

The sheer speed and vindictiveness of it disarmed opposition.

A single day to finish building the scaffold, stoke fires and sharpen knives, one day only for the Lord Mayor and his underlings to prevaricate, for merchants of the City to plead with the King, and then it would be done.

The bells roused her in the end, they would have sent her mad otherwise. She stood and stretched, went to the window and looked out in astonishment. A child was squatting in the dust of Swithin Court drawing patterns with a grubby finger, two men shaking hands on some deal; birds wheeled in a low October sky, leaves drifted, a few spots of rain fell. It was an afternoon like any other; like none there had ever been.

Arabella called Catlin to help her dress, quite steady now, everything about her unnaturally cold and still. She could help Harry during the few hours left, later would be time for reason to be overwhelmed by grief. She sent Catlin to Cheapside and she went eagerly, trying to feel horror but instead excited by the drama of it all.

Arabella sat beside Jenny while she waited for Catlin to return, staring at the sleeping face of Harry's daughter. Her features were too unformed to show any look of him; Arabella had vaguely expected to find some comfort from this scrap of Harry's life and found none at all. All the world scoured clear of comfort, a void fitted only for the revenge of Kings.

Catlin returned as dusk was falling, bursting with news. "Cheapside is like weevilled biscuit, ye can't hardly move what with soldiers having to guard the scaffold, an' half the City yelling there."

"Mistress Cornish?" demanded Arabella impatiently.

"Two gentlemen called and escorted her to Newgate. They couldn't hardly force a way through the crowd, but she were all muffled up and I couldn't see how she were taking it." Catlin sounded regretful. "The 'ole place be shut up now and King's guards on the door."

"Is she still at Newgate?"

Catlin shook her head. "I saw Will, did you know he's turned out too and everything taken by the King? He said Mistress Cornish had kin in the country and were going there after 'twas done. Tonight she stays with her childer in the house of one of Mr. Cornish's friends."

Arabella sighed with relief. Amongst so many things beyond bearing, she had dreaded that Elizabeth might claim her right to stay by Harry this last night. False right; she might be his wife in name but Harry was hers in all else, and had been since before she could remember.

The turnkey at Newgate admitted her for a mere ten guineas: the night before a prisoner faced execution he was allowed wife or harlot as he chose, and wine enough to set thought reeling. Another ten guineas to be split between upstairs jailers, two more for a scrawny hag whose purpose she never discovered. Chill passages, dirty flags, steep stairs; everywhere a stench like Cheapside kennel before the fire. Arabella kept her eyes on the turnkey's back as he climbed ahead of her up a circular stair, and thought only of how Harry was close at last.

A cell door, lock double-barred by rusty iron. A guard lounging outside eyed her in morbid speculation, wondering how she felt about spending the night with flesh so soon to become carrion. More coins to him, so he would leave them undisturbed until dawn.

He said something and she replied, she had no idea what. Then he heaved at the iron bar and the door screeched on its hinges. It closed behind her, bar thudding in its socket, while she strained her eyes in the gloom of a single candle. He was over by the slit window, she saw shadows change shape as he turned only three paces away, the cell was tiny.

"Who is it?" His voice was light, uncertain, so she scarcely recognised it.

She did not move, this width of floor all he had now, it was for him to cross it if he wished. "It's me, Harry."

He tried to say her name, but his mouth was too dry. Then chains clinked as he moved and she was in his arms, iron painful across her breast as he held her like a drowning man. She welcomed the pain but had not expected to find him chained, although she should have done, since James was set on draining the last drop of his revenge.

"Ah, Bella," he said at last on a long, soft breath, and she felt the tremble in his hands. "I should have known—I think I did know you would come."

"As I have come each day, but they would not let me in before." She did not say that tonight she had also waited for Elizabeth to go, but he probably understood well enough.

She felt him swallow, his whole body was strung tight, the beat of his heart panic-fast through crumpled cloth. "Now you've come I fear it is a poor shadow of a man you find. I've tried . . . I think I held firm until tonight and offered Elizabeth and my children what strength I could, but . . . I haven't much courage left."

She touched his eyes and lips, drew his face to hers. No passion, no passion left in such extremity, but love enough to drive back the dark a little. The candle showed a pallet covered with damp straw, and she pulled him down to sit beside her, the weight of such chains as he was hung with sufficient to sap his remaining strength. "How long since you ate or rested, Harry?"

He shook his head, he did not know; the bones of his face were stark in flickering light. He had drunk nothing, though, she thought with wonder, there was no smell of wine on him at all.

"Could you lie beside me?" she asked at last.

He gave a ghost of a laugh. "If we take care to arrange my Stuart harness so it does not split us both apart." He stood and moved the candle closer so they could see, the flame dipping as his hand shook. Then he held out his arms and she ducked her head beneath them: he had heavy cuffs on his legs and a chain the thickness of her arm joining them to fetters on his wrists, but with his arms about her they were able to lie tight-bound together.

She felt some of the trembling tension ebb as she held and gentled him, murmuring meaningless words as to a child.

"What a farewell," he said, voice muffled. "I gave comfort to the rest, but from you I take."

"You took my heart's love long ago, before I ever knew it. You do but have your own, as I have had from you."

"It's the fear of—of becoming no more than offal while others jeer," he said jerkily. "I could face death, knew I risked it over the charter and thought the cause worthwhile, but—" With an effort she could feel he caught himself, forced tumbling words back in their cage. He was Harry still and would not seek relief through her distress: he feared the smell of his own guts burning, the disgusting skill of disjointing knife which would sever flesh and sinew while leaving vital arteries untouched, the screaming hunk of meat he would become. "You won't come, will you?" he said after a moment. "Or feel I might be eased if you did? I shall die in the love of Christ as best I can, but will not die well. No man could. I would sooner be alone, since only rage may perhaps have some power to sustain me."

Me too, thought Arabella. How can he think there is a Christ of love to help? No sweet Jesus and forgiveness, but honest fury which wished her enemies dead was all her feeling now. She nodded. "If you would rather have it so, I will not come." She felt enormously relieved; she had intended to go if it would help, but thought there was no way to endure it.

"Adam. He was here earlier, did you know?"

"No." She realised with a shock that she had not seen or thought of Adam since he crouched on a windowsill in Old Bailey Sessions House.

"Thank God Jenny is too young to care, kiss her for me, won't you? But Adam...I said what I could, but I'm afraid for him."

"He loves you," said Arabella, but could not think of Adam now.

"And has a very great capacity for loving, too." He hesitated, moved in her arms so his chains rattled. "You were angry with me when I spoke of him while you were still weak from Jenny's birth. The trouble was, I did not know how long I would be free to choose a better time. Whatever you feel yourself, Bella, try to prise him out of grief and vengeance, or he will be destroyed."

"I'll try," she said obediently, "but he has a will like those old oak beams which survived the fire, or hadn't you noticed?"

He gave a croak of laughter. "I had, yes. I made him swear today that he would not take blood for me; I could imagine him stalking the King through Whitehall passages. But no oath or binding will save him from a hell as bad as mine tomorrow, with more to come through the years after."

Arabella lay, fighting jealousy. He spoke of Adam when she should have filled his thoughts.

He spoke of her again at once. "Sweeting, what will you do? You know that all I have is seized into the King's hand, since a traitor forfeits everything?"

"I haven't been thinking of money," she said drily.

He kissed her then and she clung to him, tears salty to the taste and neither knew whose they were. When he drew away and held her wordlessly at last, they lay in fragile peace within his chains.

Much later, as moonlight's single stripe crawled across the floor, he said again, "What will you do? The lease on Swithin Court is in my name, you will be turned out in days. The House of the Spurs too. I'm thankful I made it over to you in time, but do not try to assert possession now. No court would accept a document with my name on it as matters are at present. Get the paper sworn at once, then hide it until a better day. For the moment you are beggared by this as well as suffering all the rest. Adam and Jenny too. Elizabeth has kin in Kent, George Treby takes her and the children there for me tomorrow; they at least will not starve."

"Nor will I," she said, smiling. "Don't worry, Harry. When did you ever need to fret over me?"

"Often," he retorted. "As when I rode in and found you

half dead from gilding fumes." He was warmer and seemed more relaxed, the effort of control her presence forced on a man of his temperament bringing its own relief.

"I have a jointure from Wexford still, I shall do well enough. And one day surely James Stuart must go the way of all tyrants and your children have their own again."

"You have my draft for five hundred? Vyner will honour it, I know."

"Yes," she said gently, although it was nearly spent in bribes. "I have it, Harry."

He shifted clumsily and swore beneath his breath, iron chafing raw wrists. "Bella, I don't know how to say this, but if one day you can find a shadow of happiness with someone else, I should not feel I lost anything which was mine. Only be content that you had found a measure of ease you will hardly survive without. Providing I liked the fellow," he added, suddenly exactly the Harry she had so long known. "My blessing on it if I do, but I'll damned well haunt you if I don't."

And as dawn came, he gathered pride and steadiness again from somewhere within himself, born from the comfort of their love which saw the dark time past. This, she had given him.

"Courage," she said once. "As my father died he wanted to urge so many virtues on me, but since he could only say one word, that was the one he chose. Which is as well, when you think how my life has been."

"It has surely shown more courage than most of us discover in ourselves." He smiled wryly. "I asked Mr. Calamy, the parson of St. Lawrence Jewry, to accompany me to the scaffold and he refused. He said he was too squeamish."

"Are you sure—"

"Quite sure. I do not want you there. You have sworn and I remember your scrupulous swearings very well."

"I would break any oath if you were helped at all," she said candidly.

He shook his head. "No. As you love me, no." There were feet in the passage outside and he rolled over, lifting his arms so she could crawl out between his chains. "Go now, my love. Remember me how I am, and will be always in your heart, no matter what."

He held her once more as the door opened, lips cold against hers, then smiled, hands on her shoulders, chain across her throat. God knew what lightness cost him then. "Farewell, sweeting, feel me with you often. Do not grieve more than you can help but remember instead how much we had, and will have again, which no King can ever touch."

And she went as he wished her to go, while he held courage tight.

*   *   *

The soldiers came first, hundreds of them, where a token presence sufficed for most executions. Tramping down Eastcheap and Cannon Street from the Tower, jingling harness from the royal barracks by Whitehall.

The crowd was dense long before dawn: angry, expectant and disorderly. No one knew who had ordered it, but the City church bells began to toll long before the prisoner's procession started from Newgate, though the mayor sent messengers scampering to forbid them. The sun was not yet risen, dampness settled into bone, grief into heart and mind. A few ships in the river flew black flags; the Royal Exchange, the City markets, wharfside and lanes deserted, where life usually abounded even at so early an hour. Shutters closed. Black cloth on doors in shabby side street and rich Cornhill alike. Silence everywhere, except for Cheapside and the bells.

Arabella stood by her open window, face dry and still. She would not kneel or weep, give God or James Stuart their moment of surrender. Courage; this last short time for courage. Harry had not yielded, and nor would she, though afterwards would be another life. Not hers, not Harry's, not even courage any more; just years to pass as best she might. But for this time she was with Harry, bells dying as ignominious sled bumped over cobbles with him bound to it and dizzied by its jolts; her strength was joined to his, her love something he might yet hold to in his torment. The bells were silent now, except for St. Mary-le-Bow across the street from where the Sign of the Corncrake was trampled into dirt while Harry died in blood and horror on his own doorstep; where once she had dropped snow on his head, and they had laughed together while the mummers sang. The high, sweet note of St. Lawrence Jewry also remained, for there Harry had worshipped, and it was the Corporation's church where he had long sat in civic state as part of London's power. Away by the river too, one more Arabella did not recognise, so the sound drifted to ships incoming on the tide, was carried by water clear to Westminster and James Stuart waking to his pitless dawn.

All petitions had been disregarded, delegations excluded, mercy dismissed, so the friends of Henry Cornish made this last gesture, and James would do well to listen and be afraid. Who wins London, wins the realm; this day King James had lost the City.

~ III ~

Adam

1688–1695

> *Which way shall I fly*
> *Infinite wrath, and infinite despair?*
> *Which way I fly is hell; myself am hell;*
> *And in the lowest deep a lower deep*
> *Still threat'ning to devour me opens wide,*
> *To which the hell I suffer seems a heaven.*
>
> JOHN MILTON

Chapter One

Adam disappeared for a month after his father died.

At first Arabella did not even notice he was gone, every sensation she possessed on the treadmill of Harry's death, nor did she face what her indifference meant: that Adam had never been more to her than an imprint of Harry's love. Instead, she simply wished she was less healthy, less full of life's passions, for then she need never return from smudged days and trackless nights to face reality. But there was no escape; the weeks passed, sun rose and set, the winter came, and she was aware again.

Money was short, Jenny fretful, Catlin surly over serving a mistress as limp and dull as baled rags. And Adam was not there. Apathy vanished and instead Arabella became easily roused and irritable, nerves jangling at the most trifling upset. She remembered Harry speaking of Adam and spent days worrying about him, then her old impatience returned, sharpened by stripped control. Arabella was unused to neglect, and he was being absurdly inconsiderate.

Their house in Swithin Court was shut up by royal officials, and until Adam returned they could only haunt the doorstep and lodge in the nearest tavern, where Arabella's elegance was hopelessly out of place and insult commonplace.

Consequently, when he returned at last both relieved their feelings in a savage quarrel which neither had intended nor wanted, the years of fragile patching to their relationship peeling to the touch. Arabella had been wrong: Adam understood exactly the nature of the grudge he owed her.

Arabella longed for him to be like Harry and could not see

her fantasy for the cruelty it was, so railed at him when he failed to fill even the smallest part of the void in her life. For Adam was locked away from words again, revenge and hatred the only emotions he understood.

He searched for Rumsey and Goodenough but both were in prison on charges City magistrates did not care to discuss: Adam was not alone in seeking retribution for Henry Cornish's death. So Jeffries became his quarry: he had not presided at the trial but in Adam's mind became all judges and their injustice distilled into one vile brew, Lord Chancellor still and well fattened on his prey.

London's streets had been in turmoil ever since the day when Adam stood in Cheapside and heard his father speak from the scaffold of the City which he loved, and pray mercy on it. Then watched him gutted alive. Soldiers had beaten back the crowd while it was done, though afterwards there were riots, more frequent as time passed and injustice multiplied. Adam shouted and pitched stones with the rest, in desperate need of the release which violence offered, but Jeffries was always too closely guarded for attack.

Now, at last, after three long years, it was an open secret that important merchants had joined their wealth to the prestige of leading nobles and sent an invitation to William of Orange, the King's son-in-law, to come to England and receive the throne as the gift of a people enraged by tyranny and consequent disorder.

Too late, James gave back the City's charter, sacked priests and spoke of accepting counsel from his subjects. They took what he restored, and turned their backs on him. London would never trust a Stuart again, would lend no money, refused even to offer advice. Adam might curse merchant prudence which had shackled fury for so long, but it had been many years in the growing and no offence was forgotten. Sixteen years since the stop of the Exchequer spread ruin in the markets and destroyed Alderman Backwell: his sons were now trading in Lombard Street, the City's own finances burdened with huge debts as a long-standing consequence. Five years since the charter was seized: when Jeffries offered to reinstate Sir George Treby as recorder he refused, and only a freely elected Lord Mayor persuaded him to change his mind. Three years since Henry Cornish died, his family beggared and all his wealth seized into the King's hand: Sir Robert Clayton spoke for many of his fellows when he declined to take office as alderman again, new charter or old, so long as butcher James was King.

There was no easy forgetting, nor old ways simply found.

On the evening the charter was restored, Adam walked down King Street to Cheapside, his clogs rattling on cobbles. He had not been able to come this way for months after the scaffold was dismantled, and it was still an effort now. He quickened his steps, unconsciously holding his breath as he reached the corner. Just past the turn was the pair of houses once known as the Corncrake and Golden Spurs.

Adam stood staring at them across the width of Cheapside. When the Crown took everything Henry Cornish owned, the royal treasury offered to lease his sign to the highest bidder, and received not a single tender. Only the greatest merchants dealt in balances, and they subscribed to support the Cornish family and would not touch his property. Now one house was a tavern and the other an ordinary of doubtful repute. Adam closed his eyes, lips moving, repeating an oath he had sworn many times before. One day Corncrake and Spurs would be his, signs remade and regilded, and men trust him with their balances as once they had trusted his father. He would do it and did not care how, but first came his score with Jeffries.

Adam haunted Whitehall during the following days, sensing the end was near. No one would fight for James. He had tried to overawe London by camping soldiers on Hounslow Heath, but they were English and not mercenaries, wore cockades to London's liberty and drank destruction to all tyrants. The capital remained quiet all through the time when William of Orange landed in the West; while James hesitated over what to do, marched out to offer battle and came back, his troops run off without a fight. There would be no civil war, no Englishmen killed when their only quarrel was with their King, and rejection of all he stood for would accomplish their purpose well enough.

Throughout it all, Adam loitered patiently in the alleys surrounding the palace. The customary bustle had vanished, a single set of heels ringing on the flags cause for remark when in all of sprawling Whitehall scarcely anyone remained: courtiers, ministers, toadies and servants all run off to await events in safety.

Whitehall Palace itself was still shoddily guarded, nothing would be easy there, but soon Jeffries must bolt for safety, too. Adam stiffened, his eyes on movement by Jeffries' door, but it was only some old man begging. It was December and bitterly cold, breath coiling in frosty air: Adam sat shivering on a step, deathly tired after days of snatched rest and scanty food while he maintained his vigil. Even in such cold he had difficulty in staying awake.

The man was almost past before he recognised the walk. Jeffries might change full-bottomed wig for cast-off peruke, his robes for crumpled serge, there was no mistaking his predatory, pouncing gait. Blood thumping, Adam lurched to his feet and stumbled after him, once Jeffries looked round at the noise he made but was reassured when he saw an urchin tripped in the kennel. At sixteen Adam still looked younger than his age, except for his face. And that Jeffries could not see.

Chill receded as Adam settled to the chase, intent only on his quarry. He had to chance picking up the trail again several times; Jeffries was no fool and would soon become alarmed by a follower whether he was a boy or not. Through the passages of Whitehall, across the tiltyard, moon brilliant on deserted spaces so Adam had to wait in shadow and then run to catch up. These past days of loitering had taught him something of the Whitehall maze, but Jeffries would know it intimately. Across Whitehall thoroughfare itself, then he lost sight of Jeffries in the blind turnings behind the Wardrobe, normally a hive of activity and now completely silent. He stood, straining eyes and ears, wondering whether Jeffries was aiming for the river or merely intended to use Whitehall as a means of shaking off possible pursuit. Too risky surely to take passage from Palace Stairs tonight. There could scarcely be a Londoner who would not murder Jeffries on sight, whatever restraints still held them from the King.

Adam made up his mind and ran through a double archway by the kitchens, tripped over rubbish and sent cats yowling into darkness. Further on lay the lower court of Scotland Yard, then Scotland Yard itself, the tangle of York House and Charing Cross beyond. If he lost Jeffries now, he would never pick him out from the crowds there.

A flicker of something over to the right, possibly rats made bold by stillness but he ran again, skirting piles of wood and coal tipped ready for the kitchens. Sheds; dark entries; a buttery still open, half a dozen porters lounging there in greasy lamplight.

Adam grabbed one. "Has a man gone this way? Above average height but rather crouched, shabby clothes, trying not

310

to be seen? He cheated me of my fare and trusted I would not pursue him through the palace."

The porter shook him off and kicked him casually. "Nor would you, runt, were not everything so disordered. Chase through the palace next week and you'll be tied for flogging at the gate."

"It's this week now, and I was cheated of my fare. Did he come this way?"

"Aye," said another, gulping ale, stolen from unguarded stores no doubt. "Let him go, Ned. What of it if he seeks his own? So do we all this merry season. Through the arch and down to Scotland Dock," he added. "There's a coal barge leaving on the tide; he headed that way and will mayhap beg a passage if he's so unwilling to pay charges."

Adam muttered thanks and picked himself up. His thigh cramped painfully where the kick had landed and he was alarmed in case Jeffries went further than Scotland Dock, since he might now lack pace on a long chase. He plunged into another huddle of buildings, the backyards of the palace were endless and tonight most lamps were unlit. He lost himself in a jumble of stacked goods and locked-off passages, then saw a faint glint in the distance, instantly blotted out. It took a moment to realise that someone must have moved into the open beyond the next arch. Pray God it was Jeffries. Another arch through which the wet stink of the river blew, beyond again the shine of water.

A figure was on the quayside, looking down; as he turned, his face showed clearly in the moonlight. Jeffries. Adam stood in shadow, completely still, smiling slightly. The fox was sniffing at its earth, and when it went to ground there would be no escape.

Jeffries seemed wary, and surprisingly agile for a man who had done little for years but drink and sit in judgment. The tide was low and the coal barge well below the quayside, but he made little fuss about sliding down a rope. A slither, crunched grit loud in nighttime stillness, then a thud as he shut himself in some compartment. When all was still again Adam went in search of the barge's crew; with the tide only just turning he found them in a nearby tavern, and discovered they were bound for Long Wharf, Wapping, to load more coal. Jeffries had made a wise choice, had probably planned this days ago; plenty of ships bound for the Continent tied up off Wapping, as well as river trade.

With time to spare, Adam set out to walk the distance;

311

Jeffries would stay hidden until a suitable ship weighed anchor, in fact . . . Adam paused, thinking. If Jeffries had planned this, he would certainly have planned the rest. He wasn't carrying anything but wouldn't flee penniless, must have the extortions of a lifetime already loaded. Adam shrugged and limped on, it made no difference. He wanted money desperately to set himself on the path to his sworn purpose, could do with a couple of coins now for a hackney, but wouldn't touch Jeffries' blood loot if it was strewn in the street. In the end, he stole a ride on a cart as far as Queenhithe, then walked the rest of the way along Thames Street, through Billingsgate, where everything was slick with fish scales, past Christopher Wren's new Customs House, up the slope of Tower Hill and into St. Katharine's stews beyond.

He thought he would never last, but fear of not lasting kept him moving. He stopped once and unbuckled his breeches, probing the massive bruise he found on his thigh. The skin was split but nothing seemed broken, once he could rest it would soon heal.

Unlike Whitehall, the City slums seethed with life although it was the small hours of the morning. Sailors sprawled in the gutters stupefied by spirits, bunters were rummaging the dunghills for anything of value, harlots plucked at passers-by with increasing desperation. Thieves scuffled just out of sight, waiting for the dawn turn-out when taverns and bawdy houses threw stale-drunk patrons into the dangers of the street. No one molested Adam. He looked too young and ragged to interest whores, too poor for robbery, too frail for those who lived by kidnapping children; Adam regarded it all with loathing and thought how one day he would live in Cheapside and turn his back on squalor. He could set himself to the task once Jeffries was despatched and James turned out. He had tried these last three years and failed; surely he would be able to clear his mind of hauntings once this was done.

Yet as he thought of it, the nightmare swept over him again. His belly heaved and he vomited painfully, sweat freezing on his face. He could not forget, could not, although he knew he must if he was ever to succeed in his purposes. He leaned against an ice-slimed wall, muscles contracting on emptiness, seeing it all again. His father drawn through the mob in degradation, heaved bodily up to an ill-made platform browned by old blood, bound so he could not help himself. With what endless, dreadful repetition he had relived it these last years.

How many more times could he live it without going mad?

He forced himself away from the wall and staggered on, half running as if pursued by demons and not noticing pain. What was a kicked leg anyway, when set against the agony of a man slit from chest to crotch when they scarcely bothered to dull sensation by strangling him first at all? He reached the hovels backing the Ratcliffe highway at last, and with Wapping nearly gained his senses slid as if tipped off a wharfside, so he pitched into garbage piled beneath a tottering wall.

He had no idea how long he lay, but regained consciousness spluttering violently as someone flung a bucket of water over his head. He sat up, shuddering; the water had been sharp with ice. A woman was standing, laughing at him. "Young, ain't yer, to be stale drunk in my backyard of a Sunday morning?" She dug at him with a clog-shod foot.

Adam grunted and drew back his injured leg, struggling to collect his wits. There was something about a barge and . . . "Is this Wapping?" he asked abruptly.

"Aye. Where was it las' night then?"

He eyed her with dislike. Bullying harridan, he would gladly cram her bucket over her ugly face. His clothes stank of vomit and were already freezing to his body. "Long Wharf. Is it near here?"

"A couple o' hundred paces, three taverns an' a peck o' steps away. Not far."

Adam knew he must get moving, he would die if he lay again in soaking clothes, yet he felt ridiculously weak. He fumbled his fingers into a narrow pocket picked in the seam of his breeches where he kept five pennies, a last reserve he seldom touched. "Have you . . ." When he thought about it his stomach heaved at the idea of food and he ended desperately, "Could I sit by your fire for a while? I—I have a penny to pay."

She shrugged. "What d'ye think I am, a baker? No fire in the forenoon for the likes of us, there's a mite o' warm left in the ash, I daresay."

There were a few embers on a cracked-slab hearth, and a swarm of scabby-nosed children burrowing close by. More memories rose like stirred slime as Adam sat with his head in his hands, trying to imagine warmth. Layers peeled off his consciousness and he was no longer a young man bound to vengeance beside a Wapping hearth but a child huddled in Moll's hut, scarcely daring to believe that his mother had come

313

at last. Everything else was the same, hands over his face, fingers in his ears because he would scream, would be beaten when he screamed, if another whimpering maggot of a child crawled over his shrinking flesh. He hated them, slammed his mind shut against their filth, against food he could not eat, against foul washing boiling dry when men came for Moll and the two of them heaved like more maggots, breeches and skirts untied. They slapped him if he looked; he loathed looking yet could not help it sometimes. From the day Moll told him of his mother he longed for her to come if only he could make her want him when she did, look as Moll said fine people looked so she would take him from this place. But he was maggot flesh too; though he hid his face and hoped she would not notice, she was repelled by him. Grief throttled words and left only hopeless tears to disgust her further.

After she went he thought of so many things he might have said, and washed his face in a puddle by the pond in case she came again. Perhaps then she would realise he had tried. Some bigger boys caught him between pond and Moll's hovel and made him eat mud, snivelling on his knees. Nor did she come again.

He looked up, blinking stupidly, images fading but revulsion set into bone. This he had been and still was: sixteen years of life and he was back in a hovel crawling with nameless brats, the taste of filth in his mouth. Only his father had lifted him out of his past and seen the many things he wanted to offer and could not. Of his mother, he refused to think.

He stood stiffly and went out again, feeling clearheaded but oddly insubstantial. Today he had vengeance to exact and in this he did not intend to fail.

It was another pale winter's day; Adam had no idea of the time but from the mist thought it could not be late. Wapping was a spider web of alleys, cluttered with strange-smelling rubbish discarded out of cargoes from all over the world. There were some well-built houses where ship's chandlers and repairmen lived, a few crumbling farmhouses engulfed by London's sprawl and divided into tenements, the rest self-built hovels holding upright by each other's strength. He reached the riverbank at last, the sun red-gold behind masts and yards of shipping crowding the Thames.

Gulls yelped low over the water, a brisk wind slicing at his body as he walked; his clothes were still wet, his skin numb long before he reached Long Wharf. There were more than a score of coal traders tied up there, but his eyes were fixed on the barges amongst them, sails tumbled carelessly at the boom. These ferried coal upriver and he was unprepared for the number of them. Some he discounted as too large or too small to fit the shape he had seen in Scotland Dock, but was still left with forty or fifty which might be the one he sought. He wandered about the wharf all day, scrambling from one to the other, not satisfied until he had seen the master of each, whom he would certainly recognise from the night before.

Early winter dusk was falling when he was forced to give up at last. Long Wharf was unlit, so he would do no more good until the morrow and could easily drown leaping from one barge to the next. Disappointed and conscious of time running out, he sought out the nearest alehouse, a lopsided jumble of timbers almost afloat at high water, daubed painting of a red cow over the sticking door.

Inside, it was more inviting: casks were piled to make comfortable nooks and seats, the bar festooned with nets of onions and ship's biscuit and backed by bigger casks. Above all, it was hot. Not just warm but bursting with the kind of heat Adam had heard men speak of at East India House.

The barkeeper was a woman, massive as her kegs and looking much the same; blunt features, seamed cheeks and strong brown curls like poured ale. Adam laid down three pennies; only one left now. "How much for a pasty and ale?"

"Ha'pence me pie an' a whole boy for ale," she said promptly. "Whole boy ha'pence for dog's neck."

From her jerked head Adam deduced that dog's neck was mulled ale, and attracted by anything warm, he spent recklessly on that and pie. The tavern was crammed with seamen, some off ships moored in midstream, others from the skiffs and wherries which carried river traffic. Adam ate slowly, mopping rich gravy with soggy, underbaked crust, licking his fingers clean of each fragment. His empty belly snarled at such fare but he must not vomit, could not afford another meal if he did. While he ate, he listened to often unintelligible talk all around; he would search other taverns later, but might pick up some clue here to the barge he sought. Not many would go to Scotland Dock, which served only the palace and York House.

Some sailors at his back were talking in foreign grunts, others such strange English he only made out a dozen words. The woman at the bar shouted at everyone, and seemed to know who came from where, which ships would leave on the tide, so he decided to speak to her when he had finished. He looked up as the tap door opened, and Jeffries came in.

Adam started violently and spilled half his ale. A sailor turned and cursed him, when he looked again Jeffries was by the bar. His height set him apart when most others here were stunted from poor fare or ill-treatment, otherwise he was unremarkable in coal-stained serge so long as his face stayed hidden. He looked up once when a drunkard jostled him; then high brow, fierce eyes and unrelenting face marked him instantly, but only Adam saw and after a moment he shaded his face and ordered more brandy.

Adam stood. This was retribution as it should be. George Jeffries trapped in a squalid tavern because he needed drink too badly to stay hidden a single night. He worked his way through the bale-tight throng until he was close enough to jerk Jeffries' mug from his grasp and toss it behind the bar in a shower of brandy.

Jeffries straightened and struck out without reflection, but Adam was expecting it and ducked, so his fist thudded into a cask. Jeffries swore and grabbed him by the shoulders, while Adam smiled and made no attempt to struggle, a puppet in his hands. "What a strange place to find the Lord Chancellor of All England."

The grip on his shoulders tightened, ground into bone while still he smiled, eyes light and content on Jeffries' face, watching his expression change from fury to startled disbelief. His eyes flickered from side to side as if he wondered who had heard, hold slackening while his mind shifted instantly to plan an escape before it was too late.

"It's already too late," Adam answered his thought. "The only choice left is whether to yield up your life here or in Newgate."

"Hey," said the woman behind the bar. "What's all this? What's gone wi' ye, then?"

"It's Lord Chancellor Jeffries and what's gone with him," replied Adam coolly. "Look for yourself and see guilt on his face. He thought to find a ship to take him away from the rope he has so richly earned."

One by one heads turned at bar and keg, staring in spreading silence.

The woman stood, hands flat on stained wood, head thrust forward as if sniffing out truth. She nodded slowly and spat in

316

Jeffries' face. "Aye, 'tis 'im. I ain't never seed 'im, but 'tis written there as on a slate."

Jeffries' hand went instinctively to wipe off spittle, even as yells and kicking, iron-tipped boots broke stillness apart. Adam expected Jeffries to be killed there, intended he should be trampled into filth and thrown on the mudflats like infested meat. He waited for it to happen, pleased and happy his part was done, but the woman seized a broom and struck out viciously, not at Jeffries but at those who tore at him. The Red Cow was her livelihood and she did not want a dead Lord Chancellor to explain, no matter how black a devil he might be. In her experience the mighty did not often bear the consequences of their misdeeds, and tomorrow another Lord Chancellor would be sitting on his bench, condemning the likes of her to death. Not because he regretted Jeffries' murder, but because his rank should protect him from the rabble.

When she had beaten them into a snarling circle, she sent someone running to the Tower. "Bid 'em send a good guard, none o' them puling 'andfuls. 'E'll not try escaping." She jerked her head at Jeffries, doubled gasping against the bar, face smeared with blood. "Tell 'em there'll be murder done if they don't guard 'im well."

Adam stood by, neither pleased nor disappointed. The Tower would do. "He won't have run off penniless," he said clearly. "Ask which ship he hoped to board and I warrant you'll find good pickings there." Let them have it instead of the royal treasury.

Jeffries told them at once, he was no fool and knew he had lost his chance. Meanwhile, his hoarded loot would serve the purpose of keeping this drunken rabble from his throat during the long wait for a guard. The woman made them tie him before they ran off to the ship he named, and nodded thanks to Adam, misreading his motive. "My thanks. Be an hour or more to the Tower and back. Why don't yer go out to the ship yerself then? Owin' some reward, ain't yer?"

"No," said Adam, staring at Jeffries. "This is the reward I want."

Jeffries looked up. "God's death, how did anyone discover me here?"

"I followed you from your house, intending to do exactly what I have done. One day I will come and watch you hang."

Jeffries stared at him, eyes narrowed. He had been afraid when he faced being pulped by fists and boots; now the situation

317

had settled into something he recognised, a duel between man and man, his formidable confidence returned. "Why? Who are you?"

Adam nodded. "You guess it, don't you? I must be kin to one of those slaughtered by your courts. I am Henry Cornish's son."

Jeffries frowned. "He was not condemned in my court. Anyway, as I remember it, his sons were scarcely breeched."

"He was killed by your creatures and contriving. I am his son by Arabella Sperling, who came to you begging for his life."

Jeffries laughed contemptuously. "I remember that very well. Perhaps we should have given the pair of them a church trial for adultery too."

"Cornish?" interrupted the woman. "You mean the one what was 'anged, drawn an' quartered in Cheapside?"

Adam nodded, sickened as always when anyone spoke of it, and Jeffries laughed again, straining openly at his bonds. He only faced a tavern wife and a nameless brat harbouring inflated grief, perhaps all was not lost. "It seems that his kin as well as the City will long remember the lesson taught by his death. You should think well on it unless you want to follow him."

The woman slapped him full across the face. "'E were one of ours, against all o' yourn."

Epitaph, thought Adam dully. At last one spoken worthily, as it should be.

Chapter Two

Jeffries did not hang.

The Lord Mayor suffered an apoplexy at the thought of examining such a prisoner, and kept him confined out of the City's jurisdiction in the Tower, where he died four months later of excess, it was said, having nothing else to do but drink.

Adam did not care. His action had brought Jeffries to the end he deserved; he felt well quit of what he owed, aware that the manner of it was fitting.

After the soldiers left with Jeffries, the woman at the Red Cow let Adam stay the remainder of the night. He was shivering from reaction and accepted thankfully, waking so stiff he could scarcely move. The woman, whose name was Betsy Lambard, was standing over him holding a broom. "'Ere, move them casks an' get swep' out afore ye go." She took it for granted that no one slept by a fire without payment.

Adam rolled over and stood slowly. His eyes were bleared and he felt mentally empty; he had harboured revenge so long, and chosen Jeffries as its focus, that it was hard to become accustomed to the fact of it fairly done. He swept methodically as he did all things, grunting with the weight of shifting kegs and at the same time trying to decide what he should do next.

"'Ave a bite if ye wish." Mistress Lambard was watching him from the door. "'Tis a fresh morning to set out on an empty belly."

A fine morning too, Adam noticed, following her into the yard where she baked in a clay oven under an open shelter. The sky was thinly blue, gulls glinting as they spiralled into a brisk wind.

"A bad day on the river," she replied when he remarked on

it. "Dead easterly an' 'as been this week past. There's a shoal o' ships tied up an' wasting money while it stays foul." She swept her arm at the mass of masts, naming the nearest with the familiarity of one who has seen the same shapes come and go since childhood, adding: "See that un there?"

Adam nodded, staring at a beamy three-master.

"A dutcher out o' Harbour Grace bound for the Dam.* 'Twas the one butcher Jeffries waited on."

"The wind trapped him too, then. Perhaps there is a God of justice, after all." Adam was much perplexed on this point, when God was often so manifestly unjust; his mother certainly felt there was little to choose between God and the Devil, except that the Devil might prove more entertaining.

Betsy shrugged; to her God was a magistrate dispensing laws and neither had much to do with justice. "Ye'll be late back for yer master. An' well beaten unless 'e's a drunkard lying late of a morning."

"Not just late but listed as run off," said Adam ruefully. "I've been watching Jeffries since the King returned from the West, and I could see the end was near."

"Ye mean ye skipped ter watch White'all wivvout so much as by yer leave?"

"I knew I'd not catch him otherwise. But my master believes in the pleasures of beating and doubling hours of work as punishment, not handing wrongdoers to the magistrate. God knows what he'll devise for me this time, but I've served three years out of seven and don't want them to do again."

"Run off ten days and ye think 'e'll 'ave yer back?" She surveyed him with grim amusement. "Rot me, what's Lunnon comin' ter nowadays?"

Adam laughed and bade her farewell; he found words easily for those who accepted him as he was, and with rough kindliness she gave him two pies half trampled and unsaleable from the night before. He might need them, he reflected as he trudged back towards the City, even Mr. Milner's genius for extracting profit from misdemeanour might not overlook the ultimate sin of apprentices, that of running off without leave. Adam had forfeited his clerkship with the East India Company for the same reason; when he heard of his father's arrest he had left his ledgers immediately, then lost all reckoning of time. After the execution he had wandered London in a daze of grief, then

* Amsterdam.

run wild in search of revenge. He had not been able to explain himself to his mother, was distressed but unsurprised when she thought his neglect deliberate. She could not know how he felt, had never truly cared how he felt; it wasn't likely she would begin now. So when he eventually returned to East India House he was in no mood for apology nor could he divulge his relationship to Henry Cornish and appeal to pity. He was instantly dismissed by an outraged head clerk, astounded by a junior who vanished for a month and then walked back to his stool as if he should be thanked for returning.

When Adam saw his father that last day before he died, he had given him a few names of those who might take him as apprentice. "I intended to bind you to the trade which most interested you, to someone of worth who would teach you all he knew," he had said then. "Too many masters treat apprentices as muscle to be flogged into the worst of labour. I thought a year with the John Company would give you time to look around after nothing but home tutoring, now I wish to God I'd settled you fairly while I had the chance."

"I'll be all right," Adam insisted, and stumbled out his promise that one day the Corncrake would be his.

His father had held him then and sat in a clatter of chains. "Listen, Adam. I want you content, not tied to oaths and stale spilled blood. Live as a true man and I will be proud of you, no matter what your trade. Alone, you'll find it very hard to break into the few who deal in balances, and no disgrace if you fail. I inherited my father's name and trade, he his father's. I would somehow have done the same for you if it was your wish, now I can't. So any failure won't be yours, but mine; it takes more than one generation to build up the trust and reserves a goldsmith-banker needs."

"I will only be truly content if I do it," Adam had said, and meant every word.

He thought of his vow again as he saw the City laid out before him in spires and roofs lit by the sun, remembering how his father had laughed then and forced himself to think how best to help. The effort had eased their last time together, but nothing since. Henry Cornish's closest friends were exiled or crippled by fines, others might tattle the ultimate cruelty to his widow so could not be trusted with Adam's identity, and in Newgate he had neither paper nor pen for writing messages. After being thrown out of East India House, Adam had tried two men whose names his father gave him: one disbelieved his story and thrashed him for attempting to exploit a brave man's name, the other faced false prosecution before King's Bench and possibly believed him, but did not intend to take the additional risk of harbouring Henry Cornish's son.

Perhaps Adam was unlucky, but after that he did not try again, aware that he bore very little resemblance to his father. Instead he borrowed thirty guineas from his mother, which he thought the greatest amount he could hope soon to repay, and sought out a master for himself. For such a sum, it was not easy, and he immediately discovered what his father had known: established men bound their sons to each other, or else charged high premiums to initiate select newcomers to their secrets.

He eventually found a mercer willing to accept him, a confused and drunken man who taught him little but was delighted when his business improved under his apprentice's ruthless industry. Then, one night, Adam found his master gone, the house shut up with creditors hammering at the door. The bailiffs came, and also gaming cronies owed from three furious days and nights of gambling in Eastcheap.

So Adam hawked his indentures door to door again, and Mr. Milner the best master he could find. He dealt in grosgrains and laces, in bugle flouncing and leather for stays; Adam despised his goods but if he wished to set himself up in business in the City he must complete an apprenticeship, so resigned himself to it. Although he served a petty dealer, the great masters of the Mercers' Company were the richest in the City, rivalled only by the goldsmiths, so when his time was done the company at least would suit his purposes.

Mr. Milner's premises were in Lime Alley behind Leadenhall Market, an area untouched by the great fire and made up of rotting houses spilling into narrow lanes. Adam went through a tunnel leading to the filthy yard serving a handful of traders, the back door to Milner's shop leaning crazily on perished straps; he could hear Mistress Milner's voice raised in complaint before he was over the threshold. Sighing, he lifted his leather apron off its hook and squeezed past bales into the shop.

Milner and his lady stared at him with dropped jaws, few truant apprentices ever returned to face the consequences.

"Well, sirrah!" snapped Milner, recovering himself rapidly. "You've mighty effrontery to walk in as cool as a mackerel, expecting work after weeks run off!"

322

"Ten days," said Adam. "I'm truly sorry, but I had affairs of my own which could not wait."

"What affairs, pray? What affairs more pressing than your master's?"

"A duty I owed my father." Adam stared at him, refusing to offer further explanation; let him accept it if he would.

Milner tut-tutted uncertainly and glanced at his wife. For all his frail appearance Adam was a good worker and understood ledgered figures better than his master, and Milner had no desire to lose him. "It is too bad of you," he said peevishly. "I've given notice to cancel your indentures."

"I would be grateful if you would withdraw it," said Adam with his usual chilly courtesy. Milner would not admit unease, but sometimes his strange apprentice overawed him; his wife said quite frankly that Adam gave her the creeps.

"It's all very well," she said sharply now, "but how are we to know that you won't feel obliged to run off whenever further debts to your father claim attention?"

"My father is dead," said Adam quietly. "My duty now is to complete my time, and I will try to please you as best I may."

Milner reached for the bundled birch rods he kept for scullions and apprentices. "This once I will overlook it, since I have no time to waste on training another in your place. Hold the bar and loose your shirt and breeches."

Adam closed his eyes, fumbling at strings. He had been beaten at Moll's but that was part of childhood misery buried in the recesses of his mind; Mrs. Temple had punished by refusing him food, for economy was important to her; since then his acquaintance with violence had been confined to kicks and blows in the street, or from his fellow clerks at East India House when they found him different to themselves. Until he bound himself apprentice. He had served two ineffectual masters but beatings and foul food were so much a part of the poorer kinds of apprenticeship that they would have thought themselves odd indeed if they had restrained themselves from either. His first master became a violent bully when drunk, apparently remembering nothing of it sober; Milner felt his mastery pleasantly reassured by naked back and buttocks spread in subservience over bars in his shop. That way defiant eyes were kept turned to the wall and nothing disturbed his feeling of superiority. His wife enjoyed it too.

The bars were awkwardly placed for Adam, the upper almost

323

beyond his grasp, the lower grating against his hips; poor food over the past three years had slowed his growth again, while his shoulders thickened from heavy labour. In his own mind his appearance had changed from odd to unpleasantly grotesque.

He thought of nothing now, except how this must be endured, a part of malignant life from which he intended to wrench success but where he no longer expected mercy. Soon he was clinging to the bar to keep upright as birch cracked and whined, supple edges tearing flesh at hip and rib. His punishment would certainly have ended sooner if he had dropped to the floor, but the curse of pride kept him from such beggarly escape.

Eventually Milner decided that if he was to have his leather cut, then he must be satisfied. Also, he was gasping with exertion and wanted to recruit his strength at his favourite alehouse, leaving Adam to resume shirt and breeches as best he could.

When Mrs. Milner was also safely away, little Jemmy the parish apprentice crept out of the cutting room and helped him. "Christ," he said, eyes popping. "Ole Milner ain't never done worse'n that ter me!" Parish apprentices suffered everything worse than the freely bound, and his tone expressed the upset of his world.

Adam grunted, thinking of four years more in this place. "Go back to your work, or it'll be you too."

"Not wivvout yer or yer'll be back on them bars agen. I'll go prig some grease, yer'll stick dreffol else." Jemmy tiptoed down the passage and came back with a crock of mutton fat, which he smeared triumphantly on Adam's back.

He stuck dreadfully even with it, the damage to his shirt almost of more consequence than that to his back; he was paid twopence a week when Milner did not find some excuse to withhold it, and it was impossible to replace spoiled clothes. He possessed only two spare shirts and paper-thin best breeches, so perhaps it was fortunate he did not grow.

It was five days before he was strong enough to carry bales to Leadenhall Market, since Milner did not want his wares dropped in the mud, and by then James Stuart had fled and William of Orange had entered London, quietly and without indicating whether he intended to accept the crown. The City was alive with speculation, a deputation despatched to discuss affairs at Whitehall: by an ironic reversal of fortune, the only part of English government unaffected by James's flight was the City of London, secure in its newly restored rights. The throne was deserted, Parliament in recess and without a King there was no simple way to summon another; the towns and cities of the realm paralysed by charters forced on them by Charles and James, Stuart appointees more intent on saving themselves than in discharging responsibilities.

So William came to Guildhall and it was in the City, not Westminster, that the foundations were laid for a constitutional bargain such as there had never been before. All those who had sat in any Parliament of Charles II were summoned to sit in conclave with the Lord Mayor, aldermen and Common Council, the City thus forming nearly half of this unprecedented assembly. Later, some kind of Parliament must be summoned, but bargaining came first: after fifty years of conflict culminating in three years of James Stuart's rule, England had become cynical over Kings.

Writs went out for this Parliament from Guildhall, but unofficially it had been agreed that William and his wife Mary were to be offered the throne jointly, as undoubted rulers but by national invitation, their powers limited by a Bill of Rights. A flurry was caused when James was caught by Kentish fishermen as he attempted to escape; William said nothing, he did not often say much, but James was allowed to run off again, this time permanently to France.

Of course, the Exchequer was bankrupt and since he had no immediate prospect of being able to levy taxes, William's most urgent need was for a loan, which could only be raised in the City. For three years James had raised nothing there, because he could not; now, within a matter of days the precepts were out and bankers negotiating on security.

But first there was one matter to be settled.

At Guildhall the City's representatives made it clear that however earnestly they sought a constitutional settlement, in one matter honour came first: the injustice to Henry Cornish must be purged. William grasped immediately that the City would lend nothing and settle nothing until it was done, and their cooperation was more important than the trifling difficulty that he had no constitutional power to reverse court decisions. He made such declarations as he could immediately, and as soon as Parliament met the attainder of treason was reversed, even before the settlement was complete.

Adam stood in the crowd and heard the proclamation read

by a cryer flanked by the City's parliamentary representatives, each one a former friend of Henry Cornish returned from exile or obscurity and this day honouring him while the affairs of the nation waited.

". . . Whereas no cause whatsoever was proved against the said Henry Cornish wrongfully and foully put to death . . . this attainder utterly and forever reversed, set aside and expunged . . . to be later confirmed by Act of Parliament . . . all rights, inheritances and claims restored to the said relict Elizabeth and all descendants whatever by due process established . . ."

Adam's eye wandered along the assembled dignitaries and he wondered where they had all been that day three and a half years before; when ceremony was over and they dispersed in gossiping, satisfied groups of fur and scarlet, he pushed his way over and greeted his mother, whom he had also seen, looking very beautiful on Lawrence Jewry steps.

He bowed. "I did not expect to see you here today."

"Adam! Why not, pray?"

He shrugged. "I thought you well satisfied in your new life. I apologise if I wronged you."

Arabella bit her lip, vividly scarlet against the same perfect skin he remembered. "I am somewhat comforted by a good man in my loneliness, no more. Of course I would be here today."

Adam was silent. When they left the tavern in Swithin Court they had taken rooms over a clockmaker's shop in Fleet Street, able to bear neither Whitehall nor the City. Almost driven frenzied by unharnessed vitality, Arabella had drifted into helping the clockmaker sell his wares, and two years later Adam found them in bed together. He left the same day and had not seen her since.

"How is Jenny?" he asked eventually.

"She's well and would send her love, I know. Why don't you come back with me now and see her?"

He shook his head. He did not think he could bear it. "I should be at Leadenhall Market now. One day I will come."

Arabella hesitated; no one would ever know with what great effort she had turned her back on the past, but she had succeeded and lived as best she might. Harry never forgotten, neither love nor loyalties changed by anything she did. Only with Adam was she conscious of failing her trust, felt the need to try again. Yet her son was a stranger, as he had always been. "Adam, I haven't married again. It was just—you don't know how it feels, alone forever. Harry bade me choose someone he would like and find what happiness I could."

"And have you found it, Madam Mother?"

She flushed at his biting tone, wishing now she had left well alone. "A little. Thomas is affectionate and attentive when not immersed in cogs and escapements. I was brought up in a craftsman's household and fine work brings its own rewards. He is the best clockmaker in London and I share his excitement in his work when Kings and courts no longer interest me at all. Would you grudge me such comfort as I can find, when Harry did not?"

"I fear I am not the man my father was," said Adam sombrely. "I wish I was."

Her expression softened. "How goes it with you, Adam? Where do you live now?"

"Why, well enough, although I do not learn the things I need to know. Give Jenny my love."

He turned to go but she put her hand on his arm. "Adam, isn't there anything you will let me do to help? I—I do not lack for money since Thomas prospers, and truly you don't look well." Of course he had always been unnaturally scrawny, but in the eighteen months since she had seen him last, he had changed in many ways. It was no longer his small size you noticed, rather the expression of his face: withdrawn, harsh and queerly set for a boy his age. It was for his own sake, not hers or Harry's, she wanted to reach him now.

"I do not need your—Thomas's—money," he replied instantly. "I hope to repay the guineas I owe you soon, and will take myself off before you are further upset by my unfortunate appearance." He bowed unsmilingly and left her close to tears. Alone of men Adam remorselessly rejected whatever amends she offered, refused to make allowances or understand her needs. Arabella had lived a life of extravagant error patched by generous restitutions, and could not understand why this once forgiveness did not follow, forgot that repair of Adam's wrongs was scarcely possible. Or failed to grasp that perhaps he needed wrongs to hold to, trapped as he was in a void even worse than hers.

Adam had not meant to quarrel, had greeted her with the intention of making his peace on this day above all. But isolation turned all thought in upon itself and made compassion difficult; what right had she to speak of loneliness, after all?

Two years was not long to keep faith and now she looked as beautiful as he remembered her, her clothes in the latest style; she possessed also the indefinable warmth of a woman loved, whether she loved in return or not.

He looked at grey January sky and cursed himself for a fool. Women were like that, and sought protection where they could; he ought not to have behaved like a boor. All the same, he did not intend to go to Thomas Tompion's shop in Fleet Street and apologise, instead he wondered how quickly he could repay thirty guineas. In spite of his confident words, he could see no prospect of earning such a sum for years.

Chapter Three

He hit on a scheme almost by accident.
Like most employers, Milner was only too delighted if his apprentices went into the street at night, in fact he often locked them out when it saved an evening meal and brought privacy to the kitchen.

Adam soon became bored wandering about the City in the dark. He avoided company since he never felt easy with his fellows and there was little to do if poverty cut a man off from gaming, drink and brothels. He set his eye sometimes to chinks in rich merchants' shutters and saw a sliced line of mellowly lit parlour, gleaming with silver and polished wood; he also saw bare arms and necks of girls who attracted him when the slatterns of Lime Alley roused only revulsion. He was ashamed of himself for peering, nor did he want to admit he could be affected by creatures he despised; women betrayed and weakened, when he had money enough he would choose one well built for breeding and docile to his will.

Occasionally he allowed himself the luxury of a visit to a coffeehouse. There he could idle a whole evening away for a halfpenny, reading the newsletters and listening to snippets of other men's doings. He smartened himself up as best he could on such occasions, tearing at his hair with sharpened splinters and tying it in imitation of a wig, his spare shirt pressed under his sleeping straw for nights before he decided to go. Coffeehouse evenings were great occasions, planned a week ahead, and Jemmy kept awake afterwards by tales of what he heard there.

William and Mary were jointly crowned King and Queen in April, and Adam decided to celebrate by visiting Kester's, his favourite coffeehouse. There, merchants and shipowners met and the talk was of fine silks, fast passages and insurance rates for the Indies; politics interested him very little now that right had triumphed. Adam would be an uncritical Whig and passionate anti-Tory all his life, and nothing he heard changed it.

Kester's was emptier than usual since Guildhall fountain was flowing with wine in honour of the coronation, and there were banquets all over London. Since the weather had changed with customary April fickleness from midday warmth to frost, Adam was pleased to be able to edge closer to the fire than a poor apprentice usually managed.

". . . held up in the river these five days," someone was saying.

"You're lucky to find a bottom to carry your goods," interrupted another. "I've been to a score of husbands* before finding one with space to spare for the Levant. Richard here heard a week ago that his consignment of raisins was signalled past Greenwich, yet not one crate has been unloaded, nor does he know which ship to hasten."

"'Tis these God-blasted accredited quays and swarms of long-nosed searchers claiming percentages which are like to ruin us all." There was a general growl of agreement. "I spent two days last week being pulled against the ebb before I discovered my shipment of wines. At least I knew then which ship to grease to the quay, but still suffered delay since wharfage is lacking."

"I unload into barges," volunteered a captain, his trade proclaimed by chapped skin and hands black with tar. "'Tis quicker to grease inspectors and customs agents in midstream and unload cross-river to Southwark."

"That's all very well," observed the one who had lost his raisins. "Providing a captain troubles to inform you that he carries your goods. Most are not too displeased by delay; they send a man ashore to search out fresh cargo and only unload once they have it secured. One set of wharfage charges, you see."

Adam listened, idly at first and then with rising excitement, blood hammering, muscles tight. Chained down to drudgery leading nowhere, he had begun to despair, wondered sometimes whether his dream of goldsmith-banking was the madness

---

*Shore agents for ships.

everyone else would think it. And if that was lost, then he had nothing left. Now he thought of Wapping, of Betsy Lambard at the Red Cow who knew every ship in her reach of river; ships' captains were creatures of habit.

Merchants would pay for certain information on where their consignments lay, captains for prompt contact with outgoing shipments, as would outward shippers. He bit his lip, thinking about it, wanting to blurt out his idea, wondering what pitfalls he had overlooked.

If he could act as shippers' 'change, surely he could demand a percentage on time and effort saved? Adam sat in his corner, brain spinning, wondering why no one had thought of it before. Or perhaps they had and these men just voiced routine grumbles as all men did. He listened, urgently now, wishing he could ask them what they thought. But an idea of such splendour, such eager hope, was not to be lightly shared.

But talk had turned to a further loan William had asked for to prosecute war against the French, so he decided to expend the other halfpenny he possessed on visiting a second coffee-house; no great venture is set afoot without risking capital.

He went to Garraway's on 'Change Alley, where he knew the richest merchants went, but chose unwisely. There the talk was all of funding voyages and future profit offered against present cash; he listened, fascinated, for he had not dared come into so select a place before and this was the trade he intended to join one day, but heard nothing to his present purpose and was unpleasantly jolted when his measure of coffee cost a penny instead of the usual half.

"I've only half," he said, confused and ashamed. "I thought—"

"Garraway's is none of them cheap kens," said the potboy, glowering. He usually found a penny for himself in addition, and resented serving a grubby apprentice who could not afford the custom of the place.

People were beginning to look, fine merchants laughing when a moment ago he had dreamed they would one day ask him to finance their enterprises. Adam flushed vividly, absurdly close to tears. "I haven't anything. I thought half was enough. I'll come back at the end of the week and pay what I owe."

"Oh no, yer don't! Fine sheep's head I'd look trustin' the likes of yer." The potboy seized him by the arm and hauled him bodily off the settle.

Adam jerked free with unexpected strength and fastened

him with his disconcerting light-grey stare. "I will, I swear it. I have twopence each Saturday, I'll come then."

Several men broke into laughter at such absurdity amid their bartered thousands, one in a rich blue coat laced with gold was forced by the altercation to pause on his way to the door. He looked from Adam to the potboy, and then gravely handed over a penny. "Owe it to me instead of him, since he is too witless to recognise a good risk when it is thrust under his nose."

Adam stared at him, completely astonished. "It's no affair of yours, sir," he blurted, and then flushed again at his lack of grace. It was such a long time since anyone had shown him kindness he was more confused by it than by ill-treatment. "I— I mean, thank you, sir. If you will give me your direction I will repay you on Saturday evening." He took the coin and handed it to the potboy with what he hoped was sufficient of an air to make up for his previous shortcomings, and in a rash gesture added his own half as well.

The other bowed, only a glint in his eyes betraying amusement. "Francis Child, at the Sign of the Marygold, in Fleet Street."

"Then I am doubly indebted, sir, since you did not give me the money but judged me worthy of a loan," said Adam, somewhat overcome. Child was one of the most respected traders in balances and running cashes, the first entirely to give up dealing in plate and concentrate on banking.

Child laughed outright. "So speaks a true banker! It is loans to the unreliable one reckons secretly as gifts, and is pleasantly surprised if they are repaid. I will be at my place of business until eight of the Saturday evening." He nodded and went out, leaving Adam almost intoxicated with pleasure.

What an evening it had been! He was certain now that his idea was good, not through any process of thought but because one of the foremost bankers of the day had thought him worth a loan. No matter if it was only for a penny, it was an omen of success. He poured it all out to Jemmy lying together on bug-ridden straw under the kitchen shelf, but his reaction was disappointing.

"D'yer mean ter say t'ole skinflint tole yer ter go all the wiy ter Fleet Street ter give 'im a penny? Yer wouldn't be so pie-'eaded as ter go? A penny! 'Tis nuthin' ter 'im, but 'alf a week ter yer. Yerse safe enough, 'e'll never come 'ere a-chasin' after debt."

"Of course I shall go," said Adam with dignity.

Jemmy hunched a shoulder and sniffed. "'Tis plain as a constable's cudgel yer'll be broke two diys after yerse out o' 'prenticeship, payin' pennies ter rich swells all over Lunnon."

But Adam could hardly wait for Saturday to come. He would see, even if only for a few minutes, inside the kind of establishment he craved to own; above all he would have proved himself worthy of trust. He decided that on the Sunday he would walk to Wapping and talk to Betsy Lambard. Suddenly, the dreary daily grind was of no importance, and he forgot how close he had felt to despair only the day before.

Then on Friday Milner accused him of baling leather wrongly. "Fifty pieces Mr. Edwards ordered, and you put in thirty! He's sent round to say he can't finish cutting next week's batch of stays and will lose money unless he has twenty more immediately."

"He ordered thirty," said Adam. "He chose the hides himself and said business was poor with the court at Windsor."

Milner bridled angrily. "Don't contradict me, sirrah! Fifty, he always has fifty."

"I know," said Adam patiently. "But he said his trade was slack with the court out of London. He probably has some unexpected orders and wants us to make the delivery free by pretending it was my error."

"So it was! Do not think to escape blame by lying about it either, since it will only add a beating to loss of your wages."

Adam paled, Milner used the slightest excuse to stop payment of his twopence and Jemmy's penny a week. "I'm not lying, he ordered thirty hides. See, I scratched it above the bale." He went over to a shelf covered with snicks under different clients' marks.

"What is that to the matter, when you could point to any mark you chose and say it was thirty hides?" Milner was an unmethodical man himself and consequently placed no reliance on the systems of others. "Take him twenty more at once. And since twopence will not cover my loss from such waste of your time, I shall deduct a penny the following week as well." He bustled away to greet a customer.

"As mean as a King's general, that one," observed Jemmy. "'E's already prigged my penny for tippin' grease on the step. So I tole 'im they's so filthy yer couldn't see where 'twas an' where 'twasn' an' 'e beat me as well."

Adam jerked leather into a tight bale, unspeaking. He must find a penny from somewhere.

As he jog-trotted the length of Fenchurch Street with the bale chafing at his back, he discarded any notion of attempting to make the staymaker admit his trick. Milner would merely make him strip for the bars as well as keeping his pence, in a sweat of fear in case an apprentice's insolence had lost him his best customer. So he resisted temptation to cram the staymaker's smile down his throat, and when he returned to Lime Alley went through to the shop with the receipt. "Mr. Edwards thanks you for your prompt service, sir, and gives notice he will need fifty again next week."

Milner nodded, looking relieved. His materials in some mysterious way always lagged behind fashion, and without his stay-leather trade he would face ruin. "Get back to your cutting then, the extra twenty for Mr. Edwards has left us out of stock for tomorrow's trade."

"The extra twenty," said Adam slowly. "You didn't believe him either."

"A manner of speaking, a manner of speaking! And don't you be picking me up as if—as if you were my equal, which you're not!" Milner finished in something of a fluster, since Adam often made him feel not just equal but downright inferior, which was outrageous. It was largely because of this feeling that he missed few opportunities of humiliating his apprentice.

"Of course not, sir." Adam detested having to beg. "I should be grateful if you would give me one penny of my wages tomorrow and keep both next week, as payment for the time I lost."

"Why? Why should I indulge you when you have run me into a deal of expense, and are wasting more time arguing now?"

"I will finish tomorrow's cutting before I sleep, so you won't be the loser. Please may I then be paid my penny?"

Milner smiled. "That's better, that's better. Let's see whether you can improve on it again, shall we?"

Adam felt the muscles on his face tighten, what more could the swine want? "I am but asking for my due, and forfeit next week's wage instead."

"No, no! A little humility might serve perhaps, you are in no case to demand favours."

I suppose he won't be satisfied until I'm on my knees, Adam thought dully, and was still capable of outrage when Milner indicated that indeed was precisely what he had in mind.

Adam managed it somehow, and then spent half the night

cutting by a single flickering candle, so tired he twice dropped asleep on leather. Yet when he finished and lay in straw beside Jemmy, he felt too shamed to rest. He ought never to have knelt to Milner whatever the reason. All his happy pride in discharging Francis Child's trust was lost as he stared into darkness wondering what else he could have done. What would his father have done? He pushed the thought away, a beacon which had never before failed him a mockery now. Lime Alley was not Cheapside, bug-ridden straw an infinity away from the Sign of the Corncrake. If he wanted to survive here, he could no longer model himself on his father.

He was stricken by the thought, which was completely new to him. This devil-ridden city, he reflected bitterly, it does not deserve the sacrifices of those who fight for it. What is it after all but dungheap streets and mean-souled dealers scavenging for profit? If I intend ever to have something for myself, I must take what I need; the scrupulous are robbed, or butchered screaming on a gibbet.

He crawled out of straw, unable to lie still, and lifted the bar holding the back door in place. Outside it was completely dark, a faint spring sweetness in the air. He sat on the step and leaned against crumbling brick, staring at the movement of clouds overhead.

He heard nothing, but there was a change in the shadows and weight settled purring on his knee; his breath tightened and he cuddled the shape to his chin. He called the wire-thin cat which scavenged in Lime Alley Swithin, after a memory of happier living. It was completely wild with everyone else but came sometimes to Adam, as if acknowledging relationship, when the world threw things at both on sight, not for any reason but from habit.

"How is it, Swithin?" he whispered, soft fur against his lips. "Caught anything tonight?"

The cat whirred and pushed its head inside his sweat-heavy shirt, each bone distinct under his fingers: the wretched creature was too weak for hunting and hid from rats in fear. "I shouldn't have knelt, d'you know that, Swithin? If I'd had time to think I wouldn't have, but it's too late now." He eased his back cautiously, frowning. He could not pay his first debt of trust with money gained by grovelling, the only way to rid himself of shame was to throw Milner's penny on the dung heap where it belonged. "No, I'll not waste it," he said aloud. "I'll use it to buy food for you, Swithin. A penny, think of it! A week of fish heads for you, I wouldn't be ashamed of kneeling for your life." Swithin stretched and dug his claws carefully into his knee. Adam laughed and stroked him gently, oppression lifted by his decision.

He still had to find another penny from somewhere, though. He looked at the sky again, and nearby a bell struck three. Three hours before he must be back here, three hours to earn a penny while the city slept.

His mind perhaps on fish heads for Swithin, he decided to try Billingsgate first, and as he expected it was thronged with carts and sleds, some pulled by consumptive children harnessed around the shoulders, others by shambling ponies, breath spiralling in cold air. The ground was strewn with fish scales, baskets, rope, all the litter of bustling trade; men were shouting, basket women gossiping, boys quarrelling, horses biting and stamping, pie sellers shouting their wares. Boats unloaded against the quay: Kentish oyster catchers and Southwark punts, Essex longboats manned by twenty oarsmen in coarse striped shirts, Medway shallops pulled upriver on the tide.

Adam forgot weariness and his disenchantment with London, captivated by the vigour of the scene. A drayman bellowed at him and he jumped hastily out of the way, only to be sworn at for upsetting a creel of mackerel. "Have you any need of labour?" he asked when he had picked up the slithery pile.

"'Ow much 'ad you in mind, young sir?" demanded the man with heavy irony.

"I must be back in Lime Alley by six. All the time until then doing what you will for—for twopence."

"One."

"Two," said Adam firmly, no one paid your value unless you demanded more. They compromised on one and a half and he was initiated into the mysteries of swinging flat creels up twelve perilous feet at a rope's end. "Why don't they pack them in deep baskets?" he gasped once, hanging dangerously over the quayside to stop loads spilling in the river.

"'Tis my risk to get 'em up, that's why," said his employer, squirting tobacco juice between ropes. "T'fish keep fresh in flat, when they dies in deep, see? So who're they to care if a 'prentice or two breaks 'is 'ead? I've 'ad two kilt this year, an' another bad 'urt las' week, s'why yerse useful now, see?"

Adam could well believe that boys were killed every night. There was nothing to hold on to, hoists were incapable of precise manoeuvring, the press on the wharf so great that everyone was jostled, the ground treacherous with rotting fish.

It was done at last, precious penny and halfpenny handed over; he washed fish scales off in a horse trough and then faced the tramp back up the slope from the river to Lime Alley, triumph lost and strangling weariness left in its place. He was too tired to eat although he could not remember when he had eaten last, had intended to spend the odd halfpenny on pie. His back felt raw and pain in his chest forced him to breathe in awkward, shallow gulps. Through misted eyes he saw the clockface on St. Margaret Patten's church; five to six. He forced himself into a shambling run up Rood Lane, across Fenchurch Street, pain in his chest expanding with every step.

As six o'clock struck he staggered into Lime Alley, through the door Jemmy opened, to collapse over piled leather, pain an axe in his chest, breath almost stopped. Blackness receded slowly to admit a single thought. "Knife, Jemmy," he croaked. "My apron." Must look as if he was working when Milner came, or it would be another beating.

Jemmy slipped his apron over his head, put the cutting knife in his hand. "Christ, Adam. Yer look like cold meat."

He felt like it; I'm tired, he thought. It'll pass in a minute. It did not cross his mind that his heart had nearly failed: it beat strongly now, thumping against his ears, shaking the emptiness in his belly. Already he felt better, and was cutting leather when Mr. Milner came.

Adam looked up, fingering the coins in his seam as he bade his master good morning, triumph warm again. It had been worth it.

On Saturdays Mr. Milner shut his shop at six in the evening, most of his trade was wholesale and the busy time early in the week, when sometimes he stayed open until eleven o'clock at night. As soon as the door bar was in its socket, Adam took Milner's penny and deposited it with an offal dealer in Lime Street: he had been determined to rid himself of money he had knelt for, but now had only just over an hour to find Mr. Child's place of business before he quitted it.

He tied his hair with a strip of leather and scrambled into his change of clothes, aware that they were threadbare and he still smelt of fish, Milner had been complaining of it all day. He must wash in Cheapside Conduit on the way.

For the first time in years Adam hardly spared a glance for Corncrake or Golden Spurs as he passed, cold conduit water briefly cutting through a haze of fatigue and strain. He chanced a shortcut through Paul's churchyard and its litter of stone, even in his haste sparing a moment of wonder for the rising skeleton of Christopher Wren's great dome; he wished it complete enough to have a clock.

He found the Sign of the Marygold by Temple Bar, where the City gave way to Westminster. Its bowed front was lit by lamps and a coach was waiting by the entry, arms blazoned on its side.

Adam took a deep breath and pushed open the door, a clerk's welcoming bow turning instantly to affront. "Mr. Child asked me to call," said Adam hastily. He looked round at tall oak desks and stools, at a bright fire and settles in one corner for the convenience of clients. Child's might not sell or pawn plate any longer, but splendid examples of London craft glittered in sconces and on shelves, two men in brown velvet hovering as guards and messengers.

"Mr. Child?" said the clerk. "There's no Mr. Child here." He jerked his head at one of the brown velvet men, who came over and took Adam quite gently by the arm. Even throwing out would be done discreetly here.

"There must be," said Adam desperately. "He said he would be here until eight o'clock of a Saturday. I have a debt to discharge."

"You? A debt to Sir Francis?" The clerk laughed scornfully. "Get you gone afore Ned here loses patience."

Adam licked his lips. "Sir Francis then, I'm sorry. Ask him, please. Say it was a debt contracted at Garraway's on Tuesday."

"Best ask," said Ned judiciously, not tightening his grip. "Don't look the sort for sauce to me, and Sir Francis would be vexed if 'twas true."

Adam did not dare sit on one of the settles while the clerk was gone, the warmth of the room making him so sleepy he swayed on his feet. He stood by the door instead and hoped the smell of fish would not be so noticeable there.

The clerk returned, mouth set in disapproval. Of course rich men were eccentric, but in his opinion Sir Francis would end in Bedlam if he made a habit of opening his private room to every costermonger's brat with a tale to spin. "This way if you please, sir." Child enforced strict rules of behaviour, and a client was "sir" whatever his appearance.

Adam followed him, cheeks hot with pleasure. This was

how it would be in his establishment; he craned over the clerks' shoulders as he passed, trying to see everything.

Child's room was upstairs and he was sitting at a polished table covered with documents, working in his shirt sleeves. Frilled linen of the finest quality, thought Adam enviously. He looked up, unsmiling, when Adam entered. "Well, sir?"

"I—I have come . . . you bade me discharge my debt here tonight," stammered Adam, aware for the first time of his presumption in expecting to pay it personally. He should have folded the coin in paper and asked the clerk to deliver it. "I did not mean . . . I'm sorry to have disturbed you. I didn't think—" His voice trailed away and he stared at the floor, overcome by the old, absurd desire to hide himself from sight. He knew so little of the world of gentlemen, after all. He took the penny from his seam and laid it on the table, backing away quickly before his smell lingered.

"Never be ashamed of discharging obligation." Child ran his quill through his fingers idly. "What is your name?"

"Adam. Adam Furnival, sir." Adam suppressed the wish to name himself Cornish, but for all he knew Henry Cornish's true sons were living in the City now. He looked up, grey eyes level. "Thank you for your accommodation." He turned to go.

"Not so swiftly, since you are here. Furnival; the name is not familiar to me, yet you speak like my own sons."

"I was tutored once, though apprenticed now." In Lime Alley they mocked the way he spoke but some dark revulsion rooted in memory of Moll's hovel kept him from changing, though Leadenhall bullies sometimes stuffed his mouth with filth for what they called his whomelling.

"To what trade?"

"A mercer," he said reluctantly, it sounded well enough so long as there was no mention of stay leather. "I do not intend to remain in it when my indentures are finished."

"What do you intend then?" Child looked at his papers, suddenly impatient. He was a fool to waste time when he would scarcely be home by midnight with so much to settle first. Still, there was something about this boy which intrigued him, a combination of ruthless self-possession and defencelessness he could not reconcile in his mind, although usually swift in judgment.

Adam hesitated, it would be madness to satisfy mere curiosity when if his idea was good, then Child possessed more than enough resources to exploit it for himself. On the other hand . . . since his father's death he had shared his thoughts with no one, the wall of loneliness rising brick by brick about him. He wanted desperately to ask advice, find some easing in the harshness of his life, however fleeting. "I have an idea for making money, I hope. To—to do with ships and cargoes." He licked his lips, the elegant room suddenly seemed oppressively hot and blackness had returned behind his eyes. The desire to confide faded, he must get out before he brought himself to contempt. "Perhaps I may find accommodation from you for more than a penny in a few years' time, since I intend to deal in balances when I have capital enough."

Child nodded, not feeling inclined to amusement. The boy looked ill, but intuition told him that he would do more harm than good by offering a gift. There was almost insane pride in the disconcerting eyes staring at him from a white, sharp-boned face, and unnatural dedication too, both sufficient to wear out a far tougher frame, and charity would not help. "You may be sure I shall be willing to listen to any proposition you care to make," he said at last. "Come again, Mr. Furnival, and do not scruple to remind me of this occasion. I find that a man who repays one debt will generally repay another."

Adam bowed himself out in a flurry of thanks, aware of an incalculable stride taken towards his ambition if only he could place himself to take advantage of it. And all because he lacked a halfpenny to pay Garraway's extortionate charges.

Chapter Four

It was very dark and bitterly cold. On
such a night the Thames was a dreadful place, vapour blowing
off its surface, black water sliding past faster than a man could
walk. Every light colour seemed lost to the world, shadows
deeper black against black banks and tumbled buildings, sky
invisible, the river full of dark sounds too: sucking mud, the
gurgle of unseen depths, current slapping at moored ships.

Adam had grown to love London's river, but feared it on
a night like this. Its banks were unguarded, wharfs cluttered,
tide filling unlit wastes and passages. For over three years he
had haunted the quays from London Bridge to the Tower, the
crumbling wharves of Wapping and the smuggler's paradise
across the river from Southwark to Rotherhithe. He knew each
berth and sailor's tavern, the creeks where secret loads were
landed on tree trunks sinking into mud; which wharfingers were
grasping and which looked the other way when he earned money
on a Sunday illegally unloading ships before they tied up for
excisemen to check.

When he first thought of his idea he imagined himself making money within days, but soon discovered his error. Skippers
usually had an interest in their cargoes, merchants handled
many goods they kept hidden from rivals as well as the Customs
House; he simply could not gather information quickly enough
on the scale he realised was necessary. He understood now
why no one had succeeded in his idea before. Reluctantly, he
put aside the tempting notion of terminating his indentures with
Milner, and instead spent his evening and Sundays laboriously
accumulating the mosaic of facts he needed; sifting, checking,
following merchants secretly to warehouses and Thames Street

taverns, eavesdropping on discussions they held there with skippers and ship's husbands. They spoke of things when he was by which they would have kept tightlaced before men of their own sort, although in fact he had lost such youthfulness as he had ever possessed. His face had tightened and deep lines ran from eye to mouth: if he had known it, he now looked very like his father under the strain of the last months of his life, when only his eyes had shown the tie of blood before. Yet at twenty he was half the age his father was on the scaffold, and otherwise there was little similarity. Adam moved with the grace of light-boned men who must use balance rather than muscle to carry heavy loads, but the sense of disproportion remained: heavy, workworn hands contrasted with austere expression, wide shoulders with famished body, his mouth the same generous curve as Arabella's yet distrustfully compressed, low stature less remarkable than a kind of frozen reserve which held the world at a distance. It set him apart even from Jemmy, and infuriated Milner, although Adam was incapable of seeing why; at least after three and a half more years of savage toil his indentures had only months to run.

Adam shuddered, but not from fog or cold. As his time ran out Milner had less interest in keeping him, knowing that the moment Adam Furnival signed the books of the Mercers' Company as journeyman, he would leave. Adam had saved a few shillings from work on the wharves, but had not been paid a penny on Saturday for months; his belly was scoured by the filth he was forced to eat, he and Jemmy often kept working far into the night. The beatings continued too, worse for the hatred Milner bore him, worse because he was twenty and humiliation more unbearable than pain. He swore aloud into the blustering wind; when this was done he would never work for a master again.

The Red Cow was close by, and he left the river to plunge through a maze of passages. He knew every boardwalk in Wapping now, and decided to spend a halfpenny on ale, although he could not afford it. Three years of punishing labour, three years of cutting leather and humping bales, of walking the wharves every moment he could snatch, and he possessed only shillings to set himself up in the trade he had devised. He did have carefully hidden lists, though, of merchants and their secrets, of skippers, ship's husbands, trades and moorings; a web of contacts strung down both banks of the Thames, made up of bargees, wherrymen and tavernkeepers, as well as dumpers and truckers who unloaded cargo more or less dishonestly. He thought he could do it when the time came, longed for these last weeks to pass so he could put his fortune in hazard at last, to win or lose it all.

The Red Cow had not changed; very little changed along the river. Lamps smoked, the same jokes were repeated again and again, noise loud enough to curdle the mind.

Betsy was serving behind the bar with her usual massive calm, Adam had never seen her even mildly the worse for wear. She drew his ale, then jerked her head. "There's yesterday's pie in the back if yer fancy it." Over past months she had developed a kind of shame-faced motherliness which touched him absurdly, since no one else cared a jot how he felt providing he completed his labours on time.

He nodded and went behind the bar. "Will you be coming through later? It's too dark to see the moorings and I'd like to check on what came up with the tide." He had lists of routes, too, of destinations and goods shipped, so he would know where to start looking for specific cargoes. Surely he must succeed after so much preparation.

She grinned, showing strong white teeth. "Likely I'll be through later, ye'll enjoy yerself best wivvout me."

He frowned. "I must leave before dawn, and would like to sleep a couple of hours if you'll let me."

"Aye, I'll be through by'n by." She seemed amused by something but he was too tired and hungry to worry about it.

Betsy's kitchen was cold and damp since she cooked in the yard, but clean. Adam liked sitting there quietly and eating at his own pace, hearing good humour through a thickness of board without having to endure the uncertainties of conviviality; he had been too long solitary for chaffering to come easily, although he yearned to share some part of himself with others. No matter how brutal the world he could not forget that the only person who had taken trouble to understand him had liked what he discovered. There must be others who would look at what he offered and think it of some worth. He enjoyed laughter and lightness, often thought up matters for amusement; delighted in shape and colour, was endlessly curious; possessed a prodigious memory to harness with his industry, and thought he might be agile in debate if only words did not desert him and if anyone should ask his opinion. They never did, nor what he liked; men laughed against and not with him, jeered at the way he spoke and in some mysterious way caught the habit of contempt from one another as if it was the plague.

Yet Child had not thought him contemptible, Jemmy reckoned him odd but crept to him for comfort after a beating; Swithin had sensed compassion and came to no one else. Wharfingers respected his endurance, Billingsgate fish dealers courage at a rope's end; even his mother, who was so easily bored, had not thought him dull once they were acquainted.

Adam sighed, and then smiled as he listened to the Red Cow's timbers shudder at each slop of the tide; tonight the river was almost at the step, one day the whole crazy structure would just float away. He could picture it exactly, drinkers still in the taproom, bobbing down the Thames; which was the kind of thought others didn't find amusing. He jerked round to an unexpected sound, hands tight on the table: there were sleeping shelves fastened to the wall since the floor was often wet, and from one of them a girl was watching him.

"Hullo," she said, without embarrassment. "Are you a friend of Betsy's?"

"Yes," said Adam after a pause. "She lets me sleep here sometimes, but I didn't know there was anyone staying or I wouldn't have disturbed you."

"Oh, I don't mind! It's dull poked in here alone, and I like company. I came up from Kent, my mother and Betsy are cousins." She stretched, slowly and completely, like a cat. Like Swithin, he thought with a pang: the rats had caught Swithin the year before, his pitiful skeleton picked clean by morning.

The girl's bodice was unlaced, her hair tousled and pale strawgold, lips attractively pouted and eyes as blue as the sky at midsummer. Adam was revolted by the thought of this charming child trapped in the Red Cow, inevitably to become a sailor's doxy. "You aren't going to work here?"

"Oh no!" she said unconcernedly. "I might as well have stayed in Kent if that's all I could find. Betsy's sent word about me to some swell places where she says the gentlemen will be kind."

"You know what sort of places... I mean, why did you leave Kent?"

She swung her legs off the shelf, skirt hitched high, and crossed one knee over the other while she picked straws off her gown. He could see almost to her thigh. "D'you think I'd stay amongst a set of niggardly cow minders? Betsy came to visit us twelve months past when she were buying ale, and said

I'd the looks for better'n a haystack tumble. Don't you think so, then?" She stood and put her hands behind her head, fingers locked, watching him. Her bodice gaped wider, almost tumbling out blue-veined breasts.

Adam stared at her, his body tight. He had never bedded a woman and knew nothing of them except how the drabs whined in dark alleys while their better-dressed sisters carried the same trade into drawing room and court. His mother was no different; he had known as a child why Giles Albury came to Bear Street, and once his father was dead she crawled into the first warm bed she saw. Milner beat him; his wife looked on and laughed.

"Yes," he said gruffly. "I think you are very beautiful." He had meant to say something quite different.

She walked over and stood beside him, hips against his face. "You seen many like me, then?"

He shook his head and stood, the pulsebeat in her throat was level with his eyes, her neck and bosom flaunting. He touched her gently, overwhelmed by the offering of so much softness and sweetness.

She laughed and clenched her hands over his, driving them roughly into her breasts. "That's the way to do it, you know. Not many women enjoy being handled like you was searching out nits."

He felt a shudder of revulsion, but her nipples were hard under his fingers, desire flooding from a place where he had not known it locked before. Half hating her, her tore her bodice loose, fumbling with strings. He had felt tender a moment before but that was lost, while driving need remained.

Her fingers brushed his aside, he could feel her still laughing as she slipped out of layered petticoats. "You are green, aren't you? I thought in London they learned everything in the cradle." She giggled and loosed his breeches too, sliding her hands inside. "Never mind, 'twill be a change to act the teacher."

He wanted to weep, and carried her to straw instead. She was not soft at all but savagely demanding, thrusting at him as he had watched Moll squirm and thrust long ago.

The force of recoil from roused memory strangled him, deadening sense and craving in an instant. Thought, hand and body paralysed between one breath and the next.

She slapped his face, hard. "You whoreson sniveller! Fit for fondling and peeping, but nothing else!" She scrambled out of straw and began putting on her clothes again with sullen, angry jerks.

He lay and watched, ice-cold and wretched. She was so beautiful, yet within fair skin and delicate features was the same crude harshness he found hateful. At least he had been shaped from something his parents came to value; if matters had turned out differently he could have fathered a child this night and left it to more misery than he had ever known. He recognised neither this fear nor memory for what it was, felt shamed instead and stood, eyes averted. "I'm sorry."

She tossed her head. "I should have known better, I suppose. Where I come from the maids say 'tis the runts and freaks you need to take with your eyes shut an' ask your payment first."

Silently, he put twopence on the table and left into the dark.

*   *   *

His indentures were due to be completed at Christmastide, and as if in celebration the Thames froze over sufficiently for a great Frost Fair to grow there. The Sunday before Adam was due to go with Milner and sign the book at Mercers' Hall, he decided to take a holiday and went with Jemmy to wander and gape amongst the booths. He could not remember when he had last spent time on pleasure without a purpose, and at first it felt strange, as if he should be marking ships or shadowing those around him to discover where they kept their goods. But with the Thames frozen all trade had slowed, and he soon gave himself to enjoyment of noise and colour all around, the relief of walking slowly when usually he was hasting to catch up time.

There were vendors of gingerbread and eels, stalls of every imaginable variety tended by bawling hucksters who sent children scurrying into the throng to pull at sleeves and coattails, wheedling reluctant buyers. The crowd was thickly packed, since the best stalls huddled together as if the whole Thames was not at their disposal; gongs clanged, women screamed, thieves prigged watches and kerchiefs pursued by yells and flurries of slithering, upturned people. There were buskers' acts and puppet booths lit by flares, a wider stage set out in the very centre of the fair. Adam watched, fascinated, while a ferocious gentleman in velvet fought a duel with another dressed in armour, the lady they both wooed swooning over a draped balcony nearby. He could not hear their words but tried to imagine the gist of it, improvisation lost when harlequin and a clown appeared, since he was ignorant of their traditional roles. One day I will go to a theatre, he thought wistfully, and stand where I can hear.

Jemmy had scampered off about his own affairs, and Adam wandered on, averting his eyes from wild-beast shows where mange-ridden lions licked frozen paws, and bears eyed hounds tied ready for later baiting. He had enough of blood and baiting in Lime Alley. Sad dwarfs tumbling on the ice and a row of freaks exhibited for a penny also failed to attract him, nor a "verocious bull vot gored a man ter deff las' Vednesdiy, an' kilt free men each year since 'e ver veaned."

Drums beat and fiddles scraped, couples began to caper, slithering on ice as darkness fell; it wasn't much fun at Frost Fair without company, he thought in desolation. There were women in plenty, some barefoot on the ice, others swathed in furs, but to his mood of disillusion all had the same speculative or begging eyes. After what he considered as his failure at the Red Cow, he could not look at them without humiliation.

There was a girl in cherry-red velvet laughing amongst a group of friends while they watched the play, he recognised her vaguely as he recognised others from his observations whenever he went about the City. She looked merry and content at least, no need for begging favours there. He watched her with a tug of the heart, wishing he was at her side instead of the lumpish youth holding her arm too tight.

He pushed his way through a crush so dense that breath curled like fog over the ice, his pleasure in the day soured, and came face to face with the girl in red velvet. She looked angry and the lumpish youth was trailing after her mouthing explanations.

"No," she said clearly. "Don't trouble. I'll find the way by myself. I can see my father over there."

The other laughed and said something which made her flush. "It's not true. Go away."

"If you like, I will escort you to your father," said Adam, entranced by her candour. He forgot that women were deceivers.

She looked at him, surprised. "Who are you?"

He bowed. "Adam Furnival. I heard you were having some difficulty and offer my services if they would help."

She subjected him to serious critical examination and then smiled, dark eyes laughing. "Why, thank you, Mr. Furnival, they certainly would." She put her hand on his arm and repeated

347

to the youth, "Go away, Arthur. Mr. Furnival will see me to my father."

"Don't be more of a fool than you can help, Mary." Colour thickened in Arthur's face. "You can't jaunter off at Frost Fair with the first back-streets rapscallion who takes your fancy, like—like . . ."

"Yes, sir?" said Adam tightly. "Like what exactly?"

"Yes, I can, because I just have," replied the girl serenely. She pinched Adam's arm vigorously and he took the hint to turn his back on the fuming Arthur and push a way through the crowd.

"Good," she said with satisfaction. "I was afraid I would be really rude to him if we stayed longer. I would like to be, you understand, it was a great effort to remain courteous."

Adam laughed. "Your courtesy has a unique quality to it, ma'am. I was wondering how I would be able to rid you of him without embarrassment, my fighting not having been learned amongst gentlemen."

"I shouldn't have been embarrassed, I'd have enjoyed it. You mustn't call me ma'am, though, it makes me feel like Aunt Anne, who is a widow, and very *dusty*, if you see what I mean. I am Mary Eyles and much obliged to you." She surveyed the fair with sparkling eyes. "Do you think we have to go to my father quite at once? I was afraid to be alone with Arthur and stayed with the rest exactly as I was told I must."

"Like Aunt Anne again?" teased Adam.

She twinkled responsively. "Exactly like, but it seemed a sad waste of a splendid occasion to me. Do you think we could look at the tumblers and perhaps the fire swallower on the way?"

Adam considered that any man who entrusted his daughter to the unpleasant Arthur deserved to feel such anxiety as he might subsequently suffer and agreed with delight.

She did not seem to notice his threadbare clothes or feel the slightest awkwardness with him, as others always did. Reserve crumbled under her buoyant gaiety, a youngness of spirit he had never known, and he forgot the paralysing inadequacy which so often stripped him of words when they were most needed. They laughed over nothing and talked as if there were no dull topics in all the world, the most trivial subject full of intriguing possibilities the moment they discussed it.

They watched the tumblers and decided the fire eater was a fraud, since water was clearly dribbling out of his mouth even before the flame was near, applauded wholeheartedly when a coal heaver capered up the greasy pole as if his knees were lined with tacks. "They probably are, too," said Adam judicially. "I've seen wharf truckers climb ship's holds with spikes they strap to wrist and knee when the ganger isn't looking."

Mary demanded an explanation of these terms, listening intently while he described the relative dishonesty of truckers compared to lumpers. "To think Papa ships cloth with every tide and I never knew any of that," she said thoughtfully. "It just shows, doesn't it? I won't tell him, though, for I daresay they only make off with a little and if he doesn't miss it, why should I grudge them their livelihood, too?"

Adam swallowed, involuntary laugh lost in unhappiness as everything he had forgotten flooded back. For a brief while there had been nothing but a sense of joyous rightness, now she was a rich merchant's daughter while he picked what livelihood he could from stay leather and wharfside. He noticed, as he had not before, that she was slightly the taller. "I think we had best search for your father now," he said after a pause.

"I've said something which upset you," she said immediately. "Tell me, Adam, please."

He shook his head, but could not look at her for fear of what she would see in his face. He had beaten at the bars of loneliness so long; she loosed them within a single hour, and since he possessed no measure to set attraction and vivacity in its due proportion, she instantly filled his world. The wish to hide surfaced again out of nowhere; hide now, quickly, before she forgets a briefly amusing companion and sees a raw lout. Instead he looked at her hand on his arm, and loved her long capable fingers and clean nails: he realised it was also white with cold, muff hanging loose in her other hand. He covered it instinctively with his, then snatched back at the sight of its rough ugliness, chipped knuckles and grime-grained skin. "You should put on your muff," he said roughly.

"I prefer my hand cold and where it is," she said calmly.

Startled, he looked up. She was smiling at him, but her eyes were soft and concerned, intent on his. "I am not usually as forward as this, Adam. But I have the strangest feeling that with you I must always speak the exact truth, and never the polite nothings Mamma taught me, which are so useful when dealing with Arthur."

"Yes," said Adam numbly. "Yes, I suppose so." Everything

she said confirmed his sense of rightness, the feeling that this moment had been waiting for him since time began, yet her eager generosity destroyed response. He would remember her always, a week hence she would be in a puzzle to recall his name. He looked away and saw a plank stall he recognised. "Come, my dear. I should like to give you a present before we part."

"Won't you call one day? We live at the Sign of the Drake in Lothbury."

"I live in Lime Alley behind Leadenhall Market," he said grimly. "No, I'll not come visiting, to be thrown in Lothbury midden." He had a penny in his seam and handed it to the stall keeper, writing Mary's name in charcoal on the plank top. They stood in silence while machinery clanked, the stall keeper sweating to twist a giant paper smeared with ink. "He ought to be flogged for his clumsiness," said Adam, bitterly disappointed. He gave it to her, wishing he had another penny to make the man do it again.

Mary stared at it and then impulsively kissed his cheek. "Adam, thank you! I'll keep it always, and—and I can't believe you'll live forever in Lime Alley! I quite see you would dislike coming if you felt you would be less than welcome, though with me you never would be so! Will you come when you are happy to do so in yourself?"

"I think that will be never," said Adam with an effort. "God knows I should like to be on your step at first light tomorrow."

"But you've been telling me you don't intend to work for another master once you're free! The City isn't Whitehall, it's full of men who once lived in Lime Alleys, I'm sure you won't take long to prosper! Meanwhile, I shall keep this safe and look forward to other agreeable times in your company, such as we've spent today." She looked at the paper in her hand, and smiled. It bore a crudely decorated border and the legend:

MARY EYLES
Printed upon the ICE on the RIVER THAMES at WHITE-
HALL
December 16th 1692

Here may your name in printing set,
Remind you o'er this day,
Tho' numb'd with cold, do not forget,
The joys of ice's sway

For sure in former ages ne'er was found,
A press to print where men so oft were drown'd!

He returned her kiss on the lips then, no strangeness to it,
though great torches were pouring sparks into the night and
people jostling all around. Only awareness of his hands holding
her sweetness, her mouth curved softly under his, the lovely
finding of something he had long starved without. She did not
seem to mind, and he wondered fleetingly whether she made
a habit of kissing apprentices at Frost Fair. Then she was
walking beside him while they sought out her father.

He was a portly, self-important little man, deep in discussion
with some cronies in a tented coffeehouse; he scowled at Adam
and cuffed Mary absently towards a group of women, bidding
her find her mother so he could finish his affairs. Adam took
her across, seething with unreasonable anger: Mary had told
him she was only seventeen, although she seemed older, and
girls were disciplined by casual blows long after formal flog-
gings ended.

"Fare you well, Mistress Eyles," he said, kissing cold fingers with cold lips.

"Mary."

"Mary," he said painfully. It was exactly the right name for
her, he thought, direct and simple but lovely in its sound.

She was hustled away then by a woman wearing a wig a
foot high, trimmed with feathers and wax fruit. A fence of fur
and velvet closed about her, of perfume, paint and loud, disapproving gossip; the instant of his happiness was over.

Chapter Five

*F*or the next few days Adam laboured like a madman, stunning himself with fatigue so he might sleep without dreaming of Mary, then on the morning his indentures ended his mood changed abruptly. He saw himself quite simply as a weak fool, yielding to despair. Against every kind of odds the world could stack against him, he had found the one girl he could love—already loved—completely. Perhaps casual liking was all she could feel for him, but he owed them both the chance to try for more.

His notion that one day he might select and marry a woman well built for breeding and obedient to his will seemed utterly absurd. He intended to succeed for his father's sake, surely he could do so faster when the prize might be winning Mary. Already, without him realising it, she had helped him take an enormous step away from servitude to a dreadful past.

He was nearly out of Lime Alley and on his way; within a few weeks surely he would be able to earn sufficient money to buy clothes in which he could call at Lothbury without disgrace. For Adam had few illusions: he did not have long. Mary was young and beautiful, and her father looked grasping. The time must be close when her marriage would be negotiated, and so far she had no reason to feel anything for him.

The next day Milner walked to Mercers' Hall with him; it should have been a day to savour triumph, instead Adam was considering the first steps to riches which he must take at once, and scarcely thought of it at all.

He felt in his waistband for the papers sewn there, the lists of ships and tides and goods. This very night he would go to Wapping and start his trade.

He signed the red-bound register in Mercers' Hall, swore his oath to the company and only grasped it was truly done, his freedom and that of the City gained, when Milner arranged for a new apprentice and announced that he was going without adding any commands to Adam.

"I'll find myself lodgings and return for my traps," said Adam, feeling absurdly awkward.

Milner nodded and went off, the Mercers' clerk remarking disapprovingly that it was a poor master who did not buy his apprentice ale on the day of his freedom.

"He was a poor master, and I well rid of him," said Adam feelingly. He wished Mary could have watched him sign, so he could tell her he would come to Lothbury soon. His mother too; he had seen Arabella across the width of Ludgate Hill a few weeks back and dived into an alley to avoid confronting her. Perhaps when he could repay her thirty guineas he would go to Fleet Street and discover whether all was well with her. He shivered and set the thought aside. She might well be bedded elsewhere now.

He found a corner of attic in a court off Mincing Lane; he had eight shillings saved and when that was gone would be penniless if his venture failed.

Then Adam returned to Lime Alley for the last time, kicking rubbish irritably as he crossed the yard behind Milner's shop, the years of his life spent in this cheerless place already remote. He bundled his few belongings together and prised up the board where his saved shillings were hidden.

They were gone.

He could not believe it and felt frantically amongst plaster chippings, finding nothing. He was filled with killing fury then, and ran through to the shop with heavy, shambling steps, pain back in his chest, sweat ice-cold on his face. Milner was there and Adam did not even notice the customer leaning against the counter.

Adam grabbed him by his dirty neckband and shook him so he choked. "Give back my coins before I wreck your shop searching for myself."

Milner gobbled in his grip, in other circumstances Adam would have felt satisfaction at the sight, some requitement for the years of misery, instead he was numbed by fear for the whole future he had lost, terrified that the pain in his chest would prevent him from forcing Milner to give it him again. He choked and caught the edge of the counter, fighting for

353

breath, scarcely aware of the man he had taken for a customer mouthing words, nor of iron cold on his wrist.

The pain had been as bad as this only once before, when he ran all the way from Billingsgate after two nights without sleep. I'm tired, he thought, confused. I must rest before I set out for Wapping tonight. Slowly, torn breath mended and pain dulled; he straightened cautiously while still holding one-handed to the counter. One-handed. He stared stupidly at the cuff chained to his wrist and then lifted his gaze to Milner's smirking face, to the man beside him, who he now saw carried a ward constable's cudgel. He was a drinking crony of Milner's, Adam had often seen them together in their cups.

He licked his lips, feeling ridiculously weak though pain had ebbed to a dull ache beneath his ribs. "There's no need to chain me, I won't touch you so long as you return my shillings. If you don't, I swear before God to ruin you one day when you least expect it."

Milner snickered. "You're in no case to threaten, coming here to rob and assault. 'Tis a known thing in 'prentices just out of their time, so I asked my friend the constable to step over and protect me."

"I didn't come to rob." Adam strained at the chain holding him as if a muscle could snap half-inch iron. "You stole eight shillings and twopence I had saved in three years' toil; I will have your blood to find them if necessary."

Milner looked at the constable and shrugged. "You see? Just as I feared, threats and vi'lence, threats and vi'lence. 'Tis a poor apprentice who doesn't work as journeyman after he's out of time, but this one never served me fairly. I guessed he'd stolen from me all these years, yet went with him to Mercers' Hall because I owed him the benefit of trust. However unjustified . . . how-ever un-justified," he added, squeezing real tears from his eyes and staring at Adam in triumph.

"Werry true, werry true," said the constable, shaking his head. "'Prentices is wipers in the bosom an' those just freed is the vorst." He went to summon help and Adam heard coins jingling in his pockets. They've split my eight shillings, he thought bleakly. They'll charge me with God knows what and drink three years' savings in a week's blind. There was no one who would swear for him, no one who cared at all.

He felt lost in a kind of violent despair, possessed by deadly hatred not only for Milner and his venal friend, but for every being who had ever walked the earth, for God who created

354

humankind in His own image, or so the preachers said. Mary no longer any exception since he refused to think of her at all.

He did not struggle when they led him through the streets on a leash of chain and at the end of the journey stared about him as if wondering why he was kept waiting. "Where is this?" he asked a turnkey who stood watching. He had no recollection of which way they had come.

The turnkey spat. "You a Dutcher or summat? 'Tis Newgate."

Newgate. Adam shut his eyes, reality no longer deadened, breathing roughening as he remembered coming here to see his father, before he died a bloodied mess of meat on the same altar of injustice. He at least had suffered for his beliefs held dear, his son was scuffled into some foul hold for no purpose but the wickedness of man.

He fought frantically, mindlessly, hopelessly, when they took off the constable's chain, throwing off men double his normal strength until they kicked him senseless. Next day he was set in the whipping pillory in the press yard, hands strained into holes cut through planks. In crowded Newgate, prisoners who fought their jailers were apt to raise riots and were flogged where the rest could see.

They left him there in pouring rain a long time afterwards, perhaps the clean water saved his life, then chained him and threw him into the common hold; he was conscious only of filth in his mouth since he could not lie on the sponge of his back.

Disgust brought him to his feet the following day when he would have preferred to sink into the ease of a mind cauterised by disaster. Fetters were heavy on his wrists and ankles, the same tripping links he remembered on his father running between the two. He leaned against green-slimed wall and physically thrust memory aside. He must be free of everything but hatred in this place, stripped of scruple and pity if he was to revenge himself on Milner, which was all life still held for him.

"Where d'ye come from, cully?"

Adam eyed the man standing over him warily. He was one of the tallest men he had ever seen, and covered with crisp black hair from belly to cheekbone, skull balding above heavy brows. "Lime Alley. And you?"

He jerked his thumb, perhaps at the stinking hold, perhaps outside. "I'm Ripe Will Fogarty. My cullies want ter know 'ow much garnish ye've got."

355

"Garnish?"

"Garnish, dull boys, chippin's for the sow," said Ripe Will impatiently. "Newgate ain't run as no charity, yer know."

"I haven't anything," said Adam flatly. "Not a souse. I was one day out of my apprenticeship and my employer stole the shillings I had saved. He made sure his friend the constable was standing by when I tried to get it back."

Ripe Will nodded disinterestedly. "It often 'appens. My brovver got 'imself 'anged for much th'sime. Yer'll 'ave ter pay garnish if yer so much as puke in this plice, though."

"I can't; I haven't anything," repeated Adam. He sat in filth again; his back hurt savagely.

"Yer've a belt an' brogues. I'll spout 'em for yer."

"Why the hell should I? They'll not take these chains off for the few pence a belt and pair of brogues'll fetch."

"'Cos if I don't, there's others as'll strip 'em off yer for nuthin', see? Everyone pays garnish 'ere; yer let me do it, an' I'll do me best for ye, wrinkle yer on 'ow to live in this plice."

Adam put his head on his knees and thought about it muzzily. Ripe Will was as much a brute as the rest but once paid, presumably would defend him after his fashion, or the whole system of preying on each other would collapse. Probably he would have been skinned like a fish already if Ripe Will had not guarded a likely source of income while he lay senseless.

So the deal was concluded and Ripe Will became exceedingly drunk on the proceeds. There were several taverns inside Newgate and brisk trade in the lowest grade of spirits: many constables were also tavernkeepers with an interest in keeping the cells full. Will was a mill layer, or a thief who broke into houses with tools; he had concocted some yarn to tell the magistrate and hoped not to be hanged, as he had friends outside who would place a bribe at the right time. He had been waiting months for trial and most in the hold were in the same case. There were boys too young and men too old to scavenge a living outside prison walls; dubbers or picklocks; sneaking budgers who stole off stalls, children trained as clouters to snatch handkerchiefs out of sleeves or wigs off heads as the gentry passed; prod layers, bridle culls and nubbers. Without realising it, Adam filed away information on every kind of thievery, much as he had filed away details of shipping and cargoes. In the waistband of his breeches most of that was still sewn in safety, but he did not expect to use it now.

The common hold was airless and foetid, yet very cold in

midwinter. Men coughed endlessly, sickened and died. Adam thought he would never be warm again; without coat or boots he shuddered constantly, even his bowels quivered and his hands split and bled. He was restlessly bored too; there was no sign he would ever be brought to trial, nothing except hatred and injustice to think about. He rejected any idea of appealing for assistance from his mother, without money his message would probably not have been delivered even if he had tried. She had come to Newgate before; he could not bring her here again, and shied from any appeal to pity. She was part of the hating too; deep in his heart he blamed her for much that he had suffered. If she had remained faithful to her love he would have neither grown up in St. Mary's nor left Fleet Street for Lime Alley.

The other prisoners mostly ignored him. He was a queer 'un, a solitary who spoke like a swell. They feared his temper, though, his subtle revenges refined by idleness, and seldom reckoned thumping him worth the trouble. Ripe Will went out free as he had forecast and Adam was surprised to find he missed him. "If ever yer get sprung, cully, come to the Red Fevvers in Whitefriars," he said before he went. "I could make use ovver cunning cove like yer."

"If only I could rid me of these accursed chains, I would somehow spring myself," said Adam bitterly. "I doubt they've even put my name on the list for trial."

"Count yerself lucky then. Ye get 'anged fer prigging."

"I didn't prig anything! They didn't find so much as a half boy on me."

Ripe Will shook his head, unconvinced. In his experience a little matter of evidence was wheedled easily enough.

Adam felt alarmingly alone when he had gone and for the first time turned the full force of his formidable mind to the problem of escape. Before, he had battered himself against the fact of his imprisonment, now he was coldly determined to be out. If he had not been so heavily chained he would have tried climbing, whatever the hazards. He was small and light, there were many chimneys in Newgate as well as walls; somewhere there must be a way to find, but hung with chains it was impossible. He clinked at every step, while his wrists festered so badly he had to hold the cuffs from further chafing if he could.

He sought out dubbers who specialised in padlocks, but Newgate fetters were forged with their skills in mind and required iron to be drawn from the hinges. One or two of the best could possibly have freed him but without garnish refused to risk a flogging, and as spring came the courts burst into brief activity, clearing back lists of prisoners before recess. Hope flared that he would be called at last, but nothing happened and he returned to his scheming. If he gave up now then the pit of hopelessness was very close, insanity grinning in its depths.

He saw the gamble of a single chance one morning, had to take or leave it almost without reflection. The turnkey read a list of those for trial that day and an old man lying at Adam's feet groaned and flopped on his back. "They can't make me go, let 'em search the 'old for me if they wants to."

Adam glanced down at him. "Why? If your charge is serious they'll search for you fast enough, if not then you'll be out. Better to go now than risk a flogging."

"I were a sneaking budger, see? Some cove yelled an' I ran off from 'abit, they didn't find nothing on me. I'd as soon stay 'ere till summer's come, me woman brings in tosh an' scattle."

Understanding from this that he was a petty thief off stalls and well supplied with victuals and cheap spirits, Adam turned away. The old man was not chained, for him life in Newgate was preferable to precarious cadging in wet and cold outside. He stopped dead, thought new-forged. He could take his place, chance casual sentence and be out. "They're calling for Jones and Sivyer again. Is one of them you?"

"Aye, Sivyer. What of it? They'll not search through an 'undred nor more to find a common budger."

"No," said Adam slowly. "You're sure? They'll put you down as dead to keep their records straight. If you let this pass you may never be out."

The man cursed and turned over. "I've no 'eart for it today. 'Tis mortal 'ard budgin' for five brats an' a woman in Stocks Market. Let 'er do it awhile."

Poor woman, thought Adam. He picked his way across the cell and gave his name as Sivyer to the turnkey, to be heartily clouted for keeping them waiting. The shambling group of prisoners was then chivvied down a passage, it was all so easy Adam could scarcely believe his luck. The Old Bailey backed on to Newgate and they were kept waiting in the open yard all morning while the turnkeys cursed and rain poured out of a heavy sky. No one took any notice of Adam, his fellows had not listened to other names in the excited dread of hearing their own, the turnkeys concerned with numbers rather than faces.

When Adam's supposed name was called, everything suddenly became very swift. He was shoved up steps so he tripped on his chains and sprawled in the door beside five others. A clerk gabbled charges, constables swore to arrests made months ago without looking at prisoners they certainly could not remember now. One man tried to explain that his wife was starving and close to childbirth when he stole a twopenny loaf; no one heeded him since it was impossible to discover whether he spoke the truth or not. The judge sentenced him to ten lashes as well as branding for his insolence in pleading.

"Sivyer, Thomas."

"Yes, sir," said Adam. He had no intention of collecting lashes for some petty lack of respect.

A drone from the clerk about thieving off stalls; God, Adam thought, what if the old man lied and they found something on him? Theft of goods worth more than sixpence was punishable by hanging.

The judge scratched irritably on paper. "Branding and ten lashes." He did not look up.

Adam opened his mouth to protest, then shut it again, feeling sick. Protest would simply double the number of lashes and risk discovery as an impostor.

"I thought I'd get fifty at least," said the man who had attempted to plead a wife in childbirth, when they were back in the yard. "If they don't believe you it's usually fifty. Worth trying, though, last time I got off free except for the branding."

Adam swallowed. "Is it—does it hurt very much?"

"Lor' bless you, no! Garnish for the glitter cove and 'e'll do it not much more than warm." He held up his hand. "Three times I've 'ad it done and you can't 'ardly see nothing, can you?"

There was a faint mark on the dirty palm, nothing more. "I thought it was usually done on the thumb?" Adam wondered feverishly what garnish he could offer to cool a branding iron.

The other winked. "Even a warm iron's awkward on the thumb if a man's to earn a living while it heals, see? The only time I couldn't prig 'alf a dozen whole boys to have the iron cooled I got 'im to do it on me arm. Heals quicker and don't put off the customers meanwhile."

Half a dozen whole boys, thought Adam, dismayed. Now he desperately needed time to think, to prig if necessary off his fellow prisoners, there was none left at all. Newgate only accommodated those awaiting trial or hanging; once tried, petty criminals were dealt with and discharged at once.

Fetters were struck off first, while Adam could not take his eyes from the brazier shimmering in a corner, the hooped board where arm or neck was secured. The room stank of vomit and burned meat from the last batch through, the blacksmith made irritable by the numbers he was expected to deal with on such days. Of their six, two were to have *V* for vagrant branded on the cheek, one *T* for thief on the forehead, having already been marked twice on the hand, the other three were nominally first offenders and sentenced to the hand; the judge had been lenient according to his lights since both of Adam's companions seemed nonchalantly familiar with the rates of garnish which would ease their way past the brazier.

My hand, thought Adam, closing it convulsively, he must have been crazed to take this way out. He was scarcely thinking of ten lashes at all, obeyed automatically when told to lay the hasp of his fetters across the anvil. A cold-iron job the dubbers had called it, bone jarring as the blacksmith drove the links apart. He winced, watching in sick terror as a man was secured screaming by the neck and a glowing iron set sizzling on his cheek; did not notice when he was free of iron until the black-smith kicked him violently aside.

"Gawd, you look well corpsed," observed the bread thief. "Don't worry, 'twas just that one ain't got none o' the ready for garnish."

"I haven't either," said Adam.

"Nothin'? Nothin' at all?" he demanded incredulously. Garnish and Newgate were inseparable.

He shook his head, tongue slipping drily.

At least the greater fear took his mind off flogging. Ten lashes was not much compared to the fifty or more he had suffered in the press yard; he stood with every sinew quivering and tried to believe it would not be much worse than Milner's bars. Except that his back was incompletely healed and as sensitive as the fear riding his mind. He bit wood under his face and kept silent somehow on a mouthful of splinters.

The bread thief was just ahead of him and instead of feeling admiration, Adam hated him when he joked beside the brazier. He handed over six pennies "for a cold 'un," and then hesitated, eyes on Adam's face. He jerked his head. "Take a couple of 'em to cool down 'is, an' I'll 'ave mine one step up."

The jailer at the brazier grunted, there was a precise scale of charges, it was all the same to him.

"God, d'you mean it?" blurted Adam. "I mean . . . the swine'll heat yours now."

The other grinned and thrust his hand through the iron hoop. "Not too much or I'll complain to the beak. 'E's got 'is fourpence and we can't 'ave 'im dishonest, can we?" All the same he screwed up his face and yelped when the iron smacked home, even though his palm did not smoke as the last man's had done.

His turn next. Almighty God in heaven above, have mercy. There is no God, nor mercy; only blood wet at your waist and iron tight on your arm. He would never call on Mary now but what if he met her in the street and she saw him branded thief? And with Cain's mark on his hand he would be condemned forever to the foulest slums and the company of felons.

"My arm," he gasped, eyes squeezed shut. "Take the money to put it on my arm instead."

"Ye'll have it full heat then," replied the man with the iron indifferently.

He nodded, unable to speak.

"Well, turn your arm, beef-wit," said the bread thief amiably. "It'll clem up quicker topside."

He twisted his arm somehow, iron scraping on sores at his wrist, eyes still shut. He could not have opened them for anything short of a cold iron. It came like a driven spike, deep into flesh and muscle, leaping agony from fingertip to base of skull. He cried out then, deep in his throat, and fell on his knees when they released him to bolt the next into his place. This happened most days while the rest of London gave it no thought at all.

The bread thief helped him put on his shirt, and between them they supported one of the vagabonds to the entry. He was branded on the forehead, brow and eyes swelled scarlet so he could not see at all. A bent-backed slattern broke into wails when they came through the postern, and stumbled over to the man they were helping. He mumbled something and she wept again, wringing her hands before leading him away. The bread thief looked after them reflectively. "Poor bitch, 'ow will they thieve or even beg now, when every goodwife'll slam the door on such a face? Still, we was well out of it. I fancied we'd be 'auling 'im round 'alf London afore we prigged a mort to take 'im in."

Adam nodded, imagination cringing from thought of the fire in his arm hammered between his eyes.

The bread thief lifted his head and sniffed appreciatively. "D'you know, 'tis a fine day? Each time in Newgate I forget there's such a thing as sun. There is, though, and myself well pleased to see it again. You able to reach 'ome, then?"

Adam nodded again, words congealed by shock and pain. Yet this unknown thief had shown him there was some mercy in the world, he must say something. "I—I hope your hand heals cleanly and soon," he managed at last. "I don't know how to thank you, with a branded hand my life would have been worthless."

"Don't you be feeling puked-up for me. 'Twasn't full 'eat and I did it 'cos I wanted to, no askin' of yourn." He waved his burned hand airily and walked off, whistling.

A better man than I am, thought Adam soberly, and perhaps he offered the best reason of all for suffering in another's place: because he wanted to. A brisk April wind was blowing, tossing dust in the air. Fleece-white clouds sailed overhead, the sweetness of spring triumphing over London's stink. He breathed deeply, after Newgate the fresh softness of the season went to his head like wine and for a short while he felt almost strong.

It did not last. The wind which had revived him sent chills through his body even while back and arm burned at fever heat. His face felt stiff, legs soft and remote. He sheltered awhile behind a cobbler's booth, then, after careful consideration, set out to walk to the Red Feathers in Whitefriars.

On his way he passed Thomas Tompion's clock workshop in Fleet Street, and obsessed by careful holding to slithering senses, did not even notice it.

Chapter Six

*W*hitefriars, or Alsatia as it was often called, lay east of the Temple between Fleet Street and the river. An ancient sanctuary when friars lived there, it had since become a maze of courts and alleys filled with debtors, thieves and murderers. The friary was long vanished, and in its place had grown the last refuge of a violent and desperate rabble, who preyed on each other yet banded together to beat off intervention from outside.

It was unpaved, unlit, undrained; the houses occasionally patched but never repaired, the whole area so low-lying that cellars filled with the tide. Fevers, epidemics and fluxes were commonplace; children swarmed in large-eyed packs even if they seldom lived long after coming to Alsatia. Dogs howled and foamed and had to be beaten aside with sticks, the rats so bold they scampered over the wakeful as well as the ill and sleeping. The only water came from the Thames, sloshing with refuse and salt to the taste.

Perhaps Adam would not have detested Whitefriars quite so much if he had not feared that the rest of his life was to be spent in such places. He was not aware of this sensation, but it was there and prevented him from feeling pity for its stunted, furtive inhabitants or gratitude for their rough care of him. Subconsciously, he knew himself stunted and cursed as they were, that they accepted him because they recognised one of their own. He refused to be one of them, or to acknowledge such virtues as they possessed: instead he brooded on his wrongs and despised everything he saw. He healed slowly in Alsatia's infected air, but physical hurts were unimportant compared with those to his spirit, and this time there was nothing to sustain him. No childish belief in magic which might transform his mother's distaste to affection, no spur of ambition to deaden brutality, no cleansing love which Mary Eyles had placed in his heart. Only hatred remained, a fitting frame for pain and squalor.

Adam lay nearly two weeks on dirty straw, too apathetic to move. Strength returned and flesh knitted while his will remained paralysed: in the end Ripe Will kicked him to his feet and down to the taproom of the Red Feathers.

The tavern reminded Adam of rotting meat. The same harsh smell and buzzing flies, the same crawling life revealed to the casual glance: all around him men quarrelled, drank and tripped over bodies collapsed in corners just as they had done in Newgate.

After a while he could not bear it and went outside to sit on the step. It was night and the air cold; his mind cleared slightly but would not focus on sagging buildings and churned mud, instead he began to think of the well-dressed bustle in Lombard Street and fresh salt wind at Wapping, the mathematical beauty of St. Paul's in the building. Of Mary.

He slammed thought shut and stood without reflection.

"Back on yer feet at last," said Ripe Will behind him.

Adam turned carefully, and nodded. His senses felt as stiff as his back, as sore as his arm, but like the rest of him were working again after a fashion.

"If my Sue weren't a good-'earted lass, ye'd 'ave been kicked downstairs afore. And I'd 'ave bin right. Cag an' cat-lap ain't never done one no good."

From this Adam understood that Ripe Will disapproved of the bread and thin blue milk which was all he had been able to eat; but when he followed Will back into the taproom his precariously balanced stomach griped instantly in the foul atmosphere.

Will sprawled on a cask and bawled for ale. "Sit ye down, you an' me 'ave affairs to talk on."

Adam hesitated and then sat on another cask, he felt too strange to stand for long. I must get out of here, he thought desperately, earn a few pence and leave before it is too late.

Ripe Will drank his ale in a single draught and belched. "'Ave ye thought 'ow ye're to repay me?" He did not believe in oblique approaches.

Adam shook his head, words stacked out of reach.

"Ye'd 'ave bin cold meat wivvout the Fevvers to come to.

So ye owes me yer life as well as twelve nights' lodgin'. Thirty pound I reckon'd be cheap."

Outrageous, or very cheap, reflected Adam wryly. Depending on the value set on his life. He waited to hear the rest, brain alert now. Ripe Will knew he had not a souse to his name, and must have some scheme in mind.

"Ain'cher got a tongue?" demanded Will, unsettled by his silence.

"Yes," said Adam, and called for ale, it would be added to the reckoning. "What is it you want of me?"

"Fair payment, my young chub. No more, no less. Never say Ripe Will's a wrong 'un, but a fair 'un as wants 'is rights. I've a way of not forgettin' them as cheats me neither."

Adam believed it. Anyway, he had no intention of running off; a debt was a debt and if Will had some scheme for profiting, then he intended to share it. No scruple, only hatred left.

Ripe Will swore and banged his mug on a cask. He found talking into silence unexpectedly difficult. "'Ow d'yer expect to pay me then?"

Adam shrugged. "I expect you'll tell me."

Will let out a roar of fury. "I h'expect you'll tell me, eh? 'Ow about me leavin' yer to stew, and run up reckonings faster than ye can pay?"

"Then we would both lose. You know I've no trade but mercer's apprentice and wouldn't have kept me twelve nights without a purpose."

Will grunted, relieved to find his investment more intelligent than he seemed only minutes before. He lurched to his feet and shouted for Sue, indicating that Adam should follow.

The back parlour at the Red Feathers possessed a hearth and plank table, nothing else except the usual casks for sitting. There was slime on the floor from the last high tide and mould grew on unplastered walls. The mould was quite attractive and Adam stared at intricate skeins of green and brown to keep his mind from the rest.

Ripe Will's Sue was massively built, arms muscled like a wherryman's, skin seamed and grey as was common in Alsatia, but she was kindly when her own well-being was not at stake. She had not resented taking milk to Adam twice a day or sending a child to buy it, and greeted him with rough concern now he was on his feet. Will soon cured her of wasting time with a cuff and despatched her to fetch his dibblers' boman.

Adam stared at the mould and added Will to his list of hatreds.

Sue returned with a leather bag and tipped its contents on the table: watches, some fobs and seals, a gold tip from a cane. Adam turned at the sound and found Will watching him instead of the glitter on the board, "Well, what d'yer think?"

Adam shrugged. "Nothing." It was no surprise to find that Ripe Will was a receiver as well as a thief.

Sue giggled; Adam might resent her being clouted on his behalf, it made no impression on her. "Ye're a one, cully. What d'ye think to get outta 'im, Will?"

Will poked at the watches morosely. "'Ow much d'yer reckon this lot is worth?"

"I don't know; I'm a mercer, not a watchmaker."

"Guess then, cully. Ye can read, write even, can'cher?"

Adam decided against telling him that an ability to write and figure made him less qualified to value watches than an accomplished prig like Will, and went over to the table. Three of the watches were silver and of poor quality, the rest gold turnips of solid but uninspired craftsmanship. Except for one. He picked it up curiously, he had never seen anything like it. A delicately figured face and wafer-thin hands, thickness of case no more than half an inch. He laid the best of the turnips beside it in his palm, the one bulky and almost spherical, the other elegantly shaped to fit a waistcoat pocket.

"It's beautiful work," he said aloud. "Someone must have developed a completely new movement to produce anything so fine."

"'Ow much?" demanded Will.

Adam was staring at feather-like writing on the dial: *Thomas Tompion fecit. London.* His mother's lover, husband perhaps by now. He laid it gently on the table; it was too beautiful to throw, although he wanted to. "I don't know. Twenty pounds perhaps."

"The lot?"

"No, that one alone. The rest—it's pure guess but perhaps fifty pounds the lot." In a shop in Cheapside they were worth three times as much, but this was Alsatia after all.

Ripe Will exchanged a look with Sue, and breathed out heavily. "What if I told you a gager'll tip me five yellow boys the 'ole snaffle?"

"I'd say you were being cheated."

"Ah, an' there ye 'ave it. Prigs tip 'em to me, an' I pay

'em on the keg, at once. Then I tip the snaffle to gagers what'll ship 'em Dutch, or grig 'em flash, see? I ain't got no sale 'ere, nor chanst to find one. So I gets cheated, with nowhere else to go. Ye're different, flashlike, I reckon ye'd maybe find them as'd prig e'em direct from me."

Adam thought about it, understanding from this that Ripe Will bought the proceeds of theft for derisory amounts, but did not see why the fences he sold to should take a similar advantage of him. Adam doubted his ability to deal with White-friars fences, but it sounded a more entertaining enterprise than he had expected, and after a deal of chaffering he agreed to try.

Planning what he would do revived him, and two days later he went to the area bordering Whitefriars and the Temple, where Ripe Will's man of business resided. In the lanes leading to Temple Steps were to be found the skilled elite of petty criminality: forgers, fences, locksmiths and counterfeiters. The aristocrats of the trade, the placers of bulk goods and bodies, lived in respectable residences far removed from Whitefriars and it was Adam's job somehow to break into their trade and cut out extortionate middlemen.

Adam insisted that he must be reasonably dressed if he was to impress such men at all, but when clothes were stolen for him was surprised by his own delight in wearing even ill-fitting breeches and coat after rags.

Adam had seen Alsatia when he came, but refused to notice much. Now he did. He was used to fouled lanes and danger after dark in the City, but this was another life entirely. Near the Temple the houses had once been substantial, now they were windowless, crumbling, teeming with people. Elsewhere gaps were broken into walls where women peddled a variety of goods: occasionally meat or fish, usually home-distilled geneva, opaque in colour and so fiery men dropped in the gutter where they drank. Rain and Thames water did not have a cleansing effect on such surroundings, instead filth bubbled into an evil, knee-deep soup through which it was often necessary to wade.

On his early journeys Adam would have been lost without Will as guide and guard although Alsatia was not large. New buildings sprouted out of old as they decayed, courts intercommunicated, lanes were streams, ditches built over. Everything looked the same and the way was often blocked by dung piles, the bodies of babies showing amongst the muck. Here, when a child died, the natural thing was to dispose of it with the rubbish.

Adam felt the first sensation of reawakened pity when he saw these skeletal infants dropped heedlessly on middens; soon he was incapable of feeling anything at all.

Will handed over the bag of watches and waited for him outside the fence's lodging, his faith in the persuasive powers of book learning strangely touching; Adam spent his days climbing rickety stairs to greasy hiding kens under rafters and in cellars, astonished that men well fattened on extortion should choose to live in such conditions. He tried promises and cold sense on values, threatened the dealers with Ripe Will's power in Whitefriars; he had bargained for a quarter share in any increased profits, so did not lack invention. Nothing did any good. The fences wrung their hands and whined, or threatened violence in their turn, but had inherited a trade stretching back over centuries and knew each move in the game. The only result was that Will found his credit with priggers slipping away as other taverns in Whitefriars were granted better terms to squeeze him out.

"'Tain't no manner o' good," he said despondently to Adam after several weeks of this. "Ye've tried, so I won't add to your score 'cepting for the clothes. An 'undred yellow boys an' yerse clear, while I must settle for what them croakers offer."

"They've been after you again?"

"Aye. They'll go back 'ow 'twas before an' let me trade again. Some trade! It'll be scrapings now they got me beat." He spat reproachfully, he had thought better of book learning.

He calls it not adding to the score, but a hundred pounds is a tidy multiplication for a set of clothes, thought Adam wryly. "Will you let me try an idea of my own?"

"What is it?"

He shook his head. "I'd like to see whether it works first."

"Oh no, you don't, my cully. I'm the one what stands to lose, see? No trade for life an' the old Fevvers burned down one night, I dessay. I can kill yer if yer fails an' enjoy it, but that's no 'elp for an empty bag."

"Well," said Adam slowly. "It may sound crazy to you, but I thought to sell the goods back to their owners."

"Prig 'em back?"

"Yes. Don't you see, the owners lose most? Often goods they're fond of as well as value. If I could offer back what was stolen at a third its cost, you would profit and they recoup some of their loss."

Adam's idea was such a reversal of Ripe Will's notions that it took days of persuasion to let him attempt it, but at last he agreed. Adam tried first with Thomas Tompion's watch. He had not been able to bring himself to sell it for the two yellow boys which was all the fences offered, and the original thief remembered who he had prigged it from, since he worked the same alehouses in rotation.

The chief difficulty, as Adam realised, was that he did not want to be seen during the transfer. No one in Whitehall or Westminster knew him, and few in the City either, but it would not be long before they did if he acted openly as a thieves' go-between.

He solved the problem by following his quarry home, discovering his name, which was Adeney, and then writing a civil note offering to return his watch. He did not precisely say whether he was thief, receiver or conscience-stricken purchaser, nor demand money in so many words. Just described the watch and said he stood to lose by returning it, unless two men of sense could hammer out an accommodation acceptable to both.

They could, and did. Adam was determined to establish a reputation for trustworthiness and fair prices, so the sum settled on was a mere twenty guineas. He also intended to become the senior partner in Ripe Will's trade, not an indebted employee, so took the risk of trading the watch himself.

He chose the new church of St. James's, Piccadilly, for the handover. The location would reassure a street saunterer like Adeney, and was convenient to his house in Duke Street. Adam told him he could bring two bodyguards, and guessed he would place hirelings in St. James's hoping to seize watch and thief without losing twenty guineas, and laid his plans accordingly. The meeting was set for midnight so darkness would hide his features; but instead of waiting by the church he met Adeney on the steps of his house. No gentleman would have uncouth bodyguards sitting in his own front hall, but would summon them from the mews when he wanted them.

When Adeney appeared Adam moved forward at once, calling out cheerfully. Away from the light of flambeaux by the door, he put his hand on Adeney's arm and enquired civilly after his health.

"Why, well enough," he said, peering in the dark. A gentleman had so many acquaintances it was difficult to tell which were cronies whose features one could not precisely recall and which toadies needing a sharp set-down.

"Good," said Adam, shifting grip to Adeney's wrist. "Don't cry out or look round, I'm holding a pistol in my other hand. You have twenty guineas for me, I believe." He jerked Adeney's arm into his back and made him yelp. "Don't look round, I said."

To waiting grooms by the mews entry they seemed two friends passing the time of night together and they hung back politely.

Adeney's lips trembled, he had been drinking while he waited and wished his head was clearer. "Who are you?"

"You know who I am. I wrote to offer your watch back for twenty guineas, and you rewarded me by stuffing St. James's full of cutthroats. If you look at my waistcoat you'll see your watch in the pocket: count your fee into it in exchange and then take out the watch." He twisted Adeney's arm until he gasped with pain. "Look in the pocket, nowhere else."

Adeney stared at his men longingly, but fear and awareness that his senses were bleared by alcohol kept him silent. Reluctantly, he counted coins into Adam's pocket, on his instructions holding each one to the moonlight. "Since I can't trust you not to slip in clipped silver otherwise," explained Adam sweetly. "Now take out the watch and be sure it is yours."

"I can't see," said Adeney sulkily.

Adam hesitated. "Very well, we'll go over to the flambeaux. Call to your men that we are going inside for a moment." He could feel sweat trickling down his chest: he ought not to risk more traps, but men must learn to rely on his ability to deliver what he said, and Adeney was his first character reference. "Is it the right one and undamaged?" he demanded when they were in the light.

"Yes." Adeney slipped it in his pocket, fumbling to find the flap.

Adam dropped his wrist instantly, and gave him a shove which sent him staggering; the pistol he had been in the act of withdrawing exploded and the shot flicked through the skirts of Adam's coat.

"You double-crossing swine," said Adam into the stink of gunpowder. "You may tell your friends that I keep to my bargains when I make them." He turned and walked off, secure in the length of time it took to reload a pistol. He was round two corners before the grooms ran from the mews, jabbering in surprise.

He had expected Adeney to be armed for such a meeting, but had followed him long enough to know he was seldom completely sober: the risks had not been great and word of his doings would certainly spread. He laughed aloud, it had been an amusing evening and showed the first clear profit from his own wits and nerve.

Chapter Seven

*W*ill *was delighted by multiplying his* gain so simply and word went out that the Red Feathers would pay extra for the name and direction of the original owners of prigged articles brought there. To improve their value, Will said vaguely, and it was a while before thieves found out how he gained as much as fifty pounds for articles which he used to fence for a matter of shillings. Then a few tried the same business themselves and encountered the perilous realities of Adam's methods. The dangerous moment remained the meeting for exchange, when robbed victims felt no qualm over tricking thieves; another difficulty for the ordinary inhabitants of Whitefriars was that few could write or pass scrutiny in polite society. Adam had a variety of methods of making contact, and often frequented coffeehouses and gaming hells to check an identity. He had his own wardrobe now and a room in Covent Garden for changing out of Whitefriars clothes.

By autumn he was clear of debt to Will and able to take stock of his situation. He was sitting in the Grecian Coffeehouse in the Strand, idly listening to a member of the Royal Society expounding on the possibilities of easing long-distance travel by placing springs inside saddle padding. There was a great deal of hilarity on the subject, but last time he came Adam had listened to Isaac Newton talking about planetary orbits. He had not been able to look at the night sky since without excitement, although the mathematics of it left him groping to remember his tutoring in Swithin Court. Strictly speaking, he did not need to run the risk of becoming personally known to men he might have to deal with under the muzzle of a pistol, but his famished mind yearned for the pleasures of speculation and discussion.

London was such an exciting place for those able to enjoy it. There was still turmoil in politics and war with France, but the basic questions of liberty and oppression were settled after a fashion, the long bloodletting of religious dispute outlived at last. In its place came an almost infinite flowering of individual talent as men were freed from constraint: the wildest folly and the most profound insights investigated with equal enthusiasm.

London itself was bursting out its old confines too: the common grazing around Bloomsbury village was covered with brick kilns, squares taking shape as noble lords followed the Earl of Southampton's example of speculative building. King's Square, Soho, was the nucleus of new development north of Charing Cross, where Richard Frith showed the way by building a whole street named after himself, though Sir Thomas Bond ran into difficulties when he turned a cart track into a parade of elegant shops, and died a frustrated man. Sir Richard Grosvenor and Lord John Berkeley could be seen most nights in St. James's salons quarrelling about square footages in the squares their surveyors planned in May Fair Fields, while courtiers crowded to invest in cobbling tracks and farmyards round about. Social distinctions were unimportant in matters of profit and there was a vast excitement about it all, a pushful arrogance which no sooner had one problem solved, one development complete, before the next eclipsed it. The splendid gardens of Leicester House were already encroached upon, new roads following the lines of orangery and stables.

Adam preferred to risk discovery rather than return each night to the safety of Alsatia. He seldom spoke but listened to everything, recognised most of the leading minds of the day, marked those noblemen willing to lend on speculative enterprise and those who wasted everything on drink and gaming; all information was valuable. His own trade prospered; he tried never to use the same method of meeting clients twice, never to give the other party the chance to lie in wait for him; some tried, a few scorned to break their pledged word even to a thief, occasionally they were intrigued to meet him and stayed talking, back turned at his insistence. He had once been grazed by a bullet and was lucky to escape a pack set after him, but so far his fortune held.

Now he was clear of debt to Will; he stared at polished wood and flickering fire in the Grecian and surprised himself with the thought that he would like to return to the City. Since he left Newgate he had not once gone there, had refused goods whose owners lived within its confines, now he wanted very much to return, to try again to make good his oath to his father. It was a difficult feeling to justify when nowhere in the City did talk equal the brilliance found at places like the Grecian, and he knew now that the decadence of court life covered a multiplicity of other interests. But there was no need to justify it; the City was his inheritance and he wanted—had always wanted—to claim his place there.

He sat for a long time, not drinking, not even listening. If he stayed lucky he should accumulate a modest capital within another year. If he did not, then he could expect a quick delivery to the gallows, this time justified. He looked up and studied a man on the far side of the hearth; although the other did not know it, they were due to meet the following night to deal for stolen goods. Whatever the dangers he did not intend to give up such profitable matters yet; he was finished with being a victim to be robbed and beaten by others at their will. This time he would establish himself beyond the chance of easy loss before he tried again, risk or no risk.

Coldly, he decided a thousand pounds should do it. Then he would be safe from petty viciousness, and turn his mind to legality again.

He worked like a fiend through the winter. No risk was too great for him to take, he even delivered a set of stolen paintings to a reluctant peer who disliked his ancestors but could not let them rot in Alsatia. They were so awkward a burden Adam was nearly caught that time and thought he would have been if his victim had not rather admired his nerve and failed to urge on his followers fast enough; he was running out of original ideas to minimise the hazards of such meetings.

Reluctantly, he transferred his activities to the City, where he could run through the whole range of his deceptions again with men who had not previously encountered them. Only, he was doubly careful to keep his face hidden, his voice disguised, and never entered taverns or coffeehouses there. Here he meant to be respected one day, and did not want to be trapped a few years hence by someone's inconvenient memory.

He began to prowl the wharves of Wapping and Rotherhithe again, dressed in the rags he hated but which were necessary in such neighbourhoods. His intelligence on shipping and goods was more than a year out of date, and now a few months more should see him set up with his thousand pounds, he was turning his mind to finding profitable uses for his gains.

Then he fell ill. He often felt exhausted to the point of sickness, but apart from the smallpox as a child had never been seriously ill. Now he was, and it destroyed his painfully built arrangements. He was badly chilled waiting for a client, then although he felt unwell he went the following day to check cargoes on the quayside. His chest hurt and he could not stop shivering; the cobbles slithered beneath his feet, so lumpers cursed him for being drunk, sweat froze on his body. The idea he was ill came gradually, and he fought against it when it came. He could not afford to be ill.

His next coherent thought was that Alsatia was a long way off. If he collapsed on open Thames wharves then he would be dead within hours; somehow he must get back to the Red Feathers. He still refused most dealings with women, but a girl in the taproom there had finally overborne his reserve and slept with him sometimes. She would look after him if he could last out the distance.

He set his teeth and forced one foot in front of the other; wind cut at him rather than blew, throwing snow like sawdust in his face. He was glad of it, his body was so hot.

Then it was cold; when he reached the Feathers at last he was shuddering, hands and feet without feeling. Will's Sue screamed when he reeled inside and would have thrown him out again for fear of infection, but Will valued the unheard-of riches Adam earned too much for common sense to prevail. When Adam recovered consciousness he found himself wrapped in sacking on bare upstairs boards; he felt stiff and his chest hurt, not the fierce pain he had known a few times before, but a steady ache which sharpened if he moved. So he lay still and watched snow blowing on the floor, and presently Lizzie came. She had features like soaked bread, the same rough texture and dulled colour, but was fond of him in her fashion.

"Ye're better," she said at once.

He supposed he was, and nodded.

She held his head while he tried to drink ale from the mug she brought; he was fiercely thirsty, although he wouldn't have chosen ale. "'Ere," she said when he could not manage more. "Sue said to bring ye pie."

He wanted to refuse, but at the Red Feathers food was either pie or bread, and today it wasn't bread. He must regain strength quickly, he had a transfer of goods arranged for the following week which needed careful preparation if it was to be safely

375

accomplished. He managed to choke down some fragments before lying back, nauseated and feeling worse than before.

Lizzie finished it for him, filling her mouth and showering him with crumbs. "Dead cats they puts in 'em, I reckon. I tole Sue she oughta make 'er own. Can I get ye anything else afore the night kip rush?"

Adam thought of cold, clean water longingly but if he asked for it she would bring him a jug from the yard, floating with straw and slime. "No, thank you. Look after yourself with the Jouncer."

Lizzie giggled. "'E brought me a fevver'e prigged yesterday."

Adam sighed and closed his eyes. He couldn't be bothered with it any more. The Jouncer was a double murderer to his certain knowledge, a brute of a man. The Red Feathers was a kip house, or brothel, after dark; pennies were paid for a few minutes' privacy on the floor of the bare parlour, ha'pence for no privacy in the taproom. Adam had first paid Lizzie to keep her from the Jouncer, and found her so natural about matters he regarded as insuperably difficult that he was able to find some contentment lying with her, although that had not been his intention. There was precious little pleasure to it, though. Relief, certainly, yes; physical relief and also freedom from fear of his own inadequacy, but he could not experience more than mild affection for Lizzie and retained a morbid fear of fathering children.

He worried obsessively even while he could not stop himself taking her, until it became clear that Lizzie possessed inherited lore for reducing such risks. He learned all he could from her and applied her teaching scrupulously, but never escaped dread that Lizzie's skills might fail, nor wretchedness at how different he had once thought bedding a woman might be.

And now with the gift of a stolen feather, the Jouncer had taken his place and no doubt would beat her senseless if she did not please him.

He slept uneasily, shivering from nightmares and icy draughts on the uncovered floor, and woke to a kind of cold, white strength. He felt scraped out and lacking in substance, yet what was left of him under command again. He went downstairs the following day; taproom, stained bar and cold east wind remote, the effort of going about complicated affairs again almost beyond his grasp. Lizzie had a split lip and a bruise on her cheekbone, but looked sleekly satisfied in a way she never had with him.

One less thing to worry about, he thought bleakly, but deep inside was a ridiculous sense of hurt.

All his plans were disrupted by his illness. Drive himself as he would, he had not the energy to carry through all the precautions he usually took when making an important exchange, his mind clear but slow, exploring possibilities like a child spelling its first primer. This time he had made contact with a reputable attorney in the Royal Exchange and arranged to transfer the proceeds from half a dozen robberies at the same time; the attorney was trusted by those who wanted their property back and would bring their joint payments, but was unlikely to feel himself bound by terms made with a thieves' representative.

In such a situation, Adam usually watched his contact for some days before transfer, worked out escape routes and diversions and then varied the precise means of exchange at the last minute. This time he did what he could, was sufficiently recovered to be aware that his planning was less meticulous than usual, without being able to think what else to do. He dressed in his room in Covent Garden gripped by a sense of foreboding, wondering whether he should simply not turn up at the meeting. It was the obvious course and he considered it carefully but with surprise. It had not occurred to him before. No. He was aware of his own reluctance and knew that if he ducked out of this meeting then he would not summon courage for another. He was no longer ill, just plain frightened. He had escaped from Newgate once, avoided a handful of traps set for him this past year; one night his fortune would run out and this could easily be the time.

He was early, stupidly early because he had not been able to wait any longer, so decided to visit his banker and reckon his balance. No more shillings kept under loose boards for him; as his profits mounted he lodged them with Sir Peter Van Koek, a goldsmith-banker in Cornhill. The City was a great melting pot of foreigners as well as Englishmen come to seek their fortunes: Jews, Portuguese, Dutch and even French found little hostility if they competed fairly and paid their share of charges. Van Koek offered half a percent more than other bankers and Adam found his advice sound on investment: he always spent as long as possible in his shop and saved up questions to ask about the banking trade. Today he had no heart for more than routine enquiries, the risks of the night looming ever larger in his mind.

He possessed nearly six hundred pounds and his share of this night's exchange should add another hundred at a stroke. A few months more and he would have the thousand he had set himself safely banked. Crime and Alsatia had provided his chance if only he could last the time. He walked back along Cornhill, jostled by crowds: he ought to start his preparations for the night, would like to visit Mercers' Hall in Cheapside, where a group of merchants were taking subscriptions for a new bank under royal charter, which would be called the Bank of England if they succeeded in raising the vast sum stipulated. Van Koek advised him to subscribe, and with his yearning to succeed in banking he was tempted to hazard a little on it. Instead he saw and decided nothing, bewildered by irresolution when decision normally came swiftly to him.

"Adam!" He felt his arm held, and turned, panic-stricken. No one should know him here, except a constable who would stun him with a cudgel and put fetters on his wrists.

It was Mary.

Chapter Eight

"*Don't you remember me?*" she said, disappointed. "I see you've prospered as I said you would, yet you never came to call."

Adam was completely confused by meeting her again, and at such a time. In spite of himself he still thought of her but recognised his thoughts for what they were: a portrait in his mind and not to be confused with reality. His first instinct was to leave her instantly, his second to put his face to the wall and weep. He did neither, staring at her with words choked in his throat.

Her hand was still on his arm, tugging now. "Adam, please. Walk with me a way or my maid will run tattling to my mother, saying I accosted a stranger in the street."

He drew her arm through his automatically. Her mother, she said. "You aren't married?" he blurted, then flushed painfully. "I'm sorry, it's no affair of mine."

"Not yet, though Father has two likely suitors engaged in dealings for me. They cannot settle on how to weight settlements against a share in our trade, but will soon come to agreement, more's the pity."

Such trading happened every day but he felt only anger that she should be sold like a bale of cloth. "No," he said clearly. "No, I—" He stopped.

Her fingers tightened on his, he had not realised he still held them. "Adam, what is it? What is the matter? I can see you have done well, but—"

He licked his lips. "But what?"

She surveyed him candidly, her own soft curls instead of a wig framing the face he remembered as if they met yesterday.

A face made for laughter, generosity of spirit set ready to the touch. "You weren't afraid of me before, only regretful you couldn't call. Now, you don't want to."

"I do, very much," he said, not looking at her. "There's nothing in all my life I could want so much. Only, I can't."

"Why not? Do you remember how we said only the truth would do between us?"

"That's why I can't. I couldn't bear to tell you the truth about me and watch...liking...turn to contempt."

She laughed and he looked at her, astonished. "Adam, of course it wouldn't! Do you think you are behaving now as if contempt should be your due?"

"I don't know," he said helplessly. "I don't know anything any more, or why you should care at all about what I do."

"I don't either," she said frankly. "When really you have been rather rude. My father was so displeased by my behaviour at the Frost Fair I was in disgrace for weeks—I was angry with you then for helping me into such a scrape! But I couldn't help wondering how you fared, whether you had set yourself up in a trade you liked. It took a while to see my own foolishness, for I quite thought you would come one day to Lothbury for all that you said you wouldn't."

"No, you weren't foolish, my love." Too late Adam snatched at the endearment, mind coiled into that last day at Lime Alley when he was resolved to earn enough coins to call at Lothbury before all else. "Has no one ever warned you to beware of heedless charity?"

"Oh, often! I don't listen to them. When I was a child we used to stay at a farm near Paddington Cross and I was always dreadfully worried by the lost lambs bleating. I'd run with them in my arms to find their mother and get butted for interference every time, but never learned to leave well alone. My father said I upset the ewes and thrashed me in the end, then made me learn the psalm about presumption."

Blood beat in his face at the thought of her thrashed for tenderness. "He would be more than angry if he saw you talking to me. Your maid will tell someone, I'm sure." He glanced at the woman following sullenly at their heels.

"Of course she will, but I don't care. I find it hard to feel as I ought when she is such a sourpuss, but try to think it is her duty which bids her tell on me. It isn't, of course, she enjoys bringing trouble on others."

He laughed involuntarily. "Would it help if I did call and made your acquaintance seem respectable?"

"It would help me," she said simply. "Even though it made no difference to thrashings and penitential psalms."

He stopped so suddenly that people cannoned into them, neither took any notice. "Mary, my love . . . you mean it, don't you? You would find pleasure in knowing me better?"

She nodded vigorously. "I slipped out and went to Lime Alley one day, to be surprised by my own disappointment when they said they had not the direction of your lodging. I was forced to buy yards of trimming too! Then afterwards, I was angry with you as I said, but never quite ceased to wonder what your life held. Did you ever quite forget to wonder about me?"

"No. Never. But—"

"Well then! You have prospered and no one is likely to throw you in Lothbury midden now." She touched his velvet sleeve and laughed.

She wasn't quite the same as at Frost Fair. They walked in silence while Adam tried to force his mind past the fact of Mary beside him, and consider the difference in her manner. She wasn't the same as when she greeted him, either. Then she had been simply glad to see him, candid tongue and ready concern exactly as he remembered; now she was forcing liveliness, pretending to more affection than she could possibly feel for him.

"Is anything the matter?" he asked abruptly.

"Why should there be?"

"I don't know, but there's the feel of trouble to you. I— I'd like to help if I could."

She looked away but could not hide distress, he being the shorter. "You make me seem like those horrid designing females forever seeking to use gallantry for their purposes."

Adam frowned, his mind was sluggish today but surely she spoke in riddles? "The truth, remember? Always the truth between us. I've said I'll come to Lothbury if it will help, what is it you want of me there?"

Her expression cleared and she threw back her head as impulse seized its moment. "I have been facing a disagreeable future a long time now. Adam, would you offer for me?"

He stared at her, dumbfounded. "You don't know me!"

She gave an involuntary gurgle of amusement and was herself again. "I don't know my other suitors either, except Arthur, whom I detest."

Adam remembered the unpleasant youth he had seen at Frost Fair. "The one I saw before? He is treating for you with your father?"

She nodded. "He is the best of them."

"The best! Dear God, Mary, in all this great city there must be a fairer choice for you."

He watched her lips curve into tenderness, colour deepen in her face. "I think so, too," she said quietly, at last.

He had thought this day to risk life and liberty for the sake of profit, never dreaming that Mary would be offered in hazard too, if only he dared accept the stake. But he must choose for both of them, knowing full well the hurtful traps built into such a counterfeit proposal, for Mary saw him only as escape from others she disliked. He could fathom little of her thoughts, but perhaps she considered an absence of distaste sufficient for regard to strike deeper roots. Unsophisticated though he might be, Adam understood more of life than she. Above all, he realised he was unlike any image she could hold of him, a wanderer through life made harshly solitary by adversity.

Yet with her alone, words did not shatter dreams, only transformed them into reality. When he spoke to her he knew he would be understood, would not be diminished by incomprehension or rejection. She accepted what he was, and what he was not, and so released him from confinement.

Really, there was no choice. This was his chance, which would not come again if he refused to hazard his life's blood on it. This must be right, or there was no rightness in the world. He did not truly believe it, but wanted to, very much.

He held her, hands on slim waist heedless of passers-by. "I'll come tomorrow and ask for permission to pay my addresses. I'll be refused, of course, but the offer stands, time gained for your mind to settle. If by any chance I do not come, then forget me; it'll mean I can't come, ever."

Her face was so close to his he saw gladness grow there, and then alarm. "What is it, Adam? What should keep you tomorrow from a pledge sworn today?"

"I can't tell you. Never, do you understand? There are certain things about me you must never ask; I'll give you time to think about it, never fear. I am pledged to you, but you aren't bound to me until the day we marry. I'll understand if you can't bear it once you know me better and feel the burden

382

of places you must never tread, thoughts you may never share. This is the first of them; if I don't come tomorrow, then my love is yours always, but never expect me in the future."

"I shan't ask but hope that one day you will tell me, because you want to. That's the past, though, you can still alter whatever you planned to do tonight. For my sake, Adam, please. No matter how urgent your affairs may seem."

Her fingers dug into his arm through rich cloth, exactly where the brand had sunk into flesh. He bit his lip, something was exposed there and although it pained him little usually, pressure stabbed like metal on a rotted tooth. I shall have to do something about my arm and back to hide shame from her sight, he thought, dismayed.

He moved his arm and saw hurt at what seemed his withdrawal. "I can't, Mary. I have survived a good deal over the years with very little to live for, now I have so much I shall surely manage better still." He would need every penny he could glean to overcome opposition to Mary marrying him.

"And you look it," she flashed. "I recognised you at once, could never be mistaken, yet there is a great deal I do not recognise. You are not the same boy of whom I cherished so singular a memory since Frost Fair."

"No. That's one of the things I want you to understand beyond possibility of mistake. I never was a boy for easy cherishings, nor a child either. Only a man, very much alone but who loves you with life itself. I don't know whether it's enough for our happiness."

Her expression softened, but there was a gleam in her eye. "Speak for yourself, Adam Furnival. I'm astonished now by my boldness in what I asked of you, except I knew you wanted it; but now it's done, you aren't contributing everything and I taking."

He laughed and the moment passed, but when he kissed her fingers on parting she held his tight. "Take care. I will pray for you all night. Rest a little before you go wherever you are bound, or you won't last."

They were the only words she had spoken which suggested that she noticed physical changes in him as well as new harshness. Yet of course she must have done, for he knew himself very much altered by the many consequences of Newgate.

He had no time to rest, already dangerously late for what he must do. He was due to meet Attorney Etherington at the

Saracen's Head off Gracechurch Street and he relied on precise preparation to keep him from disaster.

He was nervous and unsettled, thoughts straying to Mary when they should have been anchored to the job in hand. He picked up his quarry as he crossed Fenchurch Street, talking earnestly to a colleague; Adam had intended to accost him there, now he hung back impatiently. Etherington could not be such a fool as to think he would do business with a man who brought friends to such a meeting.

The two men parted at the corner of Gracechurch Street, and Etherington went on alone, a single guard at his back as stipulated. He did not look nervous, rather eager and interested in everything around him, and again Adam felt premonition stir. It was no light matter for an attorney to carry gold to meet a master of thieves in the dark; he should have been uneasy.

Time was slipping by while Adam hesitated. Time when he could have made his move and did not. Etherington disappeared into the Saracen's Head and Adam walked around the courts surrounding it before returning. There was no sign of ambush, but still he lingered, watching from a doorway. Then, at last, he stopped a boy and sent him in with a message: Etherington was to leave the tavern and start walking towards Eastcheap.

It seemed a long time before he came out, a man of medium height with a keen, clever face and light walk. Another careful look round and Adam quickened his pace and spoke his usual warning not to look behind. "Turn into Fish Hill, and cross to the second court along."

Etherington's footsteps clicked calmly on. "I did not think you would be carrying a dozen oils and crate of silver with you."

"Difficult for running if you try to trap me," agreed Adam evenly. He felt more relaxed now it had begun. "Tell your guard to walk in front. You can hear I'm alone."

Fish Hill was an unlit cavern, strewn with rubbish. Adam ordered Etherington to wait and all three stood tensely, as if they were colleagues, listening for following feet. There was nothing except the usual sounds of night and after a while Adam motioned him forward again. "I will hand you a key. Unlock the door where we stop and go into the room on your right." He slipped on a mask such as women still occasionally wore, and pulled his hat low. He was certain Etherington would try to look once they were inside.

He handed over flint and steel and told the guard to kindle

a lamp set just inside the door. When the wick caught, stacked canvases and cases showed faintly in the dim light. "Check what you will before we count the guineas you have brought. Then your guard may stay behind locked doors while you arrange for carriers."

Etherington shook his head. "Strange as it seems, I do not expect to find you've cheated me. The law deals in motive, and you have taken a deal of trouble to build up a trade of trust." He poked about desultorily and turned suddenly when he was at the far end of the room.

"A long cloak and a mask," said Adam hardly. "I could have shot you for it, but you haven't gained much from breaking your sworn word. Put the gold on the table and turn your back again."

Etherington shrugged, but showed no sign of discomfiture. No sensible man kept faith with thieves. He untied a bag and counted out coins, handing one over occasionally when Adam asked to see it as a check. It was done at last, rebagged and safely stowed, silence growing oppressive. Adam moved instantly then, cracking his pistol against the guard's head and tripping Etherington in the same movement, while their minds were still on guineas and stolen goods.

He whipped through the door and stopped dead. A knot of men stood in the yard outside, cudgels in their hands. He recoiled and slammed over the locking bar. There was a window he had left open for just such an emergency, down a passage and giving on a different court. He cannoned into Etherington in the dark and both fell; Adam felt hands on his throat before he tore himself free, kicking out blindly and striking something hard. He gained just enough time to reach the window and let himself down the awkward drop, shouts sounding in the house as well as at the corner of street and court ahead. He had underestimated Etherington, he must have had men walking the streets to watch wherever they went, knowing they must come somewhere secluded to make such a transfer.

Adam used whatever skill suggested itself to escape pursuit. Normally he would have explored the whole neighbourhood minutely, this time he knew the general layout but not each passageway and shadow. Balked by a blank wall, he took to a rickety stair and sprawling, tumbledown roofs. The gold was uncomfortably heavy to carry, the bag at his waist conspiring against silent and rapid movement. He was damned if he would leave it, though. This was his stake, part of his bribe for Mary's love, while he had breath he would keep it.

Children screamed and dogs barked when he landed heavily in a courtyard, rotted timber giving under his hands. He discovered a packing shed of feathers and hastily split half a dozen bales, fleeing in a spew of white while his pursuers sneezed and slithered after him. Then they settled to their task in earnest, calling to each other and heading off escape from street to street. The lanes were like drains, dark but linking more logically than in Alsatia. It was quite possible to stop the ends and move inwards on a man alone, while the inhabitants shouted and complained but left armed pursuers unmolested.

There were at least two dozen of them, Adam decided, while he crouched behind a wall gasping for breath. With a couple of hundred guineas at stake and cudgels hired for a shilling, no doubt Etherington considered the outlay worthwhile. Booted feet went past his hiding place with a rush and turned a corner. Now, Adam stood carefully, his hand on clinking gold, and went back the way he had come. Only a hundred yards away lay Eastcheap and then the familiar maze of alleys around Lime Street. His body felt stiff and awkward, a week before he had lacked strength to leave his bed for the taproom. You will not last unless you get some rest, Mary had said: he smiled into the dark, it would take a while to become used to someone caring what he did.

It was dangerous to allow his thoughts to stray. He heard a shout as he turned into the next court and again there was a rush of feet, this time from all around. He ran, doubling through yards and alleys, down steps leading to the river; they were driving him away from Eastcheap and towards the trap of wharves and Thames mud. He mingled with some people at an eel stall and they missed him again, then lay under a deserted booth while they searched to pick up his trail. They were very thorough, and knew he was somewhere close; they would not miss him if he stayed. He took a chance and ran when the moon next went behind a cloud, chest hurting now, breath scorching in his lungs. The Custom House and Billingsgate ahead. He knew his way better here, leaped for the top of a wall and pulled himself over. He fell amongst stacked boards and lay semi-conscious while his mind screamed at him to stand. Through thunder in his ears he heard shouts again, somehow staggered across the timber merchant's yard, pulled himself over the far fence, and dropped on the other side.

It was a greater drop than he had hoped and he sprawled on fish scales. He was very nearly finished, but stripped off coat and waistcoat and picked up a fish creel, covering bagged gold with slithering, still-live fish. He had worked in Billingsgate through many nights since earning a penny for Francis Child; breathing in retching gasps, he went in search of someone he knew.

He was swinging up fish by the time Etherington's cudgel men arrived, and after a cursory search they knew their task was hopeless. Five hundred men and boys worked in Billingsgate on a busy night and they had not seen their quarry's face, lacked certainty he was there when no one would answer questions.

Adam returned to the Red Feathers with the dawn, limping, foul-smelling, but carrying his gold. He was exhausted but slept uneasily, sweating with nightmares. When he woke he lay on boards and stared at blue, serene sky. After sharing with Will, he had gained just over a hundred pounds from the night; added to what he'd already saved, it would simply have to do. He had asked Mary for one more night, not months or years of double-life she must not share. He grinned and threw back coverings; he was fortunate to have an excuse for discretion when he did not think he could face more dealings like the near disaster of the night.

He felt good, although bruised and with that sulky ache still in his chest. He whistled while he sharpened his knife and shaved, dressed in his remaining good clothes. This was the day of his happiness, sensation fresh-minted and joyous: Adam Furnival was twenty-two and in love for the first time in his life. Mary was everything he had thought unattainable; free of doubts, free of the crude harshness which was all the world had previously held for him. He did not find it surprising that two meetings should be sufficient for him to be so certain, would have considered it astonishing if he had not recognised such a self-evident truth when it was presented to him. He was bitterly experienced in the struggle for survival but remained almost childishly naïve emotionally, never having experienced a close relationship with anyone: he had loved his father but not lived in the same house with him.

Adam realised that he was embarking on a completely new phase of his life and rejoiced in it, but knew too little to wonder whether twenty-two years of isolation might not have left his senses as stunted as his body. All his thoughts were of how

387

quickly he could make a success of his new venture and so bribe Mary's father to accept his suit; he loved Mary and for him only the mechanism of their happiness still required arrangement. In Newgate he had persuaded himself that she regarded him in the light of a freak at the fair: so different as to be temporarily intriguing. But yesterday she had preferred him to other, richer men, and he was humble enough to think that perhaps he suited her purposes. Misgivings and caution had vanished in the night, since for him this was sufficient, more than he had ever expected for himself, and he offered Mary the time until they wed to find out whether it was also enough for her. She liked him a little, he was sure.

"I'm finished, Will," he said bluntly when he came downstairs. "I owe you nothing and intend to go my own way now."

"What way can ye go wivvout me an' the Fevvers? Ye may sell to flash coves, ye'll never be able to prig on yer own."

"Nor can I sell much longer without ending on the gallows. I told you, I'm finished, my ways have become too well known for safety. I'm taking my winnings while I can."

Will was regretful but unsurprised. He had not expected Adam to last so long, although a nubbing at Tyburn rather than retirement had been his expectation. He divided the gold from the night before, and even escorted Adam out of Whitefriars with his share. "Watch out for yerself," he said when they reached the Strand. "Ye've made me a warm man, I'd not like some cove to fancy 'e reckernised yer voice in an ale'ouse one day an' call a nark."

Adam laughed and clapped his shoulder. "By then I'll be warm enough myself to bribe witnesses into swearing I've a croaking throat when in my cups."

Will snorted. "Ye've gall enough to bribe the King 'isself."

Adam went first to see Francis Child. He had not intended to return to the Sign of the Marygold until he was a man of substance but knew he would damage his cause irreparably if he turned up at Lothbury as an impoverished nobody. He had enquired about Mary's father after he first met her: Sir John Eyles was an alderman and a singularly sharp trader, who might well sell his daughter to a man of unknown morals and breeding, providing the price was right.

A clerk eyed him dubiously when he asked if Sir Francis was in, and demanded whether he had an appointment.

"In a manner of speaking," said Adam easily. "He said he

was willing to listen to any proposition I cared to make. My name is Furnival, if you would take it to him."

Child's premises were even more prosperous-looking than before; Adam estimated that he must have at least twenty clerks scurrying in and out. It seemed a long time since he had been here before, clutching a hard-earned penny and smelling of fish. As I was again last night, he thought, and smiled, still held by tranquillity, an absence of strain he had seldom known. Mary had also rekindled confidence in his own abilities when he had held back from venturing himself again, pretending he lacked money when he had thought eight shillings sufficient only eighteen months before.

The clerk returned and reluctantly showed him upstairs, evidently Francis Child was more accessible than a jealous staff thought desirable. He received Adam in the same room, standing by the window so his visitor's face was in full light. Adam stood under scrutiny, smiling faintly. However discerning he was, there was no likelihood that Child would recognise an urchin from five years before.

"Mr. Furnival, I believe?" he said at last. "My clerk informed me of your message that we had done business together in the past, but I confess the occasion escapes me."

"I owed you a debt and came here to discharge it. You were kind enough to say we might deal in larger amounts in the future."

"A debt?" He frowned, banker's mind intrigued. "I do not often forget my debtors."

"A penny," explained Adam suavely. "Contracted when I lacked funds in Garraway's coffeehouse."

Child nodded. "I remember now. Sit down, Mr. Furnival. I am pleased to win a wager even if I made it only with myself. I thought that one day you would be back with a proposition worth the hearing."

Adam hesitated, then brought out his bag of gold. "I have a hundred and eighteen guineas here and a further five hundred and eighty with Peter Van Koek in Cornhill. I have come to you a year before I intended."

Child laughed. "Continue, Mr. Furnival. I am confirmed in my belief that it will be worth the listening."

So Adam sat down and explained his idea for taking a commission on putting shippers in touch with their cargo, owners with consignments due along their route, skippers with both. He had held it to himself for so long it was both a relief to discuss it and an almost terrifying risk. But he was older now and no longer thought a man like Francis Child would poach the ideas of others. "I have spent much of the past five years along the waterfront," he added. "I know how much need there is for reliable information when ships are often moored a month waiting for wharfage, then sail half empty because skippers and husbands can't discover sufficient cargo before their berth must be vacated."

Child sat silent a long time, then began questioning him on what he knew of quays and tides and owners; of freights and crooked captains, and their counterparts ashore. Adam was amazed by how much he knew of a trade which was not his own, enjoyed answering out of knowledge so painfully acquired.

"You said you came to me a year before you intended," Child said eventually. "The capital you have accumulated seems adequate without recourse to a loan."

"But you would make one if I asked?"

"If I saw the need for it, yes. So far, everything you have said suggests to me that you will succeed on your own, given time and care."

Adam was swept by elation. Always there had been a niggling doubt that if he consulted someone who really knew about trade and business, a flaw would appear in his schemes. "I want to offer marriage to an alderman's daughter," he said deliberately. "I do not think seven hundred pounds and a project for future profit will be sufficient recommendation of my cause."

Child stared at him. "You have surprised me this time, Mr. Furnival. You expect me to lend you capital without security, not for your business but to hand over to another? In consideration of marriage too, where you will incur further financial burdens, not profit?"

Adam nodded. "Yes."

"May I ask which alderman you had in mind?"

His tone was neutral but Adam had an idea he was amused, which might be in his favour. "Sir John Eyles, of Lothbury. Which is in confidence, since he does not know it himself yet."

"I cannot congratulate you on your choice. Eyles is known to be embarrassed financially."

"Is he, though?" Adam felt a surge of triumph. "In that case I may be able to scale down the size of loan I desire." It must be this which had delayed Mary's betrothal and confined the choice of suitors. Eyles would regard almost anyone with ready cash favourably.

Child laughed outright and went over to pour Madeira. "I have not agreed to lend for such a purpose, when I would surely be doing you no favour. If you wish to succeed in the City at the present time, you'd be wise to avoid alliance with a High Tory family."

Adam stared at him. "High Tory?"

"Didn't you know? Eyles was one of James Stuart's appointed Lord Mayors, and much hated for the part he played in suppressing the City's liberties. He does not fare well now we have our own again."

Adam jumped to his feet and went over to the window. His face was burning, and he laid his forehead against glass while he tried to think, hands clenched to stop them trembling. "When?" He swung round, nearly shouting. "In God's name, which year was he mayor?"

Child stared at him, a glass in either hand. He had thought his visitor unusual but a good business risk before, now he looked three parts insane. Not many people took politics so seriously any more. "Eighty-seven, I believe. There was Chapman after him before our liberties were restored."

Adam felt stopped blood flow again; he did not know what he would have done if Eyles had been the Lord Mayor who sat with the bench of judges who condemned his father. He did not know what he was going to do now; he sat and put his head in his hands, completely forgetting where he was.

Child touched his shoulder. "I suggest you drink and then go away and think over whatever has upset you so much. This no longer appears to me the normal kind of trading loan I would be willing to make, but be sure that I am willing to listen to a different kind of proposition in the future."

Adam drank dazedly, he had so nearly won and now was lost again. "What is your usual percentage?"

"It depends on the client. For the trade you described and to an unestablished man like yourself, fifteen percent."

"What if I transferred my funds from Van Koek to you and offered you twenty on two thousand pounds, to be used as security on my dealings?"

"For marriage?"

Adam nodded, unsure just what he did mean: his mind held to its task of raising money somehow even while he floundered with the purpose of it all.

"You show yourself a gambler rather than a man of affairs when you offer extortionate interest on money you agree to use as little more than a character reference. Fifteen percent, Mr. Furnival, since I am unlikely to lose and not a usurer by trade."

Adam stammered his thanks; he had avoided defeat but no longer knew whether victory would be endurable. How would he feel when he he saw Mary again, how bear himself to deal with Eyles at all?

"One thing still puzzles me," observed Child while they waited for a clerk to bring papers for signature. "But for your desire to marry you would not have come to me for another year, yet I cannot see great need for banking accommodation on the project you disclosed. Either it is successful or it is not, and I judge you a man who has his ventures well planned. Yet you intended to come, and borrow large sums if I am not mistaken."

Adam looked up, wretchedness peeled aside for a moment; Child was a very shrewd man and he enjoyed the experience of dealing with him. "I will be back, Sir Francis. I intend to go into banking and balances on my own account."

Child laughed. "And have premises, clerks and clients already set in your mind, no doubt."

He meant it in jest, although he took this strange fellow seriously enough; instead he saw his face tighten, the glint of unexpected malice in his eyes before lids dropped to hide them. "Yes, Sir Francis," said Adam softly. "I have the premises chosen, even if not my clients yet."

Chapter Nine

*A*dam walked for miles without any clear idea where he went. At the end of it he found himself in Lothbury, not far from the Sign of the Drake. I am pledged to you, he had said to Mary only yesterday, but not you to me until you know more about me: but he had not known one vital fact about Mary either when he bound himself to her.

Perhaps it was as well; for then he might have followed his first instinct and walked away from her. No amount of groping amongst the wreckage in his mind had helped him to a new decision; he still loved Mary, could no longer imagine facing another day without the hope of her at his side. Her parentage was not her fault, any more than he could be blamed because his mother was a harlot; the world would blame him, though, as Mary would feel a burden of reproach if she knew the barrier between them. He must never tell her, for her sake add to the places in his life where she must never tread; without realising it he wasn't thinking of past hatreds any more, only of how to shield her from their consequences. His mind eased and decision formed, although he did not know how or why.

The Sign of the Drake was one of the best design of City houses rebuilt after the fire, a trading counter and room for affairs in front, a spacious hallway beyond with curved stairs leading to family rooms above. Adam stood looking at panelling while a servant took his request for an interview to Sir John Eyles and wondered whether Child could be right when he said the man was in difficulties.

There was a sound behind him and as he turned Mary came into his arms with a rush. "Adam! You're safe! I'm sure I have promised the whole wealth of the City and my life to good works if only you were preserved!"

He held her closely. "Your life is promised to me."

She laughed and stepped back, demure when the servant returned. "I know; good works as I told you."

She could turn wretchedness instantly to joy again, doubt into certainty. He followed the servant through the house gripped by bleak determination to regard John Eyles as an antagonist to be outwitted rather than the blood-wet butcher of his thoughts. Yet as soon as he saw the man the images swept back, of scaffold, chains and gutting knife.

Eyles was checking samples, at once irritable and obsequious. It took Adam a while to realise that he hoped for trade and feared a creditor: Child had been right, after all.

Adam laid down his hat and cane, trying to estimate what he saw, but the samples strewn about were so much finer than anything at Milner's he found it difficult. For all his ambitions, he was inexperienced in the great trades of the City. "I have something of a private nature to discuss with you," he said at last. "I wonder whether you would ask your clerk to leave us for a while?"

"I don't see why I should when you, not I, demanded this interview. I haven't time to waste on mountebanks."

"I'm not seeking trade or payment, Sir John; indeed, I am anxious to bind myself in your debt." The words almost stuck in Adam's throat. One day he would ruin this man and find pleasure in it.

Eyles hesitated and then flapped a hand at his clerk. "Remain within call."

Adam smiled unpleasantly. Eyles was right to sense something amiss. God, why could Mary not have inherited different blood? "I have come to ask permission to address your daughter Mary," he said curtly, no point in shuffling, nor in more than barest courtesy either. Eyles would not betroth his daughter to a man he liked but to one who profited him.

Eyles goggled at him. "I don't even know your name!"

"Furnival. Adam Furnival."

"What of it, when I've neither heard of you nor want to! My daughter isn't to be bestowed on the first trumpery knave who comes to the door."

"Indeed, I should hope not. If you care to address yourself to Sir Francis Child or Sir Peter Van Koek you will find both acquainted with me, and able to vouch for my substance. I am

394

prepared to make generous settlements for your daughter. Also, I love her." He jerked out this last against his inclinations; he had not intended to expose himself by saying anything of the sort, yet was overcome by a sense of outrage. It was offensive to Mary to deal thus for her: let Eyles laugh if he would.

He did. "You speak as if the wench were a drab to be met on street corners. As I apprehend you did indeed meet her yesterday, if her maid is to be believed."

Adam could not trust himself to speak, and nodded instead.

Eyles's eyes narrowed as he thought of Francis Child and Peter Van Koek. This shambling scarecrow obviously deserved contempt, but he named rich sponsors. "What is your proposition?"

Adam turned sharply and went over to the window. I shall kill him in a moment, he thought, and the least of it would be for my father. "I ask permission to call on your daughter for the next month, at the end of which time, if she desires it, our betrothal would be announced. Unless she wishes subsequently to retract we would wed a year from this date; I require no dowry and pledge myself to invest a thousand guineas in your trade on the day of our betrothal, a further two thousand when we wed."

"At what percentage?"

Adam turned and folded his arms, face inscrutable. "None. I would not insult Mary by lending money on usury for her."

Eyles pulled at his lip irresolutely. Instinct warned him against this man from nowhere, who must be a scoundrel; on the other hand, he was unfortunate enough to possess two more daughters younger than Mary, and a thousand guineas without interest or provision for withdrawal would fill a serious shortfall in his current trading. "Very well. If Child and Van Koek will vouch for you, but only for three thousand on marriage. The amount pledged at betrothal is not repayable if for any reason you do not wed."

Adam picked up his hat, unwilling to linger a moment longer than necessary. "I will have it set down ready to sign within two days, which should be long enough to complete your investigations. Meanwhile, I should like to see Mary privately." If his cash was forthcoming, Eyles would be satisfied with the most cursory of enquiries.

He waited for Mary in a small parlour filled with clumsy furniture. Elegant plasterwork and large windows contrasted uneasily with oak and carvings of another age: Eyles considers it good enough for his women, thought Adam cynically, wondering for the first time what Mary's mother was like.

He found out a moment later. She came in and stood by the door, a delicate-looking woman with a sad, lined face. "My husband sent up the most extraordinary message," she said without preamble.

Adam bowed. "Yes, Lady Eyles. I desire to pay my addresses to your daughter Mary."

She frowned. "Do you know her?"

"Well enough to love her. I intend to give her a year to discover whether she is able to feel some affection for me."

She came to stare closely at his face. "I would not like to see her hurt, Mr. Furnival."

"Be at ease, ma'am. This may be business dealing between your husband and my bankers, it is very far from being so between Mary and myself."

She smiled then, the same glorious, wholehearted smile as her daughter. Once, she had been a beautiful woman and thus might Mary have looked twenty years hence if she had been sold off to some suitor she detested. "I'm so glad," she said simply. "I will send Mary to you now. You—you won't tell my husband I came, will you?"

"No," said Adam gently. "I hope in the future you will not feel you need to ask."

He felt constrained by meeting Mary alone after such great turmoil of mind, but she noticed nothing amiss and put up her face to be kissed as if they were already completely familiar with each other. He did not feel he made a very good job of it, painfully aware of inadequacy as he never had been with her before. Words froze again.

She took his hand. "Sit down, Adam. You look so tired."

Not a recommendation in a man paying his addresses, he thought, and sat. In truth he was exhausted, the aftermath of shock from Child's revelation and the night not yet outlived.

She touched his face. "What can you tell me, and what may I not ask?"

He shook his head, light dazzling against his eyes. Dear God, he must say something.

But he could not. Instead, she sat beside him, holding his hand and talking about a number of things he was unable to grasp.

"You're very sweet," he said at last, out of nowhere, and kissed her without any awkwardness at all. "Already I don't

know what I should do without a safe anchorage to come to."
He told her then quite simply of the bargain he had made with
her father. She had a right to know; not the shaming details,
but the time span and terms of betrothal.

"You've been cheated," she said, colouring with humiliation, "I don't know how much you have agreed to pay but
clearly it's more than you can afford. No dowry at all! It's
insulting to you more than to me."

He smiled and held her close. "Never. No bargain which
brought you to me could be other than what it is—a bargain.
But you are free, remember. A full year before you're pledged
and you will not shift me from it." And I shall need every
minute of each day to raise the sums I owe, he reflected sourly.

He left soon after although he could see she was disappointed, driven by the sense of how short a time there was to
earn such enormous amounts. He possessed the clothes he wore
and five hundred pounds he could draw on, two thousand he
could use as some sort of security, nothing else. Not even
lodgings, and a first payment of a thousand pounds was due
within a month.

He took a room behind the Custom House, convenient for
the wharves but noisy and comfortless. It was an inconvenient
distance from Lothbury too, and visiting Mary became a matter
for endurance and not pleasure. He needed to contact merchants
and shippers, ship's husbands and skippers, spend his nights
on the river checking ships and anchorages: after the first two
weeks he nearly despaired. As in all new ventures, confidence
in him and his information took time to develop, payments
came tardily while merchants waited to see if he could make
good his word.

He haunted the City coffeehouses too, especially Edward
Lloyd's in Lombard Street, where the great foreign merchants
met and dealt in shipping amongst themselves. He offered
deadlines against cargoes located or shipped, chaffered for a
bonus if he succeeded under time. Sometimes he failed and
had to pay a forfeit; gradually he began to succeed, learning
fast from his mistakes. But for all his efforts, time was too
short. At the end of the month he had to set aside his pride,
visit Child again and beg to draw four hundred guineas to make
up the thousand he owed Eyles. He brought lists of bargains
already struck and after studying them Child agreed without
comment, but warning was implicit when he signed the draft,
observing: "Remember, Mr. Furnival, that debts take longer

397

to recover than payments to make. A sound business cannot be built in a hurry."

Adam knew it, but had no choice. Four thousand pounds was a great deal of money to make in a year, and still have enough to support a wife at the end of it.

London was thriving in spite of the war, fortunes made and lost with extraordinary speed, heady excitement gripping normally sober merchants as vast possibilities of trade and profit came to seem almost commonplace. Nothing was too strange or too unlikely to be tried; Adam was only one of many setting out with very little and believing they would become rich by flair, by luck and hard work, by seizing the coattails of London's surging prosperity. Many failed and some succeeded, often only to fail again as ambition outleaped prudence. Adam was no gambler except in this one matter of Mary and intended to hold his gains once he had them, but whatever he tried, however hard he worked, he simply could not gather sufficient monies to keep his bargain with Sir John Eyles.

He did not find Mary her buoyant self when he visited her either, snatched meetings insufficient to build the relationship he craved. In early January, with eight months of his time gone, he fell asleep in unaccustomed warmth before her hearth and woke, chest tight with shock, to find her watching him gravely.

"I'm sorry," he said dazedly, hands to his face, elbows on his knees. "That was inexcusable when I come so seldom."

He heard cloth rustle and then her fingers were on his wrists, pulling his hands from his face. "It doesn't matter. But, Adam . . . it does matter that you hide from me and will not share your troubles."

He stared at his ugly, lumped hands held in her delicately shaped ones; she was kneeling in front of him, face tipped to his with a kind of angry concern. "All right," he said slowly. His words slurred for a moment, his chest stabbed fiercely, then pain dulled again. "There is a great deal I should tell you and have not. I don't think I can pay your father all I owe in the time, and he will hold me to the letter of our bargain. Child and Van Koek vouched for me because they think I could succeed in the future, not because I have resources now."

She nodded. "Do you think you should be ashamed of not being able to earn four thousand pounds within a year?"

"How did you know the amount?" he demanded, startled.

"I asked, and my father told me, as any man would who is well satisfied with his bargain. I was bitterly ashamed when I understood what you had agreed to for me, and told him so. Even my brother took my part, and was heartily cursed for it."

"What happened to you?"

"I was beaten, and left two days in my room." She smiled faintly. "For once I was glad you did not come for a while."

He sat, graven, wrists still held in her hands. He had intended to tell her of the pain in his chest, more frequent these past punishing months. The onset of another Thames winter tried him severely, the brutal discomforts of his life on three hours' sleep a night almost more than he could endure. His dream of happiness with Mary had withered under the impact of failure and he had faced what in his heart he had always feared: it was a dream and nothing more. He was no fit person for Mary Eyles to wed and by now she must realise it as well as he; with infinite sadness he had fought to the decision that he must ask Mary to release him from his pledge. Now he thought of her beaten for him, of her other suitors gone off and unlikely to be replaced as Eyles's repute declined, and knew he had not the right to abandon her and withdraw.

He looked up at last. "I promised you until we wed to make up your mind, a year at least, or so I thought. Only once before have I broken my given word, but there are worse things and leaving you here any longer is one of them, when your father's ill-temper is redoubled because of the dislike he bears me. If you do not find the prospect too distasteful, then by my reckoning the time has come to struggle as best we may together, and be damned to the pack of them."

Slowly, her hold tightened and she kissed his fingers, face soft against his hands. "Oh, Adam, yes. Neither of us can go on much longer like this, and together we will be so happy."

"I can't offer—"

"Who cares what you can offer? I am so very weary of being traded like bale goods in a warehouse, and don't you dare talk of distaste as if you meant it, either! I'm not at all a patient person, you know."

"You'll need to be patience itself with me. I'm not an attractive fellow to have as a husband, nor an easy one, although I love you more than I can say." Adam felt depressed rather than triumphant, aware that he was as little able to estimate her feeling for him as on the day they met.

"Who cares for that, either!" She surveyed him, eyes sparkling. "Adam, you must stop being so fusty about matters you

399

cannot help! It would be more useful if you would consider instead how we are to marry tomorrow."

He laughed and pulled her to her feet. Now she was herself again he realised how much she had changed during recent weeks. And as delight returned, certainty was reborn too; he swung instantly from wretchedness to absurd optimism. In spite of everything, his dream still lived.

Wherever he had placed cargoes these past months, Adam had been careful not to assist Sir John Eyles in his dealings. He detested the man and it was also a small revenge for the extortion which had hamstrung his efforts so far; above all, he knew by now that Eyles was desperate and not a shrewd trader. He should be easier to deal with than eight months before.

Adam saw him in his storeroom immediately he left Mary. "I am not prepared for my affianced wife to be beaten at your whim," he said without preamble. "Bid someone bring pen and paper and we will rewrite our bargain."

"A bargain is a bargain," said Eyles uneasily, disliking his visitor's expression.

"And can be unmade if both parties agree. I'm not leaving this room without your consent to Mary wedding me next week."

"I don't know what you mean. April was the month agreed, and three thousand guineas owed for my consent."

"Five hundred now would save you a deal of trouble with your creditors," said Adam brutally.

Eyles moistened his lips. "Five hundred now, the rest in April."

"You mistake my meaning. Five hundred now to be quit of my agreement."

He laughed in Adam's face. "I can wait, and beat Mary when she displeases me."

"No," said Adam softly. "No, I don't think so. Shall I tell you something I have told no other man alive? Under James Stuart my father was murdered by the likes of you. I cannot imagine a greater pleasure than bringing about your ruin, and never doubt that I would succeed. I know a score of forgers who could produce your signature on any document I chose, for all that I am respected now and deal with the great merchants of the City. If I wed your daughter secretly and never paid you a penny piece, by the time you brought a case against me I'd have a vault full of papers sworn to prove you the scoundrel you are. Sign a new agreement for five hundred now, and five hundred at the year's end, or I will do it. Even Mary's pleadings could not turn me from pleasure I so much desire."

Eyles signed, and a week later Adam Furnival and Mary Eyles were married by bishop's leave in St. Margaret's Church, Lothbury.

~ *IV* ~

MARY

1697–1704

Love makes the heart gentle.
HERBERT—proverbs
1651

Chapter One

Mary Furnival lay on the wide bed and watched shadows flicker in the light of a dying fire. There was movement downstairs, so Adam would soon come up; she frowned and twisted slightly to find a more comfortable position, hands on her swollen belly. He ought not to be so late, drive himself until the ashen look she dreaded came to his face. They had enough to live comfortably, a year after they moved out of tumbledown lodgings into this little house in Clement Lane.

It was a wedge of brick between St. Clement's Church and the Bull Tavern, but being near Lombard Street the neighbourhood was safe enough for her to walk out in day light and the house itself a joy after they scrubbed it from eaves to cobbles. Adam refused to take lodgers, so they had it to themselves, however tight this made their household costs: the ground floor for Adam's affairs and cooking in the yard, on the first a parlour and a slip of a back room, on the second this bedroom and another like a cupboard for the baby when it came. Mary shifted again and smiled. After three years' marriage there was to be the child she longed for. In the eaves above lived Rebecca, a maid of all work hired the week before; until then Mary had done everything.

Adam's step on the stairs now.

She turned on the bed and held out her arms when he opened the door. "I nearly came a dozen times to beg you to finish."

He sat on the bed and kissed her. "You ought to be asleep."

"Of course I wouldn't sleep until you came! So it's useless to shuffle the blame onto me when you insist on working until one in the morning." The bell of St. Clement's struck just above the roof, making the windows hum. "Two o'clock." She wanted to rail at him for obstinacy, beg him to spare himself a little, but held silent. Now was not the time, when he was already exhausted and would only be upset by anything she said.

He sat holding her, very still in the faint glow of the fire. "How are you feeling?"

She brought his hand to her face so he could feel her smiling. "Impatient. Adam, love, lie beside me tonight."

He stiffened. "You need rest."

"So do you. Don't you think we might both find it easier together?"

"I shall disturb you in the morning."

"No. I'll come with you to St. Clement's; it's Sunday, or had you forgotten? There's no need to rise at dawn, and I should dearly love for once to wake with you beside me."

There was a long silence, she could see nothing beyond his shape in dimness. The bed creaked when he stood at last. "Very well, if you wish it." His tone was hurtful, as if she was importuning him, and despite herself she felt tears on her cheeks. In most ways he was extraordinarily kind and thoughtful, which made hurt harder to endure. Until she married, Mary had lived all her life in a household haunted by its master's moods, by fear of violence when he was angry, by the need to defer to his views, by anxiety, when he was thwarted or unsuccessful. She thought it was Adam's gentleness and lack of self-regard which first attracted her and enabled her to discover his other qualities; the tough resilience of his mind and strength of will hidden by his quiet manner, his warmth and passion on the few occasions she was able to uncover either. For though he warned her of it, she had been unprepared for the fact that he was an intensely private man who never allowed her to share what she sensed were heavy burdens of mind and spirit. He never lost his temper either and in three years had not once struck her; brought up as she had been in an atmosphere of blows and in a society where physical punishment was taken for granted, this seemed very wonderful to her. Yet he could also be remorselessly unforgiving: he refused absolutely to have her father in his house though she begged him to let old grudges rest, and declined a loan with every evidence of satisfaction when Alderman Eyles was desperate for credit.

He also made her beg for his presence in her bed.

Mary wiped the easy tears of late pregnancy carefully from

her cheeks, it would never do for her to be weeping when he came. For this was a humiliation she found hard to bear, the way he forced her into being the suppliant when, if he chose to come, he was an ardent and considerate lover. And after loving he nearly always slept elsewhere, leaving her coldly desolate.

He came now, piling coal into the grate to give a fire for the morning before lying on his side of the bed without any caress first. Mary felt no nearer understanding him than three years ago, further perhaps, since she was unaware then of the contradictions of his nature. Sometimes she thought he was surprised to find her tender, startled out of response by an unexpected gesture of affection, as if he did not expect her to feel for him at all. It was alarming to find him shying at her touch after years of marriage, needlessly hurtful when he refused to discuss anything of his life before he met her. The slightest disagreement was met by silence, their occasional quarrel bringing wretchedness so obvious that she felt a brute even when the fault was his.

Mary was not sophisticated or well tutored, but she was intelligent, compassionate and eagerly generous. Adam loved her, she knew, and she refused to yield to despair when he continued to shut her away from so much of his life. She was also young enough to believe that life was full of magic keys and miraculous cures; Adam had freed her from a distasteful future, one day she would free him too, and gain full measure of the love she sought.

For she loved him now as she had not three years before, as he knew she had not and accepted it as natural. Then, she had felt pity and curiosity for one so totally removed from her experience, found him an unexpectedly amusing companion and sensed integrity; his appearance intriguing rather than unpleasant as he thought it. There were others in the City striving to reach from the gutter to riches in a single lifetime, who shared with him the consequences of ill-treatment. Instead of ungainliness Mary had come to see the fine shaping of bone and feature, admire the way adversity had not corrupted him. She enjoyed watching his expression change when she came close, the softer line of mouth and slackening of tension; for woman-like she recognised at their first meeting the enchantment she held for him, felt pleasantly flattered and considered herself the giver when she grasped at the escape he offered. That time was infinitely far distant; Mary might not have loved

Adam when she married him but she was affectionate, loyal to his interests and delighted by the freedom he had given her. She responded eagerly when his starved emotions unfolded in her warmth, and as love grew felt shamed by the unthinking arrogance of her previous attitude to him; believed herself to blame for the remaining disharmony in their relationship.

As time passed she became less sure of this, when each day hammered home how patient she must be and he continued to reject so much she offered him. But by nature, as she had told him, Mary was not patient, rather impulsive and confiding: it was impulse which had made her offer him absurd encouragement at Frost Fair and so triggered all the rest. Now she was three years wed to an unusually complex man and must somehow learn to curb her nature if they were ever to have a chance of gaining what both so greatly desired.

"Go to sleep," he said, almost roughly, when she moved closer to him now. "You need your strength for what is to come."

"I'm well, Adam. Don't worry so, when already you make me rest half the day. I want to be a wife as well as mother." It was nearly two months since he had made love to her, and she wondered whether he was glad of the excuse to sleep alone.

He pulled her to him fiercely then. "Ah no, my love. Do you think I could bear not to take any precaution which might help preserve you for me? My mother told me once that she was fortunate not to die with me, and feared a dozen deaths at each birthing afterwards."

She was silenced by astonishment. He had never mentioned his mother before; her father openly referred to him as a foundling brat and she accepted it as a likely explanation for his aloneness and aggressive pride. "Yet she survived and so will I, never fear," Mary replied at last, careful, very careful now if she wanted to learn more.

"There would be no life without you," he said against her hair.

He had not denied it, so his mother probably still lived. "Adam, is there anyone we should tell when the child is born? I know you have no dealings with your—your family, but a birth is such a happy time. Should we not at least send word?"

"You'll not wheedle me that way. Birth or no birth, your father isn't crossing my threshold. Send him word by all means, but do not bid him come; your mother is always welcome."

"We did not speak of my father, but perhaps of yours," she said quietly.

She was completely unprepared for the violence of his reaction. He snatched his arms from her and flung out of bed; in dim blue flame she could see him sitting on its edge with his head in his hands. She lay petrified a moment, then knelt and held him, clinging when he tried to push her away. His body was icy. She could feel chill through the quilted nightgown he wore even in their most intimate moments: another discontent Mary could not avoid was the way he took pleasure in her naked body yet denied his to her.

"Adam, for pity's sake, what have I said?"

He shook his head. "Go to sleep and leave me be."

Above the rafters Clement's bell boomed three; somehow, she must make him rest. It always ended thus. Whenever she came close to what she sought he shut her ruthlessly away: with love and caresses, with silence, hurt, or sheer driving weariness which struck persistence dumb.

This time she could not quite accept it, and in the end he lay back and allowed her to hold him until the shuddering ceased. "I'm sorry," he said at last. "I don't deserve such happiness as you give each moment of your life. My mother lives, but my father is long dead. Until I met you he was the only person I ever loved."

Her heart lifted to this first crack in his reserve, but she asked no more, anxious he should not feel that confidence was immediately met by more questions, and after a while, he slept.

She lay listening to his breathing, watching strengthening light pick out the bones and hollows of his face. He was twenty-five years old and looked forty. With increasing prosperity he wore a wig in the daytime, in a winter's dawn she saw that his own cropped hair was already greying above his ear.

Her labour pains began a week later, and her son born without great difficulty early the following morning. He yelled instantly, confidently, wasting no time about imprinting his personality and needs on the household.

"Lor', mam," said Rebecca when she brought him to Mary later. "He'll be a proper divil if we don't get 'im by the scruff of the neck at once." She watched complacently while he fed, bunched fists on Mary's breast as if squeezing the last drop.

"He's lovely," said Mary, the tug at her breast a pleasure unimaginable before.

Rebecca sniffed. "'E'll cut up our peace proper, you mark my words."

"Who cares?" said Mary, hugging him. "It's what a home is for, after all."

Adam came while the baby slept beside her, meticulously dressed and barbered as always; he was almost fanatically clean, as if he could not leave squalor far enough behind. He looked tired though; Mary could vaguely remember him supervising the midwife through the pain-shot night, keeping her skills free from the geneva spirits which were the sustenance of her calling. Husbands normally approached wives in childbirth only to take their leave if they were dying, but Adam was not a man to consider convention if he thought his presence necessary.

"Sit down," said Mary, rousing herself. "Has Rebecca given you anything to eat?"

He laughed and sat. "Don't fuss, woman. I can go to the ordinary when I feel like it."

He was completely sober too, realised Mary. His digestion was too delicate for him to drink much, but a birthing was an excuse for drunkenness even when a man cared little for his children, and Adam cared deeply, she could see.

"He's perfect," she said shyly.

He nodded. "I know, I looked...I couldn't help looking when Rebecca washed him. Like you, my sweet Mary."

"Like you too," she said swiftly. "The only difference being that I pray he will not have to struggle for life as you were forced to."

He did not reply; she had not realised until then that he feared fathering some monstrosity. She drowsed with his hand in hers and woke much later to find him still there. The fire had crumbled into ash and outside it was snowing hard. Mary snuggled lower, feeling enormously content and safe from all the ills of the world. "I hope you slept too."

He stood stiffly and went over to the fire. "Yes, and was thankful for an excuse not to be on the wharfside."

"How much longer must you go to each anchorage yourself? Surely you could afford clerks to watch for you soon?"

"I do have a dozen boys, and every tavernkeeper from Queenhithe to Deptford paid for reliable information. It still needs a deal of supervision which only I can give."

"And daily calls on most merchants of importance. Adam, I have tried not be a nagging wife but surely you must see that you cannot go on driving yourself so hard?"

410

For a moment she thought he would not answer, but had chosen her moment well. Between relief and delight, today he could deny her nothing. "In my reckoning I ought to survive another year, and then intend to change the direction of my trade."

"Tell me," she said quietly. "Surely I have a right to know your plans."

She lay back on the pillows watching his face, while he told her of designs she had never guessed he held, although from his voice she could tell that they were neither recent nor hastily conceived. "You think such a risk worthwhile?" she asked when he finished. "Abandon everything you have built and trade in balances and banking, where reputations are built up over many years?"

"I can't explain it, but it's something I must do. It won't be quite the step you think, or I once thought, either; I am already lending to finance ships in the building, and insuring cargoes against loss. I have been much helped by your forbearance in managing our home so frugally, and also by the peace, since high rates of insurance agreed a few months ago for fear of French privateers still have time to run but that particular risk has disappeared. New premises will simply emphasise a shift in my trade which is already taking place; information is as vital to a banker as to a shipper, so I can profit both ways."

"New premises? Adam, no! I love this little house of our happiness."

He came over and kissed her. "As I do; but a fine mansion in Cheapside will be better still, and fulfilment of a lifetime's ambition."

There was something in his voice which made her uneasy. Pride in accomplishment, yes, but something else as well. An implacable ring which would allow nothing to stand in his way. Not security, nor the comfort gained by nearly successful endeavour, certainly not her wishes. His glance fell to the sleeping child swaddled by her side. "We'll call him Henry."

Mary shivered and did not know why. "Adam, please, no. It—it is not a name I fancy."

He stared at her with depth of hostility which shook her. "Why not?"

She did not know, only instinct telling her of something wrong. "Could we not call him Francis, when you feel so indebted to Sir Francis Child?" Child was this year Lord Mayor, the latest of a series of eminent and determined men who had held office since restoration of the charter; as if the City recognised its own fault in too often shuffling the position off on nonentities before.

"If you wish; it would be a pleasant compliment. Henry Francis Furnival, it sounds well enough." His voice was flat, definite. He turned and left the room.

Mary did not dare protest again, when she had no reason for her dislike of the name, only for its effect on Adam. So their son was christened in St. Clement's without anyone but themselves and some business acquaintance present.

Adam refused to invite Sir John, so Mary's mother stayed away too, and when Mary again suggested that Adam should inform his mother that she had a grandson, he curtly bade her not to meddle in his affairs.

But for Henry Francis Furnival bellowing throughout the ceremony, the church would have seemed very bleak and empty.

Chapter Two

The Peace of Ryswick, which ended the war between England, Holland and their enemy France, brought still more prosperity to London. Elsewhere in the country the cessation of army contracts meant hardship and unemployment, a run of bad harvests adding to the misery, but freed from the daily bleeding of ships sunk on the trade routes, London thrived. Even bad harvests meant that corn must be imported and stored, and only London had sufficient facilities to handle the bulk needed. Exports required expert financing, which the bankers of the City could best provide; re-exports of silk, tobacco, sugar, rum and other products of East and West were too valuable to be despatched without a wide spread of insurance: only in the City could a merchant's clerk obtain enough signatures in a morning to make the transaction safe. Coinage was short, so the City bankers wrote notes on their own credit; investment needed for ships and agriculture and colonies, so London merchants set up correspondents throughout the country and sucked in the profits of the nation, then lent them again well multiplied, sometimes with unwise optimism. Rates of interest were coming down, buildings, squares, whole new areas of the metropolis sprang up. King William built a new palace in the outlying village of Kensington, his Queen a splendid hospital for sailors designed by Wren at Greenwich; prosperous tradesmen hid new dwellings behind the old to evade building restrictions, while there were few aristocrats too far gone in drink and gaming not to consider increasing their income by granting speculative leases wherever it might be profitable: Islington Heath, Bloomsbury Fields and Chelsea water meadow, with its horse-drawn ferry across the Thames, were joining May Fair Fields under piled brick.

There were panics, shortages and disasters, often caused by sheer exuberant optimism. But most Londoners learned fast, were ruthlessly acquisitive and unmerciful towards failure. Above all, the great merchants now managed government finances with a confident hand; let politicians squabble if they wished, the City controlled the power which mattered. After some near catastrophes the Bank of England was well settled, its directors considering acquiring their own premises as they became too splendid to continue using Grocers' Hall indefinitely. The Crown could no longer demand loans without warning, threaten state bankruptcy and plunge the delicate machinery of trade into disarray for its own selfish purposes. The Bank now settled such matters, its directors said austerely, and did so to their own advantage, and usually that of the nation too. The navy was regularly paid since it guarded trade; eventually the merchants grudgingly recognised the need to maintain an army too. Armies were not profitable, and dangerous politically, but they did win wars. The great French fortress of Namur fell in 1696 largely because the English-Dutch army did not disintegrate for lack of pay, and the Peace of Ryswick followed, in which Louis of France at last acknowledged William as King of England, the Stuarts a lost cause.

The merchants of the City congratulated themselves on their patriotism and discussed celebrating their victory with fireworks; although the bulk of the army had been Dutch, London was paymaster of them all—or regarded itself as such. The City fathers also arrested a few deluded ruffians who persisted in referring to James Stuart as King and presented William with a loyal address in which they bound themselves to murder anyone who murdered him. There was a pretty exchange of compliments, great ringing of bells and burning of bonfires (and fireworks) before London returned to its business of engrossing the trade of Europe as well as that of the British Isles. The world of course would follow, when Europe was itself reaching greedily into every corner of the globe.

Stench, filth and destitution also grew as London sucked in people from the far corners of the realm, and from Europe as well. Huguenots fleeing from persecution in France brought silk weaving to Spitalfields, provided an early governor of the Bank of England and a firm to print its bank notes; Portuguese Jews became leading financiers, Germans and Dutch bulk exporters, Baltic lightermen added to the weird jargon of the Thames waterfront. Rudimentary public services and parish organisation suited to a different life gave way under the strain of such tumultuous growth, law and order was swamped by such a teeming, shifting population. Some magistrates and officials tried to discharge their duty, the City Corporation had long been organised for urban life although not for the masses now inhabiting its rookeries, the rest gave up as success bred indifference to the sufferings of the unsuccessful.

The children even of comfortably situated parents had less than a one-in-three chance of living; a daughter born to Mary and Adam the year after the peace seemed to thrive, then took a fever and died within a day. It was the first great sadness of Mary's married life and she took a long time to recover her former liveliness. Fortunately, little Henry Furnival showed no sign of losing his grip on life: even when he tumbled down two flights of stairs the only damage was a bleeding nose.

He walked early, which simplified the journey to Lothbury when Mary wanted to visit her mother, as he was a sturdy child and heavy to carry far. Mary never mentioned this difficulty to Adam, since she was anxious not to become estranged from her family, and Adam more likely to forbid her journeys if he felt she was straining herself than permit her to receive her parents at home. The Eyleses had fallen on difficult times, Sir John increasingly short of temper as his embarrassments mounted. He made Mary welcome, though, and was proud of his grandson, even if he did say that it was a pity he had inherited his father's grey eyes, since otherwise no one would take him for Adam Furnival's son at all. Henry was a square, forthright child who bade fair to become a well-built, demanding man. Mary thought he inherited rather too much of his father's obstinacy, but did not hide it so well. He also possessed an endearing sense of fun and helped lighten the atmosphere in their Clement Lane house, which was by no means always easy.

One day when she returned from Lothbury, Mary found an elderly, tear-stained woman waiting for her in the upstairs parlour. "Being as how she seemed distressed like, mam, and me not wanting her fainting in the street if she waited there," said Rebecca. "Nor a-bothering the master downstairs, neither."

"No, of course not," said Mary hastily. "You did quite right, Rebecca." She pulled off her bonnet and went into the parlour, a little surprised to find the woman was completely unknown to her.

"I didn't know what I should do and that's the truth," said her visitor, sucking newly fashionable bohea through blackened teeth. "But I were that desperate I thought I'd come. I saw 'ee one day wi' the babby an' thought to meself ye'd be a one who'd not scorn to listen to an old woman."

"Of course not," said Mary soothingly. "Pray tell me in what way I may help you. I don't think, though, that I've ever—"

"No, mistress, we h'ain't never met, that's what brings me to despair. I can't understand it, and that's the truth. If I could, then Martha, I'd say to meself, this is what you must do. No crying about spilled milk, but cut straight to the remedy, that's me. But I don't know which way to turn, nor why I should turn at all, in a manner of speakin'. So I'm beat, see?"

"Not exactly," confessed Mary, bewildered. "I understand you're in some trouble, but not why you should think it in my power to help."

"There! I knewed that a lady with such a pretty, sweet face as your'n couldn' 'ave ut to do with such persickushun as me an' my Jack 'ave endured." Her eyes flickered slyly to Mary and away again. "Persickushun an' ruin, that's what. Not satisfied 'e weren't until we was in the gutter, an' my Jack struck with a 'plexy. 'E thought I wouldn't never find out 'oo was a-doin' it, but I did, see? Mr. Bowyer of Seething Lane and Mr. Edwards of Aldgate is old fren's. They didn't know, but found out from them as did. Took my las' shillin' for a-doing it, they did, too, the twistin' curs."

"They don't sound such good friends after all," said Mary drily.

"They tole me, didn' they? Last shillin' or no last shillin'. 'Twas your 'usband 'as been a-ruining us all these months. 'E's no better than a murderer, I say, with my Jack 'elpless with 'is 'plexy."

Mary's face felt tight. "I don't believe it."

"'Tis true, mistress. Your arxst 'im 'an see. An' while ye're at it, ye might arxst 'im why. Too late to beg 'im to mercy since 'e's put us in the boneyards an' my Jack's as stiff as a fish, but I just thought, Martha, I says, 'e might leave us be in the future if that pretty wife of 'is were to arxst."

Against her will, Mary believed her. The woman was not

crazed, nor particularly vindictive. She was desperate, frightened and genuinely puzzled. Oh, Adam, no.

"You want me to speak to Mr. Furnival for you?" she asked at last. "Do you really have no notion why he might have harmed your livelihood?"

She shook her head, threadbare wig askew.

"What is your trade? I'm afraid Rebecca did not even tell me your name."

"'Tis mercery, mistress. The best flouncing an' bugle trimming, lace from—from the Dam and suchlike places. Stay leather sometimes, though that's not quality o' course. The name's Milner, late o' Lime Alley an' now o' the Turk's 'Ead in Leaden'all."

"Lime Alley," said Mary slowly, mind flickering. She had ventured there once to enquire for Adam after the Frost Fair. "It's not an area where my husband trades, nor is mercery his business."

"'Twas a warm little shop we 'ad. All lost, an' now I'm like to lose me savin's too. I tell you, 'e's a divil that 'usband o' yourn."

"I cannot listen to you speaking ill of my husband," said Mary coldly, although she wanted to weep. "If you would return tomorrow at three o'clock, I will ask him whether there is any way in which his affairs might be hurting yours unfairly, but it is for him to adjust the matter if he wishes. Good even to you, Mistress Milner."

The woman eyed her maliciously. "Hoity-toity. You know it's true, but h'ain't willin' to chance an 'iding if you arxst 'im." She lurched to her feet, wheezing. "I'll be back termorrer, an' we'll see if'n ye've 'ad the common guts to risk it."

Mary was so much upset by this interview that young Henry took serious exception to her singing of his nighttime lullaby. Her normally true, sweet voice sounded absurdly husky and he hammered his heels on the boards of his bed, remorselessly demanding attempt after attempt.

"Be quiet, scoundrel," said Adam from behind her. "Your mother is weary and if you were a gentleman you would be letting her rest and not clamour for more."

"Father sing," said Henry inexorably.

Adam laughed. "I've a voice like a corncrake hammered into iron. One day you'll hear the sign of it creaking outside your window, and tell yourself you hear my voice in the dark."

Henry immediately insisted on hearing more of this mysterious sign, so Adam sat and told him some farrago of nonsense until he drowsed, while Mary made her escape.

When he came downstairs she was moving aimlessly about the parlour, mind blank except for the wish not to ask him anything at all.

"What is troubling you?" he asked at once. She could never hide anything from him.

"Later," she said wretchedly. "Eat and rest awhile, then there is something I must ask you."

His face hardened. "If it is to do with your father, the answer is still no."

"No, although I wish . . . Adam, I know he dealt with you harshly when you wished to marry me and needed to borrow every guinea for your trade, but it is long past now. God forgive me, I do not love him as I ought, but if I can forgive the past, could not you also? For my sake at least, if not for his."

"No." A single monosyllable like the dropping of a portcullis.

Mary was silent, biting her lip.

Adam watched her steadily, making no attempt to come closer. "You said your trouble wasn't to do with your father. I would sooner you told me now, so I may see what I can do to help."

Mary swallowed, this was no light matter to be settled with a caress and he sensed it too. "A woman came this afternoon. She told me you had deliberately ruined her, harassed her husband until he sickened of an apoplexy."

"You believed her?"

She nodded. "Her name was Milner, of Lime Alley. She did not know why you had done it and begged me to find out, to ask your price to leave them alone. I did not tell her so, but when she said where she came from I thought I need not ask why."

"There is no way you could know why," he said sharply.

"So it is true? The best use of your newfound riches is to pay off old grudges?"

She saw the colour leave his face and felt a familiar stab of shame. In this kind of quarrel she possessed all the weapons since he never offered any defence for his actions. "Perhaps. There are some debts which demand to be paid."

"How long is it since you were out of apprenticeship, Adam?"

He looked surprised. "Nearly seven years."

She went over to him then. "My love, I know you were ill-done by, but most masters do not treat their apprentices as they ought. Why, I remember my father—" She broke off, flushing.

He laughed abruptly. "Yes, I do not think I should have fancied being his apprentice either."

"But, Adam, why harbour grievance after seven years, when most men act so? If you had—if you lashed out in a heat of fury and killed him I could understand it, but—but to revenge yourself after seven years and not be deterred when you find your prey is old and ill . . . You have harmed his wife too, who had no blame."

"You think not? Well, have it so if you will." There was a cold, unpleasant glint in his eyes.

Mary felt baffled. It would be so much easier if he would rage at her, batter down accusation with excuses. "Are you satisfied now?" she asked bluntly, unable to think of any other way to say it.

"I have done what I set out to do, what I warned them I would one day do whether they remember it now or not. They have no one to blame for disaster but themselves."

"How did you manage it? Bring them to ruin in such a way that only clients could tell them who their enemy was?"

"Yes, I was clumsy there. I did not intend them ever to find out, but it isn't easy to buy up all the stay leather in London without transactions becoming known. Since they have not connected me with their former apprentice I daresay it doesn't matter, the woman couldn't read indentures and they never thought of me as a person with surname and being of my own. Certainly they reckon me dead these seven years past."

"Why would it matter if they did know who had ruined them? Buying stay leather is legal, even if cruel when the intention is to destroy others."

"You are too sharp on a detail, aren't you, Mary? I see you are about to threaten me; be merciful to Milners who deserve to hang, or you will tell them I was once their apprentice, since you perceive such knowledge would somehow damage me. Tell them if you must, I have lived enough of my life under threat."

Mary stared at him, lips trembling, misery a tight core in her heart. "I would never threaten you. Just beg you for your own sake to have mercy. Don't you see, my love, there is not one of us who does not need forgiveness?"

"Some more than others, though. Be at ease, my dear. So

419

far as Milner and his goodwife are concerned, my purpose is accomplished. What have you agreed with her?"

"That—that she will come tomorrow so I can tell her whether she need fear further loss." For the first time since her marriage, she felt an enormous distance from him.

He shifted suddenly then, as if some shaft of pain had struck home, and looked away. "I will send word that she is secure in what remains, so long as she keeps herself from me and mine. I don't wish you to suffer her presence again; she is an unpleasant woman and will not have improved with age. Don't look so troubled, my softhearted Mary. She has the proceeds of a lifetime's extortion well concealed, and will not weep for her husband now she has succeeded in her purposes."

He had not understood her meaning at all, her plea for forgiveness as the only way to draw the edge of hatred from his life. Mary thanked him for the little he had yielded, unable to decide whether he had yielded anything at all, and took her loss alone to bed.

Chapter Three

A brisk wind was blowing up the Thames, a good trading wind for bringing ships to their journey's end. Full-rigged two- and three-deckers inward bound from the Far East; swift brigs whose purposes were kept secret, when an unprofitable voyage could easily be augmented by piracy; old-fashioned galleons from the Mediterranean; beamy traders built to carry bulk and wallowing in a following wind. Thames wherries with rust-red sails and darting skiffs ferrying passengers from ship to shore; an unmasted hulk newly launched from Deptford yard and fitting out at Rotherhithe, sun reflecting off carving at poop and beakhead; line upon line of ships anchored and under tow, ships loading and unloading, ships gleaming with fresh paint and new yellow rope, ships low in the water from rotted timbers and criminal overloading.

Adam knew most of them and was able to guess at the rest. He stood with Mary in the prow of a Wapping lugger, pointing out quirks of paint and design which betrayed the port of origin, answering pelting questions on the scene around. She had never seen London from its river before and was fascinated by everything, trying to pick out St. Clement's from the dozens of spires of either bank while missing nothing on the river itself.

"I never realised how hardly treated I was before," she said gaily. "When I've been wed nearly six years and you've never brought me downriver on such a day."

"I'll pledge myself to bring you as often as you desire now I know the pleasure you find in it. I did not guess before."

She turned in his hold. "Dear Adam. The moment you know my pleasure you think how to increase it."

"I do my best," he said simply. "I don't always succeed."

421

The lugger heeled in the wake of a huge four-decker and spray slapped over open decking. Mary was glad of the diversion, for it relieved her of the need to reply. In all London there could be no more loving husband nor wife so well aware of her good fortune, yet their happiness remained incomplete. There were still parts of himself he could not offer, too many of her responses struck aside by lacks she did not understand.

But nothing must spoil today.

"There she is," said Adam suddenly. "Behind the one with the gilded lion figurehead."

Mary craned perilously over the rail. "The big ship painted grey? I had no idea she was so very large, nor so elegant either! You said a trading vessel, but she isn't in the least like those stubby beetles moored off Tower Quay."

"There are a deal of different traders. Perhaps I didn't want to frighten you as much as I frightened myself by taking such a risk." He stared eagerly downriver, wind blowing lace at his throat and billowing under the stiff skirts of his coat. Even on the river he was formally dressed nowadays, preferred to risk spoiling good cloth rather than wear anything old or shabby. Mary's expression softened as she watched him, for this was his one vanity.

He squeezed her waist. "No damage, either. The message I had from Deptford light said she was in good repair. We shall be into Cheapside before the winter is out." He glanced sideways at her and grinned. "Don't look, but tell me how many decks she has."

"Why . . . two. No, three . . . I'm not sure," stammered Mary, taken aback.

"She's been all the way to India and back, bearing our fortune with her, and you were looking at me instead of the ship which has made us rich." He shook his head. "Perhaps it isn't worth bringing you on the river, after all."

"I'll never learn to behave as the wife of a merchant should," said Mary ruefully. "Reckoning spice and counting decks to make sure I'm kept in comfort another year."

He laughed and kissed her, salt on their lips and heedless of the boatmen's sniggers. "It's the first time my face has been priced above the wealth of the Indies, so I've no cause for complaint. Never behave as other wives do, my sweet Mary."

Nor you as do most husbands, she thought. His lack of interest in other women, even when she was ungainly in pregnancy, was almost embarrassing. Increasingly, Adam Furnival was pointed to as one of the rising men in the City, his advice asked on matters to do with shipping and freights, other merchants' womenfolk flattering in their attentions. He sold and occasionally gave his advice, the women he disregarded with a brusqueness which came close to discourtesy.

He turned to say something to the helmsman and the lugger came smartly into the wind under the towering, gilded stern of the ship they watched. Mary craned up at massive tumble home and closed gunports, at . . . "Adam! You never told me! Has she—was she called that always?"

Above their heads the name was carved: *Mary Bonaventure*.

"No, originally it was *Neptune's Glory*, I believe. I made my mortgage conditional on a change of name, amongst other things."

Adam was not secretive in business and discussed most of his ventures with her. Two years before he had done rather more: he had asked her permission to risk most of their security on a ship fitting out in Dog Reach. The builder and group of merchants who commissioned her had pledged their credit too enthusiastically, stinting nothing on their design. Consequently they were desperate for funds and offered a mortgage on the hull, a half share of cargo space in lieu of interest. A loan of this nature, without even interest until a round voyage to the East should be completed, attracted few lenders when there was so much investment going begging, and Adam judged the terms very favourable if the ship was completed swiftly and no accident befell her in the hazardous oceans of the East. The risk was enormous, though, when all parties to it would be bankrupt if the voyage was a failure and Adam's mortgage consequently valueless; it would also mean two more years of extreme frugality in Clement's Lane while they waited for the ship's return.

This last decided Mary. She would never have stopped Adam from doing something he plainly yearned to do, although she might have hesitated over hazarding all he had slaved for just when easier times were close, but dreaded the move he planned to Cheapside for reasons she could not name. So she listened to his arguments and agreed to them for quite different reasons from his own; since then two more years had slipped by in Clement's Lane, and now his fortune had come home, risks triumphantly justified. The word would be about on 'Change tomorrow: Adam Furnival was not just a coming man but one who had arrived.

"They'll be surprised to find I already own a lease in Cheapside," observed Adam with satisfaction as they sailed back into the sunset, spilled gold on slack water. "Give me a few months to have the house cleaned and repaired, then we'll be set at last. Where we belong, with the sign on the wall again."

The sign on the wall again, thought Mary, frowning. "How long have you had this ambition to live in Cheapside and trade in balances?" she said aloud.

He hesitated, as if realising indiscretion. "Thirteen years."

She had hoped for so long that he would tell her more about the half-glimpsed part of his life, had waited and asked nothing, wanting the sharing to be something he offered freely. If he told her anything it would be the truth, she knew, blank refusal the only way he could avoid it under questioning, and they were too close for such rejection to be easily accepted.

In the end, again she did not ask, and the day's pleasures were soured because both knew why.

Five months later the bells of London rang in the new century, the year of grace 1700. King William was ailing as always and heard it with little joy, most of his subjects celebrated according to their natures. Cheapside conduit ran with wine, an old woman of Highgate died content because she had lived in three centuries, having been born in 1599 when the great Elizabeth reigned. Adam Furnival paced the boards of his counting room listening to his wife scream. Although her daughter died, Mary had had little difficulty in birthing either her or Henry: she took a deal of exercise, since their house was too tiny for more than one maid, and longed for a large family. Now, for no reason, this child refused to be born although Mary had been in labour nearly twenty hours.

Adam had engaged the best doctor in the City and wondered now whether he might have done better with the old midwife who had been successful before. They would soon move to Cheapside but meanwhile remained in Clement Lane because Mary wished her child to be born there. For some reason she thought the place well-omened and Adam humoured her, although his own affairs were inconveniently stranded between two establishments.

He paused and listened, heart tight. The sounds of urgency upstairs, feet, voices, a child's cry. He sat limply, head in his hands. Thank God. Thank God. The words were drawn from a well of thankfulness rather than conviction. Now he was respectable he went to church on Sundays but was not a religious man, having suffered too much to think God merciful. Nevertheless, he had made a bargain with God this night, as one trader to another, if only Mary was spared.

He sat beside her later, while she slept the drained white sleep which is not far from death. The doctor was pessimistic, shaking his head and muttering of fever if she was not leeched, of agues unless hot irons blistered evil humours from her belly. Adam threw him out, made up the fire and prepared to hold her to life by will alone. That she had in abundance, although short of blood to nourish leeches, and of strength to survive more torment; so he talked to her through most of the night, lying beside her to give warmth from his body.

She woke to the booming bells of St. Clement's. "I shan't be sorry to have bells across the street at Cheapside, instead of six feet above the roof," she said quite clearly, and drowsed again.

He rose without disturbing her, ordered Rebecca to feed her when she woke, and went to look at his new son. I should have liked a daughter, he thought wryly. How strange, when most men desire sons once there is some measure of achievement to pass on. Yet surely there was no other man whose wife had a tenth of Mary's spirit, and during the past two days he had not thought of his own affairs at all. The child was small and delicate, impossible to imagine he had caused so much trouble when the rumbustious Henry had been born easily.

Adam took Henry with him to Lothbury later in the day, the child kicking through drifted snow in a smother of white, like a schooner in shoal water. Adam had not been inside the Eyleses' house since the day he married six years before, and the changes were very obvious. Mary's sisters had been sold off to petty traders but her brother and his wife, as well as Sir John and Lady Eyles, were acrimoniously crammed into a few rooms amongst bales of merchandise, the upper stories hired out as lodgings. The goods were poor quality too, thought Adam.

Lady Eyles greeted him as if she still ruled a large establishment, voice cool with memory of the years he had not come.

He did not mind; when he thought Mary would die he had faced for the first time all the distress he had caused her by refusing to forgive her father for serving James Stuart, and if she lived had sworn to set his quarrel at rest for her sake. He didn't expect it to be easy, and it was not, since he might put enmity behind him but could not forget it; only realise that Mary mattered more to him than memory fifteen years dead.

"I have a favour to ask," he added, after he had discussed Mary's condition with her mother and made such apology as he could for neglect. "Would you keep Henry for a few days? Rebecca has found a healthy wet nurse since Mary has no milk, but above all she needs a little peace. And with Henry around that is always hard to find."

She agreed at once, although he had not realised how uncomfortably crowded the Eyleses already were. I shall have to find them better goods to sell, and shipping space as well, he thought resignedly. A loan would simply melt away with the rest.

He lay beside Mary again that night, holding her body to his when she seemed chilled, listening to a gale tossing tiles on the cobbles outside. Would that it was summer to give her the warmth she needed. He slept, being very tired, but lightly. She seemed stronger, breath even and heart beating steadily against his.

He felt the difference at once when she woke again, her body no longer limp and lips smiling against his face. "Dear Adam."

"Mary, my love."

"Is the child all right?"

"Yes, dear heart. We have a fine son."

She sighed. "May I name this one, since you named the last?"

"Whatever your fancy says. Even Clement Bell Furnival, poor little devil."

She chuckled sleepily. "No. I should like to call him Stephen."

Why Stephen? he wondered. And asked her in the morning when she woke again to seven shattering booms above the roof.

She looked startled. "Did I really say that in the night?"

He nodded. He ought to climb out of bedstraw and warm milk on the ashes; instead he lay in thankfulness and counted many blessings. Perhaps God is merciful after all, he thought. Just sometimes, when he tires of judgment. It often worried him that his father and Mary, whom he loved, believed in a righteous God, while he found it impossible.

"I didn't mean to. It must have been because . . . I'm sorry, Adam, I don't want to explain just now."

426

"It doesn't matter," he said, curious nevertheless. "I'll warm some milk." He turned sharply to her exclamation.

"Adam, your back!"

He had forgotten that these past two nights he had not worn his nightgown with its disguising quilting, thinking to keep her warmer naked.

Mary stared at him aghast; from neck to buttocks his flesh was welted and clawed, some scars an ill-healed mauve pucker, others ridged white or sunk into such muscle as remained. She saw him stiffen, then he went across to his clothes and pulled on a shirt. Neither spoke while he laid a copper warmer of milk on hot ash and he avoided her eyes when he brought it over. But he had to help her sit before she could drink, hold her against him while she did, and in familiar contact restraint was broken.

"Lie beside me again," she whispered. "Please, Adam, you must tell me now."

"A few more days, you're not strong enough for explanations yet."

"Strong enough? Don't you see that I shall fret each moment, thinking how I urged you into mercy on devils who treated you like that? For I suppose that woman Milner and her husband did it, I wish now you had done worse than ruin their trade."

"No, you don't, when even a mangy cur makes you weep. And I am no more a proper object for your pity than the Milners were; I think since we have gone so far in explanation, you had best see this before you delude yourself again." He jerked back his sleeve, where each night they lay together he had worn a bandage, pleading an old ulcer. He unwound it, and she stared horror-stricken at the seared T sunk deep into flesh. Split muscles had knotted either side and although plainly years old, it still looked painful.

She looked up into his face at last, at tight lines, compressed mouth and pride which had hidden this through six years of marriage. He was looking intently at the weave of her coverings and would not meet her eyes. "I asked you to lie beside me again," she said softly. "I hope you are not refusing me."

"You don't mind?" he demanded.

"Why should I? I judged you wrongly before, this time I should simply like you to tell me what happened."

So he told her, not yet of his father but much that had happened since. Of the Milners and their bars, of Swithin the cat and the loss of his eight shillings' savings, of his first

427

meeting with Sir Francis Child when he had never admitted before that there had been a time when he lacked ever a penny in his seam. Of Newgate and Ripe Will, the Red Feathers and how he had paid her price out of the profits of receiving. She understood then how he had been haunted by fear of some accident which would discover the brand of thief he carried, when success and effort would count for nothing and he be driven back to the gutters of Whitefriars, cast out by those who now respected him and this time taking those he loved into disaster, too.

"I've often wondered how I found the courage to marry," he confessed. "I knew there would be pitfalls, of course, but was such a callow lout, so inexperienced in love, I simply could not imagine the closeness most families take for granted. I loved you, but supposed I could set you aside from my concerns. Perhaps with another woman it might have been possible, I don't know. With you the distance I've put between us has become a nightmare." He was thankful he had been to Lothbury earlier, of his own free will.

When he had finished, she simply slipped off his shirt and kissed his arm. "Now I shan't be kept from you by a padded gown, or left sleepless because you dare not rest under my eye. Adam, I don't want to call him Stephen after all."

"I think that's something you'll have to explain," he said, smiling. He was astounded by how easy explanation had proved, by the fact she wept for him and did not mind at all.

"It seems unkind now, when there was so much about you I didn't understand. The kind of fancy women have when awaiting a birth, and no more. I thought—I thought we lacked one thing for our happiness . . . that you should be able to say the Apostle Stephen's prayer, and mean it. We listened to it read in St. Clement's, do you remember? I'm sorry, Adam, I never meant to speak of it and don't now remember doing so."

He lay puzzling over her meaning since he was seldom a close listener to long-droned sermons; but Mary was almost asleep again and he did not disturb her with questions since she was still very weak. Later, he leafed through her Bible downstairs and eventually came to the words she believed him incapable of saying, without which their happiness would not be complete.

Lord, lay not this sin to their charge.

He stared at it and then swore aloud, shutting the book with a snap. For Mary's sake he was prepared to tolerate Sir John

Eyles, but that was far removed from forgiveness. He had revenged himself on the Milners and regretted only that Mary found his actions distasteful; the hatred roused by his father's death had not softened with the years at all. Mary was grace and loving-kindness itself, yet there were some matters where forgiveness was an insult to the dead, a crime against the future.

A simple impossibility to ask it of those unable to forget.

Chapter Four

"*It is by no means so grand as you imag*-ine, and noisier than Clement Lane, except for the bells. I intend to treat for the lease of the next house, which once ran with it, and will again when I have my way. At the moment this one is sound and repaired, but not as convenient as I hoped."

There was both pride and diffidence in Adam's voice as he ushered Mary into her new home, and she determined at that moment to like Cheapside whatever her doubts, and sadness too, at leaving Clement Lane. This was what he had striven for through fourteen desperate years, a dream cherished when there must have seemed no possibility of success; it would be unforgivable not to rejoice with him in his triumph.

"It's lovely," she said, and meant it. If he had not told her she would never have known that the house had been a tavern for years. "I've never seen light panelling before, or such fine rooms. How dare you call it inconvenient when there is so much light and air, and stairs one would be a fool to fall down?"

"I wasn't sure about the panelling; it was originally dark but so ruined by tavern drunks I had the best of it planed and the rest replaced. Then I found I liked the lightness. I should have asked you, of course, but didn't want to worry you with anything."

Mary and the children had spent the summer at a farm on Islington Heights. She hated leaving Adam but was sensible enough to realise that baby Stephen might well die unless he gained strength away from London stenches in the heat. She too felt marvellously restored by idleness in fresh air, and no longer needed to pretend to health, while Henry had spent a summer of scarcely interrupted wrongdoing. He was rampaging around the house now, shouting at each fresh room he discovered.

"He needs to start being tutored, and a deal of occupation," said Mary, smiling. "Your clerks will be complaining their scratchings are disturbed now we are back." They went from counting room to kitchen, where there was the luxury of an inside hearth for cooking, and then upstairs to parlour and master bedroom, both fine rooms with plastered ceilings. Mary could faintly remember a time of prosperity at Lothbury but this house was more stylish than theirs had ever been. She looked at four-poster bed and elegant, new-style furniture, the infinity of trouble Adam had taken to have everything right for her. At smudged ink and yellowed paper of a Frost Fair printing, giving the name of Mary Eyles present on the ice, now framed beside the bed. She touched it, smiling. "I am so proud of you, love, and cannot think how you have guessed my taste so exactly. Or could the reason be that we know each other rather well?"

"Perhaps. Or it may be that I have a meekly dutiful wife, who always agrees with her husband's pleasure." He kissed her, and instantly sensation was alive, fire blazing in the dry straw of passion after a summer apart and long months before when she had not been strong enough for him to make love to her.

Henry came bounding into the room. "I slipped and look, I've blood all down my neck."

"You would have," said Mary with resignation. "The sooner you learn to mop up your own blood, the better, when you're never satisfied with less than a dozen falls each day." She washed and bandaged him briskly, trying not to be irritated by the interruption. She loved her children dearly, but there were times when she wished them elsewhere.

Within a few days they were settled into Cheapside. Apart from the kitchen and dining parlour, the ground floor was given over to Adam's affairs, and Mary soon saw what he meant by it not being as convenient as he hoped. Two front rooms were already insufficient for his purposes: he was still engaged in arranging freights and anchorages, in acting as an exchange for shipping information of all kinds, but to some extent was the victim of his own success. Dozens of others were now haunting wharves and river as he had done, Edward Lloyd's coffeehouse the recognised centre for such middlemen. At least it saved Adam a deal of exertion since clients came to him as he altered the character of his trade: he was still supremely well informed on all matters pertaining to Thames-borne trade and used his knowledge to lend on cargoes and ships. The enormous risk he had taken on the *Mary Bonaventure* changed him from being modestly prosperous into a man of considerable wealth and he continued to expand his capital by judicious lending in risks he understood. Shipowners and skippers were beginning to deposit their balances with him too, as well as finding Furnival's the best place for reducing their liability to loss. It was dangerous for an owner or shipper to bear all the chances of a voyage himself, and cargo space was usually subcontracted, or percentages of loaded freight resold to investors, so in the event of disaster losses were widely spread; insurance was becoming routine practice, as were mortgages and shares in ships. All this had been done, and was still widely done, haphazardly through personal deals; now Adam was establishing the Sign of the Corncrake as a house where such transactions might be conveniently concluded. For the Corncrake sign was back on the wall outside, craftsman-hammered and gilded in intricate detail.

"Why a corncrake?" asked Mary one day. "I've never even heard of such a bird before."

Adam hesitated. "There's no shape to fit the name Furnival, which I believe was a stinking alley hereabouts before the fire, and the corncrake was on this place long before it became a tavern."

"I could have designed a sign well suited to my love," said Mary indignantly. At every turn she seemed to discover some fresh cruelty the past had heaped on Adam; what kind of mother names her son for a foul alley and then took pleasure in telling him of it later? "How do you know, anyway? The fire was before you were born, and this place long a tavern...the King's Arms, wasn't it? How can you remember a corncrake sign from so long ago?"

He stared out of the window. "I remember exactly how it was. I had to leave it a tavern two more years, but the day I owned the lease the King's Arms came off the wall."

His voice was bleak and drained of life, eyes fixed on something she could not see outside. Strangely, she had settled into Cheapside quite happily, being determined to do so, while he often seemed trapped and alone with unpleasant thought. At first, Mary had thought he was beset by the sheer volume of his trade and became anxious about his health. Sometimes his face took on a greyish hue she dreaded, and although he never spoke of it she knew his breath locked painfully if he was upset. Yet he enjoyed his affairs, was stimulated by risk and, although astonishingly free from conceit, relished his new-won position at the centre of the City's dealings. He was most relaxed after a long day when he had been too busy to remember hauntings, was vigorous in love too, although consideration often kept him from her in an effort to avoid further childbirth. Mary was surprised to find him knowledgeable in matters which girls of her upbringing were never taught, although in most ways he was no more sophisticated than she.

She accepted now that the damage wrought by the harshness of his upbringing was permanent, but could not feel it fully explained the strain she sensed in him. He was deeply satisfied by his success, without being eased by it. Mary was delighted to be able to welcome her family to her home and grateful to Adam for what she realised was a profound sacrifice in allowing her to do so, yet a lack persisted in the centre of their lives. Only Henry established a totally uncomplicated relationship with his father: Adam was as quiet in his dealings with his son as he was in all things, and never beat him however much Mary sometimes felt he deserved it; he treated him as a responsible adult and Henry tagged along behind him whenever the opportunity offered. The two conferred and often laughed together, the household never so peaceful as when Adam allowed his son to watch his doings from a corner of the counting room.

Stephen benefited from his months in the country and began to put on weight, although less demanding and precocious than his brother. Cheapside might be noisy but the house was airy, money abundant for fresh milk and uncontaminated water brought in wood-straked bins from springs at Hoxton and Greenbury Hill, and with Stephen's hold on life apparently firm Mary began to yearn for another child. Or at least for an end to the remorseless restraint Adam exercised in their personal affairs. She said nothing, knowing the formidable strength of his will, but began to lay traps for his desire, to beguile him into unwariness or miscalculation.

She did not succeed.

He might be driven by demons she could not name, but nothing overset his judgment. "I couldn't live without you," he said simply. "Nor could your household. There are matters where I am powerless, but so far as in me lies I will preserve your life. I sorely need your help to ease my way, but will persist without it if I must." After that she abandoned her efforts, and as is not unusual in such matters, almost immediately conceived.

Adam was horrified, and Mary could not fail to notice how his other ghosts diminished under the impact of real, driving fear. Although she stayed well almost until her time, he became sleepless with anxiety and gave less than complete attention to his affairs; he was also much less often lost in unhappy abstractions of his own.

Mary was safely delivered of a daughter in the autumn of 1701, and recovered her spirits within hours.

"You see," she said gaily to Adam. "You need not worry for me at all. I could have twenty children and be well at the end of it."

"God forbid, for I should certainly expire along the way," he said, and not in jest. Privately, he thought God bitterly unmerciful to deny them the joy they had of each other, except at the risk each time of her life. There were few men of his acquaintance not already married to a second or third wife.

Soon after, the City was thrown into uproar by news that Louis of France had forbidden all imports from the British Isles into his dominions. Perhaps he intended a warning of the ruin which renewed war would bring to English trade, if so he miscalculated. When news broke that he was urging the same restrictions on his grandson, the King of Spain, Whigs and Tories buried party faction to denounce French ambitions. Then came the next shock wave: James Stuart died at last in exile, and in defiance of the Treaty of Ryswick, Louis recognised his son as rightful King of England.

The bells of London tolled, loyal addresses poured off the printing presses as Tories competed with Whigs in denunciation of the impudent French who tried to impose an unwanted, Catholic King on them.

Mary was surprised by the depth of Adam's feeling. He was not yet an alderman although soon likely to be invited to stand, but he attended the City's delegation all the way to Kensington when it presented William with a loyal address, subscribed bribe money to ensure that Whigs were elected for the City when a Parliament was called, and attended countless meetings, although politics normally bored him. When a drunken clerk reeled into their path by Guildhall and demanded a toast to

King James III, Adam knocked him down and only Mary's presence prevented serious trouble. He was shaking with rage, when she had never before seen his temper loosed.

"I hate them, root and branch," he said shortly, later the same day. "There isn't a Stuart worth a maggot's trust and I will kill any who tries to lay his hand on England and her liberties again."

"Do you think it will be war?" asked Mary anxiously.

"I hope so, since tyrants only bow to force. We've won at sea before; this time, we'll let Louis discover what wealth and a fair cause can achieve on land."

As the weeks passed he became deeply involved with the war party in the City, by no means all Whigs. Many Tories were alarmed at seeming to be traitors now their cause was backed by Louis, and anyway were only tepidly attached to James because he had been King by right. Mary knew that Adam was secretly fitting out privateers although England and France were officially at peace, his trade booming as nervous traders sought reinsurance in uncertain times ahead.

"Aren't you worried?" she asked him once. "What if a dozen ships are sunk in a week, with your credit pledged on each?"

He looked up, and ran his quill between his fingers; he often had to work late and she enjoyed helping him when she could. "I have no fear of it. The odd ship, yes. That we must face and not be dismayed, but nothing worse. The seas are ours, even the Dutch cannot challenge us there any longer and they know it. So they are our allies. The French look to the land, intend to seize half Europe as their preserve; our task this time is to teach them to fear us there as well. And we will do it, so no tyrant in the future can ever consider himself safe from us."

"With London's money?" said Mary, smiling.

"Yes. Strange, isn't it? A hundred paces down Cheapside and you can deal at the counters of a single building which will fuel defiance of all our enemies. Bagged coin and signed papers from the Bank of England will wield more power than generations of Kings in their palaces. I trust a few drafts signed by Adam Furnival will do their part as well."

They did. When William died the following spring and Louis proclaimed James III King of England, war immediately followed. Three schooner-rigged Furnival privateers were awaiting for the word of it at Erith on the Lower Thames, and Adam sent a horseman galloping there the same night. Himself, he went with the City delegation to pay homage to Queen Anne, the ruler recognised by the English, and this time he went by right. He was elected alderman for the ward of Cheap, and not even Mary knew how, when he signed his name, his eye strayed to an entry of twenty-six years before, when Henry Cornish was elected for the ward of Bassishaw. Adam Furnival swore at Guildhall to uphold the liberties of the City, to defend them against all comers at the utmost hazard of his life and fortune, and went quite privately afterwards to the church of St. Lawrence Jewry.

It was cold and smelled of wet stone. He did not pray, but stood before the unmarked niche where the remains of his father lay, throat tight. He had done it. Fortune had swung full circle and London need no longer fear Kings, while tyrants yet unborn would do well to tremble before the power generated in a few dozen crowded streets and wharves by Thames River, by men in quiet rooms who on a scrawled signature could pledge enough payment to shatter thrones and rule the trade and oceans of the world.

He still disliked walking down King Street and turning the corner into Cheapside, did not once cross his own threshold without glancing where a scaffold had stood, blood running down the timbers. He wished to God the Sign of the Corncrake stood anywhere but where it did, that Stuart vengeance was less exact in its choice of torments.

Mary attended the traditional ceremony in Guildhall but left before the banquet, where wives were not welcome. She expected Adam to show some sign of pleasure when he returned, instead he was deeply depressed and gripped by the old paralysis of words, which their years of happiness had almost cured. She was relieved next day when she realised he must be so engrossed in his work that he had forgotten an appointment in Guildhall: all the same, as a new alderman it would never do if he was late, and she ran downstairs to remind him.

A small section of the counting room had been panelled off for interviewing clients in privacy, although Mary knew that Adam was treating for the lease of the tumbledown ordinary next door so he could gain much-needed extra space. She hesitated, hearing voices and disliking to disturb him, but only this morning he had said the meeting at Guildhall was important.

He was standing, face bleached and hands flat against woodwork behind, while a woman sat very much at ease facing him. She swung round when she heard Mary enter, brows raised, completely in command of the situation: in middle age, she was dressed with a degree of fashion which immediately made Mary feel dowdy. The City abounded in rich materials, but lagged behind court elegance.

"I—I'm sorry to disturb you," stammered Mary, unable to account for the charged atmosphere of the room, or the unusual style of Adam's visitor. "Adam, I thought you would like to be reminded that you are soon due at Guildhall."

The lady laughed. "So busy about your affairs, Adam? Perhaps that is why you haven't found time to visit Jenny and me these fifteen years or more." She surveyed Mary critically. "I assume you are my son's wife?"

Mary's confusion vanished instantly; this woman had come to make trouble and cut up Adam's precarious peace of mind. "I am Mistress Furnival, and the happiest goodwife in this city."

"I am pleased to hear it, though I must confess I am also somewhat surprised, when Adam seems no more talkative than I remember him. Has he ever spoken to you of me?"

Mary flushed angrily. "If you are his mother, then he said you were alive." She went over and slipped her arm through Adam's, it was intolerable to be discussing him as if he wasn't there: through gold-laced cloth she could feel him trembling. Adam Furnival, banker and shipper of repute, reduced by this woman to tongue-tied misery.

Arabella threw back her head and laughed. Her teeth were white and perfect, her face only lightly wrinkled. "Well said, my dear. No, I'm not dead. More's the pity, don't you think, Adam?"

"What is it you want of us?" demanded Mary fiercely. She had pictured Adam's mother as impoverished and secretly blamed him for having nothing to do with her, now she looked at furs and velvet and thought of him flogged and half starved. "If you wish, I will bring your grandchildren to meet you before you go."

"I should like that," said Arabella calmly. "Who do they take after, Adam?"

There was a fractional pause while Mary prayed he would find words, any words so this evil woman could not taunt him further, then he replied quietly. "They are young and need time to become themselves. I think you will like Henry, who has all your eagerness for life."

"Henry?" she said sharply. "You called one of them Henry?"

437

"Our eldest son, yes. Stephen is the younger, and Margaret still in her cradle."

Mary looked from one to the other, Adam seemed to have steadied but tension was almost visible between him and this woman who incredibly was his mother. They did not look in the least alike, except that both were dark. She was vivacious where he was retiring; gracefully proportioned also, while Adam was built for carrying burdens and clearly had spent a lifetime carrying them. Expressions chased each other across her face, her eyes sparkled with interest, with sheer delight in being herself and admired; every gesture was part of her elegance, as well as of a firm determination to have her own way.

"You haven't introduced your wife to me, Adam," she said now. "You seem to have done remarkably well for yourself."

Mary felt his fingers tighten on hers, then he bowed and kissed them. "Yes, better than anyone but I could possibly know. Mary, my dear, may I introduce to you my mother, the Countess of Wexford?"

Mary was as startled by the title as she was by Adam's discourtesy in introducing the older woman to the younger; then she was pleased. Left to defend himself, Adam would have remained stripped of speech; he was very easily roused to protective anger by any slight to her. She curtsied but did not reply, her hand still held in his.

Arabella stared at them, a strange expression on her face. "It would seem that I have to congratulate you both. I remember Harry saying once that you had a great gift for affection, Adam, if only the right person could prise it loose. I was never able to, although I tried. Which I daresay you do not now believe; I can see your wife does not. At least allow me to be happy that you have found a contentment which eluded me."

"Thank you," said Adam in a stifled voice. "Mary, perhaps you would take my mother to see the children now?"

Mary nodded and stood back to allow the other the space she needed to manoeuvre many-panniered skirts sideways through the door.

"You know, it is so very strange for me to be here?" said Arabella, staring about her at light polish and sun flooding through large-paned windows. "I cannot lose the oddest feeling that everything should be familiar when of course it is not. I have never been inside this house since it was completely finished, and it's the one burned to ash I remember now." She tapped her kid-shod foot on the boards. "I lived nearly two years in a hole just below where we are standing."

Mary could not imagine this elegant creature crouched in a muddy hole, while her mind spun afresh with the knowledge that Adam's mother had once lived here. She had guessed something of the sort from his determination not just to succeed, but to succeed in this particular building, but still nothing fitted when clearly the Countess of Wexford had no claim on his affections. "Indeed, my lady?" was all she could think of to say. "Was—that must have been directly after the fire?"

"Yes, and mighty uncomfortable it was, too! Adam wants my lease on the next house, you know. That is how I discovered he had succeeded in all his aims, otherwise the only word I've had from him in years was a packet containing thirty pounds he owed me."

Mary met her eyes squarely. "Can you be surprised?"

"Oh no! Adam was always a boy who never forgot a grudge or neglected to requite himself on those he disliked. He rejected my efforts to make good the harm I did him, nor would he believe that I loved his father far more than a child could ever know. Adam has many qualities, but always lacked the gift of compassion."

"That's not true," said Mary hotly, forgetting how closely this mirrored some of her own misgivings. "As no one knows better than myself. Perhaps it was your lack, not his."

"Yes, of course. I do not refuse to face my own faults, you see, which are many and singularly black." She laughed at Mary's expression. "My dear, I am everything you think me and more besides. Yet I think Adam the only person who is worse off for my actions, and at least I gave him a life, which has become of infinite delight to him at last. I cannot tell you how happy I am to find it so. You must visit me one day and meet his sister."

"Yes . . . I should like to," stammered Mary, all her notions upset again. "That is, if Adam will permit it."

"He will not mind what he does not know," said Arabella lightly. "Husbands are tedious creatures if you take them too seriously. I also think there is a deal he has not told you, which you would be happier if you understood."

"He will tell me himself when the time is right," said Mary, quietly but definitely. "Meanwhile, I should like to come if I can. And I don't need Adam's consent so much as certainty that I won't distress him by coming. He has suffered enough already, and I'll only add to it unwittingly."

"Good girl," said Arabella approvingly. "I will leave you my direction and look forward to your company; although I should warn you that I am of ill-repute in my neighbourhood at present. Now, I do not usually find young children amusing, since they are as self-centred as myself, but I should very much like to see my grandchildren. Really, I don't know whether to be delighted or annoyed to find myself a grandmother! There is such a disagreeable sound to the word, all black and mourning bands, yet the prospect of seeing the next generation of one's own love is stupidly attractive."

Chapter Five

Mary found Adam collapsed at his ta-
ble when she returned from bidding her mother-in-law farewell.
He was conscious but sweating with pain and breathing in short,
hard gulps. When she would have called help, he grasped her
arm and heaved himself back somehow in his chair. "Don't
tell anyone. Send...message to...Guildhall. All right tomorrow. Please, Mary."

She laid her fingers across his lips. "Stay still, I beg you,
Adam. I must have help to carry you upstairs."

"No. Leave me...awhile. I'll walk there...later. I can't
afford the...City to think me on my deathbed. Be
here...demanding their balances tomorrow."

Mary wavered, not knowing what to do. Strain aggravated
his condition, she knew; less serious attacks had subsided before when he rested. Above all, he never suffered them when
his mind was tranquil. She might do more harm by upsetting
him than by yielding to his will, however great the madness
seemed: doctors bled patients too frail to protest, redoubled
torment with hot irons and rough handling. Adam had hidden
his body even from her for years, he would force himself to
his feet, anything, rather than be examined by a prying phy-
sician, his delicate digestion collapse under forced dosings of
fashionably bottled filth. He had saved her from this after
Stephen was born and kept her alive with his love; instinct told
her that her presence was his best chance now.

She sat, speaking occasionally in a voice which sounded
strangely in her ears, trying not to worry him with her anguish,
holding him lightly when she longed to use her grasp somehow
to haul him back to strength. After a while the dreadful choke

441

of his breathing eased, greyness ebbed from his face and his eyes flicked open. "I'm sorry to give you such a fright."

She swallowed, relief bringing tears where desperate fear had kept them away. "Oh, Adam, I thought—I thought—"

"Not this time. Not for a while, I hope, while life remains so sweet." His eyes closed again. He was still in pain, she could see, but so exhausted that sleep would soon bring relief. He dozed through the rest of the day and, as he had promised, walked upstairs in the evening, indeed seemed almost himself again and made light of her anxiety. "I've had these attacks much of my life. My days for humping bales are over, but I'm fit enough to scratch a quill across paper for a good while yet."

"So long as all goes well." Mary was unable to free herself from panic at the thought of life without him. "Adam love, now we are so rich, can't you take things more easily?"

"No. Affairs don't tire or even worry me unduly. I should be wretched, and no fitter, if I divided my time between coffeehouses and parlour gaming. And when I work I cannot do it with less than my whole mind. Besides, it wasn't trade which upset me, as you well know."

"Don't think about it," said Mary swiftly.

"Not now," he agreed. "But I think perhaps I have refused to think clearly about a great many things for too long. There's much I need to straighten in my mind at last. What did she tell you?"

"Your . . . Lady Wexford?"

"Don't worry about me so dreadfully," he said gently. "Yes, my mother."

"Nothing, except she had tried to repay the wrong she did you. She wanted to tell me more, but I preferred that one day you would tell me yourself."

"I will, and that's a promise. First there are a few things I need to work out for myself."

"She asked me to visit her. Would you mind? She lives off Holborn and gave me her direction."

"No, I don't mind. I'm not sure yet whether I can bear to come myself. Do you know, she's hardly changed at all? Looking at the two of us I should think a stranger would be puzzled to decide which was the older."

Mary was enormously relieved. Although obviously still unwell, he gave the impression that some deep discord in his nature had been resolved, and time would do the rest.

When she came, his mother had brought the deeds of the

next house, so there was now the link of rent he owed her; another link too, a splendid silver flagon she sent as a belated wedding gift the day after her visit. Mary exclaimed at the workmanship, and after some hesitation Adam pointed to the maker's mark, RSP, and admitted the smith was his grandfather.

"This was my mother's most cherished possession," he said, holding it gently. "I don't know how she brought herself to part with it, but perhaps wants it to come home once I have the House of the Spurs repaired."

"She wants you to have it," said Mary.

He looked at her strangely, but did not reply. She knew he wrote to his mother in thanks, but he did not suggest a visit.

Several weeks passed before Mary decided to go to Holborn on her own. She hoped from day to day that Adam would make good his promise and tell her all she longed to know, and several times thought he was close to doing so. Then something would happen and he would sheer away from the subject, or stare out of the window in abstraction until she wondered how much longer she could hold back the questions tumbling in her mind.

No. She refused to yield; he must tell her of his own free will, and because he wanted to.

The Countess of Wexford's lodgings were three interconnecting rooms on the ground of a house in Warwick Court off Holborn, and not nearly so grand as Mary expected. There were knots of people hanging about the narrow pathway too, jostling her rudely when she went to pull the bell. Their silence was disconcerting when troublemakers usually jeered and quarrelled; Mary told herself she was imagining menace, but was absurdly relieved to be inside and away from their stares.

Arabella hugged her impulsively. "I'm so glad you came! I began to wonder whether you ever would."

"I wanted to, but first Adam and then Stephen were not well. I apologise for not sending a message first, I'm fortunate to find you at home."

Arabella laughed. "I vow I don't dare leave the premises at the moment! So Adam let you come, did he? I confess I wasn't sure he would."

Mary flushed. "I haven't told him which day it would be. I thought it best for him not to think about it while I was away."

"Quite right! As I told you, there is a great deal husbands are best off not knowing. All the same—" She glanced out the window, the shadow of trouble on her face. "I wish someone knew you were here today, and would come to escort you home."

"Those people outside? I thought perhaps there was a gin shop hereabouts, and—"

"And wondered why I chose to live in such a place? It is respectable enough usually, but I've been thinking I ought to move again although I dislike being put to such a pother because some riffraff have taken a dislike to me."

She brushed aside Mary's questions and sent for wine and biscuits, brought by a sour-faced maid who regarded Mary with open curiosity.

"You mustn't mind Catlin," said Arabella airily. "She helped deliver Adam, you know, and though I've turned her off a dozen times, she always comes back."

So far as Mary could see, for all Lady Wexford's title and stylish clothes, Catlin was the only maid in the place. The room was well furnished, but there were also indefinable touches which told of straitened means. "How long have you lived here, ma'am?" she asked curiously.

"Do you think that in time you could bring yourself not to call me 'ma'am' or 'my lady'? It makes me feel so very depressed. I've lived here two years, and before that two years in the Strand. Then, let me see. Yes, I moved there from Fleet Street, where Adam thought I still was until he discovered differently. He has a splendid system for gathering information, hasn't he? I was living there when he walked out on me; he was sixteen, I suppose, and discovered I was living with a clockmaker."

Mary laughed involuntarily, her hostess's idea of light conversation was unexpected, to say the least. "And were you?"

Arabella looked surprised. "Of course. I'm not a saint, you know. Though nowadays I find men more amusing in the drawing room than in bed." She sounded regretful. "Jenny is quite different, and betrothed to the most respectable young man she met while staying with my Wexford connections. I find him intolerably dull, but she seems very happy. It's strange that both my children should be so straitlaced in matters of pleasure, for of course I could tell that Adam would be really shocked at himself if he felt even slightly drawn to any woman except you. Not that you aren't everything he could wish, of course," she added hastily, "but it just goes to show, doesn't it? People talk a deal of nonsense on matters of inheritance."

Mary regarded her with fascination, thinking that probably it was their mother's unconcern with morality which had influenced Adam and his sister so strongly. "Henry sent more messages than I can remember. He often speaks of you and would dearly like to visit you one day." Henry had recognised another reckless spirit instantly, and at six years old was male enough to succumb to his grandmother's charm.

"I think perhaps he is best away from here, don't you? I will take him to see the wild beasts in the Tower or some such thing, which will suit him exactly. I—" She was interrupted by a crash of glass and a stone thudded against the wall.

There were shouts from outside, the sound of running feet, then silence.

Arabella jumped to her feet and threw up the empty window frame in a shower of splinters, shaking her fist and shouting until Mary hauled her back. "Have a care, ma'am! You may stir up something worse than stones if you enrage them."

Arabella thrust out her lip, scowling. "And you think I should sit back like a well-brought-up miss, and let them do as they will?"

"I think you should exercise a little prudence, however unfamiliar it may be."

She smiled then, ruefully. "Unfamiliar indeed. I wonder sometimes how different I would have been if Adam's father had lived. They think I am a witch."

Mary was startled, having just come to the conclusion that some idle rogues were amusing themselves at the expense of a woman they considered a whore. "A witch? In God's name, why?"

"I dabble in their lore a little, when life becomes tedious," explained Arabella blithely. "I lived two years ago with a man who studied herbs and remedies, and he taught me all he knew. It was vastly diverting, and since then I distil some of his potions and offer help if I am asked. I am quite successful too, but three months ago a girl I cured swore I had bewitched her. The cats around here follow me, too, because I feed them, poor things. And then a few days past a goodwife begged me to say a spell over her daughter and I was fool enough to do so."

"A spell," repeated Mary, carefully. "What happened?"

"I dosed her well and she recovered, but since they expected a spell I said one to please them. They believed it, you see, and an easy mind helps anyone to health." She glanced at Mary,

445

and laughed. "Adam is a good example. Anyway, the child recovered, but the mother caught the infection and died. Her husband says I transferred the disease out of spite because they paid me insufficient. I did curse her for it, of course."

Mary stood back from the window, looking out. Half a dozen men were busy with something on the far side of the court; dusk was falling and she could not see what it was. "You must come back with me to Cheapside tonight."

"Oh no! They'll soon become discouraged when nothing happens and I would be a danger to you if we left together. Besides, they would pillage an empty house. If they refuse to go away, I shall terrify them by screeching incantations; I can look very alarming, I promise you."

"You mustn't," said Mary, aghast. "Don't you see, that would give the proof they lack? Convicted witches are hanged, even if nowadays most judges disbelieve accusations if they can."

Arabella shrugged. "I was threatened with burning for treason long ago, and escaped. I won't do it unless I must."

As the evening darkened, instead of dispersing the crowd grew larger and more threatening. At first, Arabella begged Mary to go, but soon it became obvious that anyone leaving the house was in danger. There was no rear entrance, and even a man who lodged upstairs was roughly handled when he attempted to enter: the watch hovered uncertainly by the entry to the court but soon decided it would be safer to know nothing of the disturbance.

"Poltroons!" said Arabella indignantly. "Catlin, you'll have to slip out by the area steps and run for a magistrate. They won't molest a servant, surely."

"They'd call me your familiar and strip me naked to look for Devil's mark. You're the witch, my lady, you fly on your broomstick to find a magistrate!" She marched out and could be heard slamming pots in the background.

"She is often very disagreeable, but has never yet run away when I needed her," said Arabella defensively.

Mary immediately visualised a succession of scrapes down the years, in which Catlin had disapprovingly assisted. Neither her mother-in-law nor her maid seemed alarmed by the fracas outside, as if it was different only in degree from countless mishaps in the past, but both crowd and noise were increasing steadily. Arguments, presumably on the next course of action, were accompanied by blows, while aimless rushes flowed about the courtyard. A bonfire had been lit in one corner and by the light of the flames Mary could now see that they had decorated an obscene effigy and were preparing to burn it.

One of the men had a pot of gin and was shouting at the rest, the court full of jostling faces, shaken fists, jeering mouths. The effigy caught with a flash of yellow flame, evidently well soused in gin: there was an angry roar, as a spectacle it was exciting but too swift to satisfy.

A black-browed fellow wearing velvet cast-offs thrust his companions violently aside and thumped on the entry, shouting.

"The witch! The witch!" Everyone was yelling something different, but beneath it all the same word echoed.

"Is there no way out of the back? Surely there must be a yard or something?" demanded Mary.

Arabella smiled; she looked excited, as if boredom was her worst enemy and danger welcome. "No, I've just these three front rooms. It's always so dark away from the sun and not worth paying extra for space elsewhere."

There was a ripping crash from the door into the hallway and an immediate rush from the outside. "Back!" said Mary urgently, shoving Arabella in front of her. "Into the furthest room and out of the window while they're looting." Arabella was still protesting about abandoning her possessions and how the mob would certainly be awed by a spell, but Mary took no notice. The next room was a bedroom, dominated by an enormous double bed; perhaps Lady Wexford was not yet reduced to liking men only in the drawing room. A short passage led to a dark hearth room, where Catlin was standing with a brass ewer in her hand, looking furious at the disturbance.

"Out of the window," said Mary, brushing aside argument. "It's our best chance." She wedged a chair under the door handle as she had at each one they passed. She no longer felt frightened, but angry. The children were too young to manage without her, and Adam . . . Sweet Jesus, help me. He must not be left alone again, because a drunken mob mistook her for the familiar of a witch.

They nearly managed it. Doors and furniture were crashing behind them, Warwick Court almost deserted as the prospect of loot and destruction made the mob forget witch hunting for a while. Then someone saw them and shouted, others shouted, and Mary felt hands seize her, thrust her from one rough grasp to another, twirling in mockery until her senses spun and she fell. A red-bearded, rank-smelling fellow with leather sleeves rolled above muscular arms scooped her off cobbles as if she was nothing, and thrust her violently towards the fire.

She was very frightened now; houses, cobblestones and flames still revolving sickeningly. It needed the most enormous effort not to struggle when nothing would be achieved except further to inflame lust, to strive for calm which alone might bring a glimmer of reason to drunken baiting.

The crowd was much smaller than it had been; some had slipped away, sensing serious trouble, most of the rest were prancing in Arabella's silks and laces, or slashing at her furniture with the mindless pleasure of those who have lived a lifetime without any glimpse of beauty. The man with the gin was still there, though, slobbering incoherent words. The general effect seemed to be that they should burn the witch as well as her effigy, and violent argument broke out. Witches were good for sport, for stripping and searching for marks set by the Devil on buttock and belly, and if they were unlucky enough to die under such handling then tormentors ran down the nearest alley and hoped for the best. Deliberate murder was another matter, which magistrates would not overlook. Men were hanged for it, the guilty usually denounced because otherwise the nearest innocent were taken in their place.

"Run when your chance comes," said Adam quietly. "Don't argue and I will bring my mother."

Mary started violently. He was standing immediately behind her, wide shoulders and short stature unmistakeable even in flame-shot shadows. Her lips framed his name, but no sound came. She turned back to the scene by the fire, mind whirling. He was unarmed, since City merchants kept their word as a matter of sound trade and despised duelling, policed their streets as adequately as they could and consequently seldom carried even decorative weapons. And the exertion of fighting or running could easily kill him.

The gin drinker had just burned himself when he nearly fell into the fire, and created a diversion with his screeches. Mary saw Arabella jerk herself loose and knew what she would do: she lifted her hands above her head, torn silk trailing from her arms, and began to utter curses in a fine, carrying voice. There was an instant of recoil; if she had not been so closely amongst them, strange words and compelling presence might have been enough to cow their persecutors for a few vital moments, but a dozen brawny men were ashamed to be routed by a single woman, however evil, when they were close enough to strike her with their fists. Anger and lust rippled through those closest to the witch.

Mary twisted frantically in her captor's grasp, but Adam was gone.

She saw him again almost immediately, close by the fire and standing quite still; for a dreadful moment she thought he recognised justice in such an end for his mother. He would let her die and do nothing.

One of the men hit Arabella on the mouth to silence her, and a shocking silence fell, each looking at her and thinking of her flesh in his grasp, Arabella herself staring at blood on the hand she put to her lips.

"I offer you all a reward for your good work in digging a witch out of her earth," said Adam clearly. He threw a fistful of coins across the court.

They fell with a jingle on stone and woodwork, bounced off walls, disappeared into piled filth, lodged in clothes and chinks between cobblestones.

"You'd best shift your whids, my cullies, and snaffle 'em quick unless you're minded to share dibs with the rest," he added coolly, his tone pure Whitefriars.

They scrambled then for more riches than most had ever held at one time, scuffles breaking out as those inside the house came hurtling out again. If they thought of it at all, each assumed that another kept their captives secure. Mary ran as Adam had told her so as not to confuse him in the darkness, but waited by the entrance to the court, relief overwhelming when he reappeared.

"Out into Holborn," he said when he saw her. "We're safe wherever authority cannot pretend nothing is happening." He had his mother and Catlin with him, and in the light of tavern flares Mary could see he was smiling.

"My rooms," protested Arabella when he called up a hackney. "For God's sake, Adam. I can't leave everything I possess to be trampled in the gutter."

"It would take more than a pocketful of coins to save the little you have left," he replied curtly. "Thanks to your own generosity the one item worth the risk of a life is safe in Cheapside, so for once virtue is well rewarded." He dropped her arm and held Mary instead; she was shivering with reaction and abruptly he stripped off his coat, tucking it around her shoulders and holding her to him. They made a strange, bedraggled party in Holborn thoroughfare.

449

"Ye've been and gone and cooked yerself this time," said Catlin with gloomy relish. "Lost everythin' and me wantin' me wages tomorrow afore I goes. I'm not stayin' any longer where I'm likely to be struck down by my own hearth, and go chowsin' out of windows at my time of life."

"There is nothing like a fright for making everyone snappish and disagreeable when it is over," observed Arabella when they were all in the hackney. "If you have some good brandy, Adam, I am sure we'll be surprised how quickly matters appear in quite a different light."

In the darkness, Mary laid her head on Adam's shoulder. "How did you come to be there exactly when we were so desperate?"

"You were late, and Henry told me where you had gone when no one else could inform me. I came to escort you home since this isn't a safe neighbourhood after dusk."

"Although you would have to cross my threshold to do so?" snapped Arabella, showing herself no more proof against the aftermath of shock than anyone else.

"Do you think anything would weigh with me against Mary's safety?" demanded Adam, astonished.

There was a croak of laughter from Catlin and the rest of the journey was completed in silence.

Once back in Cheapside, Adam sent servants scurrying for hot punch and food while Mary took Arabella upstairs to search through her press for something to wear. The two were similar in figure and although Mary saw her mother-in-law make a private moue of distaste at the styles she was offered, she had the grace to make no comment beyond a somewhat pointed compliment on the quality of the cloth.

For herself, Mary felt stupid with exhaustion. Adam bullied her into eating and drinking but warmth and reaction made her drowsy, the memory of brutal faces and derisive hands mercifully blurring in her mind.

Memory leaped at her in the night. She woke with a scream, sitting bolt upright and staring into flames. They faded, and instead she was shuddering in the darkness of a pit.

"Hush, my love," said Adam. She felt him move beside her, heard the scrape of flint. After a moment tinder and then candle wick caught and blackness retreated. He lay back, cradling her to him. "Weep, or whatever else will ease you. There is little I don't know about nightmares."

Mary looked at the familiar shadows of their room, at

Adam's beloved face faintly underlit, and the image of horror faded. "The worst terror was thinking of you left alone again. It angered me that it could happen in such a foolish way, and rage helped me keep me on my feet, not courage."

"You must have seen for quite a while before how ugly the mob's mood was becoming; it had needed courage then, not to leave my mother to face the consequences of her folly alone."

"As it would have been safer for you just to deliver me when you threw those coins, left her and Catlin to take their chance. There was an instant by the fire, wasn't there, when you wanted to?"

He smiled faintly, hand stroking her hair. "Perhaps. I hope not. My father was executed, you know, on the corner of King Street and in sight of this, his own house. For a long time I chose to think she didn't care."

"Your father? Then . . . Adam, you mean your father was Henry Cornish?" As soon as Mary said it, she knew this must be right. She had only been eleven at the time and her own father a supporter of the King, but even so, she could remember the fear and fury aroused in the City when one of their own was drawn and quartered in sight of Guildhall and his own place of business. But she had not previously connected that place with her own home, the stories of butchery with familiar cobbles outside. Nor the anguish of the Cornish family with Adam.

He told her then, quietly and unemotionally, adding, "All these years I have blamed and hated anyone I held responsible for what happened. I suppose I always will." She felt him shift, memory still scarcely bearable. "I cannot forget, nor do I want to; if any man deserves to be remembered in this city and by his descendants, it is my father. It was the sheer filth of his death which tore me apart. The memory of sinew, guts and blood pouring off timber, that was what overset my mind. When my mother . . . went with another man I nearly killed her. Now I realise I was to blame for that part of it. When I saw him in Newgate my father made me swear I would not go to watch, and afterwards I would look to my mother. He made her promise too: she did as he begged her, remembered him with love and was able to patch her life together again as he had wanted for her. I broke my word and went, thinking I honoured him and despising her for not going, but truly it was a thing only an animal should see. It nearly turned me into one, as he feared it would when he made me swear."

451

"At least he wasn't alone when he died," said Mary slowly. "However brave a man may be, surely at such an end one of his inheritance close by would give a shadow of comfort, even if he didn't know from whence it came."

"I should like to think so, but no. I know now how he felt, how I should feel myself: only privacy from those you love could allow you to remain a person in their minds. There is no way to outlive such a memory, somehow you have to face it every day of your life and try to see courage and the cause of liberty advanced, instead of a butcher's shambles."

Mary was silent, appalled by the suffering Adam and his father had endured. Silent, too, because having begun to speak of matters he had never before put into words, he was anxious to rid himself of it all. He was sweating now, hands cold on her body as he relived brief happiness at Swithin Court, and then reached back to that earlier time when he grew up in a world he loathed, when it seemed the mere sight of him was enough to disgust the only person he was told belonged to him. "She . . . my mother told me long after that it wasn't me she disliked so much as being reminded of her own mistakes. She loved my father, and I was a—a mockery of her love. I didn't believe her, of course. I understand now, I suppose; it was a little difficult then, even after she took me in."

Sweet Jesus, she thought, it would be impossible. As impossible as this detached tone now. How will I face his mother in the morning without stripping flesh from her bones? And she dared accuse Adam of lacking compassion.

"So I requited her in her own coin," he added after a silence. "My father bade me look to her, knew and loved her well enough to understand she could not live alone, yet I left her and wished to do so. I've just told you I could have killed her then, but that's not quite true. Thinking about it these past weeks I've realised I wasn't sorry to find her less faithful than myself, well satisfied by an excuse to requite my wrongs. I blamed her for much of the harshness of my life, but think now that nothing is ever so simply explained." He laughed. "I don't suppose she will stay anywhere so dull as Cheapside for long, but am better contented by offering the care I owe her than by all the years of revenge."

The candle guttered and went out, the bell of St. Mary-le-Bow tolled five, and outside were the sounds of London rousing to another day. Adam had been lying holding her for a long time, now he moved and kissed her, hands no longer offering and receiving comfort but rousing passion.

As he had learned, so she must too. The past was irretrievable; hatred, remorse and humiliation were part of it and could not be set aside. Yet it must be accepted or the future would be corrupted too, and for them the future held so much if only they could free themselves from what was done and finished.

I will try, thought Mary firmly, though that woman deserves to be whipped at the cart's tail. For Adam's sake. And also because however much he might be reconciled to his mother, Mary sensed that Adam would never feel much affection for her. Whereas she could not help warming to Arabella, in spite of everything.

Chapter Six

*Even inside St. Paul's, it was stifling*ly hot. Lord Mayor, sheriffs and aldermen sweated in fur and velvet, tempers so frayed by discomfort that there was nearly an unseemly brawl when it was discovered that City dignitaries had been ousted from their usual places by peers and court officials. The moment passed when the disputed stalls mysteriously disappeared during the course of the quarrel and were replaced only after their discomfited lordships had seated themselves elsewhere. Consequently, a certain smug complacency had settled on the City side of the cathedral, while the peers were still audibly grumbling during the entry of Her Majesty, Queen Anne, who came in her own person to grace the service of thanksgiving for the great victory of Blenheim, won by English troops under the Duke of Marlborough. Of course, Prince Eugene and his Austrians had played a part too, but this was not felt to detract overmuch from the most splendid victory of English arms since the days of Agincourt.

And Eugene was as dependent as Marlborough on loans raised in the City.

Mary looked down on the scene from the gallery reserved for aldermen's wives: at plump Queen Anne glowing with heat so the red of her face clashed with her purple gown; banners of the City companies draped to disguise the remaining scaffolding inside St. Paul's; peers in their robes, the scarlet splash made by the City Corporation, the cold, steel glitter of the Sword of State laid on the altar. At Christopher Wren's masterpiece all around her, twenty-nine years so far in the building and soon to be complete. Its dome and great gold cross were visible almost everywhere in the City, already part of the familiar landfall for ships inward bound up the Thames.

Mary glanced at Henry sitting beside her. He had declared his intention of sailing in one of his father's privateers at the earliest opportunity, and considered himself seriously wronged by his parents' opinion that seven years old was too young for such a venture. He was studying the scaffolding in the dome consideringly, head flung back, eyes narrowed in calculation, and Mary sighed. She would have to watch him like a jailer after the service or he would be trying to convince them that hanging by his knees from a scaffold pole instantly qualified him to be a ship's boy.

At least Stephen seemed quieter, although Mary doubted whether his will would prove any more malleable. Even little Margaret showed a tendency to agree with whatever her family proposed and then pursue her original course with undiminished amiability.

The congregation sat back with a grunt of relief to drowse through an inaudible sermon. Wren's acoustics were excellent, but with the Queen present the preacher felt compelled to face her and turn his back on everyone else. In their own ward churches, where they contributed to the parson's upkeep, the merchants of the City would have been offended if they failed to obtain full value for their outlay, on this occasion they were paying to entertain Her Majesty and mark a national triumph, and felt satisfied if it was worthily done. A few lapsed into leisured calculation on the quality of the hangings to be sure they had not been cheated, while others contemplated the massive stones of St. Paul's. It was the considered opinion of the City that Wren had employed their money to good effect, although for years they had been unsure of it and consequently fractious over such matters as a triple-skinned dome and false walls which the architect insisted were necessary to perfect his design.

Mary's gaze wandered down the lines of familiar faces: there was a continual flow of shippers and merchants through their Cheapside home these days, and few men important enough to be seated for thanksgiving were unknown to her.

It was strange, although the Sign of the Spurs had joined that of the Corncrake on their wall and Robert Sperling's flagon was set in a glassed sconce by the entry, most people referred to Adam's place of business as Furnival's, as if they instinctively acknowledged an achievement which was uniquely his.

455

He seldom urged his views or became involved in City faction, nor was he interested in the jobbery of politics; yet his signature on a paper was regarded as one of the best half dozen guarantees in the City, his word on a bargain or advice on shipping sufficient to clinch most disputes. It would create an ugly scandal if his fellow merchants discovered that Adam Furnival was a branded thief, but they would judge him now as one of themselves and might well leave their balances in his care.

Mary could see Adam now, leaning slightly forward in his seat, hands clasped, face contemplative. He did not look particularly well, fulfilment and ease of mind had come too late to mend damage wrought by the years, but Mary tried not to worry about him when she knew he was deeply content, at peace with himself as never before. In the end, love and patience had healed what could be healed and the rest was in God's hands. She worried, all the same.

He came to meet her when the service ended at last, the Queen borne away to the sound of drums, fifes and huzzas down Ludgate Hill. Tonight there would be bonfires and fireworks throughout London and a banquet at Guildhall, but first they were going downriver to greet a Furnival privateer which had been signalled past Deptford the night before, flying the Corncrake flag to indicate a prize taken.

"Great news," said Adam immediately he saw her. "I had it by messenger just before the service. Gibraltar has fallen to the fleet."

"Where's Gibraltar?" demanded Henry. "Will you send a privateer there?"

"I'll send merchantmen secure about their trade one day, and if you show your worth then the best of them under your command, scamp. It will be the base we need to guard half the trade routes of the world, and double traffic on the rest."

"A finer victory than Blenheim?" asked Mary, smiling. She had seldom seen him so openly delighted.

"Blenheim was necessary to cut a tyrant back to size. God forbid we should ever see our future as paymaster to armies marching and killing around Europe. Ships and trade are London's lifeblood."

"And privateers!" shouted Henry, running in circles on the brick pavement of New 'Change. "Privateers with me on board!"

"If you keep your neck unbroken long enough," said Mary tartly. "I saw you looking at scaffolding and wondering what St. Paul's would look like from a hundred feet up."

"I sincerely hope the time for privateers is over before he's grown," remarked Adam, when Henry had run ahead to investigate the lugger waiting for them at Queenhithe. "There should be adventures enough on the trade routes to satisfy even him."

Mary laughed. "You'll never keep him in a Cheapside counting room, although some of the ideas I've heard put to you there are greater fantasy than any tales of deep-sea monsters or pirate gold."

"And will bring their own destruction; London has a deal to learn yet about the use and misuse of her great wealth. We now have the power to be tyrants ourselves, and reap the hatred of those we dispossess. One battle won, and lines are already drawn for the next."

"There is no end," said Mary. "Sometimes I find it a very comforting thought."

Note on the Trial of Henry Cornish

Henry Cornish was hanged, drawn and quartered on 23rd October 1685, and his head exhibited on Guildhall roof as directed by his judges; but the City was apparently so disturbed that his family was allowed to claim the fragments of his body within a few days, and they were buried in St. Lawrence Jewry.

Legal standards at seventeenth-century treason trials were abysmal, but even contemporaries were scandalised by the methods used in this particular instance. State prisoners were seldom allowed counsel, although judges were meant to give some guidance to the defendant; it was very rare for solitary confinement to be imposed prior to the trial, and several diarists commented on the indecent haste with which Cornish's arrest, trial and execution took place within a week. Two independent witnesses were required for condemnation of high treason, but in Cornish's case Goodenough and Rumsey did not allege the same treason, both were already at the Crown's mercy and working their passage to a pardon, while Goodenough was proved to cherish a bitter personal grudge against the prisoner. Sheppard, a key figure in the Crown's case, owed Cornish money and contradicted the evidence offered by Rumsey when Cornish examined him under oath.

I have necessarily compressed a considerable amount of evidence and cross-examination but the course of trial, and the main points of the Crown's case, were as depicted. Elizabeth Cornish did force her way into the King's presence and received the half-promise I have given; Cornish's (legitimate) son did succeed in producing a mass of witnesses under impossible conditions.

Bishop Burnet in his memoirs described Cornish as a "plain, warm, honest man," and feeling in the City remained so strong that William of Orange pledged himself to reverse Cornish's attainder even before the affairs of the realm were settled.* He must have been told that the City's support depended on justice for Cornish, even though he was three years dead and the City's Orange sympathies not in doubt. The attainder was formally reversed by Act of Parliament in June 1689.

Not only was his attainder of treason reversed and restoration of property to the Cornish family ordered, it was also directed that all record of the trial should be "wholly cancelled, taken off the file, or be otherwise defaced and obliterated to the intent that the same may not be visible to after ages." In spite of this direction, a more or less verbatim report of the trial did survive and numerous pamphlets circulated under William and Mary giving accounts of it, and of Cornish's last words on the scaffold.

Sir John Hawles, Solicitor-General to William, wrote his own commentary on the case a few years after, in which he tears apart the evidence offered against Cornish, exposing the untrustworthiness, malice and contradictions of the witnesses, as well as the partisan attitude of the judges and harsh treatment of the prisoner. He points out that Cornish's defence was weak since he produced no witnesses for his political probity, but adds that "anyone could plainly see he was so beset that any defence he or anyone for him could make, would have availed him nothing."† Anyone who is faced with the necessity of

---

*A series of riots occurred in the City 1686–7, chiefly anti-Catholic in character, which seem to have centred on Cheapside—possibly no coincidence. In 1687 even the Tory Court of Aldermen refused to vote an address of thanks to the King when he broached the subject of returning their charter.

Sir John Shorter, whom James was constrained to make Lord Mayor in 1686 for lack of anyone else willing to accept so invidious an office, is described by Evelyn in his diary as "a very odd, ignorant person, a mechanic, I think."

†Sir John Hawles went on to say: "...he was very rudely handled. How often was he snubbed and bid hold his tongue? How often did he beg the patience of the court, to hear him and his witnesses? And when he was heard how was all he said ridiculed? If he said he was innocent, he was bid remember [those before him who were condemned believing the same and]...told few believed him. If he said the matter sworn before him was improbable, how was he ridiculed of improbability, improbability, improbability? If he prove he is an honest man, he is told it is all appearance. If he says he was [forced to] employ Goodenough, he is told that is a branch of the plot; if he called a witness to prove he received the sacrament [according to the Church of England] he is told it was simply in order to qualify himself to be

460

proving he has not committed treason rather than defending himself from accusations that he has, is likely to encounter serious difficulties.

Nevertheless, when one reads through the proceedings it is difficult to avoid the impression that a great deal of evidence is going by default. The judges several times derisively drew Cornish's attention to the sort of plea he should be making. They were, after all, lawyers, their professional senses aroused by incompetence even if their judgment was already made.

Cornish persisted in bringing forward witnesses to his business standing and honesty, about which there was no doubt, and failed to call any who might have substantiated his political loyalty. One judge commented that he ought to call some former fellow aldermen of the Whig administration, but he did not do so. Another odd circumstance is that under Cornish's cross-examination Sheppard clearly exonerated him from any part in the Rye House Plot or in fomenting insurrection, yet insisted on the part Cornish played in defending the City's charter, when this was scarcely calculated to help him with his judges. Rumsey corroborates the assertion that Cornish was on his way to chair a meeting to discuss the defence of the City's charter when he came to Sheppard's house. Also, although Cornish denied ever having financial or treasonable dealings with the Duke of Monmouth, his reply to a question as to why therefore he came to see him (if he did come to see him; the witnesses contradicted each other on this vital point) is extremely elliptical. The impression of a man telling the exact truth, but not the whole truth, is very strong.

Motive, therefore, as always, seems very important. Granted that Cornish was no lawyer and could be expected to make errors in conducting his own defence under conditions of extreme difficulty, it is still surprising that he failed to press some of the very damaging admissions he extracted from Sheppard. Goodenough and Rumsey would say anything they were paid to say; Sheppard was not quite in the same category and seems to have tried to reveal such of the truth as he was allowed, and it was safe, to admit. Cornish appears uncertain of some court procedures, but was clearly an able and determined man: he was very quick to seize on the discrepancy in Rumsey's evidence though he had no record of Lord Russell's trial before

---

sheriff; and such was his usage before, and at his trial, so it was afterwards. To order him to be tied when he was sentenced was an indignity not used to persons of his quality...and even the cheerfulness of his countenance at condemnation was seen as cause for reproach."

461

him, such as any lawyer would have insisted on being admitted into evidence. It was blatantly untrue that an official record was not evidence, or that judges could not corroborate a prisoner's statement.

Motive for the Crown, too, is baffling. James was a vindictive man, but just why should the Crown be so anxious to kill, in the most agonising and humiliating way, an ex-alderman of the City of London, who at that time was not actively opposing royal policies? The prosecution never suggested that Cornish had done anything but trade peacefully since the spring of 1683—two and a half years previously.

The very strong animus against Cornish dates from 1680–1, when he was a sheriff of the City just after the worst period of the Popish Plot. Probably he was partly responsible for the fiasco of Shaftesbury's acquittal by a Whig jury, since sheriffs could pack juries and he had only just quitted office; certainly he was a leading protagonist in the disputed elections which followed.

Above all, however, it seems clear that Cornish headed opposition within the City to the attack on their charter. He was a member of the committee of five appointed in 1682 to consider the City's defence, was turned out of office under the new charter in 1683, was one of those who presented a petition to the King in the summer of the same year. He also played a leading part in the debate which forced the King to seize the charter rather than having it surrendered once the courts had declared it forfeit.

Cornish was thus left very exposed to royal vengeance once the new charter and officers were forced on the City, and was constantly harassed in 1684–85. He was fined on derisory charges and stated at his trial that he had been four times in prison that year, and each time released for lack of evidence.

This background would explain some of the inconsistencies of his trial. He might well have had dealings with Monmouth, not over any uprising, but as an important political figure with access to King Charles's inner councils. "The Protestant Duke," as Monmouth was nicknamed, was popular in the City (as was Shaftesbury) and would have been a valuable and quite legitimate ally in the fight to keep the City's liberties—which coincided with the beginnings of the Rye House Plot.

By the time of Cornish's trial, however, Charles was dead and Monmouth recently beheaded for leading a rising in the West. Cornish might well have felt that it would not benefit him to reveal discussions with Monmouth on the charter, while such revelations could further damage the City by appearing to implicate leading figures there in Monmouth's subsequent treason. This would account for the way Cornish failed to exploit Sheppard's admissions, which virtually established his innocence, while still leaving open the question of what exactly he had been doing at Sheppard's house when Monmouth was there. Everyone agreed he was in a great hurry as he had an important meeting to attend, that Monmouth was at Sheppard's house secretly, yet Cornish knew he was there and was shown upstairs to meet him. This part of the evidence has the feel of truth. It would seem likely to me, if unproveable, that he came to discuss City tactics with Monmouth, or possibly to receive some reply from Charles via Monmouth about the charter, which he needed for the following meeting. He then left and the conspiratorial business proceeded. He may have suspected there was something else on hand, indeed he would be a fool not to with such people as Rumsey and Ferguson about, but was no lover of Stuarts and cannot have felt unduly concerned.

This interpretation would also explain why he failed to call other aldermen to support his political loyalty. It was in any case minimal; he was obstinately uncompromising on the charter while they mostly continued in office after its seizure. His close allies and friends had either fled or faced heavy fines already. It was stated at the trial that he had to go to the charter meeting "because he was the only alderman in town." This is patently absurd: he may have been the only one left who was willing to take the risk of presiding over such a meeting, and his fellows could well have stressed this to save their skins if called as witnesses. At best, his fellow aldermen's testimony would be unhelpful, at worst it would make the past Corporation of the City look like a pack of conspirators—an impression to be avoided at all costs in the first year of James's reign.

His behaviour thus becomes consistent, instead of appearing foolishly naïve—which we know he was not. He appears to have started his trial thinking he could not possibly be condemned on such evidence, and also in a towering rage: William Penn, who attended his execution, comments on his "strong anger and natural resentment at the way he had been treated." However, he must very quickly have come to the conclusion that he was lost, and as a last service to the City he loved decided to avoid tearing it further apart with faction, to die alone rather than expose others to the same retribution.

There are many plaques in the City of London commemorating its famous citizens; none is set at the corner of King

Street and Cheapside where Henry Cornish was hanged, drawn and quartered in circumstances of extreme barbarity, as a consequence of the fight he made for its liberties. He lost, but his cause triumphed. The hatred generated by his trial and death directly contributed to the restoration of the City's charter and to London's unwavering support for William, as well as the prominent part played by the City Corporation in the smooth transference of government and Bill of Rights which followed.

With a measure of liberty gained, half a century of political upheaval drew to a close, which had drained so much effort and wealth from economic endeavour, the City's normal function. The scene was set for unparalleled British expansion in the eighteenth and nineteenth centuries, in the course of which the City of London was to become the centre of world trade and finance. London bankers were not carrying out any new function when the army which had to be hastily cobbled together to face Napoleon after his escape from Elba could only be paid by means of a loan from the City. N. M. Rothschild handled it, raised three-quarters of a million pounds to pay British, Dutch and Prussian troops at Waterloo and charged a mere £700 interest on the deal. Rarely has so far-reaching a victory been so cheaply financed. Or so swiftly: without the City it is doubtful whether Napoleon would have encountered any opposition at all until his power was securely re-established.

London did not forget the basis on which its strength was established, either. Nearly a hundred years after Henry Cornish died, Lord North's government asked for a loan to prosecute the war against the American colonies, and the City fathers flatly refused. It was, they said, an unjust war against the liberty of the subject and they would have no part in it. Nor did they. The war was fought and lost on inadequate government finance, and when it was over the City immediately reopened trade with the independent United States of America. At a profit, of course.

About the Author

Patricia Wright is a novelist with a remarkable talent for rich characterizations and vivid recreations of historical eras. She lives in Sussex, England, where she is currently at work on her next novel.